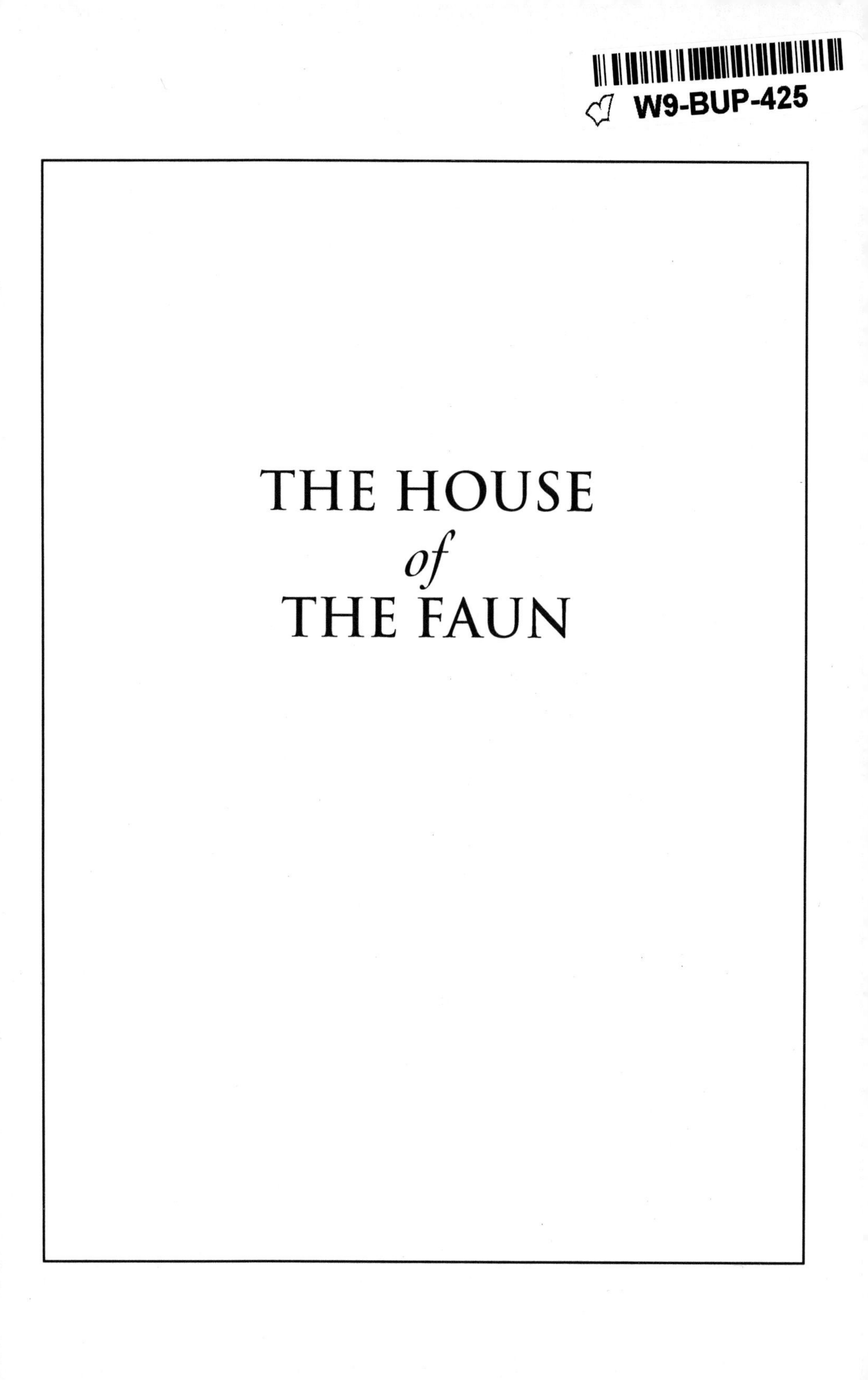

THE HOUSE *of* THE FAUN

THE HOUSE *of* THE FAUN

A NOVEL OF POMPEII

Carolyn Doggett Smith

iUniverse, Inc.
New York Lincoln Shanghai

The House of the Faun

iUniverse books may be ordered through booksellers or by contacting:

iUniverse
2021 Pine Lake Road, Suite 100
Lincoln, NE 68512
www.iuniverse.com
1-800-Authors (1-800-288-4677)

ISBN-13: 978-0-595-40519-0 (pbk)
ISBN-13: 978-0-595-84884-3 (ebk)
ISBN-10: 0-595-40519-3 (pbk)
ISBN-10: 0-595-84884-2 (ebk)

Printed in the United States of America

ACKNOWLEDGMENTS

For reading all or part of the manuscript and making many valuable suggestions: Barbara Dillon, Clinton Doggett, Marie Doggett, Nicholas Doggett, Trudy Doggett, Connie Fiedler, Lynne Glikbarg, Megan Lynch, Madeleine Morel, Theresa Sanders, Wade S. Smith, and Sara Watt.

For guiding me through the final revisions: the skilled and understanding staff at iUniverse, especially Rachel Krupicka and Susan Driscoll.

And for not only reading multiple drafts but always providing encouragement when I needed it: Guy, Jeanie, and Larry.

My heartfelt thanks to all of you. I couldn't have done it without you!

MAJOR CHARACTERS

The House (and Farm) of the Vettii

Claudius Vettius, a wine merchant

Julia, his wife

Marcus, their son

Aurelia and Julilla (Julia), their daughters

Petronius, the cook

Ariana, a kitchen slave; later a maidservant in the House of the Faun

Alomila, her mother, a slave at the farm

Publius, the manager at the farm

Sextus, the cook at the farm

The House of the Faun

Lucius Tullius, a prominent citizen and city official

Clodia, his wife

Gaius, their son

Manlius, the house steward

Kineas, tutor to both Marcus Vettius and Gaius Tullius

Timon, Quintus, Junius, Tertia, and Claudia, household slaves

The City Government

Suedius Clemens, an administrator sent to Pompeii by the Emperor Vespasian*

Paquius Proculus, a city official

Statius Rufus, a rising politician and member of the *Comitia*

Nabucco, his manservant

Caecilius Jucundus, a city official

Munatius Faustus, a retired member of the *Comitia;* prosecutor in the trial of Statius Rufus

Larcius "Lupus" Licinius, defense counsel in the trial of Statius Rufus

Nigidius Vascula and Melissius Aper, members of the *Comitia* and close friends

Other Citizens of Pompeii and Nearby Towns

Julia Felix, a landlady, gossip, and matchmaker*

Phidias, an architect

Cornelia Jucunda, a widowed landowner living in Herculaneum

Caecilia, daughter of a Roman financier with a villa on Capreae

Pomponianus, the owner of a villa in Stabiae*

Gaius Plinius the Elder, admiral of the fleet at Misenum and author of *Naturalis Historia**

Gaius Plinius the Younger, his nephew*

A glossary of Latin terms and place names may be found at the end of the book.

*Clemens, Julia Felix, Pomponianus, Vespasian, and the two Plinys are historical figures; the others, and all their actions, are fictional.

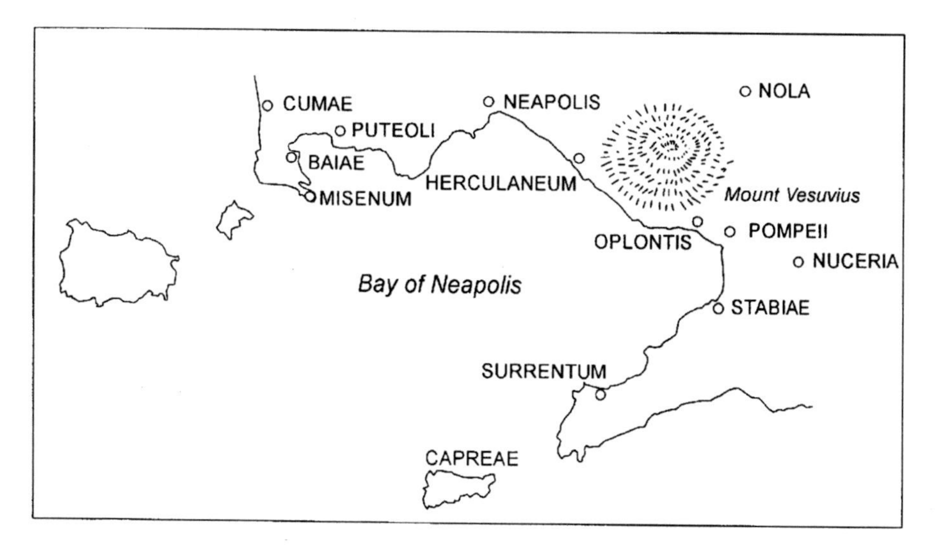

Pompeii and the Surrounding Area

Latin has no word for “volcano.”

PBS, *Pompeii: The Last Day*

PROLOGUE

In the years between 57 and 59 A.D., in the seaside city of Pompeii, three children (among many others) were born: Gaius Tullius, the son of Lucius Tullius, one of the city's wealthiest and most prominent men; Marcus Vettius, the son of Claudius Vettius, a successful wine merchant and would-be scholar; and Ariana, the daughter of Alomila, a slave in the household of the Vettii.

About a hundred and fifty years previously, Pompeii and many other Italian towns and cities had banded together to defy Rome's dominance and been decisively defeated by Roman legionaries under the leadership of the dictator Cornelius Sulla. Sulla had settled some of his veterans in Pompeii, and for many years their presence upset the balance of power in a city that had long been governed by magistrates from the established Samnite families of the region. The animosities between the two groups of citizens gradually diminished, and now Pompeii, ideally situated for both commerce and agriculture, thrived as never before.

Above the city loomed Mount Vesuvius, its flanks covered with forests and vineyards. People thought of the mountain as a benevolent deity, its arms spread wide to bestow gifts of plenty upon them—game, timber, grapes, and much more. They paid scant heed to the thin plume of smoke rising from its summit; there may have been a fire within the mountain, but it posed no threat to them. They knew what a true fire-mountain looked like: Mount Aetna in Sicily, which thundered constantly, sending flames high into the sky and belching forth fiery cascades of boiling rock and burning sulphur that flowed down its flanks and destroyed everything in their path. No such danger threatened Pompeii, though the city, along with others nearby, was subject to frequent earthquakes, most of them little more than tremors, but some strong enough to cause considerable damage and loss of life.

In 62 A.D., the region was devastated by a huge earthquake, and in Pompeii many buildings, both public and private, were damaged or destroyed. For the next several years, great efforts were made to rebuild, though some structures, notably the surrounding wall, were not repaired. To some leading citizens, the quake presented an opportunity to rebuild on a scale they might never have considered if disaster had not struck. They developed an ambitious plan to expand and embellish the Forum and completely rebuild the Basilica. The rebuilding provided incomes for many laborers, but the city's renewed prosperity stemmed mainly from the abundant produce grown in the fields and vineyards that adorned the slopes of Vesuvius to the north and the Campanian countryside to the east and south. Pompeii's fifteen thousand souls never lacked for food or drink.

In 70 A.D., Pompeii had thirty-three bakeries, one hundred and thirty taverns and snack bars, a dozen fulleries, thirty-nine wool-processing plants, and more than six hundred shops. Pompeiians raised grain, grapes, olives, sheep, and flowers. They made and sold bread, wine, olive oil, wool, perfume, and garlands of flowers. Dog biscuits were baked fresh each morning at the bakeries, as well as bread and rolls of wheat, barley, millet, and oats. Each day, loaded carts entered the city through its seven noisy, congested gates, bringing in produce to be sold in the market or delivered directly to wealthy households. Vendors set up stalls along the roads, where pedestrians stopped to look and buy before passing through the gates. Inside, they found shops of all kinds on the commercial streets, with open fronts, wares displayed on shelves, and painted signs on the walls advertising merchandise and prices. The gods seemed indeed to be smiling on the small city nestled at the foot of the mountain towering above it.

Ten years after the great earthquake, Gaius, Marcus, and Ariana, though not yet grown, were no longer children. And soon their lives would be intertwined in unforeseen ways. This is their story.

I

MARCH, 72

Ariana skipped lightly over the sidewalk of large stone blocks lining the Via Stabiana. Her feet were bare, the soles toughened by years of running along the sidewalks of Pompeii. In winter she might wear sandals, an old pair outgrown by one of the master's children, but during the rest of the year she went barefoot. In winter also, when she was sent to fetch a bucket of coals, she might throw across her shoulders a makeshift shawl cut from one of the mistress's cast-off *pallae*. Its soft rose color echoed the rosy glow of her complexion, healthy from so much time spent outdoors. The first time she wore it, the mistress had noticed and looked sharply at her, then shrugged and turned away. After all, what harm could it do if a slave girl ran around town wearing a scrap of worn-out wool?

Today, though, she wore only her tunic of coarsely woven linen. She was not yet thirteen and her breasts were just beginning to bud, so she did not yet need to wind a piece of cloth around them for support. Her shiny, unruly black hair streamed out behind her. She never had time to tend it, what with all the errands she had to run and all the other tasks set for her by Petronius, the old cook, who was too fat and lazy to do much besides the actual cooking. And as the youngest slave in the household, Ariana was the one who could most readily be spared from more important tasks.

It had rained the night before, and the early-morning sunlight gleamed on the roof tiles. The streets were full of muddy water, along with scraps thrown from doorways, avidly sought by pigs and dogs. Ariana went the long way around, keeping to the main streets—the Via Stabiana, one of the three main roads that traversed the city from north to south, and the Via Nola, one of the two major east-west routes through the city. At the corner of the Via Nola, she paused for a moment to look toward the northern gate and the broad-shouldered mountain that rose in the distance beyond it. It was an early spring day, cool but sunny, with a light blue sky forming a glowing backdrop for the snow-topped mountain and the thin wisp of smoke rising from its summit.

At most intersections and at intervals along all the main streets, large stepping stones allowed people to cross to the other side while still permitting carts to make their way along the cobbled surface. Ariana ran across, turned right onto the Via Nola, and continued on her way; after a moment she came to the small lane on the left that led to the bakery. She turned and ran the last few yards. She loved going to the bakery, even though this was an errand she had to run almost every day. She loved the smell of the bread as it came from the oven, loved to sit on a bench, nibbling on a morsel of fresh bread given to her by the baker while one of his assistants bundled three of the circular loaves for her to carry home. Then she would watch as the donkeys plodded slowly around the four large mills in the center of the workroom, pushing against wooden poles that turned the huge grinding stones.

She was aware of the looks the baker's assistants gave her and wondered what they meant. They didn't look only at her budding chest or her abundant black curls. Their gaze lingered on her slim legs and especially her face, which was not only pretty but always changing as something new caught her interest and attention. She was like a nymph or a dryad, a thing of sky and sunlight with a touch of the divine.

But she was a slave. Anyone who saw her knew it, even though she was not branded or marked in any way. No one not a slave would be dressed in such poor clothing, with no adornment, nothing to bind back her hair. She was the daughter of Alomila, a Sogdian woman whose mother had been imported to Rome by a slave merchant; the mother died shortly thereafter, but the merchant kept the child and raised her with his other slaves. When she was about sixteen years old he brought her to Pompeii, where he made a nice profit on her sale to a wealthy family with high aspirations. Alomila had been assigned to care for the mistress of the house, but it had not been long before she caught the master's eye.

A year after entering the household, Alomila was with child. No one would acknowledge who the father was, though many guessed. It was given out that Alomila had lain with one of the other slaves, a handsome, dark-haired youth. The allegedly guilty slave was sold, and Alomila was banished to the family's farm outside the city walls to bear her child and remain there, working in the kitchen and laundry. There Ariana was born and spent her childhood, tending the chickens and garden, exploring the nearby fields and woods. She never gave a thought to who her father might be, and even if she had asked, no one would have enlightened her.

When she was almost ten years old, she was summoned to the town house to help in the kitchen. She would ride in the donkey cart that brought fresh produce to the house each morning. Her mother wept over her, clutching her to her breast until the last possible moment. Ariana wept too, but her sadness was tempered by excitement at the prospect of something new, new territory to explore.

Now, as she returned to the house with the bread, she held the loaves close to her, walking slowly so she could enjoy their warmth and aroma as long as possible. On the way she took a short detour in order to pass the House of the Faun, the home of one of the wealthiest families in town. Usually the door was open and she could glance through into the atrium. She could not see the whole room, but she could see the *impluvium* in the center, where a small statue of a faun—a young satyr—stood on one side as if dancing with its reflection in the water. The faun seemed to return her look with an enticing smile. She would imagine that he was her friend, that when they had finished their daily tasks they would meet, perhaps just outside the Vesuvian gate, where they could look down the slopes toward the sparkling sea in the distance.

But of course this was sheer fantasy. Even if the faun had been real, they could not have met. She was free to choose her routes through the streets when sent on errands, but otherwise she could not leave the house. Nor was there any question of "escaping": Where would she go? If she went to be with her mother at the farm, she would simply be retrieved and taken back to the town house, perhaps with a whipping to discourage her from running away again.

In Pompeii slaves did almost all the work. They stoked the fires at the baths, pounded the clothes at the laundries, cooked, cleaned, repaired roads, and taught children their letters. Carpenters, bricklayers, plumbers, doctors, artists, musicians, and secretaries were slaves. Most domestic slaves were paid a small wage, which they could save and eventually use to buy their freedom. Some masters taught their slaves trades, and some gave them money to start businesses. Slaves could buy their freedom with money accumulated from outside jobs, or they might simply be freed by their masters after ten or fifteen years, provided they were at least thirty years old. Freedmen and women made up a large segment of Pompeii's population and accounted for most of its food vendors, tavern-keepers, and shop-owners. But Ariana gave little thought to the possibility that she might eventually become a freedwoman—it was too vague, too distant. Anything could happen in twenty years. She was far more interested in the possibilities offered by each new day: the sights, the sounds, the smells she might encounter in the streets and alleys of Pompeii.

In the Via Nola she paused again to look at a long crack running diagonally down the outer wall of one of the houses. For some reason the wall had not been repaired after being damaged in an earthquake two years before. Ariana remembered that time—the wild barking of the dogs, the sudden rumbling noises, the shaking walls and floors, everyone panicking and running outside and praying to whatever god or goddess came to mind. There had been several quakes at about the same time—none as severe as the big one ten years earlier, but enough to strike fear and dismay into the hearts of many of Pompeii's citizens. Although they were accustomed to frequent tremors and small quakes, these stronger ones were another matter. Some of the wealthier citizens watched bitterly as their brightly painted walls crumbled and their beautiful mosaic floors heaved and cracked, the money spent on expensive repairs after the last quake wasted as those repairs would have to be made all over again. Those who lacked strong ties to the city, who had not lived there for generations, sold their houses and land and moved away, and moderately rich people like her master bought them, hoping thus to advance their standing in the social and political world of Pompeii. Claudius's new house was only one or two *insulas* away from the old one, the so-called House of the Golden Cupids, but it was much larger.

When at last she returned to the house, going directly to the kitchen, Petronius yelled at her: "What took you so long? With all your dawdling, the bread will be stale! Hurry up and take one of those loaves and a bowl of olives to the master. Hurry!"

She obeyed, saying nothing. It was always the same, every day. "Crabby old bastard," she said to herself when she was well out of earshot. She entered the master's *tablinum* as quietly as she could. He was intent on the scroll he was reading. Not wanting to disturb him, she stood still and looked around the room. It was small but beautifully decorated with paintings of mythological scenes copied from Greek originals. One wall was entirely taken up with cubicles for scrolls. The master sat at a polished wooden table, with two carved wooden chairs facing him. A bronze lamp stood beside the table. Because candles were expensive, most Pompeiians used oil lamps, both small ones that could be placed on a table and larger, beautifully crafted ones on stands.

Claudius looked up and motioned to her to place the food on a smaller table at one side of the room; there was a pitcher of wine there already. She turned to leave, but he stopped her with a gesture and seemed about to speak to her. After a brief moment, however, he shook his head and indicated that she could go.

Claudius Vettius was a proud man, but he was also intelligent and thoughtful. Although the Roman *paterfamilias* had absolute control over the lives of his slaves, Claudius knew he would receive prompter, more willing service if he provided decent living conditions and avoided extreme punishments. The crucifixions and deadly floggings suffered by some wayward slaves did not occur in his household. The worst that could be expected was a moderate whipping, perhaps ten lashes.

He had been about to speak to Ariana in a conversational manner, as if she were his daughter—which he knew her to be—but he had stopped himself. Patrician families in the Roman Empire did not acknowledge bastard offspring. The most he could do for her was to make sure she was safe and well fed. *I can't acknowledge her,* he thought, *but I can at least make sure she comes to no harm.*

As Ariana left the room, she almost ran headlong into the mistress but managed to turn aside in time, flushing in embarrassment. Julia Vettia ignored her, not even slowing her pace as she entered the *tablinum* and began speaking to Claudius before he even knew she was there.

"What are you going to do about Marcus?" she demanded.

Marcus, their son, had a tendency to be absent when his tutor was due to arrive. Each time, Julia had to send a slave to the gymnasium to haul him home to his lessons. It had happened again that day, and she was furious. "This has to stop, Claudius. You're going to have to beat some sense into him."

Suddenly she realized whom she had passed in the doorway. "You weren't talking to that girl, were you?"

"No, of course not," he said. "She just brought me some bread and olives, as usual."

"Make sure you don't!" she snapped.

Claudius sighed in exasperation. "We've been over this a hundred times, Julia. I won't break my word. As for Marcus, tell him to come see me when he's finished with his lessons."

◆ ◆ ◆

Marcus Vettius had his father's slim good looks but shared none of his interests. After his thirteenth birthday a few months earlier, there had emerged in him a streak of rebelliousness that had not been evident before. He seemed unable to sit quietly while his tutor read to him from the works of Cicero or Horace. *Integer vitae scelerisque purus ...* who but his father could be interested in such useless stuff? Nor could he concentrate on writing the short essay he was assigned each day. Instead, at every opportunity he ran outside, often to the gymnasium, where he watched the men as they exercised, and imitated them as best he could. He could not wait to become a man. But that would not happen, in a formal sense at least, until he was fifteen, when he would dedicate his childhood toys to the family gods and don the pure white toga denoting Roman citizenship.

Today he had witnessed a wrestling match between two of the best athletes in Pompeii, and he had been exhilarated by the skill—and trickery—he observed. One of the men had finally succeeded in throwing the other to the ground; he immediately leaped to his feet and the two men embraced. It was at this point that a slave tapped him on the shoulder and informed him that his tutor was waiting for him at home.

Marcus grumbled at the intrusion, but he knew better than to protest. He raced home and sat through the day's lessons, sweating and fidgeting the whole time. At the end of the session, Julia dismissed the tutor and told Marcus to report to his father in the *tablinum*, and with some trepidation he did so.

"Come in, Marcus, and have a seat," his father said.

He entered slowly and sat. Claudius finished reading a scroll that was unrolled on the desk before him; he then rolled it up and placed it in its cubicle on the wall behind him, then turned and looked at Marcus for a moment. Marcus attempted to look back, but he soon dropped his gaze.

"Your mother is displeased by your recent behavior," Claudius began.

"Yes, Father."

"I don't have time for this, Marcus. For the next month you'll not leave this house without my permission. If you're caught outside the doors, you'll be whipped. Is that understood?"

"But Father ..."

"No buts. Is that understood?"

"Yes, Father."

"You may go now."

Head drooping, Marcus left the room and sulked his way to his chamber, where he threw himself down on the bed. *Men don't weep*, he told himself as tears trickled from the corners of his eyes. *Men don't weep*. The tears ceased.

Marcus desperately wanted to be a man. He wanted to be free to choose how to spend his time, not required to sit through endless lessons. He resented his parents, especially his father. He was actually ashamed of Claudius. His father might be a successful businessman, but he spent much of his time reading works of literature and philosophy—not a manly pursuit in his son's eyes. Marcus sympathized with his mother's desire for social prominence, but it meant little to him. As for his sisters, as far as he was concerned they were there to be either teased or ignored.

The other members of his family might have been surprised if they had accompanied him in his forays through the city. When he spent time with other boys, he was cheerful and pleasant, with a wry sense of humor. When he encountered his father's business associates, he was polite and respectful. But when he reentered the House of the Vettii, he seemed to wrap himself in a cloak of resentment. He hid himself away in his *cubiculum*, whiling away the time with fantasies about what he might do when he was a man.

◆ ◆ ◆

Ariana returned to the kitchen, stopping briefly to scoop a dipper of water from the large basin just inside the door. "What took you so long?" old Petronius growled at her as usual. And as usual she said nothing and went to work sweeping the floor. She thought of her mother, whom she had not seen for over two years. She remembered their last day together, before she was taken away and brought to the House of the Vettii. Alomila had held her hand and walked with her along the paths that divided the fields, frequently hugging her and weeping, but also talking with her, trying to prepare her for life in the master's household.

"The most important thing, Ariana," she had said, "is to keep your mouth closed and your eyes open."

"Why, Mama?" she had asked.

"Because then you'll be wiser than anyone else."

This had not meant much to her at the time, but in the ensuing years she had come to recognize the value of keeping silent and paying close attention to everything around her. She had sensed the central facts of the Vettius household: Julia sought social advancement, while Claudius wished to lead the quiet life of a scholar. Their son, Marcus, was a source of frustration for both of them. Their daughters, Aurelia and Julia (known as Julilla), were virtually ignored.

It was Julia who had goaded Claudius into buying the new house when it came on the market after the earthquakes two years earlier. It had more style than the House of the Golden Cupids, she insisted. It would be an asset in their climb to the top of the Pompeiian social ladder....

Ariana shook her head to banish thoughts of the mistress and went back to her memories of her mother. As they were walking back to the farmhouse, she had thought of one more thing she wanted to ask Alomila:

"Mama, why did you name me Ariana? I don't know anyone else with that name."

Alomila stopped walking and stared at her. A strange look crossed her face, a mixture of sadness and pride. Then she took Ariana's hand and led her to a bench in the yard. It was next to the goat shed, and they sat there in the warm sunshine, leaning against the wall of the shed, as Alomila told Ariana the story of her origins.

"Ariana is the name of a vast land far from here," she said. "A proud land where many tribes—Arachosians, Bactrians, Sogdians—roam with their herds, and warriors fight on horseback. My mother's people lived there, had lived there for hundreds of years."

She closed her eyes and leaned her head back, dreaming of a life she could never know.

"Go on, Mama, tell me more," Ariana urged.

"They had always lived the same way," Alomila continued. "They lived in large tents with beautiful carpets and cushions, and they grazed their herds on the vast plains, moving, always moving, in search of new pastures. They drank fermented mare's milk and made flat bread patties from ground grain, which they used to scoop up their food—curried lamb and chickpeas, for the most part. In the hot summer months they might go high into the mountains, but in the winter they came down to the sheltered valleys. They held festivals where the young women danced and made eyes at men from neighboring tribes, and in due course married them and bore them sons and daughters. It was a good life.

"Then one day everything changed. From the west came a great army led by Alexander, a Greek who wished to conquer the whole world and came close to doing so. The Sogdian horsemen rode out to meet him, banners flying and trumpets blaring, but they were no match for the army of Alexander. Like Media, Parthia, and all the other lands to the north and west, Sogdiana fell. Alexander established a base at Marcanda and began converting the nomadic Sogdians into city dwellers.

"In each land he conquered, Alexander took a woman as a concubine, but in Sogdiana he saw Roxana in the line of dancing women at the winter festival. She was the daughter of a local baron, and she had marvelous long black hair, bright eyes, and a proud bearing. He loved her at first sight and married her, but he didn't take her with him when he continued his march through the eastern lands. It was from this Roxana that my grandmother was descended. Whether her ancestor was Alexander's child or the child of a later marriage, I couldn't say. In any case, her proud ancestry did her little good.

"Over the course of many generations, the condition of the Sogdians worsened. At first they prospered under the rule of Alexander's governor, but the country proved difficult to defend, and eventually it was conquered, first by the Seleucids in the west and later by marauding tribes from the east. Stripped of their herds, the people struggled to farm the arid soil or became merchants and traders. Marcanda was situated on a major trade route, and those who had the wherewithal for trade did well. The rest suffered many hardships, but the worst of it was that they were easy prey for raiders who stormed into their villages, placed them in chains, and sold them in the slave markets. My grandmother was one of those poor souls."

Alomila sighed and grew quiet, thinking of her mother, whom she had known for only a few years. Finally she said,

"This is what my mother told me when I was a young child. I don't remember much from those years, but I do remember her telling me her story and the story of her people. It was important to her that I know where we came from, even if we could never hope to return."

Ariana leaned her head on her mother's shoulder and thought about what she had been told. She could hardly believe her ears. A descendant of the Princess Roxana! It couldn't be true. It must be a story invented by her grandmother to pass the time. But then again, slaves came to Italia from all parts of the Empire, people of all races, each with his or her own story. Why could it not be true?

"Mama," she said. "What about *your* name? I haven't met anyone else with your name, either."

"My name?" Alomila smiled. "My mother made it up! When she was unhappy she would try to calm herself by closing her eyes and reciting "a-lo-mi-la" over and over. It was a sort of charm for her, and when I was born it became my name."

"I will name my daughter Alomila," Ariana said, smiling back at her mother.

◆ ◆ ◆

"Ariana!" Petronius's shout shattered her reverie. "What are you doing? Get busy and strip these beans. I need them right away. Hurry!"

With a barely suppressed sigh, she returned to her daily tasks, putting aside the memory of her mother's story but promising herself that later she would think about it again, going over every detail and wondering what it might mean.

◆ ◆ ◆

The mistress's personal maid—the small, shrewish woman who had replaced Alomila—appeared in the doorway. Speaking to Petronius, she pointed at Ariana and barked, "The mistress wants to see that one."

Petronius raised his eyebrows and looked at Ariana. "Well, don't just stand there, go!" he yelled.

Ariana dropped the beans and followed the maid without a word. They left the kitchen and passed through the *viridarium* to the back of the house. Julia's chamber was part of a three-room suite with its own small peristyle open to the sky. The walls were beautifully painted with birds and flowers. Momentarily distracted by the entrancing scene, Ariana jumped when the mistress spoke.

"Stop your daydreaming, girl, and look at me!"

Ariana obeyed, looking straight at Julia without blinking. *She's going to be a beauty,* Julia said to herself. Despite her feelings about the girl, she couldn't help admiring her lustrous curls and startling dark blue eyes. Her mother's eyes.

"What were you doing in the *tablinum* this morning?" she demanded.

Ariana was surprised. It was not the first time she had taken fresh bread to the master. Why would the mistress be wondering about this now?

"Well, answer me!" Julia insisted.

"I ... I brought bread and olives to the master," Ariana stammered.

"Is that all?"

"Yes, Mistress."

"You did not speak to the master?"

"No, Mistress."

"Well, make sure you don't. I don't want him to be disturbed any more than is necessary. I don't want to see you loitering in the *tablinum* or the *triclinium.* Do you understand?"

"Yes, Mistress."

"You may go now."

As she made her way back to the kitchen, Ariana wondered what had prompted the mistress to summon her on this day of all days. Then she remembered almost running into her as she left the *tablinum.* She had noticed Julia's angry glance as she passed. She could understand her not wanting the master to be disturbed while he was working. But why the *triclinium*? She went there only when Petronius told her to carry some of the dishes from the kitchen—which happened only when there were guests and extra hands were needed.

It was true, she would have loved to linger in the *triclinium* and look more carefully at the paintings of gods and goddesses that adorned the walls. There was Apollo with his lyre and Artemis with her bow and quiver; on one side a bull was led in for sacrifice; on the ground, a snake writhed; above, a bacchante danced to the sound of drums. On the few occasions when she had been able to stay in the room for a moment, she had imagined that she was the bacchante. She was dancing in the forest, under the sky, to the sound of drums and flutes …

"What took you so long?" Petronius shouted at her.

Shaking her head, she went back to work on the beans.

◆ ◆ ◆

An hour or two after Marcus's encounter with his father, Claudius's manservant appeared in his doorway.

"Your father wishes you to accompany him to the baths," he said.

Marcus was still lying face-down on his bed. He did not respond.

"Now!" the man said, and left.

Marcus rolled over and sat up, still sulking. He found a clean tunic, slipped it on, and buckled his sandals. Then he walked slowly toward the *tablinum,* where Claudius awaited him.

"I'm going to the baths," he said, "and you're coming with me. If you keep your ears open and your mouth shut, you may learn something."

Marcus followed Claudius as they walked along the Via Stabiana toward the Stabian Baths. They could not walk abreast unless they descended into the middle of the street, where passing carts splashed through the mud. To Julia's dismay, Claudius did not frequent the new Forum Baths, where he might rub shoulders with the city's most powerful men. Nor did he go to the Central Baths, even though they were closer than the Stabian Baths. At the Central Baths, he would have met many of his fellow merchants and perhaps returned home with a profitable deal or two in the works. But though not averse to increasing his wealth, he did not like conducting business transactions in public. Instead, considering himself a part-time scholar, he sought out Pompeii's more intellectual citizens at the Stabian Baths.

Situated in the southern section of Pompeii, not far from the theater and the temple of Isis, the Stabian Baths were the city's largest bath complex and included a gymnasium and swimming pool as well as the men's and women's baths. As was his habit, Claudius paused in the central courtyard to admire the elaborate decoration of the inner walls, which were painted with false windows, doorways, porches, and balconies to suggest a row of two-story attached houses. The artist had favored red and yellow, producing a bright, lively scene.

Once inside the baths, Marcus forgot to sulk and looked around eagerly. He had always been fascinated by the baths, with their multiple chambers and pools. He wished he could go off on his own and explore, but one look at his father—who seemed to be able to read his mind—made it clear that this was not possible, at least not today.

In the spacious changing room, they undressed and placed their clothing in a niche in the wall. A slave handed them cloths for drying themselves, and they proceeded to the *tepidarium,* where they sat for a while to get used to the warmer temperature. Claudius sat in the pool of lukewarm water at one end of the room.

In the steamy *calidarium* they sat on a bench until they became uncomfortably hot; they then returned to the *tepidarium* to dry themselves and apply ointment. Claudius signed to one of the attendants to give him a massage.

As the slave rubbed his father's back, Marcus looked around and again wondered how the temperature in the different rooms was controlled. Claudius had pointed out that the floor of the bath was raised on stacks of bricks so hot air could circulate under it, as well as in hollow spaces between the walls, to warm the rooms. He had described the *hypocaustum*, the large room between the men's and women's sections that provided steam and hot water to both, but Marcus had never had a chance to see it for himself. He made a mental note to remedy that omission, and soon.

Maybe I could sneak out at night sometime, he mused, his thoughts wandering as he waited. *I could bribe the door slave, he's really just a boy. I could run down here and look around and run back. No one would know ...*

"Marcus?" He jumped. His father was standing beside him, looking at him quizzically. "What are you dreaming about?"

"Nothing, Father," he mumbled.

They went through the door at the end of the room to enter the *frigidarium,* a small, circular room in which a series of steps led down to a pool of very cold water. Like most of his fellow citizens, Claudius believed that a plunge in cold water not only cleansed the body of sweat and ointment but also cleansed the skin. Marcus was not convinced. He disliked the cold water and entered it slowly and reluctantly. He would have preferred to simply sit on the top step and look up at the ceiling, which was painted to imitate a starry night sky. Then he would let his imagination take hold: It was night; he was walking alone through the streets of Pompeii. He was a man, going to meet a beautiful woman, one who loved him and never told him what to do or not to do ...

After bathing, they dressed and went outside to walk under the roofed peristyle. A slave brought Claudius some wine. As they approached the end of the colonnade and were about to turn back, they encountered Lucius Tullius, an *aedilis* and one of the wealthiest and most highly respected men in Pompeii. It was Lucius and his family that lived in the House of the Faun.

"Greetings, Claudius," he said. "And Marcus. It's good to see you!"

Julia will be thrilled, Claudius thought. "Greetings, Lucius. What brings you here? I thought you preferred the Forum Baths—closer to the Forum, more convenient ..."

"Ah, yes, but far less satisfying. Where else but here can one bathe while looking up at the night sky?"

"True, and that's one reason I prefer these baths. They're also less crowded."

"Yes indeed," Lucius agreed.

They walked together toward the entrance, exchanging opinions about the news of the day. Marcus trailed behind. At the entrance Lucius said,

"Unfortunately, I must leave you here. I have to return to the Forum."

"I, too, have business to attend to," Claudius replied. "But it was good to see you. Let's dine together soon."

"That would be delightful," said Lucius with a smile.

◆ ◆ ◆

Pompeiians did not eat a formal midday meal; their main meal, often a lavish one, was dinner, which could begin as early as midafternoon and continue late into the night. Those who were out and about at noon would buy a snack from one of the many food vendors who thronged the Forum and could be found on almost any streetcorner near the center of town. Those who were at home might grab a handful of olives and some bread, or perhaps some cheese, figs, or nuts, accompanied by a cup of water. In the House of the Vettii, when Claudius and Julia were at home they usually ate a little fruit and perhaps one or two barley rolls. Each day Petronius gave them what they requested, sending a slave to each of them with a dish and a jug of water or wine. He then left Ariana to clean up the kitchen while he lay down for his afternoon nap in a little cubicle opening off the kitchen. Ariana did not mind the work. It was the only time of the day when she could be alone.

The kitchen in the House of the Vettii was typical of those found in most Pompeiian houses. It was larger than many, but still somewhat cramped. It contained a basin of water with a sink beside it, an oven, and a waist-high hearth of brick and tile; fires were built in a pit on top of the hearth and charcoal stored underneath. There was never enough charcoal—one reason Ariana was often sent out for more. On nails driven into the walls hung colanders, ladles, spoons, and baking pans, and herbs and smoked meats hung from the rafters. Next to the kitchen was a pantry where oil, wine, olives, dried fruit, and other foods were stored.

A pile of dirty plates had accumulated, some from the evening before, some from that morning. Ariana scraped the leavings into a rough clay bowl to give to the dogs. The two large hounds that spent the day lying sprawled out on the floor of the atrium seemed to have a sixth sense. As she filled the bowl, they appeared in the doorway, gazing up at her in eager anticipation. She gave them the food and watched with a smile as they devoured it. She did not touch them, though. They were guard dogs, not pets.

She carried the dishes and bowls to the sink, dipped a rag in a mixture of water and ash lye, and scrubbed them, then poured clean water over them and set them on the kitchen table to dry. When she was finished, she carried the bowl of dirty water to the *viridarium,* poured out the water at the base of one of the bushes, and wrung out the rag. The garden was, of course, open to the sky, and on sunny days Ariana would turn her face up to the warming rays of sunlight for a moment or two before returning to her chores. On rainy days she would pause in the shelter of the surrounding peristyle to watch the rain falling, its patter merging with the splashing of the fountains in the garden.

As she entered the kitchen, she dipped the rag in the water basin; making sure she was alone, she used the wet rag to clean herself, starting with her face and working downward. When she was finished, she wrung out the rag again and spread it on the floor in a corner of the room to dry.

She took the clean dishes and bowls from the table and placed them on shelves in the pantry. Then she sat on a bench beside the table, waiting for Petronius to wake from his nap. This was her chance to sit still, to think, dream, perhaps even doze a little—though she tried to avoid actually napping, as it made old Petronius furious. Often she sat and thought about her childhood on the farm. She did not really miss her life there—the city was so interesting—but she missed her mother. If only she could go visit her, even if it were just for an hour! But when she had shyly raised the idea with Petronius, he had laughed. "Who do you think you are, that you can imagine coming and going as you please?" he had said. "You were brought here to work in this house, and here you will stay."

And so she had stayed, spending most of her time in the house, though she was grateful for the many errands she was required to run. There was so much to see! She knew all the main streets, side streets, and back alleys of the western half of Pompeii, from the Porta Vesuvio in the north to the Porta Stabiana in the south. No one dictated the routes she followed when ordered to fetch bread or olives for the family's meals or charcoal for the small bronze braziers used to warm the master's *tablinum* or the mistress's chamber. And that was why she ran or skipped when running those errands: It gave her a chance to expand her knowledge of the city by taking detours, as she had done that morning to glance through the doorway of the House of the Faun, and still return to the House of the Vettii before she was missed. But she was never sent to the farm; there were men with donkey carts for that.

Mama must miss me as much as I miss her, she thought. *I wish I could see her! Maybe I could sneak out at night sometime. I could let the door slave kiss me, I know he wants to. I could run down to the farm and hug and kiss her and then run back. No one would know ...*

She shook her head. She knew it wasn't possible. There were guards at the city gates and watchdogs at the farm. She would surely be caught and whipped. She sighed and turned her thoughts to the work she would have to do that afternoon. Most likely Petronius would set her to shelling peas. But perhaps she would be sent on another errand. It was warmer now, and it would be pleasant to be outdoors for a little while.

She was in luck. Petronius woke from his nap and stumbled sleepily into the room where she sat, looking up at him expectantly as though eager to get back to work. He said nothing as he fumbled around in the pantry, seeing what was available for the evening meal. Food—dried fruit, salted fish, pickled vegetables, and the like—was stored on shelves, fish sauce and wine in amphoras on the floor. Petronius determined that there was enough bread and plenty of olives. Meat—mostly mutton—and poultry were brought in regularly from the farm. He would stew some mutton in wine, with herbs and spices added. But he needed olive oil, and supplies were low. He handed Ariana a large pitcher and sent her to one of the shops on the Via Dell'Abbondanza.

"Get this filled and bring it back right away!" he snapped.

Though the pitcher was heavy, Ariana was delighted to be given another errand that would take her out of the house and into the streets. In fact, the errand was a long one, for the Via Dell'Abbondanza was in the southern part of town and she would have to pass the entrance to the Stabian Baths to reach the oil merchant's shop.

As she left the house, she encountered the master and Marcus returning from the baths. Respectfully, she stood aside to let them pass. They went by without a word, though Marcus shot a glance in her direction. *Pretty girl,* he thought. *Too bad she's a slave! Still, she might be worth a kiss or two ...*

Because of the weight of the pitcher, Ariana could not run along the Via Stabiana, but she walked quickly, pausing frequently to make way for the men walking together in pairs, discussing business or politics and paying her no heed. After turning onto the Via Dell'Abbondanza she slowed her pace, taking in the sight of men and women going in and out of the shops, taverns, and *thermopilia*. She especially loved the *thermopilia*, with their marble-topped counters punctuated by round depressions filled with pots containing hot foods and spiced wine, kept warm on a burner that was always lit. The vapors rising from the different foods filled the air and whetted her appetite. Seeing the longing in her eyes, one of the proprietors beckoned to her and held out a dipper full of lentils simmered in chicken broth. She put down the pitcher and raised the dipper to her mouth, delighting in the warmth and flavor of the broth. She thanked the man with a smile, picked up her pitcher, and continued on her way to the oil merchant's shop.

The sunlight was slanting golden along the walls as she made her way home, slowed considerably by the weight of the oil in the pitcher and the upward slope of the terrain. Just before she turned from the Via Stabiana onto the street leading to the House of the Vettii, she took a last look through the Porta Vesuvio at the mountain in the distance. Its snowy shoulders glowed in the afternoon light, and the sky behind it was a vivid dark blue. She thought she had never seen anything so beautiful. *What gods dwell there?* she wondered. *With such a fine home, they must look with favor on the towns and farms below them … including the farm where my mother lives. How I miss you, Mama …*

She roused herself and hastened to the house, arriving breathless in the kitchen with her burden.

"What took you so long?" growled Petronius, as usual.

◆ ◆ ◆

Before the evening meal, all the members of the household, slave and free, gathered to sacrifice to the household gods—the *Lares* and *Penates*—and pray for their continued protection. The *lararium* was located in a small atrium to the right of the entrance, between the main atrium and the kitchen and pantry. It was an elaborate shrine containing images of the household gods as well as one of the goddess Fortuna and one of Bacchus, the god of wine; these two, Claudius believed, were the protectors of his lucrative business. Sometimes, after performing the sacrifice, Claudius would say a few words to the assembled group. This evening he gave them a brief lecture on obedience, perhaps with Marcus's recent behavior in mind.

On these occasions Ariana would stand at the back with the other slaves; with no one watching her, she was free to admire the huge vertical loops of the serpent painted just above the altar. It looked as if it was bounding along the ground, oblivious to the far less vivid gods and goddesses portrayed above it. *Why a serpent?* she wondered, *and why such a big one?*

Every day, as she went about her work, she mused over questions like these, and indeed, the rich decoration of all the rooms in the house gave her much food for thought. When finally she was free to go upstairs to her little *cubiculum* and sleep, her dreams were filled with the gods and goddesses, men and women, and animals of all kinds, large and small, that peopled the walls of the House of the Vettii.

II

MARCH, 72

The House of the Vettii was lavishly decorated in the most modern style. Not so the House of the Faun. Its decor had not been changed in over a hundred years; the wall paintings, designed to resemble rows of different-colored marble blocks between columns and pilasters, had been repeatedly restored to their original brilliance by the best painters in town. The current master, Lucius Tullius, was the great-grandson of the Marcus Tullius who had been Pompeii's most famous citizen and was rumored to be distantly related to the orator Marcus Tullius Cicero. It was he who had built the Temple of Fortuna Augusta, donating to the city not only the temple but also the land on which it stood.

The House of the Faun was the largest in town. It occupied an entire rectangular *insula,* so no other buildings abutted it, and it enclosed not one, as was usual, but two peristyle courts—gardens surrounded by elegant colonnades. While its wall paintings were strictly traditional, the floor mosaics in the rooms where guests were received were elaborate and beautiful. One of them, set in the hallway between the two courtyards so it could be viewed from both, portrayed a famous battle from the Persian campaign of Alexander the Great. Another, at the entrance to the *triclinium*, depicted an immense hippopotamus facing a crocodile on the banks of the Nile. In the center of the atrium was an *impluvium* filled with rainwater; the roof above it sloped inward toward an opening of equal size, the *compluvium*, where waterspouts in the form of lions' heads gathered the water and poured it into the pool. The floor of the pool was covered with colored tiles in a diamond pattern. A small fountain gushed from the center, and on one edge stood the exquisite bronze statue of a smiling, dancing faun, his arms raised, his hair a mass of wayward curls.

On the floor of the vestibule was a mosaic of comedy and tragedy masks surrounded by garlands of flowers and fruit tied with ribbon. Just outside, colored tiles set into the pavement spelled out the greeting *AVE*, welcoming all who crossed the threshold. Across this pavement now stepped the master's son, Gaius

Tullius, accompanied by a slave with a jar of oil and a *strigil.* They were bound for the gymnasium, where Gaius would take his morning exercise.

Although the gymnasium at the Stabian Baths was larger, Gaius used the one at the Forum Baths because it was nearby and he would have a chance to bathe and eat a small meal before his tutor arrived. He ducked in through the back entrance on the Vico delle Terme to avoid the more public entrance on the Via del Foro and the temptations of the shops and *thermopilia* surrounding it. As he walked along the peristyle to the changing room, he noticed a larger-than-usual group watching the wrestling. Though he was a bit late for a lesson with the boxing master, he paused for a moment to watch the contest.

Wrestling was taken very seriously in Pompeii. Though the best wrestlers were slaves imported from the northern provinces, they were given many of the privileges of freedmen. They were well fed and not required to do other work besides train and increase their strength and skill. If they won their matches, on which heavy bets were often placed, their masters might reap a considerable sum, and sometimes the wrestler was given a portion of the winnings.

The wrestlers contended naked, oiling their bodies and rubbing them with fine sand to offer a better hold. They stood upright in the Greek fashion, trying to grasp their opponent on the upper body and throw him to the ground (tripping was permitted, but not gripping the lower body). The first to throw his opponent to the ground three times was the winner. The two struggling here were among the best in town, but as it was a training match, there was no betting and the contest was a friendly one.

As he turned to continue on his way, Gaius noticed Marcus Vettius amid the onlookers. *What's he doing here?* he wondered. *He has the same tutor I do; he must have his lessons in the morning.* Just then he saw a slave come to fetch the truant youth. *Uh-oh, someone's in trouble! And look at the sour expression on his face!* Shrugging, he went on to the changing room to prepare for his boxing lesson.

Gaius stripped and placed his clothes in a niche in the wall. Naked, he could be seen to be in the middle ground between boy and man. As he approached his fifteenth birthday he was still growing. His build was ordinary, neither slim nor heavily muscled, but good habits had made him strong and healthy. His best quality was his pleasant face, quick to smile, a trait he inherited from his father Lucius, who was not only one of the most influential but also among the best-liked men in Pompeii. Gaius was utterly devoted to him.

Binding his fists and forearms with leather thongs provided by the young slave who accompanied him, Gaius went in search of the boxing master, whom he found with the other men watching the wrestling. "One moment," the man said. "They'll be finished soon and there'll be room for us over on the other side."

Like wrestling, boxing had come to the Romans from Greece, where both were part of the games played at the Olympic festival. It was a soldier's pastime, designed to enhance efficacy in battle. Boxers fought in the open, surrounded by spectators. There was little leeway for movement; the goal was simply to batter the opponent until he admitted he was beaten. There were, however, certain tricks that a skilled fighter could employ, such as maneuvering his opponent so he faced the sun.

Gaius was strong and quick to learn, and soon he was landing as many blows as his teacher, who laughingly yielded the round. Gaius knew the man fought lightly with him—it would be unwise to harm the son of Lucius Tullius—but he was nonetheless pleased. "The gods smiled on me today," he said. "Surely they will favor you tomorrow."

He sat on a bench in the shady peristyle while the slave oiled his body and used the *strigil* to scrape off the oil and dirt. Then he took a quick bath in the *tepidarium* pool before dressing and going home for a light meal of bread and dried figs.

◆ ◆ ◆

As Gaius entered the house he encountered Lucius, who had just seen the last of his clients to the door. "Father!" he said happily. Lucius turned and smiled. "Greetings, Son! How was your boxing lesson?"

"It was wonderful, Father, though I'm sure Servius holds back a little. Otherwise I'd have some big bruises to show you."

"No doubt he holds back, Gaius, but even so the exercise is good for you. Exercise your body in the morning and your mind in the afternoon, and your good will at all times."

"Yes, Father," Gaius said, smiling inwardly. Lucius loved to make such statements.

They strolled around the *impluvium* and paused beside the statue of the faun; as was his habit, Lucius patted the faun's head affectionately. "Father," Gaius said hesitantly, "Father, could I go to the Curia with you sometime? I'd like to sit in on a meeting of the *Comitia*, to listen to the speeches. Could you take me with you, just once, when you aren't too busy?"

Lucius looked hard at him, surprised. "Of course I'll take you with me, Son, if that's what you wish. I didn't know you were interested in the speeches of old men!"

"Kineas says it's important to listen to what wise men say, and to learn to speak like Cicero," Gaius responded.

Lucius laughed. "I wouldn't say our leaders are especially wise, and they certainly don't speak like Cicero, but it won't do you any harm to hear what they have to say. Would tomorrow morning suit you? I don't want to interrupt your lessons."

"Oh, yes, Father, thank you!" Gaius assented happily, and dashed off in search of food and a fresh tunic.

◆ ◆ ◆

Lucius paused in the atrium, looking out at the small formal garden in the first courtyard. He loved his house, to which he had devoted a great deal of attention, hiring the best painters to restore the wall paintings, which had been damaged during the great earthquake, and continually seeking out fine statues of marble and bronze to place in the gardens and peristyles. The house had been spared the worst effects of the quake, but even so, repairs had been necessary as a few of the columns in the peristyles had buckled and fallen, and part of the upper floor had collapsed. He had supervised the repairs himself.

He thought back to the terrifying day of the quake: a February day a little over ten years ago. About midday, a long, muffled roar shook the city; no one knew what it meant until the earth began to tremble and buildings to collapse. Many buildings in Pompeii, Herculaneum, and other nearby towns were ruined, some seaside villas collapsed, and huge gulches had opened up in the countryside, one of which swallowed a whole flock of sheep. A nearby reservoir broke, adding floods to the chaos. Some people were killed, but not as many as might have been the case if the quake had struck at night. But it—and the ensuing tremors—occurred during the afternoon, when most people were outdoors, in the streets or the Forum or working on their farms. Still, the shock was great, and for several hours many remained confused, wandering through the streets and lanes, unable to help themselves.

Afterwards, those who were most frightened, or had suffered the most serious losses, moved away, but the greater part remained to rebuild and resume their lives. Wealthy families could leave the city and live elsewhere for a year or two while their homes were repaired, or, as Lucius had done, remain in their houses and endure the plaster dust and the coming and going of workmen. Those who were less well off moved in with relatives and continued to operate their shops and taverns. Life was too good in Pompeii for them to be tempted to leave, despite the constant risk of quakes, large and small. And besides, the repairs and rebuilding would provide income for the city's plasterers, painters, mosaicists, and other workmen for years to come.

It never even occurred to Lucius to leave. The Tullii had been the most prominent family in Pompeii for generations, and it would take much more than a few broken columns and a little plaster dust to convince him to live anywhere else.

Shaking his head to dispel the distressing memories, he walked through the central courtyard to the larger *viridarium* at the back of the house, where he found his wife, Clodia, seated on a bench set charmingly in a small alcove of flowering oleanders. Her face was tilted upward toward the faint warmth of the sun; thrushes chirped in the avaiary nearby. He sat next to her and took her hand.

"How are you feeling today, my dear?" he inquired gently.

"No worse than usual," she responded, resting her head on his shoulder. Since the birth of their second child, a daughter, several years earlier, Clodia had been in poor health, a condition that had worsened when the infant died after only a few weeks. There had been no more children, and little else to distract her from her lingering sadness.

They sat together in silence for a moment. Then Lucius said,

"Your son is a credit to you."

"Ah, no, Lucius," she answered, "he's a credit to *you*. He's so much like you, and you're so good to him."

"He wants to go with me to the Forum," Lucius continued, not wanting to contradict her. "I said he could. I don't think it'll do him any harm, and it might do him good. At any rate it may prevent him from growing up with any illusions about our so-called leaders." Never overtly critical in public, Lucius occasionally shared his views with his wife, confident that she would keep them to herself.

"That would be a good thing," she agreed with a smile.

Clodia Tullia may have been a semi-invalid, but her mind was as sharp as ever. She was rarely seen in public, but behind the scenes she did everything she could to help maintain Lucius's reputation as one of the most capable and respected men in town. Of course, his descent from an ancient and renowned Samnite family provided a solid foundation for that reputation, but with his own resources of wisdom and generosity he had done a great deal on his own to enhance it. No one challenged his position as *aedilis*—commissioner of public works—and many came to him for advice. He also scrupulously avoided taking sides in the political disputes that often roiled the city's political life, and with Clodia's assistance he held frequent dinner parties that included guests from all the factions that were active at any given time. Reclining in his *triclinium*, enjoying his fine Samnite wines and intelligent conversation, they forgot their petty rivalries, at least temporarily.

He smiled back at her, grateful as always for their mutual understanding. Then he stood and looked around the garden for a few moments, noting the new buds forming on the boxwood hedges and the fresh shoots pushing up through the soil around the fountains. He was proud of his garden, not only directing the gardener but even taking over some of the planting himself. He turned to Clodia and said,

"Before very long it'll be much warmer, and it would be good for you to spend some time outdoors. Suppose we hire a couple of litters and go for a ride through the countryside in a week or two. Would you like that?"

"I'd like that very much," she replied.

He bent and kissed her cheek. "I'm going to have a bite to eat and go back to the Forum for a couple of hours, and then to the baths. I'll be home for dinner. If I decide to bring anyone with me, I'll send a man to let you know."

◆ ◆ ◆

After several years of poor health, Clodia Tullia was no longer beautiful, but she was still attractive. This was due in part to the fine fabrics she chose for her garments and the skilled hairdresser she employed. But it also stemmed from her resolve to maintain the reputation of the Tullii. Her appearance was simply part of the overall plan. It was she who insisted that the décor of the House of the Faun be maintained in the old Republican tradition, not changed with every shift of artistic fashion as was common among Pompeii's wealthiest families. She was proud of the house's famed mosaics, and she instructed the slaves to wash them carefully every day with a soft cloth and water. She saw that the slaves were clean and decently clothed, not forced to wear cast-off garments and rags as was the case in many other houses. She spent much of her time seated in the *viridarium*, not only enjoying the garden with its fountains, small statues, and well-tended plantings, but also thinking about what she could do to advance the fortunes of the Tullii.

Clodia ate little, though Lucius had asked the cook to make sure fresh fruit and other delicacies—whatever was in season—were always close to hand wherever she might be. So now, on a small table near the bench on which she sat was a basket of dates and dried apricots. Lost in thought, she absently reached out and took the first thing her fingers touched, a date, and nibbled at it. *Sweet,* she thought, *sweet. How sweet it is! And how sweet it would be to have a daughter. If only she had lived … How I would have loved her. And when she became a woman I would have betrothed her to the son of one of the best families, someone like Gaius, and given her a magnificent dowry, and …* And once again, as she did almost every day, Clodia wept for her lost child.

◆ ◆ ◆

Among the well-off families of Pompeii it was fashionable to have a Greek tutor—whether purchased or hired—to instruct their sons after they had completed the rudimentary schooling that all boys, and some girls, received. The Tullii were no exception. Lucius had sought recommendations from numerous friends and acquaintances before settling on Kineas, an Athenian philosopher-scholar who had been brought to Rome as part of the Emperor Augustus's efforts to infuse the empire with the artistic, intellectual, and cultural traditions of Greece. After many years in Rome, Kineas, now fluent in Latin and conversant with Roman historical and literary writing, had retired to Pompeii to enjoy his later years in a milder climate and less strenuous surroundings. To support himself, he tutored several Pompeiian youths, including Marcus Vettius and Gaius Tullius.

His session with Marcus that morning had been frustrating; the boy had obviously been distracted by some inner turmoil and Kineas could barely hold his attention. Marcus was bored by all things literary, even the Greek and Roman epics with their stirring scenes of battle and shipwreck, their gods, heroes, and monsters. But he did have a good grasp of mathematics, and had Kineas only known it, he could have aroused the boy's interest by telling him about the theories of Euclid and Archimedes, about how aqueducts worked and the underlying structure of the city's encircling walls. But Claudius had instructed him to focus on Horace and Cicero in hopes of instilling in Marcus the same love of poetry and oratory that motivated his father to spend many hours in his *tablinum* with his scrolls while Julia fretted over his apparent lack of ambition.

Kineas's sessions with Gaius were entirely different. In fact, he didn't feel as if he was teaching the youth; instead, they were having an ongoing, animated conversation. Today, as it happened, they were discussing the same ode of Horace that Kineas had had so much difficulty getting Marcus to listen to that morning. *Integer vitae scelerisque purus*—"The good man with a clear conscience …"

"That sounds like my father," Gaius commented.

"Yes, it does," Kineas agreed. "It's men like Lucius that Horace had in mind when he wrote this ode, don't you think?"

"Yes, and he was also suggesting a contrast between such men and others, men like …"

The tutor interrupted. "Gaius, I'm sure your father would agree with me when I tell you it's not a good idea to make negative remarks about anyone, even in private. Suppose someone overheard you saying the name you were about to say and reported it to him. It could create difficulties for your father, and indeed for your family. Do you understand?"

Contrite, Gaius replied, "Yes, I do, and I'm grateful to you for pointing this out. My father has always emphasized that it's important to avoid giving offense. I just wasn't thinking."

"That's all right, Gaius. You're young, but you're learning fast. You'll be as fine a man as your father, I'm sure of it. But now tell me, is there another ode you'd like to consider?"

"Yes, actually," Gaius answered with a smile. "I was just thinking about the one where Horace talks about the end of winter: *Solvitur acris hiems grata vice veris et Favoni*—'The mild west wind melts away the harsh winter …' It seems appropriate for today, when we finally have a little warm sunshine after a lot of cold rain. Though winter's never really harsh around here."

"Have you thought about what Horace is trying to say in the rest of the poem?"

"Oh, sure, that's easy. It's the same idea that shows up throughout lyric poetry: 'Make the most of each day, rejoice in the springtime, enjoy the pleasures of youth, and so on, because death comes much too soon.'"

"Don't take those ideas too lightly," the tutor warned. "You'll be surprised by how quickly youth passes and the cares of manhood arrive. And as for death, it can come at any time—from illness, accident, perhaps another earthquake like the ones we witnessed a couple of years ago—so it really does make sense to make the most of each day."

"Thank you, Kineas," said Gaius. "I'll remember what you've said."

◆ ◆ ◆

On the occasional days when there were no guests, Lucius, Clodia, and Gaius ate their evening meal together. If the weather was pleasant, they did so in the large *viridarium* at the rear of the house; if not, they would sit in a small room that opened onto it, where they could look out at the garden in the fading light yet not be chilled by the evening breezes.

As warm weather was still some weeks away, they were now seated in the intimate little room they favored; a brazier in one corner supplied the warmth Clodia needed. Their meal finished, they continued to sip wine and converse about the events of the day—which, for the most part, were the events of Lucius's day. Gaius was not excluded, however; both Lucius and Clodia were keenly interested in his activities, and in his thoughts and feelings about them as well. While he enjoyed considerable freedom in his day-to-day life, he had not yet pulled away from his parents as is common during the years between childhood and full adulthood.

"There was quite a bit of grumbling in the *Comitia* today," Lucius commented. "Several members are upset about the use of blocks of stone from the curtain walls to repair houses damaged in the earthquakes. There are places where so many blocks have been removed that you can practically walk through the walls and into the fields beyond."

"Why are they concerned, Father? There's been peace in the Empire for as long as most people can remember. We don't need those walls any longer, do we?"

"It's true, we've been at peace since the days of Augustus. But nothing lasts forever. The grumblers feel that as long as we have the walls, we should maintain them. Also, they think it makes the city look bad: 'What will the people of Herculaneum think when they see our walls in ruins?' Actually, I tend to agree with them on that point. Just as we get more respect from other people if we dress well, our city will get more respect from its neighbors if its walls are intact."

There he goes again! Gaius thought, but he kept his amusement to himself.

"How are the grumblers going to prevent people from taking the stones?" Clodia put in. "It's been going on for years. And why didn't they say anything about it before?"

"They're calling for an edict," Lucius replied. "And as for why they've suddenly gotten excited about the matter … well, I think there's something else going on."

"And what might that be?"

"Certain individuals … a certain individual … is trying to get himself noticed."

"And who is that?"

Lucius paused for a moment, his expression serious. "I know I can trust both of you not to repeat this to anyone. Actually, it'll probably be known before long. It's Statius Rufus."

"Rufus!" Clodia exclaimed, not bothering to hide her disgust. "But why?"

"I think he's trying to get support for a run for *aedilis* next year. In his heart he knows he's too young and inexperienced, but he feels that if he has the backing of a sizable portion of the *Comitia* he can win. This business with the curtain walls is just a means to an end: It's a way of forming a faction—an anti-Samnite faction, I might add."

"You mean he's rousing the non-Samnite members of the *Comitia* to oppose the ones from Samnite families?"

"Yes. He says the Samnites have too much influence and it's time for some new blood. He claims that the Samnites—that *we* cannot tolerate change, that we don't really care about the welfare of the city and its people, and so on. Typical political maneuvering; I can't tell you how often I've heard that kind of talk."

"What's so important about whether a family is Samnite or not?" Gaius asked.

"Surely you know, Son, that the Samnites were the original people of this region," Lucius answered.

"Yes, Father, but that doesn't really answer my question."

It was a mark of Gaius's comfortable relationship with his parents that he could speak so frankly to them. Instead of becoming annoyed, Lucius explained further:

"The Samnites were here before the founding of Rome and long resisted Roman rule. They were known for their love of freedom. During the civil war between Marius and Sulla, they had hopes of recovering their independence, but they were defeated by Sulla."

"Yes, Father, but …"

"Let me finish. That was a bad day for Pompeii, even though it could have been worse: At least the city wasn't sacked and devastated like Stabiae and some others. But Sulla made Pompeii a *colonia* and allowed about two thousand of his veterans to settle here. They're the ones who built the *palaestra* and the amphitheater; they loved gladiatorial contests. Many of their descendants, like Rufus, don't think much of the Samnites. The veterans were able to keep the Samnites out of power for a good fifty years. Eventually, though, balance was restored. Until recently there hasn't been much to fight about: Since Augustus brought peace to Our Sea, Pompeii has been prosperous, and the distinctions between veterans and Samnites have faded."

"But you take pride in being a Samnite," Clodia pointed out. "And some of the most respected men in town are Samnites. One look at that Rufus tells me he's not of noble blood!"

"To be honest, Clodia, it's *you* who take pride in my being a Samnite. But you're right, there are still distinctions. However, they're more social than political. Any male citizen of Pompeii, whatever his birth, has the right to seek political office."

"Will you pass the edict?"

"I think we should, but we probably won't. Once people have taken sides on a question, they tend to dig in their heels and stop listening to reason. The Samnites won't agree to the edict because they don't want Rufus and the other upstarts to gain a victory, and the anti-Samnites will use this as evidence that the Samnites are a bunch of stick-in-the-muds. We'll be playing into Rufus's hands, but there's no way to stop it."

"I can't believe that!" Clodia objected. "Can't you speak out, tell them what Rufus is trying to do?"

"Oh, they all know what Rufus is trying to do. That's not the issue."

"Then what is?"

"The issue is that every politician is more interested in his own advancement than in anything else. No one can speak openly against Rufus without looking as if he's guilty of the very thing he's accusing Rufus of—that is, of trying to create factions for his own benefit."

"Well then, how about acting behind the scenes?" Clodia suggested.

"That may be possible," Lucius agreed. "Perhaps we could ask certain members of the *Comitia* to dine with us someday soon."

III
APRIL, 72

Julia Vettia was having a dinner party. That is, Claudius Vettius had asked some friends to dine with him, but it was Julia who had selected those friends and made all the arrangements. Her instructions to Petronius were extensive and involved several days of preparations. Ariana was kept busy the entire time, running errands, scrubbing floors, peeling and chopping vegetables, pounding spices, and running more errands.

It was about two weeks after Ariana's thirteenth birthday. Already she was growing tall, and she was more beautiful than ever. And more and more she felt the eyes of men upon her, following her as she made her way through the city to fetch a jar of oil or a bucket of coals.

Two days before the day of the dinner, she awoke with an unfamiliar pain in her lower belly and streaks of blood between her legs. Left to herself as she had been for so long, she had no inkling of the reason for the bleeding and was overwhelmed by a panicky fear that made the pain worse. She crept into the kitchen and found one of the rags used for cleaning. Returning to her bed, she stuffed the rag between her legs and covered herself with the thin blanket that was all she was permitted.

She had been very quiet, but even so Petronius must have heard her, for he called to her from his chamber beside the kitchen. "What are you doing in there, girl?"—his usual morning greeting. When she did not reply, he sensed that something was wrong. Ariana was usually the first of the slaves to rise, seizing the opportunity to spend a few moments in the *viridarium* before anyone else was up and about, then going to the kitchen in search of a little bread before starting on her daily tasks. When the cook heard her moving around, he would wake up and embark on his own daily routine.

Petronius got out of bed and went to find her, grumbling about how much trouble she was always causing. When he saw her huddled in her bed, he thought at first that he had been mistaken and had not heard her in the kitchen. Then he heard her muffled sobs. Pulling the blanket off the weeping girl, he gruffly asked her what she was crying about. She continued to weep, too frightened to answer. Petronius reached out and shook her shoulder, saying "Answer me! You can't lie around here weeping all day."

Without saying a word or ceasing her sobs, she sat up and showed him the bloody rag.

Petronius knew little of women, having always preferred boys, but he knew enough to understand the cause of Ariana's distress. "Stop your weeping, girl, that's nothing to worry about," he said. "It means you're a woman and can bear children. It will come every month unless you're with child."

His words fell on deaf ears. The girl had never heard about this aspect of womanhood, even in conversations overheard in the house or on the streets. She stared at him in disbelief and her sobs intensified.

Petronius finally realized that he could not handle the situation himself. The girl needed the advice of an experienced woman, one who could explain what was happening and show her how to deal with it. He thought of Julia's maid, but immediately dismissed the thought; the woman obviously disliked Ariana and would probably do more harm than good. Petronius also recognized that it was to his advantage for Ariana to be healthy and content, so in an act of unusual kindness he arranged for her to be taken to the family's farm outside the city. Her mother would do what needed to be done. He gave strict orders, however, that she was to be brought back the next day.

Later that morning Petronius sought out Claudius in the *tablinum.* Since it was rare for Petronius to leave the kitchen, Claudius knew immediately that the circumstances were unusual. He set aside his scrolls and gave the cook his full attention.

"Master," Petronius began. He had earned his freedom many years earlier and the correct form would have been *Patronus*, but he had chosen to maintain the old forms. "Master, forgive my intrusion …" Claudius cut him off.

"Don't mention it. What have you to say to me?"

Petronius explained what he had done and asked Claudius's forgiveness for having acted without first obtaining his permission. "I thought it was urgent," he said. "There wasn't anything I could do, and something needed to be done. That girl is very useful to me."

Claudius thought for a moment. Then he told the cook he understood that the situation was highly unusual and Petronius could be excused for acting as he had. "Just don't speak to Julia about it," he said, "and make sure the girl is back at work tomorrow."

Petronius nodded and left the room. *So she's become a woman,* Claudius mused. *I wonder what lies in store for her.*

◆ ◆ ◆

Lucius Tullius was the first of the guests to arrive. Julia received him warmly, chatting with him amiably as she led him through the atrium to Claudius's *tablinum.* Claudius greeted him happily and drew him to his writing table, where a new scroll lay open.

"I'm glad you could come a little early," he said. "I've been eager to show you my latest acquisition. It's a new rendering of Ovid's *Metamorphoses,* and look, the scribe has left a little space between the words to make it easier to read. I suppose in the long run it uses more paper, but it's worth it!"

... *and you can afford it,* thought Lucius nastily. Then he checked himself. *Of course he can afford it. So can I. Why begrudge him?*

Claudius was a wine merchant, and very wealthy. His business, which consisted mainly of buying and selling large quantities of the local Vesuvian wine, was immensely successful. Even so, the speed with which, at Julia's urging, he had bought this house after its owners moved away had startled those who cared about such things. There was nothing wrong with the House of the Golden Cupids; in fact, as its name suggested, it had a certain distinctiveness that was lacking in the present House of the Vettii. But the wall paintings of the new house were at the height of current fashion, and Julia was determined to make an impression. Which she did.

Though not beautiful by the usual standards, Julia was tall and had long, dark brown hair that she submitted to the hands of a skilled hairdresser each day. And each day the hairdresser found a new way to pile some of that hair on top of Julia's head and surround it with a different arrangement of thin braids and ringlets, some of them false, finishing it off with embroidered ribbons or a gold filigree cap. That, along with Julia's habit of coloring her eyebrows and accenting her green eyes with powdered antimony, created an image that fell little short of majestic, an image that was enhanced by the finely crafted jewelry of gold, emeralds, and garnets that she wore at all times, and the scent of roses that accompanied her everywhere.

To humor his host, Lucius bent and examined the scroll. "It's a fine scroll," he said. "Is Ovid the one they called 'Naso,' for his large nose?"

"Publius Ovidius Naso was his full name. I don't know anything about his nose," Claudius retorted, a bit irritated. "Perhaps his nose was larger than yours or mine, but his poetry—well, just listen to this:

> And since I am embarked on the boundless sea and have spread my full sails to the winds, there is nothing in all the world that keeps its form. All things are in a state of flux, and everything is brought into being with a changing nature. Time itself flows on in constant motion, just like a river. For neither the river nor the swift hour can stop its course;...

"That *is* excellent," Lucius agreed, "and how true!" He watched as Claudius rolled up the scroll. Then he asked,

"Just out of curiosity, who else is joining us tonight?"

"We ... I've also invited Vascula and Aper," Claudius said. "They should be here soon."

Looks like Clodia and I don't need to have a dinner party of our own—Julia's doing it for us! thought Lucius. Nigidius Vascula and Melissius Aper came from established Samnite families and were moderately wealthy. Both had contributed funds for the new Forum Baths. Lucius understood that Julia wanted to associate Claudius (who had also made a contribution) with these well-regarded men. He chuckled at the thought that in her efforts to do so she had created an ideal situation for Lucius Tullius to begin his behind-the-scenes campaign against factionalism in the *Comitia.*

"Oh, and Rufus is coming too," Claudius added.

So much for that idea! I can't accomplish anything with Rufus here.

The other guests arrived shortly thereafter, removing their sandals in the vestibule. Julia made them welcome, inquiring about their wives and children as she led them to the *tablinum,* where they greeted Claudius and Lucius and made small talk while Julia went to make sure everything was ready in the *triclinium.*

◆ ◆ ◆

Alomila had been a great comfort to Ariana. She had held her daughter for a long time without saying anything; then, when the tears stopped flowing, had helped her bathe, given her a clean tunic, and shown her how to adjust the rags to absorb the bleeding. She had found some discarded clothing that could be torn up to produce an adequate supply of rags. And she had explained the basic facts of womanhood.

"You were just a girl when they took you away," she said, "and when the time was right to speak to you about these things, I couldn't because you weren't here. I could only hope some woman in Claudius's household would befriend you and help you through this."

Ariana shrugged. "There are only a few women in that household, and none of them are friendly." *Imagine me going to Julia like this!* she thought. *Or her maid!*

Once past the crisis, Ariana and Alomila made the most of the few hours available to them. They told each other every detail of their lives in the past couple of years, but they avoided any talk about the future. As far as either of them knew, they would both remain slaves of the Vettii, Ariana in the city and Alomila on the farm.

They slept together in Alomila's narrow bed, warming and comforting each other. The next day, as Petronius had arranged, Ariana was brought back to the House of the Vettii in a donkey cart, along with the day's supply of produce.

◆ ◆ ◆

Now Ariana was putting silver bowls full of water on the small tables that had been placed beside the three ivory-inlaid couches that surrounded a larger table in the center of the *triclinium.* Earlier she had carried a brazier to one side of the room and filled it with burning charcoal. Oil lamps imported from Greece glowed in the corners, held up by bronze statues of nude youths; their light flickered over the wall paintings and made the figures seem alive. A row of cupids shown in the various stages of making perfume seemed to be actively engaging in their assigned tasks. She thought she could see them crushing the essences, steeping them, stirring and decanting them, and finally bringing them to a seated goddess for her approval. She watched the goddess sniffing the fragrance and considering it. Would it be the right one for her?

"What are you doing here, girl?" Julia snapped, making her jump. "I thought I told you not to loiter in this room."

"I'm sorry, Mistress. I was just arranging the water bowls."

"Well, the bowls have been arranged and you may go!"

Ariana went back to the kitchen and set to work placing food on trays, which would be carried to the *triclinium* by the kitchen slaves according to Julia's instructions.

◆ ◆ ◆

Unlike wealthy Romans, who were constrained by the demands of a conservative Senate to avoid conspicuous displays of *luxuria,* the Pompeiians operated under no such constraints. The feast ordered by Julia could not equal the famous banquets of Lucullus, but it was certainly lavish. It began with the *gustatio*: a plate of appetizers, including green and black olives, eggs, toasted pomegranate seeds, and Syrian plums. In a separate warmed dish were small sausages. Fortunately, each guest had brought with him two napkins, one to tie around his neck and one to keep nearby to be used to wipe his fingers after dipping them in a water bowl.

Claudius ushered his guests into the *triclinium* and, since they were roughly equal in rank, allowed them to distribute themselves on the three couches as they wished. Vascula and Aper, always inseparable, reclined together. Lucius would have liked to recline next to Claudius, leaving Rufus to himself, but that would have been too obvious, so he smiled at Rufus and stretched out beside him.

"That leaves you all alone, Claudius," he said with a laugh. "Didn't you invite someone else to keep you company?"

Claudius smiled back at him. "Actually, Julia will be joining us for part of the meal," he replied. "She'd very much like to hear about what's been going on in the *Comitia* lately."

A brief silence followed, in which each man concentrated on the delicacies before him and studiously avoided looking at the others. After a moment, Lucius turned back to Claudius.

"My compliments," he said. "These little sausages are very tasty."

A slave brought in silver wine cups and a pitcher of wine, handed a cup to each of the men, and poured.

"Your wine is excellent, as always," Rufus remarked.

As always? How often does he come here? Aware that there was much he did not know, Lucius resolved to keep quiet and avoid political subjects as much as possible. He could not, however, control the conversation.

"Why is Julia interested in the debates in the *Comitia*?" Vascula inquired. "They're really quite boring, if you ask me!"

"Except for today's," Aper put in, with a glance at Rufus.

"Julia has never been content to pass the time the way most women do, shopping, gossiping, or gambling with knucklebones. She's always been interested in the affairs of men, particularly those having to do with governance. In truth, if she were a man I believe she would make a good politician," Claudius said by way of explanation.

This exchange was cut short by Julia's entrance, followed by a slave bearing baskets of hot bread flavored with fennel seeds, and another with a tray of delicacies including chickpeas, dates, and African figs. These were to accompany the main course, or First Table, which consisted of a selection of roast meats and fish—hare, goose, and mullet. As the slaves were carving these and placing bite-sized pieces on each of the tables so all the guests could sample them, Petronius himself entered with a platter bearing a roast suckling pig surrounded by thrushes in a honey glaze.

"What a magnificent feast!" exclaimed Lucius in genuine admiration. *It will be hard to match this ...*

"I am honored by your friendship and pleased to entertain you," answered Claudius, using the customary formula. But Lucius knew he meant it. Claudius was nothing if not honest. Lucius was somewhat less sure about Julia. *Is she up to something,* he wondered, *or is this just display, intended to impress ... and succeeding!*

At this, Julia took her place beside Claudius. She wore a *stola* of fine white wool with an embroidered border. Her necklace was a golden double-link chain; her earrings were gold with pendant emeralds. Her *stola* was fastened at the shoulders with gold *fibulae,* and like most wealthy Roman women she wore several rings. "Is everything satisfactory?" she asked, smiling.

"More than satisfactory!" said Vascula and Aper simultaneously, then looked at each other and laughed.

Claudius offered a small sacrifice to the Lares, and a slave brought him a pitcher of wine so he could pour the libation. There followed several minutes filled with the silence of contented feasting. Then Ariana entered, swiftly and silently, to remove the water bowls and empty them. She returned with the bowls and a pitcher of water, placed the bowls on the end tables, and refilled them. She left the room immediately, not even glancing at the wall paintings and well aware of Julia's disapproving look.

I've seen that girl somewhere, Lucius thought. *Oh, I know—she's the one who sometimes looks in at our doorway as if she'd like to dance with our little faun! How pretty she is. Julia doesn't seem to like her very much; I wonder why.*

◆ ◆ ◆

In the kitchen, all was chaos. Extra hands had been hired or borrowed for the occasion, and everyone was getting in everyone else's way. Petronius had managed to keep order during the first hour or two, but now he was losing control. Finally he told everyone but Ariana to go and wait outside the house until they were called. He would prepare the dessert himself, with Ariana's assistance. There would be time, as Claudius had planned some entertainment for the interval between the main course and the dessert.

Since returning from the farm, Ariana had been even quieter than ever. She seemed to have turned inward, though her natural curiosity had not abated. She obeyed orders without complaint, but she also took every opportunity to spend time by herself, time she spent wondering what was to become of her. She knew her days as a kitchen slave were numbered. The household would soon put her to some other use, and it was likely that at some point she would be married to one of the other slaves.

Now, however, as she and Petronius arranged the delicacies on silver platters, she turned to him and said,

"I want to thank you for what you did for me. It was good of you."

"Don't speak of it," Petronius answered gruffly. "It was necessary. Go call the slaves and tell them to carry these trays into the *triclinium.*"

◆ ◆ ◆

Typical of Claudius, the entertainment consisted of recitations from Virgil, presented by Cossius Libanus, a self-proclaimed "bard" who claimed to be related to the historian Sallust and indeed lived in the house Sallust owned over near the Herculaneum gate. This Cossius made a living of sorts reciting and playing the lyre at dinner parties in the better houses of Pompeii, though his sources of income had dwindled since the latest series of earthquakes had frightened some of the wealthier families into moving away. More eager to please than ever, Cossius had rededicated himself to memorizing works by the most popular authors—especially Ovid and Catullus, whose lubricious poetry was greatly favored by the younger men, those whose dinner parties often included dancing girls and flute players. But Cossius could also recite many of Horace's odes, as well as works by Lucretius, Propertius, and Sallust himself. And, of course, Virgil. If one walked past the House of Sallust during the late morning or early afternoon, one could hear him practicing, reciting to the statues in his garden the works he had been hired to present that evening.

Now Cossius entered the *triclinium,* struck a pose, cleared his throat, and when he had the attention of the guests, started in on the *Aeneid: Arma virumque cano …*

Lucius was bemused by this choice of fare. Everyone knew the beginning of the *Aeneid:* "I sing of war and the hero …"*;* it had been the mainstay of tutors and the bane of young scholars for generations. He could probably have recited it more intelligently than Cossius, with his stylized gestures and mawkish expressions.

What's Claudius doing—what's he trying to tell us? Why would he choose the Aeneid, *of all things? Why not that new rendering of the* Metamorphoses *he's so proud of? Or is this Julia's doing?*

Lucius pondered these questions as Cossius proceeded with selected portions of Virgil's epic: the departure from Troy, the arrival in Latium, the establishment of Rome. Then it came to him: *Tradition! It's about tradition. Claudius—or more likely Julia—is saying, "We're the old families, the backbone of the Empire, the ones who should be in charge of things because we understand tradition, we know what's right and what isn't. The rest are upstarts, planted here by Sulla because he didn't know what else to do with them."*

He glanced at Rufus, but there was no sign that the young rusty-haired man was thinking along the same lines. He was sipping his wine with appreciation, apparently more interested in its fine quality than in the recitation. *With that reddish hair,* thought Lucius, *he might be descended from Cato. If so, the idea of tradition should have some meaning for him. But I see no sign that it does. Besides, at least one of his ancestors was one of Sulla's veterans. Why did Claudius invite* him? *Maybe Julia's heard that he's an up-and-coming member of the Comitia, someone it would be useful to know …*

Lucius's musings were interrupted by the end of the recitation, which Cossius marked with an elaborate bow and a broad smile in response to the polite applause of the host and his guests. As he left the room, a lyre player entered; his assignment was to provide gentle background music for the conversation accompanying the dessert. During the same interval, slaves removed the soiled tables and replaced them with clean ones.

Dessert—the Second Table—arrived a moment or two later: dates and dried apricots, pastries with a wild-duck filling, several kinds of nuts, and a tray of honeyed oat cakes in animal shapes. The guests indulged happily, frequently dipping their fingers in the water bowls. The wine—now mixed with honey—continued to flow and the conversation grew animated, covering everything from the weather to the latest gossip about those not present. Then Julia, looking around the room with a smile, asked,

"And what's been going on in the *Comitia* lately?"

The amused glance that passed between Vascula and Aper was unmistakable, but no one gave any sign of having noticed it. There was a brief silence, and then Lucius, seeing an opportunity, spoke up:

"There's been a lot of talk about the stones being taken from the curtain walls to repair damaged buildings," he began.

"Oh, that!" Julia interrupted impatiently. "That's been going on for years."

"Yes, I know," said Lucius. "But now there are large gaps in the walls, and some members of the *Comitia* are calling for an edict forbidding the removal of any more stones."

"Will you pass the edict, do you think?"

"I can't answer that, Julia. There are arguments on both sides, and the question will have to be discussed thoroughly before any decision is made. Speaking for myself, though, I would be in favor of an edict, so long as the penalty for violations isn't too harsh."

There, he thought. *That should take the wind out of Rufus's sails.*

Because he was reclining next to Rufus, he could not see his face without turning to look at him, but he felt a sudden movement suggestive of surprise. Sensing his guests' discomfort, Claudius changed the subject, telling the others about the scroll he had shown to Lucius and asking them to let him know if they encountered any other noteworthy editions. They agreed to do so, and the conversation turned to literature and the arts. Because Vascula and Aper had made contributions to the new baths—and it transpired that the others had as well, including Rufus—there was an animated discussion of the style of decoration that had been chosen for the inner walls.

"I love the head of Oceanus crowned with crabs' claws that looks down from the ceiling of the changing room," Vascula ventured, and as usual Aper agreed. There was less agreement about the frieze of cherubs competing in a chariot race that ran around the walls of the *frigidarium.* "Cherubs driving chariots!" Rufus said with some distaste. "Hardly a manly image! But I like the scene in the *tepidarium,* with Zeus in the form of an eagle capturing Ganymede."

Does he prefer boys? Lucius wondered. If so, it would not put him at a political disadvantage in a society that welcomed love in all its forms. *It would be useful to know, just because it's useful to know anything about a potential opponent. Certainly Claudius doesn't share that propensity, judging from the décor of this room.* Lucius looked appreciatively at the paintings surrounding him, which portrayed mythical and legendary lovers: Perseus and Andromeda, Apollo and Daphne, Dionysus and Ariadne.

"The paintings in this room are just as beautiful," Lucius said to Claudius and Julia, favoring them with his winning smile. "But my goodness, that one in the vestibule is—well, what can I say?" The painting showed a dignified man pulling aside his *pallium* with his left hand to reveal an enormous phallus, which he was weighing with a scale held aloft in his right hand.

Julia blushed, and Claudius laughed. "You know what that's for," he said. "It's supposed to avert evil. The idea is that such a sight will disarm visitors, cleansing them of whatever evil thoughts they might have."

"Well, it certainly disarmed *me*!" Lucius laughed back. *And actually, it may have cleansed me of evil thoughts. But I wonder about the others, especially Rufus.*

Claudius was reminded of another painting, one that guests never saw. *It's a good thing no one goes into that little room off the kitchen, the one where Petronius sleeps,* he thought, with a surreptitious glance at Julia. On one wall of that room was a graphic portrayal of the master of the house having his way with a young servant. *I wonder why Julia didn't have that one painted over. That could be me and Alomila, that lovely girl Julia banished to the farm. Her daughter—our daughter—has the same blue eyes and wonderful dark hair. And she's now a woman, though a very young one. Men will be looking at her, if they aren't already. How can I protect her?*

The evening wore on as the guests continued to enjoy the pastries, the music, and the conversation. And of course, the wine. Perhaps Julia had enjoyed it a little too much, because now she looked across the room at Rufus and said,

"Statius, I understand you're developing quite a reputation in the *Comitia* for your outstanding oratory. I would love to hear a sample of your skill. Would you consent to declaim for us? I'm sure Claudius has a scroll of Cicero's most famous speeches, or perhaps you've committed some of them to memory …"

This was too much for Rufus. His face turned almost as red as his hair, and he stammered a reply. "I'm sorry, Julia, it's really too late in the evening for oratory, and I must be going—I have some matters to attend to." He stood hastily and bowed to Claudius. "If you don't mind, Claudius, I'll just get my *pallium* from the door slave and be on my way."

Vascula and Aper stood also. "It *is* late, Claudius," said Aper, "and we should be going as well. It's been a very enjoyable evening."

"Yes, it has," Vascula agreed. "We must dine together again soon."

"Wait just a moment," said Claudius. "I'll see you to the door."

"I'll join you," said Lucius, who dreaded the thought of what Claudius would have to say to Julia when he returned. The five of them strolled through the atrium, where the guests retrieved their cloaks and went out into the night, guided by slaves with torches.

So much for preventing factions! thought Lucius. *What could she have been thinking, embarrassing him like that? He'll probably think one of us put her up to it, knowing he's not that great a speaker. And because the rest of us have Samnite connections … Poor Claudius! All he wanted was to have dinner with some intelligent friends …*

But here was his welcoming house, and his loving wife was waiting for him. He set aside his worries and went in, patting the dancing faun on the head as he walked by.

IV

APRIL, 73

A little over a year had gone by since Julia's dinner party, and Ariana, now fourteen, had reached her full height and womanly development. Her breasts, though small, were well-formed. Her legs were long and slim. A few months earlier, there had been an awkward stage during which her arms and legs seemed too long for the rest of her body and the bottom of her tunic hung so far above her knobby knees that Petronius knew something had to be done. Without telling Ariana, he sought out Julia and asked her if by any chance she had an old tunic that could be spared for the girl's use.

"The one she's been wearing for the last three years is much too short, and the male slaves are looking at her with too much interest to suit me," he said. "If she's to go on helping me in the kitchen, she's going to have to be more decently clothed."

"That girl is nothing but trouble," Julia grumbled, but she found a reasonably good tunic and gave it to him. He in turn gave it to Ariana, who did not ask where it had come from. With strips torn from her old, worn-out tunic, she braided a belt to cinch the new one at the waist, and with some smaller strips she made a thin band to bind back her hair, which had grown very long and wavy. When she reappeared in the kitchen Petronius gave a satisfied grunt, but it soon became clear that her new garb did nothing to discourage the glances of the young men in the household, including not only the kitchen help and Claudius's manservant, but Marcus as well.

In fact, it was astonishing how much time Marcus was spending at home these days. He was no longer late for his lessons, though as always he fidgeted continually as Kineas attempted to interest him in history, geography, literature, and philosophy. For a while, the tutor was able to hold the boy's attention with Caesar's account of his exploits in Gaul—especially the descriptions of siege engines like the stone-hurling *ballista,* which spurred the boy to try to construct a miniature catapult of his own—but before long Marcus reverted to his old habits. He would pretend to be listening, but at the end of the lesson he would practically run from the room, saying he needed to go to the kitchen for a drink of water.

There he would see Ariana at work, scrubbing the floor or chopping vegetables. He would stand in the doorway watching until she looked up at him; then he would ask her for a dipper of water. As she gave it to him, he managed to touch her hand with his, and as he slowly drank the water he gazed at her until she blushed and turned back to whatever she had been doing. He would go on his way, leaving her disturbed and unable to concentrate. He was attractive, but his bold looks troubled her. After a few such encounters, she began trying to avoid him. When it was almost time for Marcus's lessons to end, she would remind Petronius that they were low on oil or bread or charcoal and tell him she would be glad to go out and get whatever he needed.

But how can a slave evade the attentions of a determined master? Marcus guessed her intentions and knew where she was most likely to go, and on more than one occasion he succeeded in intercepting her and walking beside her as she made her purchases and walked briskly home. No more detours for her; she hurried back to the house and sought refuge in the kitchen, where Petronius's presence put a damper on the boy's pursuit. But later, when the household gathered for the evening devotions, he would stand near her and let his arm brush against hers while she stood immobile, not wanting to attract attention by moving away from him.

As the weeks passed, Marcus found more and more ways to be near Ariana and speak to her or touch her. Though she did not respond to his advances, she knew it was only a matter of time before he succeeded in having his way with her. She thought of confiding in Petronius, who had been much kinder toward her lately as he realized that she would not be serving in his kitchen much longer. But she was shy and embarrassed, and each day she delayed, hoping Marcus would turn his attentions elsewhere.

Then one day help came from an unexpected quarter.

◆ ◆ ◆

Kineas was no fool, and he had quickly surmised the reason for Marcus's abrupt departure at the end of each day's lessons. For a while he gave the matter little thought, being more concerned with the difficulty of getting the boy to absorb at least a little of what he was trying to teach him. Besides, most young men chased pretty girls; it was the nature of the beast. But something about this particular situation bothered him, and it went beyond Marcus's failings as a scholar. And then one day he realized what it was and knew he must intervene. Without a moment's hesitation he went to find Claudius, who was in his *tablinum* as usual, going over his accounts.

"Forgive the intrusion, Claudius," he said, "but I must speak to you on a matter of some urgency."

"Of course, Kineas. Please sit. What is it?"

"It's about Marcus ..."

"Naturally, what else would it be about?" Claudius smiled, but Kineas went on as if he had not spoken.

"... and the girl who works in the kitchen. Marcus is decidedly interested in her; in fact, I believe he is actively pursuing her in order to ..."

Claudius had turned pale and was gripping the edge of the table with both hands. *Oh gods, no! She's his sister!*

"I'm sorry to trouble you with this," Kineas continued uneasily, pretending not to notice Claudius's distress. "But I don't think it would be wise for Marcus to have his first sexual experience with someone in his own household. If you wish, I could accompany him to the *lupanar* and see that he ..."

It was all Claudius could do to remain calm. He knew Kineas was trying to act in his and his family's best interests, *but oh gods, what am I going to do? This must be stopped at all costs, but I can't tell Marcus why.* He took his hands from the table and placed them in his lap, looking down at them as if considering Kineas's offer. Then he said,

"That would be most kind of you, Kineas. In the meantime, I'll speak to Julia and see what we can do to prevent the matter from going any further. Thank you for bringing this to my attention."

Relieved, Kineas left the room as Claudius leaned forward and hid his head in his hands. The Emperor Caligula might have married his own sister, but any respectable Roman citizen would condemn such a union, and many had been deeply shocked by the mad emperor's action. Brother-sister marriage was a rarity, a practice associated with the Egyptian pharaohs; it was unknown in the Roman Republic and not condoned in the considerably more permissive Empire, Caligula's example notwithstanding.

◆ ◆ ◆

Claudius knew he had to discuss the situation with Julia, but it would not be easy. They spent little time together these days; relations between them had become increasingly strained since the disastrous dinner party at which she had embarrassed Rufus. He found her and her maid sorting through a pile of clothing, choosing the lighter-weight garments in preparation for the warm weather that would be arriving soon. Julia turned toward him with a look of irritation but said nothing when she saw the look on his face.

"I wish to speak to speak with you alone," he said. She gestured for the maid to leave.

"What is it?"

"It's about Marcus."

"What about him?"

"It seems he's become extremely interested in Ariana. Kineas tells me he's been pursuing her actively, and Petronius confirms that he's been spending a lot of time loitering in the kitchen."

Julia dropped the *stola* she was holding and strode toward him angrily, her cheeks flushed and her eyes flashing. "I *told* you that girl would be trouble! I *told* you she shouldn't be brought here. Why did you do it? What were you thinking? Couldn't you have predicted this, with all your reading of Ovid and Catullus? She should have been sold long ago, or at least sent back to the farm, but no, you couldn't let her go, you sentimental fool."

Claudius remained silent throughout this outburst, only interrupting to ask her why she hadn't spoken to him earlier if it was so inevitable that Marcus would be attracted to the girl.

"She's *your* problem, not mine," Julia snapped in response. "*You* brought her here; *you* should have prevented Marcus from even seeing her, let alone … Anyway, that's neither here nor there. I want her out of my house. Immediately!"

"May I remind you, Julia, that it's *my* house, and if I so desired, I could require *you* to leave it immediately?" Claudius pointed out.

"Don't play lord and master with me!" she retorted. "You caused the problem, you've got to solve it, and you've got to solve it right away. She's got to go."

"All right, Julia," he said with a sigh. "But I'm going to do it *my* way, and you're not going to interfere. I'm not going to sell her to the first slave merchant who comes along. I'm going to make sure she's safe and well cared for."

"Yes, of course you are!" Julia replied, still angry. "You care more for her than for your own children …"

"Stop this, Julia," he said, suddenly contrite. "I know I've been at fault. But please bear in mind that Ariana has done no one any harm and has always worked hard and asked for very little. She's not the cause of this situation, and I expect you to respect my wishes and not take out your feelings on her."

"Not the cause? How naïve can you be? Have you *looked* at her lately?"

"Julia, I know she's grown into a lovely young woman. But she's done nothing to invite Marcus's attentions. Petronius attests to that."

"I don't care!" Julia replied. "I don't want her near me. Or Marcus. Or you. I want her out of here. Do you understand?"

"I understand perfectly," Claudius said with a sigh. "And as I told you, I will do what needs to be done. And ..." he looked her in the face, sternly, "you will say or do nothing to interfere with my actions. Is that clear?"

"Perfectly clear," she said defiantly, giving him a final angry glare before turning back to her work.

◆ ◆ ◆

A few days later, Claudius encountered Lucius Tullius at the baths. As was their custom, they spent a few moments strolling under the peristyle, sipping a little wine and chatting about recent events—conversations that had become more animated as the Samnite and anti-Samnite factions had gained ground in the *Comitia*. After Lucius had filled him in on the latest maneuverings by the anti-Samnites (still led by Rufus, despite his unsuccessful bid for the office of *aedilis*), Claudius mentioned the problem of Ariana.

"She's a good girl and a hard worker," he said, "but Julia considers her too attractive and a distraction for the men in the household. She wants her sold."

Claudius looked down at the marble floor as they talked. He was not sure how much Lucius knew or guessed.

"I will honor Julia's wishes," he continued, "but the girl has earned a place in a decent household. I don't want her to be sold to someone who will use her for breeding or for his own pleasure, without any consideration for her well-being. If you know of a household that's looking for a good female slave, perhaps to be trained as a maid for the mistress ... Or at least if you could recommend a reputable merchant, one who ..."

"Say no more!" said Lucius. "As it happens, Clodia's maid recently bought her freedom and went to live with a sister in Herculaneum. Clodia has considered two or three women as possible replacements, but hasn't liked any of them. Why don't you send your Ariana to her? If, as I suspect, she's the girl I saw filling the water bowls at your dinner party last year, she's not just attractive but quite beautiful, and Clodia loves to surround herself with beauty." He spoke warmly, his face alight; anyone could see that he was completely in love with his wife.

Claudius was overcome with hope and gratitude. "Lucius, what a wonderful idea!" he burst out. "Please ask Clodia if she'll take a look at the girl. She'll need some training, but I'm sure she would be suitable. She's very willing and …"

"Say no more!" said Lucius again. "I'll tell Clodia you'll be sending Ariana to us in the next day or two, if that suits you. After that, it's for Clodia to decide."

"Thank you, Lucius!" Claudius replied. "You're a friend indeed!"

◆ ◆ ◆

"We must find some better clothing for you, my dear," Clodia said. "I can't have you attending me in those rags."

Ariana looked down at her tunic and blushed. Though she had been wearing it only a few months, it was worn thin and the edges were frayed. She had been so busy during those months that she had given hardly any thought to her appearance. Now she saw that it was indeed a rag.

"You'll also need to bathe," Clodia continued. "I'll have the slaves bring warm water for the tub, and while you're bathing I'll look for something you can wear. I've got some sandals you can have, too—it looks as if our feet are about the same size."

Ariana had never bathed. Though she tried to wash herself every day, it was not the same as immersing herself in a tub full of water. When the water had been poured into the tub and the slaves had left the room, Clodia said,

"Don't be shy. Take off those old clothes and get into the tub. Here's something to wash yourself with. Take all the time you need. I'll come back in a little while. Oh, and when you're finished you can dry yourself with this." She placed a large, soft cloth on the floor beside the tub.

Though the life of a slave in Pompeii was not usually one of great hardship—and many slaves actually received a small wage that they could spend or save to buy their freedom—it was certainly not a life of leisure or luxury. As she sat in the warm water with her knees drawn up to her chin, Ariana could not believe her good fortune. A warm bath. Clean, new clothes. A mistress who cared for her feelings and appearance as well as her ability to perform the tasks set for her. *What did I do to deserve this?* she asked herself in a daze.

◆ ◆ ◆

When Ariana was clean and dressed, Clodia took the girl's hair in her own hands and twisted it into a knot at the back of her neck. Then with a comb she arranged a few curls over her forehead and stepped back to admire the results. Ariana had been transformed from a none-too-clean slave girl to an attractive Pompeiian maiden. "This will do for now," Clodia said, "but soon we'll find some better clothes for you, and I'll have my hairdresser tend to your hair—there's so much of it, and it's ragged at the ends. It will have to be trimmed, but not too much."

Throughout these activities, Ariana did not say a word.

◆ ◆ ◆

The next morning she was allowed to sleep as long as she wished, not knowing that Clodia had taken the opportunity to speak with Lucius before he left for the Forum. She had explained her wishes with regard to her new maid, and Lucius had consented. "Just keep her close to you for a while," he said. "Claudius was quite eager to get her out of his house."

When she awoke, Ariana was confused at first, not knowing where she was. Then, with a happy smile, she remembered. She sat up in her bed—a larger, more comfortable one than she had ever slept in before—thinking she should throw on a tunic and run to the kitchen to find a bit of bread before seeking out the mistress and asking what services she desired. Just then a young female slave entered her *cubiculum* and said,

"The mistress wishes to see you. Please get dressed and join her in the *viridarium.*"

Ariana looked around her and saw the clothes she had been given the day before hanging from a hook beside the bed, with the new sandals on the floor below. On a small table nearby were a basin of water, a cloth for washing, and a comb.

A comb! Never in her life had she owned a comb. She tried to pull it through her hair, but despite Clodia's attentions on the previous day, it was too tangled. She tied it back and washed her face, then dressed and went to find her new mistress.

"Good morning, Ariana," Clodia greeted her with a smile. "Did you sleep well?"

"Very well, Mistress," Ariana replied, returning her smile. "And thank you Mistress … thank you for the nice little room and the comfortable bed. I've never …"

"Say nothing of it, my dear," Clodia said. "I want you to be happy and comfortable. Here, have an apricot."

She gestured toward the nearby basket of dates and dried fruit. Shyly, Ariana complied. Then Clodia began speaking to her of her duties.

"I won't be asking much of you at first," she said. "You'll need time to learn how we do things here. Later I'll show you around the house. It's quite large, but for the most part your tasks will keep you in the rear part of the house. I have a hairdresser, so you won't have to arrange my hair, but I would like you to watch what she does so that you can—shall we say—make repairs when necessary. I'll have her take a look at yours and see what can be done, but after she's trimmed it and arranged it in an appropriate style, it'll be your responsibility to wash and arrange it yourself.

"I would also like you to take care of my wardrobe, making sure everything is clean and fresh and ready for my use at any time; you'll need to make sure the lighter garments are close to hand during the warm weather and the heavier *stolae* and *pallae* available in winter. My previous maid took excellent care of my clothes, and you'll find everything in good order. Feel free to ask me if there's anything you need to know about their proper care."

"Yes, Mistress," said Ariana, still savoring the first apricot she had ever tasted.

"I spend a lot of time here in the *viridarium,*" Clodia continuted. "I like it here; the sound of the fountains calms me and helps me think—or dream, as the case may be. My dear husband has asked the cook to make baskets of fruit or olives available to me at all times; he wants me to eat more, I think, but I do well enough as it is. Please share these with me if you feel hungry."

"Thank you, Mistress," said Ariana, overcome and a bit dazed by Clodia's generosity. She glanced at the dates but looked away quickly, not wishing to appear greedy. But the truth was, she was very hungry.

Clodia, knowing that young people are always hungry, gestured toward the basket and said, "Please, have some dates and another apricot. It'll do you good."

Thus encouraged, Ariana reached out, gingerly picked up a date, and popped it into her mouth. The look of bliss on her face made Clodia laugh.

"I think we'll do very well together, my dear," she said.

◆ ◆ ◆

That afternoon Clodia took her to see the main rooms of the House of the Faun, explaining the purpose of each. In the atrium she waited while Ariana looked around, taking in the *impluvium* with its little dancing faun, the corresponding opening in the roof, and the sedately painted walls, along one of which stood the sculpted busts of the family's male ancestors.

"This part of the house isn't usually used by women," Clodia informed her. My husband has his *tablinum* here, and on most mornings the atrium is filled with clients hoping to speak to him. See, here's the table where they put their petitions." She gestured at a carved marble table supported by winged lions that stood before the entrance to the *tablinum* as if to guard it. Each morning Lucius's clients—unemployed freedmen and others who visited him each day to receive a small present of money—a *sportula*—or seek his assistance in some private matter—gathered there. Only the most favored clients gained access to the *patronus.*

"You'll have few occasions to come in here," Clodia said. "I may ask you to take a message to my husband in the *tablinum*, but most of our time will be spent in the rear portion of the house."

She led her back around the inner courtyard, with its small formal garden, to the larger *viridarium* beyond it, and showed her the *triclinium* that opened onto it.

"When there are guests, I will expect you to accompany me in the *triclinium,*" she went on. "Though I don't attend all my husband's dinners, I do spend a little time in the room during the early part of the meal to make sure the guests are comfortable. Of course, when we give dinners for mutual friends, I try to be present for the entire evening. This, by the way, is the summer *triclinium*. The one we use in winter is next to the *tablinum* and opens onto the inner courtyard.

"I'll also want you to come with me when I visit friends and acquaintances; again, because my health is not all it should be, I don't leave the house very often. But when I do, I would like you to walk beside my litter and tell me what you see. I've heard that you're an inquisitive young woman, and you may provide me with new insights into matters I've long taken for granted."

Ariana was not quite sure what Clodia meant by this, but she was happy at the thought of going outside the house and seeing the familiar streets of Pompeii. But then Clodia said,

"I know you're used to running around town fetching things like bread and oil, but you will not be doing that while you stay with us. I'll occasionally send you out with a message or an invitation to a friend, but most of your duties will be performed within these walls."

Ariana tried not to let her disappointment show, but Clodia was nothing if not astute, and she reassured her: "Don't worry, I won't keep you cooped up in here like a pretty bird. During the afternoon, when I'm resting, you may go for short walks in the neighborhood if you wish. But please don't go out for the first week or two. Claudius and Lucius have informed me that this would be unwise. I'm sure you understand."

Ariana blushed and looked down. "Thank you, Mistress, I do understand."

"I'm going to rest now," Clodia went on. "While I do, please look through the clothing you'll find in the chest in your *cubiculum.* That's the room you slept in last night. Most of the slaves and freedmen sleep upstairs, but I've always wanted my maid to sleep near me, so my husband agreed to let her, and now you, use that room. It's next to the pantry, so you can sneak in there and get a snack if you get hungry!" She smiled, and Ariana smiled back.

"Thank you, Mistress," she said. "I'll try to leave some food in there for the rest of the household!"

It was a measure of her sense of ease and comfort that she could already exchange little jokes with her new mistress.

"My previous maid took some of her garments with her," Clodia continued, "but there are several good *stolae* and a couple of *pallae* in the chest that you can have. The *stolae* will have to be shortened, of course, and if you need help altering them to fit you, please let me know."

Ariana just looked at her, speechless with gratitude.

"Don't be silly, girl," Clodia laughed. "As I told you yesterday, I want you to be dressed in a fashion worthy of this household. I'm sure you know my husband is a highly respected man, a member of a good family and a leader in the city government. I wish everything—and everyone—in this household to dress and behave accordingly."

"Yes, Mistress, of course" Ariana responded.

"Now I'm going to take a little nap," Clodia said. "But before I do, please feel free to tell me if there's anything else you need or desire."

"Oh, no, there's nothing. Everything is wonderful," Ariana stammered. "But Mistress, I just want to ask you one thing."

"What's that, my dear?" Clodia asked.

"After I've learned my duties and gotten your wardrobe in order and everything … maybe in a few weeks … could I perhaps be allowed to go visit my mother?"

"Certainly!" Clodia exclaimed. "It would be remiss of me not to allow a mother to see her daughter …," *to watch her as she matures, as she becomes a woman, grows more beautiful each day …* She turned aside to hide the tears that trickled from the corners of her eyes. Quickly wiping them away, she turned back and said,

"You may visit your mother once every three months, beginning three weeks from now. If Claudius Vettius permits it, you may stay with her overnight. And when you see her, please convey to her my compliments on the fine young woman you've become."

Without waiting for a reply, Clodia walked swiftly from the room, leaving Ariana standing there, overwhelmed with gratitude but also aware of the emotion she had aroused at the mention of her mother. *What could that mean?* she wondered. *I must find out. I don't want to cause any distress to this sweet, kind woman.*

◆ ◆ ◆

Not many days had passed before Ariana, exercising her natural curiosity, had explored almost every part of the house—even the atrium, in the quiet afternoon hours when Clodia was resting and Lucius was absent at the baths or the Forum. She often lingered in the hallway between the two courtyards, gazing at the mosaic of Alexander and dreaming about her mother's ancestors and their life on those vast Asian plains.

One morning she came upon a young slave washing the mosaic floor with water and a soft cloth. Going up to him, she asked him his name. "It's Timon," he answered. "I already know yours; we all do. Welcome to the House of the Faun!"

She smiled at him. "Timon—that's a Greek name, isn't it?" He nodded. "Several of us are of Greek ancestry, but you'll find that we come from many different lands. There are about forty of us in this house; don't try to learn all our names at once—you'll know them all in time. And you'll find that each of us has a story to tell and would like to hear yours."

She thanked him and offered to take his place, explaining that she wanted to examine the mosaic more closely. Surprised, but not unwilling to be relieved of the task, he handed her the cloth and went off to enjoy a few moments of rest. Ariana bent over the small stones, gently washing each portion of the work and wringing out the cloth before going on to a new section. She was particularly interested in the features of Alexander and spent some minutes on her knees just gazing at his face. It was there that Gaius encountered her.

With her *stola* draped in a circle around her kneeling form and her hair hanging loose down her back, her face pensive as she wondered about her possible forebear, she presented a picture of beauty such as Gaius had never seen before. He was deeply moved by the simplicity and quiet repose of her posture. He approached her and touched her lightly on the shoulder. Startled, she looked up at him and blushed, gathering her skirts and preparing to stand and flee. But he restrained her.

"The mistress probably wouldn't want you to be doing this," he said, "and you risk soiling your clothing. But I'm sure you knew that. So why are you so interested in this mosaic?"

Still taken aback, but appreciating his honest query and friendly smile, she began telling him about her interest in Alexander and her mother's stories about her ancestors in Sogdiana and possible descent from the Princess Roxana. Then, realizing that she had been talking to him for several minutes, she blushed again and said,

"But Master, these are just the dreams and stories of a slave. They cannot interest you. Please forget you saw me here."

"Please don't call me Master. I'm Gaius. And don't be embarrassed. I loved hearing your tale and would like to hear more. I have to go to the gymnasium now, but maybe we could speak again sometime."

He turned to go, but then something occurred to him, and he turned back and looked at her closely.

"You know, I think I may have seen you before," he said. "Now where …? Oh, I know: You're the girl who used to look in our doorway sometimes. You looked as if you wanted to come in and dance with our little faun. Isn't that right?"

Again she blushed. "Yes, that was me," she said shyly. "They used to send me to the bakery for bread, and I'd look in on the way home."

He smiled at her. "If it had been me, I'd have done the same thing!" he said, and went on his way.

◆ ◆ ◆

That evening there were no guests for dinner, and Lucius, Clodia, and Gaius met in the winter *triclinium* to dine together as was their habit. Spring had arrived, but it was not yet warm enough to sit outdoors. The brazier was not lit, however, and Clodia sent a slave to ask Ariana to bring her a shawl. Ariana complied, and as she placed it around Clodia's shoulders she thought to herself, *How pleasant and friendly they seem. Wouldn't it be lovely to be able to sit with them, to have a mother and father and brother to talk to …* But though the three of them smiled kindly at her, it was obvious that her place was elsewhere. A little sadly, she left the room and went to the kitchen, where the cook had set out a plate for her. She sat on a bench beside the table, gazing at the lovely mosaic of a cat capturing a bird that decorated one of the walls.

Had she only known it, Clodia was having similar thoughts. *I know it wouldn't be proper, but would it do any harm for Ariana to join us on some of these quiet evenings? It would be nice to have her here with us, like a daughter almost ...*

Knowing where such thoughts would lead her, she shook her head and turned her attention to the conversation between Lucius and Gaius. As usual, Gaius was intensely interested in the doings of the *Comitia*, and indeed he accompanied his father to the Curia whenever Lucius would allow him to. Now they were discussing the worsening conflict between the Samnites and the anti-Samnites. Lucius had made every effort to prevent the two factions from forming or gaining strength; he had spoken privately to almost every member of the *Comitia*, earnestly warning of the possible consequences of such an arbitrary and unnecessary polarization of the city council. And every man he had spoken to had agreed with him and pledged not to join one faction or the other, not to support the proposals of one faction at the expense of the other's—in short, not to fan the flames of factionalism. But they were only human, and they could not resist the temptation to advance their own goals by siding with those who promised to help achieve them. As a result, the *Comitia* had not passed an edict regarding the curtain walls. In fact, for the past few months it had issued no edicts at all. It was hopelessly deadlocked.

"I've been told that the Emperor Vespasian is thinking of intervening," Lucius was saying.

"How would he do that, Father?"

"Well, I suppose he could send a small army and simply take over the city," Lucius said, half-jokingly. "But I hear he's thinking of sending an administrator, someone who has no interest in either faction and will make sure things get done."

"An administrator!" Clodia broke in. "Do you mean someone who would be ranked above the *aediles*—above you and Proculus—and even the magistrates?"

"I suppose so," said Lucius. "I think, actually, that he'd replace all four of us, at least temporarily. He would issue edicts, and the *Comitia* would approve them—or else."

"Or else what?"

"I have no idea. I haven't thought about it very much, since it's just a rumor. But it seems to me that if Vespasian's taking an interest in us, it can't be a good thing. While he's no Caligula or Nero, he's still the Emperor, and he's used to having his way.

Anyone he sends here to restore rational government is likely to be something of a dictator, in effect if not in name."

They were silent for a while, drinking their wine and listening to the fountains in the garden just outside. Then Clodia said,

"Lucius, there's still time. There must be something you can do. Do the members of the *Comitia* know about this plan of Vespasian's?"

"I don't think so," he replied. "I heard about it from Claudius, who heard about it from another wine merchant who's just come back from Rome. But I don't think it'll remain a secret for very long."

"Well, can you address the *Comitia* and warn them? Tell them if they don't get back to governing the city, someone else will come in and do it for them? And how long will this 'administrator' stay? Something tells me that once he's here, he won't be leaving soon."

"You're right, Clodia," Lucius agreed. "There's a clear danger here, and I'll do whatever I can to avert it. Meanwhile, tell me …"—he clearly wanted to change the subject—"how's your new maid working out?"

"Oh, she's a lovely girl," Clodia said, "and she's learning fast. The only problem is that she wants to spend more time outdoors, roaming the streets the way she did when she was younger. But this I can't allow, though I do let her take short walks while I'm resting."

"I can sympathize with her," Lucius said. "Even though I walk to and from the house and the Forum and the baths almost every day, I find that most of my time is spent indoors, and now that it's getting warmer, I'd like to be outdoors more. It would be pleasant to go for an excursion in the countryside, don't you think? Perhaps we could hire a couple of litters and go for a tour. We could take her with us; I'm sure it would put a light in her eyes and a bloom on her cheeks!"

"Father, that's a wonderful idea!" Gaius said, though he chuckled inwardly at Lucius's "light in her eyes and bloom on her cheeks." "Would you like that, Mother? Do you feel well enough, now that spring is here?"

His excitement was contagious, and Clodia could not help responding with a loving smile. "Of course, if the two of you would enjoy an excursion, so would I. And we can take Ariana with us. In fact, she has said she'd like to visit her mother. We could leave her at the farm on the way back into town."

And so it was decided.

V

JUNE, 73

In the weeks since Ariana's departure from the House of the Vettii, Marcus had been glum and sullen most of the time, though he had shown renewed interest in some of his former pursuits, especially watching wrestling and boxing matches in the gymnasium. Kineas continued to tutor him, despite his almost complete lack of interest in the subjects Claudius considered important. Literature in particular failed to move him. In desperation, Kineas returned to Caesar's Gallic wars, spending an inordinate amount of time on the siege of Alesia, its defenses, and how they were finally overcome. As before, this piqued Marcus's interest for a while. He was fascinated by the thoroughness and extent of the siege works Caesar had built to surround Vercingetorix's mountaintop fortress and starve out its ninety thousand defenders: an encircling wall with towers overlooking a deep trench, concealed pits filled with sharpened stakes and iron hooks to prevent a breakout, a similar ring of fortifications facing outward to forestall any attempt to break the siege. Marcus absorbed every detail, even constructing a model of the fortress and Caesar's siege works, and Kineas hoped that in the process his student might have absorbed something of the rhythm and muscularity of Latin prose. But he could not persuade the youth to read history or philosophy; Marcus flatly refused, claiming that these were useless subjects suited only for old men who had nothing better to do with their time. When *he* was a man, he would do something worthwhile, not sit around all day reading scrolls like his father. He wanted to be an athlete or a soldier. What use were a bunch of dusty old scrolls to someone with his ambitions?

In vain, Kineas reminded him of what he had learned from Caesar's account and pointed out that good military leaders paid close attention to the writings of their predecessors in order to apply what they had learned and avoid their mistakes. Marcus merely shrugged.

Then one morning Kineas remembered his promise to Claudius. After a frustrating hour with his inattentive student, he rolled up the scrolls and put them away.

Then, before Marcus could dash from the room, he touched him on the shoulder and asked gently,

"Marcus, you've been very restless these past few weeks. Have you had dreams that disturb you?"

Marcus looked at him in surprise, then looked down and said nothing.

"Have you been dreaming about women, Marcus? And waking up with dampness between your legs?"

Marcus gave him another surprised look and nodded sheepishly.

"Don't be embarrassed," Kineas reassured him. "That's perfectly normal. In fact, it would be surprising if it *didn't* happen. It simply means you've reached full manhood. You're too young to marry, but you could lie with a woman and have children."

Marcus looked at him in amazement. "Do you mean I'm a man?"

"Of course you are!" Kineas replied. "Whatever made you think you weren't?"

Marcus shook his head, saying nothing. Kineas waited a moment. Then he said,

"If you want to find out what it's like to lie with a woman, I could take you to the *lupanar* and introduce you to Africanus, who runs the place. He's used to helping young men learn the ropes, so to speak. And your father has given his permission."

Marcus nodded, again saying nothing.

"If you wish," Kineas concluded, "we could go there this evening."

Kineas's session with Gaius that afternoon was, as usual, vastly different from his morning session with Marcus. As usual, Kineas did not feel compelled to instruct his charge; instead, tutor and student engaged in conversation, for all practical purposes as equals. Over the years, they had held many such discussions as Gaius became increasingly immersed in the writings of the best Latin authors, from the stern moralists of the Republic to the libertine verse of Catullus. They had studied not only the *Aeneid* but also Virgil's *Eclogues.* They had taken time out to laugh at Plautus's bawdy comedies, and not long ago they had spent some time with Ovid's *Metamorphoses.* The young man had a knack for going right to the heart of a work and displaying an acute understanding of its meaning and implications. He would read the assigned piece the evening before and arrive in the *oecus*—the room off the atrium where he had his lessons—fully prepared to tell Kineas what it was about and why it was important—or, alternatively, to probe his tutor for a fuller understanding of some point he had not grasped, usually for lack of experience, not intelligence.

It would not be long before those pleasant sessions ended, as Gaius would turn sixteen in a few days and was old enough to continue his studies on his own; besides, he was spending more and more time with his father in the Forum and often sat listening while Lucius received clients in his *tablinum.* There was no doubt in his mind that he would become a member of the *Comitia,* and perhaps *aedilis,* in his turn; he could wish for nothing more. And unlike Marcus, he well understood that a broad-based knowledge of history, literature, and philosophy would be invaluable as he pursued his goal.

So now, in their last few sessions, Gaius and Kineas were once again considering the works of Horace. Though a Greek, Kineas had developed a profound respect for Horace, considering his works emblematic of all that was good about Rome and the Romans.

"Don't worry, Kineas," Gaius was saying. "I'll definitely go on reading and rereading Horace over the years. He seems so real to me—he's like a friend."

"I hope you'll study other authors as well," Kineas replied. "There are several we haven't gotten to …"

"Don't worry," Gaius said again, laughing. "My father and Claudius Vettius have become good friends, and Claudius has promised to lend me any of his scrolls I might want to study, provided he's had a chance to read it first! He keeps up to date with all the best writers—it's his passion, you know—and he'll probably make sure I'm up to date as well."

"I'm glad to hear that," said Kineas, wishing Marcus was a little more like his father. "In the meantime, what do you have to say about Horace, now that he's been your friend for so many years?"

Gaius responded eagerly. "Well, I have an idea about some of the odes, the ones in which he talks about the sea. I wonder if you'll agree with my interpretation."

"What is it?"

"It has to do with how Horace feels about the sea, how he describes it and its effects on those who dare to sail upon it."

"Yes, go on."

"He mentions the sea a lot, and in a lot of different contexts—in connection with sailors, ships, boats, sailing, storms, shipwreck, drowning, and so on. But most of all he uses it as a metaphor for unpredictability. For him, the sea is something that constantly threatens to erupt in stormy waves and overwhelm whoever is rash enough to sail upon it. This is especially true in Book One, where no fewer than thirteen of the odes touch on this aspect of the sea."

Kineas was fascinated, but he tried not to show it. Though the young man was justly proud of his achievements, he had been brought up to speak and act with modesty, and the tutor approved of this training.

"Look at the third ode," Gaius went on. "The sea is *non tangenda*—off limits; the gods have forbidden men to cross it. The man who first set sail and risked the storms and other dangers of the sea was unbelievably bold—both fearless and impious. And this ode is addressed to none other than Horace's good friend Virgil. Horace is asking the gods to protect Virgil on his voyage, but he's also implying that Virgil shouldn't be setting sail in the first place. What I'm wondering …" Here he paused and looked shyly at Kineas. "What I'm wondering is …"

"Well, what? Come on, out with it!"

"I wonder if Horace is suggesting that Virgil was attempting too much in undertaking to write the *Aeneid.* Wait, let me explain." (This in response to a surprised gesture by Kineas.)

"Look at Ode 14," Gaius went on. "It's about a ship that's carried out to sea by 'new' storms—in other words, this has happened before. What does that ship represent? The state? Love? The poet himself? I think it might refer to the poet. Look at Ode 28: The sea ended the life of the philosopher Archytas, and *Me quoque devexi*—'I, too, was seized.' Who else could that be but Horace?"

"That makes sense," Kineas agreed. "Go on."

"Things start to change at the end of Book One. In Ode 32, Alcaeus—who you told me was Horace's model—moors his boat after it's been tossed by storms. This is the first hint that a poet can cross the sea safely.

"Now listen to this." Gaius was becoming excited as Kineas seemed to be following his argument without objections. "In Book Two the sea is still threatening, but there are differences. In Ode 10, Licinius is advised not to sail too far out to sea, but he's *not* told to avoid the sea altogether. Then in Ode 20 the poet will dare to look upon the Bosporus, though only from above. So you see, in Book Two the sea is still something to be feared, but it's not something to be avoided entirely. What I think this implies is that moderate risks are acceptable—and that includes moderate risks taken by a poet.

"In Book Three there are more changes. In Ode 1, we're told that a man who wishes for only enough to live on will not be made anxious by the stormy sea. In Ode 2, the poet implies that he would be willing to embark in a fragile boat, as long as his traveling companion is pious. But now we come to Ode 4. Listen to this (you remember, he's addressing the Muses): 'With you beside me, I would gladly set sail/Across the raging Bosporus.' So from the anxiety he expressed in Book One, Horace has progressed to caution in Book Two and confidence in Book Three. In other words, in Book One the sea was an obstacle to Horace as a poet, and he didn't fully approve of Virgil's crossing it. This has changed. Horace now has the confidence to write new kinds of poetry—*carmina non prius audita*—and presumably he would approve of Virgil's doing so as well. And look at this: In Ode 28, Horace has become so confident that he actually celebrates Neptune's festival. And finally, in Ode 29, he no longer feels the need to have the gods calm the waves. Now he can safely cross the sea in a little boat—after all, if Alcaeus could do it, why can't he? That little boat represents self-confidence."

Kineas was silent for a few moments, considering how to respond. Then he said,

"Gaius, your analysis is truly impressive. However, I'm still not entirely sure what you think Horace is trying to say with this sea imagery."

"I'm sorry, I should have explained further," Gaius replied. "It's like this. Horace's treatment of the sea gives us insight into his philosophy of life. That philosophy has two main aspects. One is moderation: Observe the mean, stay within your limits, and you'll live well. The other is confidence: There are times when it's necessary or desirable to transcend limits and take risks. So it is with the poet, whether it's Alcaeus, Virgil, or Horace himself. The sea is unapproachable as long as the poet lacks confidence in himself. When he's ready to take some risks, it becomes a challenge."

"Yes, I see," said Kineas. "Congratulations, Gaius, this is an excellent piece of scholarship. I hope you'll share it with your father and Claudius. And Gaius ..."

"Yes?"

"You'd do well to consider Horace's philosophy your own. Moderation and confidence—those are good qualities to have."

"Thank you, Kineas," Gaius smiled. "As I said, I think of Horace as a friend."

◆ ◆ ◆

"Lucius," Claudius called out, coming up behind him as he strolled along the Via Stabiana. "Lucius, I've been meaning to talk to you. I wanted to say how grateful I am to you for providing a good home for my ... for the girl, Ariana. And I was wondering if you could tell me how she's getting along. Is Clodia satisfied with her?"

"Satisfied! My dear Claudius, it's *you* who's done *me* a favor. The girl is beautiful, which is a pleasure in itself, but she's also very sweet and thoughtful. She anticipates Clodia's wishes and makes her comfortable without her having to say a word. And Clodia's much happier. She's eating more, she's more cheerful, and I think her health is improving. The other day we went for a tour of the countryside, taking some wine and cheese and olives along so we could spend the day outdoors, and the whole time Clodia and Ariana were chatting with each other as if they were mother and daughter …"

He broke off suddenly. Though he never spoke of the death of his second child, her memory lay close to his heart, and in the silence of the night he, too, sometimes shed tears for the loss he and Clodia had suffered. Claudius fell silent as well, and the two of them walked together to the corner of the Via Nola, where Lucius turned left to traverse the last few steps to the House of the Faun while Claudius continued on his way to the House of the Vettii.

◆ ◆ ◆

Ariana, too, had blossomed in her new surroundings. The day in the country had indeed, as Lucius had predicted, "put a light in her eyes and a bloom on her cheeks." Better food, and more of it, had given her a healthy glow, but never having eaten large quantities of food, she had not developed the habit of overeating and thus remained slim even as she developed a woman's figure. Her hair was dressed simply but elegantly; Clodia would not allow her to pile it up on top of her head in the latest fashion, but her hairdresser showed Ariana how to pull it back in a twist, leaving a few loose strands on each side to soften the lines of her face. Her clothing consisted of the abandoned garments of her predecessor, but with Clodia's help she had trimmed and shaped them to create several simple but flattering *stolae*, which she belted with braided lengths of wool from a worn-out *palla*. When she looked at her reflection in the small polished copper mirror Clodia had given her, she saw herself transformed into an attractive young woman with glistening black hair and dark blue eyes. *Whose eyes are those?* she often wondered. *Are they Roxana's eyes? Or Alexander's?*

Her visit to her mother, and the assurance of future visits, had given her a sense of security and a deep gratitude that was reflected in the care she took in satisfying Clodia's wishes. In fact, however, Clodia made few demands on her, and she found herself spending a great deal of time sitting with her mistress in the *viridarium*, enjoying the warm sunshine. During these times, Clodia increasingly confided in her, speaking of her pride in her husband and her hopes for her son.

On one occasion, she even mentioned the child she had lost, and as always the tears came to her eyes. Without thinking, Ariana went over to her and put her arms around her, murmuring words of comfort and holding her until finally she raised her head and wiped away the tears.

"I'm sorry, Mistress, I didn't mean …" Ariana stammered.

"No, my dear, it's all right. Thank you. You're very good to me."

"Oh, no, Mistress, it's *you* who are *much* too good to me!"

In the afternoons, while Clodia rested, Ariana went for walks. Not wanting to encounter Marcus, she avoided areas she knew he frequented and went exploring in parts of Pompeii she had not seen before. Going east on the Via Nola, she discovered a whole district of merchants' houses into whose entrances she peered curiously. Traveling north on the Via Stabiana, she arrived at the Porta Vesuvio and looked out at the immense mountain with its snowy peak. She was not allowed to venture outside the gates, but she promised herself that one day she would walk in the countryside, exploring the woods and streams as she had as a child, staining her fingers and lips with the juice of blackberries as swallows swooped and darted overhead.

◆ ◆ ◆

Dusk was fading into evening as Kineas and Marcus arrived at the *lupanar.* The brothel was a small, two-story building strategically located at the junction of two alleys not far from the Forum. Africanus met them at the entrance, bowing respectfully. His palm had been liberally greased by Kineas that afternoon, and he gave no hint of noticing Marcus's state of mixed embarrassment and excitement. All other customers would be directed to the upper floor; nor would there be any giggles from the girls as the youth made his choice. Africanus had done this before.

"Africanus will see to your needs," Kineas reassured Marcus. "You can trust him. And if you decide you wish to stay here tonight you may do so—but if you do, I recommend that you go directly to the Forum Baths in the morning. You can bathe, get something to eat, and watch a little wrestling. I'll meet you at home at the usual time."

Marcus mumbled something in reply and followed Africanus into a dimly lit room surrounded by five small *cubiculi,* each containing nothing but a bed covered with a thin mattress. The walls of the central room were painted white except for a section of the north wall, which contained a picture of Priapus in front of a fig tree. There was nothing unusual about this—Priapus appeared with great frequency in wall paintings throughout the city. This one, however, sported a huge double phallus.

Marcus glanced up and noticed that the upper part of the room, above the doors, was decorated with a frieze containing a series of pictures portraying … He stifled an exclamation. *What are they doing? I didn't know you could do it like that. Or like that!*

"Do you see anything that interests you?" Africanus asked. Nothing in his tone of voice indicated that he knew exactly what Marcus was thinking.

As the youth seemed to have lost the ability to speak, the older man led him gently into one of the *cubiculi.* Then, stepping back into the main room, he clapped his hands twice. Three slave girls entered the main room and stepped to the door of the chamber where Marcus waited. They had been imported from the eastern reaches of the Empire and specially groomed for this purpose. In the dim light and to the young man's unschooled eye, each seemed more alluring than the one before.

"You may choose any of these three lovely young ladies to be your companion this evening," Africanus told him. "They're all very well trained, and I'm sure you'll be happy with any one of them. Or all three if you wish!"

"No, just one," Marcus mumbled, blushing to the roots of his hair. "That one." And he pointed at the one who looked most like Ariana.

VI

AUGUST, 73

It was midsummer, and the streets of Pompeii were dusty and hot. The treeless avenues offered no shade, and the narrow alleys stank. Business and government came to a standstill as people stayed indoors or gathered at the baths. Evening brought some respite as the sun slid into the sea and an onshore breeze caressed the city. Then the somnolent streets and silent houses came to life; slaves rushed to bring chilled wine to their masters; children ran around the courtyards, playing tag and hide-and-seek; and even more than at other times of the year, friends dined together in the pleasant evenings, *triclinium* doors flung wide to welcome the breezes and the moonlight.

Clodia and Lucius held several dinner parties that summer. Lucius was still trying to persuade his colleagues in the *Comitia* to abandon their factional ties and work toward compromise before Vespasian, increasingly impatient, sent his dreaded administrator to take over the city government. But even Lucius's well-developed leadership abilities were not up to the task. Rufus and his cohorts had convinced themselves that the old Samnite families were trying to take full control and exclude the descendants of Sulla's veterans from city governance. Lucius knew it was just a matter of time before the administrator arrived.

Gaius was usually present at his father's dinners, and Clodia, as was her custom, attended for part of the evening, quietly listening to the conversation and directing the serving staff to bring in wine, water, and new dishes at the appropriate times. She took particular pleasure in arranging the flowers, which grew in great abundance throughout the region and were used liberally at banquets and festivals. Ariana stood at her side as she reclined next to Lucius, ready to assist her if there was anything she needed. And so it was that on several evenings Gaius saw her there, standing like a statue as she silently awaited her mistress's bidding. *She looks like a goddess!* he thought.

On one of those evenings, Lucius had invited a rising young poet, Eumelos, to entertain his guests with selections from Catullus and, if he wished, one or two of his own lyrics. The young man, whose name attested to his Greek origins but whose parents, seeking to expand their olive oil trade, had brought him to Pompeii as a child, had rich curly hair, a sweet face, and an assured bearing. He began with one of Catullus's best-known poems, "To Lesbia," with its scarcely-disguised echoes of Sappho:

Him rival to the gods I place,
Him loftier yet, if loftier be,
Who, Lesbia, sits before they face,
Who listens and who looks on thee;

Thee smiling soft. Yet this delight
Doth all my sense consign to death;
For when thou dawnest on my sight,
Ah, wretched! flits my laboring breath.

My tongue is palsied. Subtly hid
Fire creeps me through from limb to limb:
My loud ears tingle all unbid:
Twin clouds of night mine eyes bedim …

Gaius was mesmerized. He had read some of Catullus's work, and that of Ovid and other poets who often wrote of love, but love poetry had never made much of an impression on him. Love was for another time; he was far too interested in his day-to-day pursuits to give it much thought. But here he was, listening to Catullus speak of love while a goddess stood across the room from him. And now Eumelos was reciting another famous poem by Catullus: *Vivamus, mea Lesbia, atque amemus …*

> Let us live, my Lesbia, and love, and not give a penny for the lectures of strict old men. Suns can set and rise again; but for us, once our brief light has set, there's a night of unending sleep. Give me a thousand kisses, then a hundred, then another thousand, then a second hundred, then yet another thousand, then a hundred, then, when we've made many thousands,…

Gaius was beginning to feel the sensations described in the first poem: a delicate tingling, little tongues of fire, a pronounced breathlessness. Unable to help himself, he glanced across at Ariana and was stunned when she returned his glance. Murmuring an excuse, he hurriedly left the room as Eumelos launched into "The Marriage of Peleus and Thetis."

Later, as the guests were departing, Claudius lingered behind and asked Lucius if he could spare a moment; he wished to consult him on a personal matter.

"Of course, my friend," said Lucius, leading him into the *tablinum.* "Please have a seat. Would you like some more wine?"

"Oh, no, thank you, Lucius. I've had plenty, and it was very good. And your kitchen, as always, did you proud. That pheasant with mushroom and goose-liver stuffing was delicious, better than anything old Petronius can come up with."

"On the contrary, I think Petronius serves excellent dishes," Lucius objected, smiling. "But if you wish, I'll send over a slave with instructions for preparing the pheasant—that is, if Petronius wouldn't be insulted!"

"That would be very kind of you."

"So tell me, Claudius, what's your concern, and what can I do to help?"

"It's about Marcus. I don't know what to do with him. He's almost fifteen years old, but sometimes he acts like a child, He pays no attention to his lessons, he mopes around the house, he spends hours out in the streets, I don't know where. And you and Gaius seem to get along so well, and Gaius is such a fine young man … well, I was wondering if you could give me some advice."

Lucius thought for a moment, then responded, speaking slowly and cautiously.

"I hope you won't take offense at what I'm going to say …"

"I won't take offense. Please be honest with me."

"I don't know if I can give you much advice that will be useful. Raising children is such a challenging task, especially boys, and especially during the years between childhood and full manhood …

"Yes, I know," Claudius interrupted him, a trifle impatiently; as their friendship had grown, he had become aware of Lucius's fondness for tendentious statements.

"By the way, I hear Marcus has achieved full manhood, if you know what I mean."

Claudius was startled. "Where did you hear that?"

"Oh, just idle gossip among the slaves."

"I ordered them not to say anything," Claudius muttered, his face red.

"Don't worry, it won't go any further," Lucius reassured him. "But as for your larger concern, it seems to me that you need to spend more time with him. Give him something to look forward to—perhaps an evening at the theater. Go with him to the *palaestra* and watch some of the wrestling matches. I know, contests of strength don't appeal to me either; I'd much rather watch the foot races or the javelin throwers, but Marcus apparently loves to watch the wrestlers, and he may be gaining some skill himself …"

"He's been *wrestling*?" Claudius asked in amazement.

"Of course. You didn't think he'd be content to stand on the sidelines forever, did you? He's also been seen at the gladiatorial school. Don't worry—he was just watching some of the training sessions. And he wasn't alone; several other boys were there. It's a favorite gathering place for them."

Claudius shook his head, embarrassed by his lack of understanding of his own son. He began to realize he knew almost nothing about him. All the time he had been pushing Kineas to fill the boy's head with literature and philosophy, Marcus's thoughts had clearly been elsewhere. Kineas had told him this repeatedly, but Claudius had never considered allowing the boy to pursue other courses of study. He remembered Marcus's interest in how water traveled from one room to the next in the baths, in how the *hypocaustum* functioned; Kineas had mentioned the boy's interest in siege engines and techniques. Maybe he should speak to him about finding a new tutor, a mathematician. On the other hand, perhaps it was too late to speak to him at all. Still, it was worth a try. He looked gratefully at Lucius.

"If I understand you correctly, Lucius, you're saying I've been neglecting the tasks of a father. No, don't worry, I'm not offended. Your advice is sound, and I'll act on it right away. Thank you. Thank you so much."

"That's quite all right," Lucius responded. "Goodnight, my friend, and good luck."

◆ ◆ ◆

Lucius had not missed the look that passed between his son and his wife's maid during the recitation of Catullus's love poems. Nor had it come as a surprise. He had been expecting something of the sort and was prepared to deal with it. On the morning after the dinner party, he asked Gaius to stay with him in the *tablinum* after the last client had left.

"Gaius," he said, "I saw you leave the *triclinium* last night, and I think I understand why. Would you like to talk about it?"

Gaius, who was mature for his age and usually able to control his emotions, suddenly seemed unable to speak. He looked mutely at his father and blushed.

"You don't have to say anything if you don't want to," Lucius continued. "But I believe you're showing some of the signs of young love, and I must say I'm not surprised. Bringing such a beautiful girl into our household was bound to offer a temptation, and you'd be within your rights to make love to her. But I would prefer that you not do so, for several reasons, some of them obvious, some of them private concerns of my own."

"Father," Gaius stammered. "Father, I hope I'll never do anything that would displease you ..."

"I know, Son, but the forces of nature may be too strong even for you. You may not be able to help yourself. However, I don't want to send Ariana away; your mother depends on her, and I'm sure you've noticed how her health and spirits have improved since Ariana's been with her. I won't try to command your feelings, but I ask that if you do feel anything for the girl, you refrain from acting on those feelings. I must warn you: If it ever becomes evident that she's with child, she'll be sent away. As you know, I don't place great emphasis on my Samnite lineage, but it's important to your mother, and for her sake I won't tolerate anything that would detract from our family's reputation. We can't afford to have people gossiping about us, even if the girl's just a slave."

"I understand, Father," Gaius said.

There was a brief pause; then Lucius said gently,

"If you wish, I can arrange for you to spend a night at the *lupanar.* Africanus is very sensitive to the needs of young men ..."

"Oh, no, Father! I mean, thank you, but I don't need that. I can take care of myself."

Lucius nodded and turned back to the petitions piled on the table in front of him. Gaius left the *tablinum,* his thoughts reeling: *Within your rights ... forces of nature ... with child ... sent away.* He was overwhelmed by all the implications that could arise from a single glance between two young people on a summer evening. He left the house and walked abstractedly to the gymnasium, where he sought out the boxing master. Surprised, Servius agreed to go a few rounds with him, but Gaius was out of practice and not concentrating. He soon allowed himself to be maneuvered into facing the sun, whereupon Servius landed a blow to his face that knocked him backward onto the sandy floor. The boxing master, more surprised than ever, pulled him to his feet and examined his face, where his left eye was already half closed and surrounded by a livid bruise.

"I'm so sorry! I didn't mean to hit you so hard!" he apologized, knowing full well that the fault was not his.

"It's all right, Servius," Gaius replied with a smile. "I'll take this as a lesson that I must be more alert and not let my thoughts wander. Anyone who asks me where I got this black eye will be reminding me of that. You've done me a favor, my friend."

And he turned and walked away, removing the leather thongs from his hands and heading for the *tepidarium*. Today he would take a plunge in the *frigidarium* as well.

◆ ◆ ◆

Ariana was aware that Marcus was following her. One afternoon, as she walked down the Via Stabiana toward home, she turned around to take a last look at the mountain in the distance, its sloping shoulders bathed in a soft orange glow. As her gaze lingered on the mountain, the nearer countryside, and finally the Porta Vesuvio, she noticed Marcus standing in the archway, staring back at her. Hastily she turned and continued on her way.

Marcus had not set out to follow her. He had been investigating the city's decaying defense system—a curtain wall punctuated by three-story guard towers at strategic locations and surrounded by a deep trench. Someone had told him that signs of the attack on Pompeii during the War of the Allies could be seen in the northern walls, and he had gone to investigate. His informant had been correct: There were numerous round impressions in the stones, made by Roman artillery over a hundred years earlier.

Marcus was planning to explore the entire system—walls, gates, and towers—when he spotted Ariana and was brought to a standstill. *She's more beautiful than ever!* he thought, and he felt the familiar fire in his limbs, the fire that said "I must have her." But he did not move a muscle until she turned onto the Via Nola and disappeared.

In midafternoon on the next day, guessing that Ariana went for her walks while her mistress napped, Marcus hid in a doorway near the intersection of the Via Stabiana and the Via Nola and was rewarded with the sight of her heading north toward the Porta Vesuvio and then turning right into the northeastern sector of the city. He followed at a distance, ducking into doorways whenever she slowed her pace or seemed about to turn around, but she did not look back. She continued her walk as usual, and repeated it at intervals over the next few days, always stopping just inside the northern gate to look out at the mountain in the distance.

Marcus had learned her route and become adept at keeping out of sight as he followed her, more closely now as he became more confident. But before long his confidence betrayed him and she caught a glimpse of him. She continued on her way as if nothing had happened, but she knew immediately that this was not the first time he had followed her, and guessed that it would not be the last.

To test her theory, she left the house at a different time the next afternoon and chose a different route, stopping occasionally to look over her shoulder. There was no sign of Marcus. But on the following day she returned to her usual habits, being careful to give no sign that she knew he was there. She stopped as usual to admire the view through the Porta Vesuvio, then went back down the Via Stabiana toward the House of the Faun. As she turned onto the Via Nola, she stopped and looked back. As she had expected, there was Marcus ducking into a doorway just half an *insula* away.

Over the next few days, realizing she had seen him, he began following her more openly. She found this so unnerving that she finally decided to confront him. The next time she sensed his presence behind her, she turned and walked quickly toward him. He stood and watched her approach, smiling at her angry expression. As she drew near and began to speak, he grasped her arm and pulled her into a shadowy doorway. Before she could resist, his mouth was on hers in a rough kiss, his arms around her, holding hers against her sides as she struggled to free herself. Finally she managed to twist her face aside, but he placed one hand over her mouth and with the other reached inside her *stola* and felt her breasts. But now her arms were free and she managed to push him away. He let her go with a laugh.

She was speechless at first, her lips bruised, tears in her eyes. She beat at him with her fists, but he merely grabbed her arms and pulled her toward him again. This time, however, she struggled so fiercely that he gave up the effort.

"Don't touch me! Stop following me! Why won't you leave me alone?" she cried.

"Because you're mine, Ariana. Mine!"

"No!" was all she could say as she whirled and ran back to the House of the Faun, Marcus's laughter echoing behind her.

After that incident, she gave up her afternoon walks and remained in the house while Clodia rested. Sometimes Ariana napped as well, but she had never needed to sleep during the day and found that instead of resting she spent the time lying on her bed and staring at the ceiling. Her usual good spirits deserted her and she became moody and introspective. *Is this all there is for me?* she wondered. *Am I going to spend the rest of my life in this house, tending this woman as she grows older ...* Then she would berate herself for her disloyalty. How could she complain when Clodia had given her so much?

Clodia was a kind and perceptive woman, but even if she had lacked these traits she could not have helped noticing that Ariana was out of sorts. One hot afternoon, as they sat in the shade of the peristyle beside the *viridarium*, Clodia leaning back with her eyes half closed while Ariana mended a *stola*, Clodia said to her,

"Ariana, my dear, you haven't been yourself lately, and you haven't been taking your afternoon walks. Are you feeling unwell, or is something troubling you? Don't be shy; you can speak freely to me."

Ariana looked at her feet and mumbled something about the heat, but Clodia persisted.

"Ariana, I know it's hot. It's summer in Pompeii! But until now that hasn't stopped you from going out every afternoon. Come now, tell me what's bothering you."

At that the tears sprang from Ariana's eyes and she told her everything. Clodia listened in silence, then put an arm around the girl's shoulders and said,

"Don't worry, my dear, I'll speak to Lucius and he'll put a stop to this nonsense."

"Thank you, Mistress," Ariana said gratefully. "I don't know what I'd do without you."

"Nor I without you," said Clodia with a smile. "Come, let's find something more interesting to do than mending. How would you like a new hairstyle?"

Ariana enjoyed looking attractive, but she had never paid much attention to the details. One tunic or *stola* was a good as another, as long as it was clean and mended, and she had given little thought to the intricacies of women's hairstyles. But she submitted to the attentions of Clodia's hairdresser as she and Clodia spent an hour or so trying out various arrangements, seeking a compromise between the simple styles favored for young girls and the more elaborate creations worn by Pompeiian matrons. Eventually they settled on a becoming style in which a thick braid encircled the top of Ariana's head while a mass of curls framed her forehead and the remaining hair fell loosely beside her face and in back. Ariana admired herself in a mirror and smiled happily. Dismissing the hairdresser, Clodia went into the small room where she kept her clothing and returned with an ankle-length white *stola* and a lovely rose-colored *palla*, which she gave to Ariana, saying,

"It's time you wore a long *stola*, my dear. Your legs should be covered, for modesty's sake. And try on the *palla* as well. I know you won't be wearing it for a couple of months, but let's see how it looks on you."

Astonished, and yet again overcome by her mistress's generosity, Ariana slipped the *stola* over her head and cinched it at the waist, draping the *palla* loosely over her shoulders. The effect was spectacular, especially as the glow in her cheeks echoed the flattering shade of the fabric. Clodia was very pleased with herself.

"You look absolutely stunning," she said. "I could not have wished for more had you been my own daughter."

And for the first time since the death of her child, Clodia did not shed tears for her loss.

It was this scene that greeted Lucius and Gaius as they returned from the Forum and strolled to the rear of the house in search of a cool place to rest and refresh themselves with chilled wine and a handful of olives. At the sight of Ariana in her new glory, both men stopped in amazement. Lucius advanced to look at her more closely, then stepped back and said,

"My dear girl, you look like something out of Ovid's *Metamorphoses,* one of his matchless maidens—perhaps Daphne, who was pursued by Apollo. Only if I were Apollo, I would not pursue too closely, in order to avoid having you turn into a tree!"

Emboldened by the friendly attention she was receiving, Ariana spoke up. "Master, you're too kind. Daphne was beautiful—at least in the wall paintings I saw at the other house. She was shown with Apollo, but not as a tree! How in the world did she become a tree?"

Gaius laughed. "Haven't you heard the story of Apollo and Daphne? Oh, of course—you couldn't have. Well, it so happens that Claudius has lent me his copy of the *Metamorphoses,* which I've been studying lately. If it's all right with you, Mother, I could fetch it and read to you while you rest here in the shade."

No one objected. It seemed the perfect way to while away the remaining hour or two before the evening meal. Gaius returned with the scroll and quickly found the story of Daphne. Scanning it, he picked out the most eloquent portions and began reciting, beginning with Apollo's first sight of Daphne, at which he fell hopelessly in love. Cupid took aim at him,

> ... and love's arrow
> With fire of lightning pierced his bones;
> Apollo walked as in a tower of flames.

(At Apollo's approach, Daphne fled),

And ran with floating hair through deep-green forest;
Nor would she hear of lovers or of men,
Nor cared for promise of a wedding day …

(Pleading with her father, the river god Peneus, she asked him to make her an eternal virgin like Diana. Peneus agreed, but before he could keep his promise),

… as September fields of wheat and straw
Take fire from a careless traveler's torch
Left smoldering in the wind that wakes the dawn,
So did Apollo's heart break into flames,
The sterile fires that feed on empty hopes.
And while he gazed at Daphne's floating hair
That fell in tendrils at her throat and forehead …

At this, Gaius could not help taking a quick look at Ariana's new hairstyle, and his heart broke into flames like Apollo's, but with a massive effort at self-control he continued:

He looked into her eyes and saw the stars.
Though staring does not satisfy desire,
His eyes praised all they saw—her lips, her fingers,
Her hands, her naked arms from wrist to shoulder …
Yet she ran from him swifter than light air
That turns to nothingness as we pursue it,
Nor did she stop to hear Apollo calling:
"O daughter of the deep green-shadowed River,
Who follows you is not your enemy;
The lamb runs from the wolf, the deer from lion,
The trembling-feathered dove flies from the eagle
Whose great wings cross the sky—such is your flight
While mine is love's pursuit.…

(Apollo said a lot more, trying desperately to persuade her to stop and listen to him proclaiming his love, but she),

… distracted,
In flight, in fear, wind flowing through her dress

> And her wild hair—she grew more beautiful
> The more he followed her and saw wind tear
> Her dress and the short tunic that she wore,...

Gaius paused for moment, choosing to skip Ovid's description of the girl as 'a naked wraith in wilderness.' Then he continued with the chase, telling how Apollo, like a greyhound chasing a hare, drew ever closer,

> ... until his lips
> Breathed at her shoulder; and almost spent,
> The girl saw waves of a familiar river,
> Her father's home, and in a trembling voice
> Called, "Father, if your waters still hold charms
> To save your daughter, cover with green earth
> This body I wear too well," and as she spoke
> A soaring drowsiness possessed her; growing
> In earth she stood, white thighs embraced by climbing
> Bark, her white arms branches, her fair head swaying
> In a cloud of leaves; all that was Daphne bowed
> In the stirring of the wind, the glittering green
> Leaf twined within her hair and she was laurel.

As Gaius finished his reading, the others sat spellbound. Even Lucius and Clodia, who were familiar with the ancient tale, were speechless at the beauty and pathos of Ovid's rendering of it. Finally Lucius said,

"You read very well, my son. It seems your time with Kineas was not wasted."

Gaius was breathless, not merely as a result of his recitation but because he could not help identifying with Apollo in his fruitless chase. After a moment he said,

"Thank you, Father. Not a day with Kineas was wasted, and I'm grateful to you for giving me such an excellent tutor."

The four of them sat in comfortable silence as a slave brought them a basket of fruit. Made mellow by the golden light of the setting sun, they sat together for another hour or two, sharing the evening meal and chatting quietly as dusk descended into night. No one commented, or even seemed to notice, that there were four of them at dinner rather than three.

◆ ◆ ◆

In the ensuing weeks, as summer ripened into autumn, the four of them often dined together in the fading light. Gaius recited to them from scrolls he was studying, and in this way Ariana was introduced to the rich world of Latin literature—and even a few Greek writings in translation. She wept at Hector's farewell to Andromache and little Astyanax; sighed in sympathy with poor Ariadne, abandoned by Theseus after rescuing him from the dreaded Minotaur; laughed at the antics of the slave Pseudolus in Plautus's comedies; and giggled at Catullus's endless and hopeless pursuit of the coy Lesbia. And always there was Horace, Horace with his love of the simple life, his fondness for the countryside, his piety and propriety leavened with intelligence and humor. Although Ariana would have preferred to hear more legends and myths like that of Daphne and Apollo, she listened attentively to Gaius's renditions and interpretations of Horace's odes, knowing how keenly the young man admired Rome's greatest poet.

Gaius enjoyed these evenings immensely. He knew he was falling in love with Ariana, but he was willing to wait a while before approaching her; besides, he respected his father's wishes. Though there were times when he felt the physical symptoms of love described by Sappho—

> My tongue sticks to the roof of my mouth
> Flickering flames lick my skin
> And I can't see
> And there's a roaring in my ears
> And I'm drenched in sweat
> And trembling seizes me—

he managed to disguise them as emotions aroused by the passages he was reading; or he would make an excuse and leave the room, seeking relief in private.

As for Ariana, she was too caught up in her day-to-day existence to think about love—except as something she wanted to avoid in the form of Marcus. *If he chases me, there won't be anyone to turn me into a tree!* she told herself. *And I don't like him or want him. He's handsome, but there's something sinister about him …*

Her feelings for Gaius were more complex. He was about her height, neither slim nor heavy. He was not handsome in the ordinary sense of the term, but no one would have called him unattractive; his honest face and warm brown eyes, his sincerity and thoughtfulness caused everyone to like him. But Ariana knew she did not merely like him. Certain feelings arose in her when she thought of him—warmth flooded through her body, and she felt unfamiliar desires, a desire to be close to him, perhaps to receive the sweet kisses described in Catullus's lyrics. Whether she loved him, or ever would, she could not tell; her mind slid away from such thoughts. *I'm a slave,* she reminded herself. *There could never be anything between us. But if he touched me … if he wanted to kiss me …*

Lucius and Clodia were aware of Gaius's feelings, but they trusted him to behave honorably. Besides, they enjoyed his recitations and their peaceful evenings together as much as he and Ariana did. Clodia had spoken to Lucius about Marcus's pursuit of Ariana, and he had set her concerns to rest.

"I don't think that'll be a problem any longer," he told her. "Claudius has begun taking him to the theater, and he tells me the boy's enthralled by the mechanics of theatrical production, especially devices like the crane and sling used to deliver the *deus ex machina.* I hope these outings with his father will help him get over his moodiness and stop following Ariana around. It's time that boy grew up and found something worthwhile to do with his life. He may not want to be a merchant like his father or a budding politician like our Gaius, but it's clear he has an aptitude for all things mechanical; Claudius tells me he's always building little models of things like siege works and catapults. Not that there's any need for such things nowadays, but there are other possibilities. I hear there are some problems with the waterworks …

And with this the two of them set aside the problem of Marcus and turned to their own concerns, which were becoming more urgent with the impending arrival of Vespasian's administrator, Suedius Clemens.

VII

NOVEMBER, 73

And where was Julia Vettia while all this was happening? Julia was having an affair with Statius Rufus.

It had begun, as such things often do, almost by accident. Claudius had told Julia she should apologize to Rufus for embarrassing him in front of the other distinguished guests at their dinner party. Embarrassed herself, she had declined at first, but Claudius had insisted. Then she remembered that Rufus lived in a part of town where several jewelers and metalsmiths had their shops. *Well, at least the trip wouldn't be a complete waste of time,* she thought. So finally she had shrugged, thrown a *palla* around her shoulders, taken a slave with her bearing a gift of good Chian wine, and gone to seek out Rufus at his house, having earlier sent a messenger to find out if he would receive her that afternoon.

Rufus's house was unusual in that it was actually one of three houses that had been combined some sixty years previously to form a much larger residence. There three related households, all descended from one of Sulla's veterans, shared access to an immense central garden surrounded by a two-story peristyle. Rufus, who was single, occupied the section near the main entrance, which was arranged in the traditional fashion with an atrium surrounded by a *tablinum*, several *cubiculi,* and other small rooms where business could be conducted. This suited his needs as a member of the *Comitia* and lately as leader of the anti-Samnite faction. In the mornings, he received clients in the atrium, and later in the day, if he wished to spend some quiet time with friends, they could pass through into the *viridarium* and stroll around the peristyle court, or dine in the *triclinium* opening onto it. The largest section of the house, situated next to Rufus's but with a separate entrance, was the home of Rustius Verus, Rufus's uncle, and his family. Verus, a fellow politician who had never had much success despite numerous campaigns for *aedilis* or *duovir,* had retired from politics. The rear portion had formerly housed the family of a third, rather obscure relative of Rufus, but now it served as servants' quarters, with the result that many rooms in Rufus's and Verus's sections were unused.

As she approached Rufus's doorway, Julia noticed that a nearby shop specialized in emerald jewelry. *I'll take a look in there after I'm finished here,* she said to herself. Then she went into the house.

In the vestibule, she paused to admire the stylish black-and-white mosaic of a dolphin; then she passed through into the atrium, where Rufus greeted her. She gave him the wine and dismissed the slave who had carried it. Rufus led her into a side room whose walls were magnificently decorated with paintings of half-naked bacchantes carrying offerings for their lord Dionysus. *Suggestive,* she thought. *He lives here alone; I wonder ...* Abruptly she suppressed her thoughts and turned to the task at hand.

"Statius," she began, somewhat hesitantly, "I hope you'll forgive me for my indiscretion the other night. I assure you I didn't mean to embarrass you. I suppose I may have had too much wine ..."

"Please, Julia, think nothing of it. I probably had a little too much myself"—he glanced appreciatively at her peace offering, knowing how much it would have cost—"and your husband provides superb vintages."

"Well, I *am* sorry. I shouldn't have put you on the spot like that. It's just that I'd heard you're really making a name for yourself in the *Comitia* and I thought ... You know, I'm very interested in political affairs, even though Claudius insists they're really very boring—as if he had any idea; he goes to the Forum only to meet with traders and exporters. He doesn't know what's going on in the *Comitia,* or anywhere else for that matter."

"Actually, he's right," Rufus said. "A lot of it really *is* boring. It's only occasionally that anyone has anything worthwhile to say, and even then they don't usually say it very well. No Ciceros here, I'm afraid."

She could think of nothing else to say, and after a moment, noticing her interest in the wall paintings, he offered to show her the garden and some of the other rooms. She assented with pleasure, and he led her back through the atrium and into the *viridarium.* There they stopped to admire the rectangular pool in the center, with a niche on the far wall that contained a fountain in the form of a bronze sculpture of a satyr pouring wine. Water flowed from the wineskin into the basin, but it was easy to imagine that the satyr was pouring wine for guests to enjoy.

The back wall of the peristyle was covered with paintings of deities and legendary figures like Perseus and Andromeda, Hercules and Hesione. In the *triclin-*

ium was a scene from Euripides's *Iphigenia in Tauris;* Julia gazed at it for several moments before turning to Rufus and saying,

"These paintings are beautiful. I would be most grateful if you could tell me who painted them."

"I'm flattered," Rufus said, "but your house is every bit as beautifully decorated. As for the artist, unfortunately he's no longer living."

"Oh, too bad," Julia said, and then, at a loss for further topics of conversation, she took her leave. As she walked before him, looking around at the magnificent paintings and elegant bronze statues in the atrium, he noticed how tall and stately she was, and as her *palla* swung loosely from her shoulders he glimpsed her form, still youthful even after bearing three children. *Why not?* he thought. *Claudius has his nose buried in those scrolls of his; he'd never know the difference!*

He saw her to the door and went back into the house to get ready for a trip to the baths. When he emerged a few minutes later, he saw her in the jeweler's shop, examining an emerald pendant set in gold and suspended from a gold chain. It was clear that she coveted it and was in the process of bargaining over its price. Rufus went into the shop and reached past her, taking the pendant from her hands as she stood frozen in surprise. "How much?" he asked the man. "Twenty-five *denarii*," he responded without a moment's hesitation. "You shall have it," Rufus assured him, and turning toward Julia he carefully passed the chain over her piled-up hair and down to her shoulders, adjusting it so the pendant hung just above the neckline of her *stola*, in the cleft between her breasts. Then he stood back to admire her. "That suits you very nicely," he said. "It brings out the green of your eyes."

"Oh, Statius, thank you, but I can't accept this," Julia said, reaching up to remove it.

"Please take it, Julia," he insisted. "Consider it a token of our friendship." And he looked into her eyes and smiled. His meaning was clear, and it was equally clear that she understood it.

"I see you're interested in fine jewelry," he continued. "So am I. I also know the owners of these shops quite well. If you'd like some help finding the best pieces at good prices, please feel free to call on me. I'm usually home at this time of the day."

"Thank you, Statius, I'll do that," she said, and turned for home.

◆ ◆ ◆

Two days later, in midafternoon, she came to his doorway, unaccompanied this time. He greeted her cordially, but before she could reply he was holding her in a close embrace, his hot, moist lips on hers. She made no protest as he led her to his *cubiculum*, whose walls were decorated with erotic scenes like those in the *lupanar,* only painted by a much more accomplished artist. There he unwrapped her like a gift, carefully removing each garment and draping it over a chair. Then he shed his tunic. Her eyes opened wide at the sight of his orange-furred body and eager erection.

Rufus's skills as a lover were more highly developed than his ability as an orator. Though Claudius was a patient and virile partner, Julia had never experienced what Statius Rufus had to offer. Gently and deftly he brought her to such a peak of pleasure that she couldn't help crying out, and when she put a hand over her mouth and looked around, he told her with a laugh that he had dismissed the servants for the afternoon. Then he entered her, and with slow, sure strokes brought her back to the peak she had reached a moment before, and joined her there.

In the ensuing weeks Julia developed a consuming interest in jewelry and metalwork, and on several occasions she arrived home with a flushed face and disheveled hair, triumphantly displaying her latest treasure: a golden brooch in the shape of a clamshell; a silver cup decorated with fantastic winged figures. Her disposition improved markedly, and she left Claudius to his scholarly pursuits without complaint.

As spring merged into summer, Julia found herself becoming obsessed with Rufus, and her visits to his house were more frequent. Before she had crossed the atrium, she would have shed her *stola*, leaving her undergarments for him to remove with his caressing hands. She became increasingly adept at lovemaking as they made a game of imitating the positions portrayed on the walls of his chamber. "You have the best *lupanar* in town," she teased, kneeling astride him as he lay stretched out on his back. She was fascinated by the orange furze on his chest and loved to run her fingers along the ribbon of hair that extended downward from it. She stroked it repeatedly, then moved farther down and stroked lower, watching in amusement as he responded in predictable fashion. Then he would reach up and gently pinch her nipples, driving her wild.

During the lazy summer afternoons they would couple ecstatically, then lie together on the rumpled bed, drinking chilled wine and talking idly about everything and nothing. One day he asked about her childhood.

"Oh, it wouldn't interest you, it was entirely conventional," she protested.

"No, tell me, I want to know."

"There really isn't much to tell," she said, "but if you insist ... Before I was married, my name was Julia Poppaea."

"Don't tell me! Quintus Poppaeus was your father?"

"Yes, and yes, we're kin to Poppaea Sabina. My father boasted of it; my mother and I were embarrassed. That woman ..."

Poppaea Sabina had been the Emperor Nero's second wife. Though nowhere near as vicious as her husband, she had not endeared herself to those around her, including him. It was rumored that in a jealous rage he had killed her by kicking her in the stomach when she was pregnant. Then, in a show of remorse, he had come to Pompeii and offered a gold oil lamp and pearl and emerald earrings in the Temple of Venus.

"Julia, we can't help who we're related to!" Rufus protested. "Our birth is in the hands of the gods—or, as I like to think, a matter of pure chance. You could have been born in my household and I in yours. That's why it galls me when the old Samnite families put on airs. They're no better than you or me!"

Sensing that the conversation was entering dangerous territory, she quickly changed the subject.

"Yes, well anyway, we never lacked for anything, and I had a happy childhood. When we were little, my brother and I—we were only a year apart—we used to play together. We'd run around the atrium and jump into the *impluvium,* or we'd play hide-and-seek—our house was huge, and there were lots of places to hide. We'd make our pet turtles race each other by poking them with sticks. Or we'd sneak into the kitchen, and while one of us distracted the cook, the other would snatch a loaf of bread or a handful of dates, whatever was there, and than we'd escape to the *viridarium* and share our loot ... Now that I think about it, I don't think the cook was deceived at all!"

She was smiling, lost in her memories. He had never seen her so relaxed, so free from the constraints of the role she played, the role of a wealthy Pompeiian matron. He kissed her softly and said,

"Your house ... That's the one they call the House of Menander, isn't it? Why is it called that?"

"Oh, that comes from the paintings in the *tablinum.* Menander is shown on one wall and Euripides on the other. I don't know who started calling it the

House of Menander—perhaps some tipsy guest after a good dinner! It's really the house of the Poppaei."

"But Quintus sold it after the quakes, didn't he?"

"Yes," she said, and turned away, her mood now somber. "I don't understand it. I'll never understand it ..."

"Don't be too hard on him," Rufus said soothingly. "A lot of people were very frightened; I can't blame them for leaving. And besides, isn't that how you got your lovely new house?"

"You're right, Statius," she admitted, and said no more. But Rufus, still curious, persisted.

"Tell me one more thing?"

"What?"

"Why did you marry Claudius? I must say the two of you don't seem quite right for each other. And Quintus was a rich financier; you probably could have married just about anyone he chose for you."

"Well, Claudius was handsome and quite well off, and of good character, and my parents favored him, and at that age I didn't think of asking for anything more," she told him. "But what about you? Why haven't you married?"

"Because you weren't available!" he said with a grin.

"Don't be silly, Statius. We hadn't even met! Seriously, why aren't you married? Considering your political ambitions, it would seem logical to marry and have children. Having a family makes one appear more respectable."

"I don't know, Julia," he said, suddenly serious. "Maybe it's because I don't have much experience with family life. My parents were childless until fairly late, and they were very surprised—and probably not overjoyed—when my mother got pregnant at the age of forty! Anyway, she died giving birth to me, and my father raised me alone, with the help of a wetnurse and later a tutor. Except for them, I had no one. Even my father, though he meant well, didn't know what to do with me, and even if we'd been close it wouldn't have mattered, since he fell ill and died when I was about thirteen. So I began seeking company outside the house, making friends at the gymnasium or the baths, getting introduced to sex at the *lupanar,* going to the young people's dinner parties—you know the kind: The men recline and feast, the hired girls dance, and then the girls sit beside the men and let them kiss and fondle them until everyone is drunk and rolling on the floor ..."

"Yes, I've heard about them," Julia interrupted. "But surely, when it came time for you to marry, your uncle or some other relative could have helped you make a suitable match."

"Perhaps," he said, "but I wasn't interested. I never lacked for female companionship—none like you, of course—"

"Of course!"

"… and I had gotten interested in politics and was putting everything I had into winning a seat on the *Comitia.* You know how it is: The people don't vote for someone who promises to support a public building program or reduce taxes or improve the quality of the roads. They vote for someone who is thought to be of good moral character. So all you need to do is get several reputable citizens to vouch for your character, and bribe a few others to cast aspersions on your opponent's character, and you've got it made."

"So why didn't you win the race for *aedilis* last year?" Julia asked. "You couldn't have had a problem making the necessary bribes."

"I chose the wrong race," Rufus replied. "I thought it was obvious that Paquius Proculus is getting too old for the job. But I couldn't get anyone to say a word against him. He's from one of those old Samnite families, the ones everyone looks up to regardless of the merit of their members. I couldn't touch him."

She made as if to answer, but he rolled toward her and put a hand over her mouth. "Don't say anything, Julia, I don't want to talk about it anymore. In fact," he added, "I have a better idea: Let's not talk at all."

◆ ◆ ◆

As the summer progressed and Julia's absences became increasingly frequent, even someone as preoccupied as Claudius was bound to notice. One day she returned late, missing the evening meal, and went directly to her chamber. There she hastily unpinned her hair and donned a fresh *stola*; then she went to sit in the *viridarium,* calling for Petronius to bring her some bread and wine. Claudius found her there.

He could hardly believe this woman was his wife. With her hair loose, she looked at least ten years younger. She somehow managed to appear both flustered and serene at the same time. Patting the bench beside her, she looked up at him and said,

"Come, Claudius, let's sit here for a while and enjoy the evening."

He obeyed, and they sat there for several moments without speaking. Then he asked,

"Where were you today? Surely the metalsmiths' shops were closed during the afternoon. They can't hope to do much business on these hot days, even if they put up awnings to provide a little shade."

"Yes, they were closed," she replied. "I'd forgotten. There's a necklace of lapis lazuli I saw last week that I decided I wanted, and I went to buy it, but the shop was closed. So since I was halfway there, I went to the public gardens on the other side of town, looking for some shade and a change of scene."

"And how were they?" he persisted.

"Well, they weren't very shady, and there was a gusty wind that blew my hair around, but it was still pleasant. You know, they have a vineyard there where you can get some wine. I must say I appreciate the thoughtfulness of whoever decreed that the gardens should remain open to all, and that no one may build a house there. Every city should set apart a place like that for its people."

And with that she allayed his suspicions, at least temporarily.

◆ ◆ ◆

After her conversation with Claudius, Julia became more circumspect. She went less frequently to the jewelers' shops, and in order not to be seen entering Rufus's house, she arranged to meet him in the *pergula* above one of the shops. This was the room where the shopkeeper ate and slept. Rufus paid him handsomely to be absent on those days, and paid him even more to keep silent about it.

But the days were growing shorter and colder, and even with coals burning in a brazier in a corner, the room was chilly and they made love under a pile of blankets. As if echoing the climate outside, their ardor cooled as winter approached. Without anything being said, her visits became less frequent; often ten days would go by before she would seek out Rufus in their *pergula*. And though Rufus continued to welcome her gladly and to satisfy her craving as well as his own, he often seemed distracted, failing to respond when she spoke, or lying lost in thought as she tried to arouse him. Finally she asked him why he was so preoccupied.

"I have to go to Rome," he said.

VIII
DECEMBER, 73

A clever and astute man, Suedius Clemens timed his arrival in Pompeii to coincide with the Saturnalia, the winter festival during which all business was set aside in favor of parties, gift-giving, and general goodwill. Not having a temple specifically dedicated to Saturn, the Pompeiians opened the week of festivities with a ceremony in the Capitolium, the large temple dedicated to the sacred triad of Jupiter, Juno, and Minerva, which all Roman colonies were required to worship. Everyone attended: men, women, and children; masters, freedmen, and slaves. Thus, on a brisk midwinter morning, much of the population of Pompeii was present either within or outside the great temple that dominated the north end of the Forum, flanked by triumphal arches, one of them topped with a bronze statue of Augustus driving a four-horse chariot. As a member of the College of Augustales, Claudius sat with his colleagues on the platform before the richly carved altar, leaving space for the *pontifex maximus* to walk up the short staircase leading to it and pass between them. Also seated there were the *duoviri,* Caecilius Jucundus and Octavius Quartio, and the *aediles,* Lucius Tullius and Paquius Proculus; and with them was Clemens. Below them were the members of the *Comitia,* including Statius Rufus.

In this way, Clemens succeeded in inserting himself into Pompeiian government on an occasion when no one was interested in questioning his presence, since the thoughts of all were turned toward the grand public feast that would follow the sacrifice of an unblemished ox to Saturn. Already, delicious aromas were rising from the various booths and tents that had been erected around the edges of the Forum square. Knowing that his popularity was directly proportional to his brevity, the *pontifex* got through the ritual statements as quickly as possible and signed to his attendants to slit the ox's throat and catch the blood in a large golden basin. The carcass was immediately carried outside to be cut up and placed on spits over a large fire; meanwhile the blood was poured out at the foot of the altar as prayers were offered up to the god to maintain the safety and prosperity of the city and its people. The *pontifex* then led the other priests and the Augustales in procession down the stairs and out of the temple, thereby signaling the beginning of the feast. Inside, the councilmen milled around, each anxious to make Clemens's acquaintance without appearing too eager. Lucius, considering such efforts undignified, left the political jockeying to his colleagues and went outside to exchange a few words with Claudius.

He found him standing with Julia, Marcus, and their two young daughters near a table covered with delicacies of all kinds—dried apricots, pastries, little sausages kept hot over a small fire. The fresh air and hours of waiting had whetted everyone's appetite, and they were all nibbling away happily. To look at them, one would not have suspected that this was a family with serious problems. Lucius was well aware of Julia's affair with Rufus, but he would be the last person to tell Claudius about it. Claudius would have to figure it out for himself, and eventually he surely would. *And then what? Will he divorce her? I doubt it, actually. I suspect he genuinely loves her, despite her domineering nature, or perhaps because of it ...*

He took Claudius aside and asked him what he thought of their new administrator.

"He seems pleasant enough," Claudius said, "but we don't yet know what he has in mind for us. From what I've heard, he has a strong interest in public works. That will probably affect *you* more than most."

"Yes, so I expect," Lucius agreed. "But we won't find out for at least a week, and perhaps even longer. Did you know he's planning to hold games in the amphitheater to celebrate the new year—and, of course, his arrival?"

"No! Really?" Claudius was surprised. Winter games were not unheard-of, but most such events took place in warmer weather. It made no difference to the gladiators, of course, but the spectators were another matter. However, if Clemens held games, all the citizens of Pompeii would be expected to attend them.

"That's what I've heard," Lucius replied, "but we shall see what we shall see."

At that point, Clodia, with Gaius and Ariana in tow, strolled over to join them. Gaius whispered something to Ariana, and the two exchanged a quick smile.

"Greetings, Claudius," Clodia said with a smile. "We haven't seen much of you lately. How have you and your family been getting along?"

"Very well, thank you ..." said Claudius, his voice fading. His eyes were on Ariana. *By all the gods,* he was thinking, *she's even more beautiful than I thought she would be! My daughter. How I wish I could acknowledge her!*

Clodia went on as if unaware of his lapse.

"We'll have to dine together soon, the four of us. Perhaps Marcus and Gaius could join us as well. They're both fine young men. How quickly the time has gone by!"

She continued with similar platitudes as Claudius came to himself and responded in kind. Meanwhile Lucius surreptitiously looked over at Marcus and then at Ariana. *They look so much alike! If I ever had any doubts, I don't now. How painful this must be for Claudius.*

After a few moments, Clodia turned to Lucius and said,

"My dear, I'm rather tired and would like to go home. Would you send for my litter?"

He did so, and after politely taking leave of Claudius, he, Gaius, and Ariana walked beside the litter as Clodia was carried home. None of them had noticed the angry expression on Marcus's face as he gazed first at Ariana, then at Gaius.

In the Forum, the feasting continued, and soon tables were set up for the gambling games that were permitted only during the Saturnalia. Coins changed hands rapidly and in large numbers as the citizens of Pompeii indulged themselves, their happiness increasing steadily as the afternoon wore on and ever-greater quantities of wine were consumed. Clemens mingled with the crowd, sampling the food and wine and chatting with people of all ranks. Some of the councilmen followed him around; others, more conscious of their dignity, went their own way. But here and there they clustered in small groups, comparing their impressions of the new administrator and speculating about his intentions.

◆ ◆ ◆

During the Saturnalia, slaves were freed from their duties, and in some houses they were actually served by their masters. It was also customary for each household to choose a "king" to preside over its private festivities. Lucius and Clodia honored the custom, but as they preferred to maintain the orderly routines of their home even during the holiday week, they limited the "king's" reign to a single day, the second day of the festival week. In past years, each of them had had an opportunity to rule the household for a day; this year, as a result of a conspiracy among Lucius, Clodia, and Gaius, they awarded this prerogative to Ariana, informing her of their choice early in the day.

"Oh, no, I couldn't!" she protested. They insisted, however, telling her she had earned the honor through good and loyal service to her mistress.

"Really, we're indebted to you," Lucius added. "You've brought a ray of sunshine into this house, and we're all the better for it."

Gaius merely grinned. *There he goes again ...*

Still protesting, Ariana was finally persuaded.

"But you must give me time to think," she insisted. "Meet me in the atrium in an hour."

Thereupon she retired to her *cubiculum* and, deciding she needed to look the part, donned the long *stola* that Clodia had given her, throwing the rose-colored *palla* over her shoulders. She had no jewelry, but she took special care with her hair, arranging it in the most becoming fashion she could devise. Meanwhile the others had set up a sort of throne in the atrium, placing a cushion on one of the bronze chairs. When she entered, she found the entire household assembled there. Lucius took her hand and led her to her "throne," and as she seated herself they all knelt before her. Looking up at her, Gaius knew he would never love another. *She's a goddess!* My *goddess! She'll be mine one day, I swear it!*

"Please rise!" Ariana begged, more flustered than ever, and as they did so, Lucius said,

"Now, Queen of the House of the Faun, tell us your commands for this day!"

Ordinarily, such occasions were opportunities to engage in pranks of all kinds, such as ordering the cook to kiss the kitchen maid or the master and mistress to dress in each other's clothes. But Ariana had something else in mind.

"Hear ye, hear ye, all ye who belong to the House of the Faun: Here are my commands."

She was beginning to enjoy this.

"Master,..."

"No, Ariana," Lucius interrupted. "You're the mistress today. Call me Lucius."

"Lucius, you will go to the bakery and purchase five loaves of bread fresh from the oven. Gaius, you will go to the market and buy all the sausage pastries you can carry. Mistress,..."

"Not 'Mistress.' 'Clodia'!"

"Clodia," Ariana continued, blushing, "You will go to the kitchen and help the cook arrange baskets of olives, dates, figs, and whatever else is available so Timon can carry them into the *triclinium.* The rest of you, arrange the benches and tables in the *triclinium* for a feast; bring in a brazier—someone'll have to run out for a bucket of coals—and bowls of water. Manlius, go to the cellar and find a couple of good jugs of wine.

"When each of you has performed his assigned task, we'll meet in the *triclinium* for a midday feast. There I'll give you my commands for the afternoon and evening."

Smiling, they rushed to carry out her orders. As they were leaving, she motioned to Gaius to stay behind.

"Gaius," she said, blushing yet again, "while you're running to the market, think about your scrolls and choose one to read to us after we've eaten. Something beautiful, not too short, nor too long either; your mother will need time for a rest before the afternoon's activities."

"Yes, my Queen!" he said, half mockingly, half lovingly. A look of understanding passed between them, and then he turned and went on his errand.

At noon they held their feast. The couches and chairs were gathered in a circle around a large table on which the food was set out. They gathered as equals, serving themselves and each other. No one had to cook or wash anything except a few wine cups. As "Queen," Ariana was seated in the place of honor. When the baskets and platters were almost empty, she tapped her cup on the tabletop to get everyone's attention.

"Shortly I will give you my commands for the rest of the day," she said, smiling. "But first I order Gaius to recite to us from a work of his choice."

Lucius and Clodia were pleased; they had both enjoyed those quiet summer evenings when Gaius had read to them as they dined in the fading light. The other members of the household had not been present on those occasions, though some of them had occasionally stood nearby and listened for a moment before returning to their duties. Now they, too, looked forward to Gaius's recitation.

Ariana was especially eager to hear what he had chosen. Would it be something new from Ovid? One of Catullus's love poems? (She hoped not; she was afraid she would be unable to hide her feelings.) *It'll probably be another of Horace's odes; he's really fond of them.* To her surprise, though, Gaius had not selected a work by any of those familiar favorites. He had borrowed a scroll of Propertius's works from Claudius, and he introduced his reading thus:

"Our Queen Ariana has instructed me to recite to you, something not too short and not too long. In obedience to her command, I offer you this lyric by Propertius, titled 'Love's Image':

He was a genius deft and wise
Who pictured Love in boyish guise.
He knew how senseless lovers are
To let small frets great pleasures mar.
A god with human heart he drew,
Tempestuous wings he gave him too

Well knowing that we lovers toss
On waters where wild currents cross,
And neither can we ever know
The quarter whence the wind will blow.
A quiver from each shoulder hangs
And shafts he holds with barbed fangs
Because he strikes us unaware
That any enemy is there.
Once hit we're never free from pain;
In me his arrows still remain,
His image haunts me everywhere,
But he has lost his wings, I swear,
For from my heart he ne'er takes flight
But wars upon me day and night.
What boots it, Love, with me to stay
Whose life-blood has been drained away?
Since a boy's form you manifest
A girl should take you to her breast,
'Twere meter that your poisoned dart
Should rankle in a virgin heart.
'Tis not myself your chastenings try
But the mere ghost that once was I.
If to destroy this ghost you please
Who will recite you songs like these
that humbly glorify your name
Since Cynthia's beauties they proclaim,
Her tapered hands, her graceful tread,
Her jet black eyes, her golden head!

When he had finished, no one spoke; no one wanted to break the spell he had cast. *I believe we have a potential orator here,* thought Lucius. *Not to mention a potential lover.*

Ariana had bowed her head while she listened, and the others had been looking at Gaius as he spoke, so no one had seen the expression on her face. *He's telling me he loves me, and I love him. But what can we do about it?*

Reminding herself yet again that she was still a slave—even though today she was "queen" of the House of the Faun—she pushed those thoughts aside and went on playing the role expected of her.

"Thank you for your excellent recitation, Gaius," she said with a smile. "Now, here are my commands for the rest of the day.

"You, Clodia, will go to your room and take a nice long nap. Lucius and Gaius, you will join me for a walk along the Via Stabiana to the Porta Vesuvio, where we will go through the gate and admire the view of the mountain and the countryside. The rest of you may spend the afternoon any way you wish: You may rest here, or go to the Forum and take part in the festivities, or visit relatives or friends. But you must all return here by sunset, at which time we will have a simple meal and then proceed to the theater. Manlius, please go to the theater ahead of time to reserve places for all of us. The rest of you, leave the *triclinium* arranged as it is now, since we'll be dining here together this evening."

◆ ◆ ◆

They strolled north along the Via Stabiana, chatting amiably. As there was no cart traffic that day, they walked three abreast in the center of the road, Lucius between Gaius and Ariana, an arm around the shoulders of each.

Along the way, they encountered several friends and neighbors and paused to exchange greetings. Heads turned as Ariana passed, decked out in her new finery and blushing more intensely than ever. When they arrived at the gate, the guards interrupted their dice game to smile and wave them through.

Outside the walls, they stopped to enjoy the view. Ariana was entranced. There in the distance was Vesuvius, its peak covered with snow, its shoulders sloping gently downward on either side. Below the huge mountain, the farm lands spread out to the east, but on the west they descended to the coast, with its scalloped bays and a multitude of fishing boats drawn up on the shore. There was the sea, and a misty horizon. Before her were fields, woods, and vineyards in their winter quietude. *How peaceful they look,* she thought. *And how much more beautiful they must be in the summer!*

"Thank you for bringing me here," she said to Lucius. "I've always wanted to come here ..."

Her voice trailed off as she remembered once again who she was. But Lucius smiled fondly at her and said,

"You may come out here any time you wish. I'll speak to the guards."

Her look of gratitude was all the reward he needed.

◆ ◆ ◆

Theirs was not the only household that had decided to attend the theater that evening. It seemed as if half of Pompeii was there, though that was not possible in a theater that could accommodate five thousand spectators. There were three tiers of seats, with the lowest tier, closest to the stage, reserved for public officials and leading citizens. Lucius led them along the row of seats reserved for them, followed by Clodia. Despite being "queen" of the household, Ariana attended Clodia, carrying her cushion and helping her arrange her *palla*. Gaius deftly managed to seat himself beside her. They sat without speaking, full of anticipation as they admired the rear wall of the stage, with its permanent backdrop in the form of a palace with arches, columns, niches for statues, and water gushing from fountains.

The evening's fare began with a short farce, a favorite entertainment of Pompeii's less cultured citizens. They loved to watch and laugh at the antics of stock figures: Pappus the Idiot as a candidate for office, or Bucco the Hunchback turned gladiator. But on any night at the theater, the main offering would be a comedy or tragedy—most often a comedy. The play presented that evening was an old favorite, Plautus's *Miles Gloriosus*, an uproarious comedy uproariously enjoyed by an audience that was already giddy after two days of celebration and license. Roars of laughter erupted at one episode after another in which the swaggering soldier was flattered and duped. If they had wished to do so, Gaius and Ariana could have held an amorous conversation without being heard, their voices drowned out by the shouting, laughter, and clapping of the exuberant audience. But they said not a word. Nor did they make any effort to touch each other, not even the slightest pressure of elbow against elbow. They were so acutely aware of each other's presence that no word or touch was necessary. Neither of them saw Marcus Vettius seated with his father a few rows above them, but Marcus saw them. In particular, he saw Ariana in her fine robes, her face flushed with pleasure and her eyes shining. *I* must *have her. I* will *have her!* he vowed. *Gaius is after her, I can tell. I've got to get her away from him. She can't stay in that house all the time, she's got to go out sometimes, and then I'll find her and tell her I love her. I won't do what I did before, I'll be gentle and ask her to let me kiss her, and then maybe she'll let me touch her, and then maybe ...*

His fantasies took flight as he imagined what might follow.

◆ ◆ ◆

The next morning, Ariana rose, donned her everyday dress, and went about her duties as usual. However, she could not help noticing the smiles that greeted her wherever she went. Everyone from Manlius, the house steward, to Quintus, the youngest of the kitchen slaves, smiled broadly at her. Even Lucius and Gaius, who had risen early and were on their way to the Forum, greeted her with smiles and compliments. Laying a hand on her shoulder, Lucius said,

"My dear girl, you were an excellent 'queen' yesterday! Would that every household had such a one, one who sheds beauty and happiness on everyone around her!"

Not sure how to respond, Ariana blushed and smiled back, saying nothing, and Gaius stifled a chuckle at his father's effusions as the two went on their way.

She went to the kitchen and prepared a pitcher of warm water, which she took, along with a bowl and a soft cloth, to Clodia's chamber. Half awake, Clodia turned toward her.

"Come over here, Ariana," she said drowsily. "Let me look at you."

Ariana set down the pitcher and bowl and knelt beside her mistress's bed. Clodia reached out and pulled her close, hugging her like a daughter.

"My dear," she said, "you're the best queen or king we've ever had. Thank you for giving us such a happy day!"

"It was my pleasure, Mistress," Ariana replied.

"But you don't need to be a queen to make *me* happy," Clodia continued. "You make me happy every day, just by being yourself. Promise you'll never leave me. Promise!" And she held her even closer.

"I promise," said Ariana, as if she had any choice in the matter. Nor did she consider leaving the House of the Faun. She was happy there, as happy as she could expect to be. There was nothing to warn her of the pain and sadness that awaited her.

IX
JANUARY, 74

The citizens of Pompeii had hardly had time to return to their everyday lives before the new year arrived, and with it the games proclaimed by Clemens. So on a cool, sunny winter day, most of the city's population gathered in the amphitheater to witness the opening ceremonies and the first of the contests.

Pompeiians were justly proud of their amphitheater, which was the oldest of its kind and in fact was being imitated on a grander scale in Rome; the Flavian Amphitheater—so huge that some called it the Colosseum—was under construction and scheduled to open in a few years. Pompeii's amphitheater had been erected over a hundred years earlier, under the sponsorship of Quinctius Valgus and Marcus Porcius, who were then at the summit of their careers in local government. It was a huge gift, way beyond what was typical in a small city like Pompeii. But Valgus was immensely rich; he had profited from Sulla's proscriptions after the War of the Allies, and had endowed similar public works in several cities and towns in the region; in one of them, he had donated money for the walls, the Forum, the Curia, and a cistern. Porcius, one of Sulla's veterans who had become a major wine producer, had a similarly large fortune and had made similar donations—all for the purpose of acquiring the largest possible following for a political career in Rome.

The amphitheater had been constructed in the southeastern corner of the city, partly so the surrounding wall could be used to support the huge structure and partly because there were few other buildings nearby, making it easier for large crowds to enter and leave the area. There were thirty-five rows of seats, which provided enough space for twenty thousand spectators, the most important citizens occupying the rows in front and the lower classes relegated to the back, with poorer views. In the summer, an awning was stretched on long poles above the seating area. The spectators were often raucous, as this was the only place where they could express themselves politically through vocal protests, protected by the anonymity of the crowd. Vendors paid the city a fee to sell refreshments—cakes and sweets, honeyed wine, hot sausages—from stalls set up just outside the entrance. Some had portable ovens; others walked among the crowds, selling fritters from trays.

The main reason for building the amphitheater was to attract visitors from surrounding communities—especially veterans who had settled in nearby towns like Abellinum and Nola. Sulla's veterans, many of whom had spent some time in Rome, were avid viewers of gladiatorial contests and combats between men and beasts, and the amphitheater had been built with their needs in mind. The older residents of Pompeii, especially those of Samnite heritage, were less enthusiastic about such bloody forms of entertainment, but it was necessary for them to attend; the absence of leading citizens would be noticed and would put them at a political disadvantage. And the gladiators were enormously popular; their names appeared on walls throughout the city. ("Thrax is the heart-throb of all the girls.") It would be extremely unwise to show disapproval in any way.

If they had any inclination to voice their distaste, the more refined citizens of Pompeii had a further motive to remain silent. About fifteen years earlier, the *duovir* Livincius Regulus had arranged a gladiatorial show for the people of Pompeii, Nuceria, and other nearby towns. As often happened at such events, taunts were exchanged by veterans from Nuceria and Pompeii; taunts led to stone-throwing, and before long swords were drawn. The result was a massacre in which many Nucerians were killed and others taken home wounded and mutilated. The Emperor Nero had instructed the Senate to investigate the affair, and as a result of its efforts, Regulus was exiled and Pompeii was barred from holding any similar gathering for ten years. Not long thereafter, however, Nero had rescinded the order and Pompeii had cautiously resumed holding games.

Most gladiatorial contests were held in the spring and summer, in connection with regular feast days; the Games of Apollo, for instance, were held in early July. But sometimes games were held to commemorate special events, such as the consecration of a temple or the funeral of an honored citizen. Drawing on this precedent, Clemens had proclaimed a three-day series of contests, declaring that they marked not only the beginning of a new year but also the initiation of a new era in the governance of Pompeii. He did not elaborate on the nature of that "new era."

Clemens was fortunate in that while the day was cool, there was little wind, and the steady sunlight streaming into the arena warmed the stone benches, enhanced by the warmth emanating from braziers placed at intervals along the lower rows for the benefit of the wealthier and more prominent citizens, many of whom were wearing two or three tunics or *stolae* under their cloaks and had brought cushions with them. Several of the lower rows had been roped off for members of the *Comitia* and other public officials; their wives, with their attendants and children, were seated in the rows just above them. Gaius and Clodia, with Ariana beside her, were among them. Unnoticed, Marcus had found a seat from which he could watch Ariana without attracting attention.

The games began with a procession that included the combatants, the animal trainers, a number of musicians, and a criminal who would be put to death during the interval between the morning and afternoon events. It was led by the games' sponsor, Clemens, clad in a toga with a purple border to signify that he was the representative of the Emperor Vespasian. After circling the arena, the procession dispersed and Clemens went to the place reserved for him, where he stood motionless for a moment. The shouts and chatter of the crowd subsided as Clemens raised his left arm and declared,

"Let the games begin!"

No sponsor in his right mind would begin the games with gladiatorial contests. The gladiators were saved for the afternoon, by which time the spectators' excitement would have reached fever pitch. The mornings of game days were devoted to other entertainments—mock fights, animal displays, and the like. Some of these, such as staged hunts, required large numbers of wild animals, especially lions and bears, which had to be imported. Clemens had decided against doing so for this event; it would not have been worth the cost. He knew his audience: The Samnite families were proud that the original gladiators had come from their region, and the descendants of Sulla's veterans were avid viewers of bloody battles of all kinds. Pompeii had a well-regarded gladiatorial training school, and it was rumored that some women of good family had had, or were having, affairs with gladiators. So Clemens had opted for a few animal acts followed by a series of mock fights in which heavily padded "gladiators" went at each other with whips, clubs, and fists. Some in the crowd amused themselves by urging on one contestant or another; others simply gossiped or sought out the food and wine vendors.

The midday break was given over to the execution of the criminal, in this case a murderer. There were a variety of ways of carrying out executions, including crucifixion and *damnatio ad bestias* (casting the criminal into the arena with violent animals). But the Emperor Nero had come up with a new way of disposing of criminals while entertaining the masses: reenactments of mythological tales in which the "hero" was actually killed. Again with his audience in mind, Clemens had arranged for a reenactment of the return of Agamemnon from Troy, complete with a large tub of water in which "Clytemnestra" pretended to bathe

"Agamemnon" and then covered him with a net so "Aegisthus" could stab him to death as he struggled, his frantic cries for help falling on deaf ears. Even the elite members of the audience, who ordinarily would leave during this interval to have a meal, stayed to watch the drama.

"Inventive," said Claudus to Lucius, who merely nodded. He had noticed that Rufus had managed to seat himself near Clemens and was leaning toward him, presumably to compliment him on the entertainment. *He's up to something,* Lucius was thinking. *But what?*

After the execution, there was a good deal of milling around. The vendors were mobbed; bets were being made; and the noise level was rising rapidly, along with the level of anticipation. "Now for the real thing," said Aper to Vascula. The two of them, inseparable as always, had made a series of bets, each opposing the other, on the afternoon's contests. Unless something out of the ordinary occurred, they would each break even. They joined the small group of friends standing around Claudius Vettius and teasing him because some of the gladiators had been supplied by one Aulus Vettius of Ephesus. "Another profitable business venture?" asked Aper with a grin. After numerous denials, Claudius acknowledged that the Ephesan was a distant relative. "But I have nothing to do with him!" he insisted.

Clemens had been strolling along the aisle surrounding the arena, exchanging pleasantries with anyone he chanced to meet, high born or low. Some of the councilmen, including Rufus and a few other members of his faction, took the opportunity to chat with him; others, including Lucius, did not want to be seen chasing after the new administrator like beggars hoping for a handout. This may have been an error of judgment; time would tell.

Under cover of the noise and activity, Julia strolled past Rufus, then turned and looked back at him with a smile. She was dressed in her finest clothing, her long *stola* cinched by a broad gold belt; she wore a diadem of pearls complemented by a pearl necklace and teardrop earrings. She carried her *palla* casually draped over one arm. "Are you at home in the afternoons these days?" she asked, moving close to him. "Certainly," he smiled back at her, angling his glance downward toward her shapely breasts, "once the games are over and the *Comitia's* back in session."

When Clemens returned to his seat, the crowd immediately fell silent. Clemens raised his arm; the gate at the end of the arena opened, and the first pair of gladiators entered. The answering roar was deafening.

There were three types of gladiators—four if one counted the *bestiarii,* or animal handlers. The so-called Thracians wore wide-brimmed helmets with visors, high greaves on both legs, an arm protector, and a small shield; they carried short, curved swords. Spartacus, the leader of the great slave revolt a hundred years earlier, had been a Thracian—that is, a gladiator who fought in the Thracian style.

The *secutores* wore egg-shaped helmets with round eye-holes, a greave on one leg, an arm protector, and the oblong shield and short sword of the legionary. Their name, meaning "chaser," probably came from the fact that they were often paired with the third type of gladiator, the *retiarius,* whose tactics included running. A *retiarius* fought with a large net and a trident; he had no helmet but wore an arm and shoulder protector and carried a small dagger.

Typically, a gladiatorial contest paired combatants of two different types; pairings of *secutori* with *retiarii* were especially popular. This first contest, however, pitted two Thracians against each other. Since both were heavily protected, the combat lasted much longer than most, with a great deal of clashing of sword on shield and much maneuvering for advantage. Finally, with a lucky blow, one of the combatants severed the wrist of the other. As blood poured from the wound, the ill-fated man attempted to defend himself with his small shield, but the victor beat it aside with his own. The loser held up an index finger to concede defeat, and the victor stood ready to deliver the final blow.

The crowd was evenly divided, with some calling out for the kill while others shouted for *missio*—reprieve. To the disgust of the former, Clemens granted *missio,* thereby avoiding the need to pay for another gladiator to replace the slain one. The bleeding man was carried from the arena to an uncertain future: His wound would be treated and would probably heal, but he would never fight again. The victor was given the usual prize, a wooden sword, which he raised in salute to Clemens before turning and leaving the field as the spectators roared their approval. A greater prize, freedom, awaited him after a few more victories.

The ensuing contests were more traditional, consisting of a series of matches between *secutores* and *retiarii.* These involved much more strategy and a great deal of running, since the *secutor* had to avoid the net at all costs. Once snagged in the net, he would be helpless against the *retiarius's* trident. On the other hand, the *retiarius* wore very little protective gear, and hence was vulnerable to a quick stab of the *secutor's* sword. Regardless of which combatant prevailed, the outcome was bloody. After one or two of these battles, Clodia buried her head in Ariana's shoulder, tears pouring down her cheeks. "I can't bear it any longer!" she cried. Ariana put an arm around her and held her close for a moment. Then she said,

"You seem ill, Mistress. Let me send for your litter and take you home."

Mutely, Clodia agreed. Ariana dispatched a slave for the litter and another to inform Lucius of their plan. Lucius sent back to ask if she wished him to accompany her, but even though his presence would have been comforting, Clodia declined, knowing how important it was for him to be seen. Her absence could be excused, his not.

Clemens had saved the best for last: The "heart-throb," Thrax, would face another local hero, Priscus, Thracian against *secutor.* Again, both combatants were heavily protected, though their gear differed in several respects, leaving more points of vulnerability. Both had been captured in wars on the fringes of the Empire and sold to a purveyor of gladiators, who in turn had sold them to the master of the Pompeiian school, where they had received their training. They had often faced each other in practice matches. Both knew, however, that this day was different: One of them must die. And both were prepared. Gladiators were trained not only in how to inflict death but also in how to accept it. They had sworn the gladiators' oath—*uri, vinciri, verberari, ferroque necari*—they would submit to be burned, bound, beaten, or killed by the sword.

They entered the arena, raising both arms and turning in all directions to face the audience, ending with Clemens. Then they faced each other, separated by the referee's thick wooden staff.

They circled each other warily, each looking for an opening, for any possible advantage, however slight. For a while, there was little action; a few short, sharp thrusts were easily parried. Then Priscus aimed a massive blow at Thrax's head, which the latter barely avoided while launching a similar blow at Priscus's mid-section. The impact caused Priscus to stagger backward, but as Thrax followed, his sword raised to deliver the final stroke, Priscus fell to his knees and thrust upward before Thrax could deflect the thrust with his small shield. Thrax managed to swerve aside and thus escape certain death, but he suffered a grievous wound, and for a moment he stood still as if paralyzed.

In that moment, Priscus struggled to his feet and prepared to strike again, but Thrax suddenly came to life and lunged toward him. Both men struck simultaneously, and both parried the blows with their shields. There followed a rain of blows on both sides, with neither man able to penetrate the other's defenses, until Thrax succeeded in striking Priscus's shield arm, wounding it and causing him to drop his shield.

At this point, the referee thrust his staff between them. When one combatant lost his shield, the other must discard his. The fight would continue with swords alone.

The gladiators were evenly matched. Both were strong and swift, and both had been thoroughly trained. Sword clashed on sword with little effect. But time was passing, and the combatants were tiring. Pretending to move to the left,

Priscus quickly shifted to his right and slashed at Thrax's unprotected shoulder, leaving a deep gash and bringing him to a standstill. He took advantage of the moment to strike the sword from the other man's hand. Again the referee intervened, and the contest resumed without weapons of any kind. Blinded by rage and fatigue, the two men pummeled each other until Thrax succeeded in pinning Priscus to the ground, but Priscus refused to concede defeat and struggled to free himself and continue the contest.

But once again the referee intervened. Dazed, both men rose to their feet as the crowd went wild. Amid the uproar, Clemens raised both arms, spread wide apart, and the referee, standing between the gladiators, seized an arm of each man and raised it above his head. The match had ended in a draw, a highly unusual outcome. Both gladiators were awarded wooden swords and granted their freedom. And while some of the spectators were disappointed because all wagers were canceled, most were pleased to have witnessed such a stirring combat. Clemens's reputation was firmly established.

◆ ◆ ◆

The next day, Clodia was unwell and did not attend the games; Ariana stayed home to care for her. Gaius also stayed home. He had gone to the *tablinum,* where Lucius was attending to a few matters of business before setting out for the amphitheater, and asked his father if it was really necessary for him to attend. He had acquired some recent writings by Pliny; he believed he could learn more by studying them than by watching gladiatorial contests.

"It's not really necessary for you to be there," Lucius agreed, "and I wish I could say the same for myself. I've never enjoyed these brutish forms of entertainment. But most people do—I suppose it stems from all the wars Rome has fought, against so many enemies, some as vicious as the animals we see slaughtered in the arena. I would prefer to stay home and receive clients, or go to the baths or the Forum—anything rather than sit on a hard stone bench and watch men killing each other. And today, I hear, there's a pair of women scheduled to fight. I'm glad Clodia won't be there to witness such degradation! But as *aedilis* I have to be there. My absence would definitely be noticed. Yours probably won't, but if anyone asks, I'll say you're ill—that you and Clodia both ate tainted food sold by one of the vendors. I'm sure you'll have a much more enjoyable day than I will. When I get home this evening, I want you to tell me what old Pliny is writing about these days!"

And with this he donned his *pallium* and set out for the amphitheater.

◆ ◆ ◆

Gaius settled down in the *oecus* where he had formerly met with his tutor. After the cessation of his lessons with Kineas, he had converted the room into a sort of *tablinum* of his own. Chairs and a table were already there; all that was needed was storage for scrolls. For this purpose, Gaius had obtained a number of large wooden buckets; in these he stored the rolled-up scrolls vertically, about a dozen to a bucket. He then arranged the buckets against one wall, starting with Aeschylus and ending with Zeno. As long as no one moved the buckets around, he could easily find any work he was looking for.

Gaius spent an hour or two perusing Pliny's treatise on oratory. *I need to learn as much as I can about public speaking,* he told himself, *but I'm not sure I can learn about it this way. Maybe I'd be better off studying some of Cicero's speeches.* He went over to his storage buckets and found Cicero's *In Catilinam.* The great statesman's diatribes against his arch-enemy Catiline were considered among his most powerful orations—and indeed, they had eventually led to the man's conviction and execution for treason—but Gaius soon wearied of the intensity of Cicero's accusations and the self-satisfaction underlying them: Cicero knew he was brilliant, and was convinced he was saving the Republic from grave danger. Gaius rolled up the scroll and returned it to its container, intending to give Pliny another chance to hold his attention. And then, unbidden, Catullus's famous plea to Lesbia came to his lips: *Da mi basia mille ...* "Give me a thousand kisses, then a hundred, then another thousand ..."

As if in a dream, he rose and went to the kitchen. There he found Ariana rummaging in a cupboard for a piece of bread, a few olives—whatever she could find to serve as a midday meal. Hearing his approach, she turned to face him.

It was inevitable, had been inevitable since the day she came to live in the House of the Faun. They had both known this moment would arrive someday, and they had both been willing to wait until it presented itself. The moment was now.

Slowly, wordlessly, they came together and embraced. They stood there a long time, barely breathing; then they moved apart and, still silent, gazed into each other's eyes. He drew her toward him again and kissed her with the utmost tenderness. Suddenly she was on fire. Waves of heat passed through her, over her, an ocean of fire that did not burn, of waves that did not drown. She tightened her arms around him and returned his kisses. *Da mi basia,* he was thinking, *Oh, Ari-*

ana my love, da mi basia! As for her, the power of thought had deserted her entirely.

"Is Mother expecting you?" he asked after a while.

"She's asleep," she said.

They held each other and kissed again and again. Then he took her by the hand and led her to his *cubiculum* just off the atrium, closing and latching the door. They lay on his bed, wrapped in each other's arms, drinking each other's kisses like honeyed wine. An hour went by, perhaps two; they were in a trance. But finally Gaius came to himself and reluctantly freed himself from her embrace. He sat on the edge of the bed and looked down at her flushed face and shining eyes.

"I love you, Ariana. You and only you!" he said, bending over for another kiss.

"And I love you, Gaius," she whispered, reaching up to encircle his neck with her warm arms. But then she turned away, hiding her face in her arms.

"What is it?" he asked gently, thinking she might be overwhelmed by the suddenness of their encounter. But he was mistaken.

"I'm a slave, Gaius. A slave! You can't love me!"

He leaned over and put his arms around her.

"Ariana, listen to me. I love you, no matter what. You may be a slave now, but I'll find a way to change that, I promise. Now, tell me again, do you love me?"

"Oh, yes, Gaius, yes. I only wish ..."

"Shhh," he said, putting a finger to his lips. "Don't think about it."

He stood and held out his hand to help her rise.

"Ariana, my love, we must be careful," he said. "There won't be many days when we're alone in the house, but we may be able to meet somewhere else ..."

"At the Porta Vesuvio!" she broke in. "I always go there when I'm out walking."

"At the Porta Vesuvio," he agreed. "If I can meet you, I'll leave a scroll unrolled on my table instead of putting it away. Go through the gate and wait for me outside the walls. I'll spend a little time at the baths so people see me there, then I'll come and find you."

◆ ◆ ◆

Though subject to imperial decree, Pompeii was self-governing for the most part. The *duoviri* or magistrates made legal pronouncements and administered public funds, as well as presiding over meetings of the *Comitia.* The *aediles* were in charge of administrative tasks like road maintenance and supervision of markets.

The *Comitia,* or city council, was made up of one hundred councilmen or *centumviri.* Under most circumstances, these officials constituted all the government the city needed. Rome rarely interfered in Pompeii's internal affairs.

This general rule was broken, however, when public order was threatened. After the brawl in the amphitheater between the Pompeiians and the Nucerians, the *duoviri* then in office had been replaced, and Nero had appointed a prefect to supervise them. The emperor had also suspended the games—and then reinstated them, thereby demonstrating his omnipotence and reinforcing his popularity.

So when Vespasian sent Suedius Clemens to restore order to their city's government, the Pompeiians by and large did not view his action as an attack on their autonomy. They lived under imperial rule, and imperial intervention was to be expected under certain conditions. Indeed, some members of the *Comitia* saw Clemens's presence as an opportunity to advance their own interests; Rufus was one of them. Others, and especially Lucius, were less optimistic. Distressed and frustrated by the factionalism that had paralyzed the council and led to Vespasian's decision to appoint an administrator, Lucius was one of the few who felt that Clemens's arrival was inauspicious. Far from healing the rifts that had developed in the past few years, the presence of an administrator, one who could dispense favors and issue edicts that might benefit one side or the other, was likely to make the situation even worse. But Lucius kept his doubts to himself. Only Clodia and Gaius knew what he was thinking.

On the morning after the games ended, Clemens addressed the *Comitia,* laying out a series of issues on which he proposed to take action, from restoring order to the tax registers to reclaiming land that had been appropriated by corrupt speculators. He made no mention of Samnites or anti-Samnites, nor did he give any indication of favoring one side over the other. He did, however, issue his first edict: Removal of stones from the city's walls would cease immediately; in fact, the worst breaches would be repaired. And he appointed Statius Rufus to the position of *procurator.* It would be Rufus's responsibility, and that of three assistants selected by him, to enforce Clemens's edicts, as well as to collect taxes and assess fines for minor offenses like damaging roads or water pipes.

◆ ◆ ◆

"How did you do it?" murmured Julia sleepily, snuggled up against Rufus in their *pergula* on an especially cold winter afternoon.

"Do what?"

"You know, get Clemens to appoint you *procurator.*"

"Oh, *that*. That was easy."

"Well ...?"

"I went to Rome ..."

"Yes, I know. I missed you."

"I missed you too," he said, running his hand along the length of her body, then stroking her thigh. "You're beautiful." And he moved on top of her, kissing her avidly, preventing her from speaking. Finally she turned her head aside.

"Come on, Statius, you're trying to distract me!"

"And succeeding, too!" he said, grinning as she moved under him, parting her legs and granting him entry to the warm, moist place he sought. But after a few highly satisfying moments, she repeated her question.

"Tell me! I really would like to know."

"You won't tell Claudius?"

"Claudius and I don't have much to say to each other these days."

"Does he know about us?"

"I don't know, and I don't care!"

"Well, maybe you should. What would you do if he divorced you?"

"Marry *you*!"

He did not respond and, somewhat disappointed, she returned to her original question.

"So what did you do in Rome?"

"I talked to someone I know, a client of Clemens. I asked him to put in a good word for me, to tell Clemens about me, tell him I could be useful to him. And he did."

"In return for what?"

"Never mind what," Rufus replied, and would say no more.

X

MAY, 74

It was a blissful springtime for Gaius and Ariana. They had found a small wooded area not far from the Porta Vesuvio, and every few days they met there and spent an hour or two together.

At first, they were shy with each other; so much had passed between them in silence that they had difficulty finding words to express their feelings. They held hands and wandered through the trees, occasionally stopping to embrace for a moment, then continuing their aimless wandering. Finally they found a dry, grassy spot on the far side of the woods, with a good view of the mountain and a sun-warmed boulder to lean against. There they sat, shoulder to shoulder, desiring nothing more than to be near each other.

Gradually they began sharing their thoughts and feelings. He recalled how, long ago, he had noticed her peering through the doorway of the House of the Faun as she returned from her errands.

"I never dreamed I would end up living there!" she said, still amazed at her good fortune. And then, after a moment:

"It *is* a charming little statue!"

"Yes, it is," he agreed. "It's been there forever. Have you noticed that Father pats it on the head every time he walks by?"

"Yes, I've noticed!" she said, and they both laughed happily.

After that, the words flowed more freely, punctuated by kisses. He told her what he could remember about his childhood, which had been a happy one.

"I always felt that I could go to Father or Mother if something troubled me, and they would comfort me and advise me. Actually, it was usually Mother who did the comforting and Father who did the advising. You know how he is ..."

"He's a good and wise man."

"Yes, he is. I can't imagine better parents."

"They've been very good to me. I wasn't really unhappy in the other house, but it was nothing like this. Your mother treats me almost like a daughter. I sometimes forget I'm a slave."

With that she fell silent and turned her head away. After a moment, he realized she was weeping quietly. He reached over and gently turned her face toward him.

"Ariana, my love, my goddess! Please don't weep. I promised you we'd find a way to be together, and I'll keep my promise. We'll find a way. Be patient and trust me."

And he put his arms around her and held her until the tears stopped flowing and she rested her head on his shoulder.

◆ ◆ ◆

As the weeks went by, they grew to know each other better. There were no longer any constraints between them. She told him about her childhood on the farm—a childhood he could barely imagine, as he had never spent much time outdoors. She told him her dream of walking through the countryside and picking blackberries, and he promised her they would do so late in the summer, when the berries were ripe. She told him about her mother, and how she had wept when Ariana was taken from the farm to serve in the kitchen of the Vettii's house in town, and how sweet Clodia was to allow Ariana to visit her from time to time.

"And your father, did you know him?" he asked.

"I know nothing about my father, and Mama won't tell me anything, just that he was sent away somewhere—who knows where?—and she was sent to the farm."

"And you don't know why?"

"No, she won't tell me."

"That's very strange, and sad," he said. "And it makes me realize even more how lucky I am."

"I suppose it's sad for Mama," she agreed, "but as I never knew my father, it makes no difference to me. Besides, your father is very kind to me."

"Perhaps for Father, and for Mother as well, you're taking the place of my baby sister who died," Gaius suggested. "They've never said any such thing, but do you remember those evenings the four of us spent together in the *viridarium?* They enjoyed having you there, and they really *did* treat you like a daughter. But no one outside the household must know, of course. We're such a respectable family, one of the original Samnite families ..."

A note of bitterness crept into his voice, and he remembered his father's warning: *If it ever becomes evident that she's with child, she will be sent away. … I won't tolerate anything that would detract from our family's reputation.*

"What's wrong, Gaius?" she asked. The more time they spent together, the more she became attuned to his moods. He did not answer, but took both her hands and folded them in his. Finally he said,

"Remember our first day together, how I said we must be careful and you agreed? What I didn't tell you is that some time ago Father guessed my feelings for you. I suppose it wasn't difficult: I doubt if I can look at you without it showing! Anyway, he warned me not to make love to you; he said if you were with child you would be sent away."

"He would do that? Oh, of course he would. He'd have to! Just like Mama was sent away …"

They sat there in silence; neither could think of anything that would offer any consolation. Finally they turned toward each other and kissed for a long time, the sweetness of their embrace providing some comfort as they struggled to come to terms with their situation.

◆ ◆ ◆

By tacit agreement, they avoided meeting in the house and limited their trysts to an hour, two at most, so Ariana could return before Clodia rose from her afternoon nap. As spring merged into summer, they spent less time in conversation and more in contented silence as they sat together on the grass and watched the clouds drift by above the tall mountain and the spreading countryside below it. Occasionally, one or the other would point to something—a pheasant scratching around in the underbrush, a butterfly alighting on a nearby bloom—and they would share a smile of pleasure. Sometimes they turned to each other with love in their eyes and embraced, kissing again and again as if striving to surpass the count set forth in Catullus's poem. Then, sated, they would lean back and close their eyes, holding hands and absorbing the sun's warmth for the brief time remaining to them.

Gaius had obtained a scroll of epigrams by Valerius Martialis, a young poet who was attracting considerable attention in literary circles. To amuse Ariana, he would memorize one or two of them before leaving the house, then recite them to her as they sat together in the sun.

"Listen to this!" he said, shaking his head. "What a wit! Listen:

Diaulus, recently physician,
Has set up now as a mortician;
No change, though, in his clients' condition.

"And this one:

Aper the archer's rich wife, struck
Through the heart by his own shaft, was killed.
All sports consist of skill and luck:
She was unlucky, he is skilled.

"They say Martial's the most talked-about poet in Rome; I can see why! Oh, I forgot, here's another one:

They're mine, but when a fool like you recites
My poems I resign the author's rights.

I have to assume he's not talking about me!"

"No, he's talking about that so-called bard, Cossius!" Ariana assured him. They both laughed. She smiled at him, sharing his excitement at his new discovery. Anything that gave him pleasure was pleasing to her.

One lazy afternoon, Ariana pointed to the plume of smoke emanating from Vesuvius's summit.

"I've always wondered about that smoke coming out of the mountain," she said. "What does it mean?"

"Vesuvius is a fire-mountain," Gaius said. "A mountain with a fire within it. What you see is the smoke escaping from a vent in the rock. There are other mountains like it in other lands. There's one in Sicily, called Aetna. Aetna's a lot worse than Vesuvius—it's three times the size of Vesuvius, and it's constantly sending flames and clouds of smoke and ash into the sky and rivers of burning rock down its sides. In fact, the poets refer to it as the forge of Vulcan. The Greeks believed that the Cyclopes fashioned lightning bolts there, for Zeus to use when he got angry."

"It must be a truly fearsome sight," she said.

"It must be, though I doubt if anyone has gotten very close to it. Not like here. If we want to, we can climb to the top of Vesuvius. All it does is send out a little smoke."

"Well, I hope that's all it ever does," she said with a laugh.

◆ ◆ ◆

As the weather grew hotter, they retreated under the trees, finding a secluded spot where he spread out his *pallium* and they lay on it, gazing lovingly at each other, or kissing, or holding each other in a long, warm embrace. He loved to lie on his side, an elbow on the ground and one hand supporting his head as he looked down at her and stroked her forehead and hair; then he would bend over for a kiss. One day, as he bent down to kiss her, she looked past him and saw Marcus standing just a few paces from them, staring at Gaius with a look of intense hate. She gasped and pushed Gaius away, getting to her feet as fast as she could—but Marcus was gone.

Trembling, she knelt beside Gaius and stammered: "Marcus. It was Marcus. He was watching us. Oh, Gaius, what are we going to do?"

"I'm going to find him and break his neck!" replied Gaius, standing up and slinging his *pallium* over one arm.

"Wait, no, don't go after him!" she begged.

"Don't go after him? Do you want to just sit here while he tells everyone he meets that Gaius Tullius is making love to a slave girl?"

His words stung, and she could think of nothing to say. Angrily he strode off toward the Porta Vesuvio, leaving her kneeling on the ground, sobbing.

◆ ◆ ◆

In recent months, Gaius had been taking his exercise at the *palaestra,* the large, rectangular training ground adjacent to the amphitheater. It was much more spacious than the small gymnasia associated with the baths, and though he had to walk all the way across town to get there, it was worth the effort. It had been built at the command of the Emperor Augustus to give Pompeii's young men a place to meet and train so they would be prepared if they were called up for military service—though in these days such training was no longer necessary, as battles were fought by the Empire's professional troops. There one could engage in a variety of athletic pursuits—including foot races and javelin throwing as well as boxing and wrestling—then rub down and relax in the shady peristyle surrounding the tree-studded exercise field, or perhaps go for a swim in the large pool at the center of the field.

Having seen Marcus at the *palaestra* on several occasions, Gaius decided to confront him there. He did not have long to wait. On the day after the encounter in the woods, he saw Marcus at the edge of the field watching a wrestling match. Overcome by anger, he walked up behind the youth and grabbed him by the arm, spinning him around to face him.

"You will not spy on me ever again!" he shouted.

Stunned by the suddenness of the onslaught, Marcus did not reply but struggled to free himself from Gaius's grip.

"Answer me!" Gaius persisted. "Swear you'll stop following me!"

Angrily, Marcus tried to push Gaius away, without success.

"You can't have her, she's mine," he muttered. "Leave her alone!"

Infuriated, Gaius assumed the boxer's stance and began pummeling his opponent, who was smaller and much less skilled. Marcus tried to return the blows, but he could not get close to Gaius, and in a few moments it was over: Gaius delivered a jarring blow to the side of Marcus's head that knocked him to the ground, unconscious.

Gaius stood still amid a silent throng of onlookers, aghast at what he had done, yet not regretting it. Then Nigidius Vascula and Melissius Aper emerged from the crowd. Vascula lifted Marcus from the ground and carried him to the peristyle, laying him on one of the marble benches and calling for water. Aper took Gaius by the arm and led him to the entrance of the House of the Faun.

"Are you going to tell your father what happened, or shall I?" he asked grimly.

"I'll tell him," Gaius replied.

Bad news travels fast, and when Lucius came home he had already heard about the fight and its outcome. Summoning Gaius to his *tablinum,* he spoke in a voice of ice.

"Your behavior is inexcusable, but I'll listen to what you have to say."

"I have nothing to say, Father. It's a private matter."

"Nothing that damages the reputation of the Tullii is a private matter. What do you think people are saying about my family, about my son, who attacked a smaller youth and knocked him senseless? What do you think they're saying?"

"They must realize there was provocation."

"What provocation?"

"As I said, it's a private matter."

"It is not!" shouted Lucius. "As master of this household, I insist you tell me what led to this outrageous conduct. Then I'll decide what action to take."

Thus compelled, Gaius told him everything.

As he spoke, Lucius gradually regained his composure. After Gaius had finished his account, he sat for a moment in silence. Finally he said,

"You're right: There was provocation. But there's still no excuse for what you did. The matter could have been handled in some other way …"

"What other way? What would you have said if I'd come to you and told you what had happened? What would you have done?"

"Frankly, Son, I don't know," Lucius admitted. "But that doesn't change the fact that your behavior was unjustified. In the morning you and I are going to visit the House of the Vettii and you're going to apologize to Marcus. And there will be no more meetings outside the Porta Vesuvio. I'll speak to the guards."

"Father …"

"There's nothing more to say. Leave me now."

◆ ◆ ◆

With both fathers present, Gaius apologized to Marcus—a grudging apology grudgingly accepted, as neither youth had a choice in the matter. One side of Marcus's face was blotched and puffy, one eye swollen shut. With the other, he glared angrily at Gaius. *This doesn't end here.*

The deed done, Gaius nodded to Claudius and left the house. Lucius followed Claudius into his *tablinum* and offered his own apology, which was considerably more gracious than his son's. Then he told Claudius what Gaius had told him.

They were closeted together for almost an hour, at the end of which Lucius rose to take his leave. Claudius stood also, preparing to escort him to the door. Just then Lucius reached out and placed a hand on his friend's shoulder.

"I don't wish to intrude in your private affairs," he said, "and what we've discussed won't go beyond these walls. But this is a serious matter, my friend, and I feel compelled to advise you to tell Marcus the truth about Ariana's parentage. Before it's too late. I'm sorry to have to say this, but you can imagine the potential consequences if …"

"Say no more, Lucius, I know what I have to do," said Claudius. "Tell me, though, you're not going to send her away, are you?"

"No, I'm not. At least not now," Lucius assured him.

◆ ◆ ◆

Marcus lay on his bed with a cloth soaked in cold water covering his face. Beneath the cloth, tears of rage and frustration seeped from his eyes. Claudius had summoned him to his *tablinum* and told him, without elaboration, that Ariana was his sister and he must cease his pursuit of her. Crushed, and furious with his father as well as with Gaius, he had stormed out of the room and flung himself onto his bed.

I don't believe it, it can't *be true,* he was thinking. But in his heart he knew it was. During the Saturnalia, he had seen them standing near each other, his father and Ariana, and the similarity in their build, their features and coloring, had been evident. He had squelched the thought immediately, but it had been lurking in the back of his mind ever since. He wanted her, had wanted her for a long time. Yet his father's words had taken away his hopes. And when he remembered his behavior toward her—and his fantasies about her—he felt embarrassed and humiliated.

But he still wanted her. Now, trying to sort out his feelings, he began to realize he was obsessed with her. Why did he want only Ariana when there were plenty of pretty girls in Pompeii, many of whom had sent promising glances in his direction? He believed he loved her. But now he wondered if he could ever love her as a sister. He knew he could never hate her, but could he stop wanting her as a woman?

He would have to stop pursuing her, would have to start thinking of her as his sister. But his sister was a slave in another man's house, and the master's son could have his way with her if he wished. He seethed with anger. If he could not have Ariana, he would make sure—somehow—that Gaius Tullius could not have her either.

XI

JULY, 74

A shadow had fallen over the House of the Faun, a shadow in the form of a deep, pervasive silence. Lucius and Gaius spent as much time as possible outside the house, though not together. While Lucius followed his usual daily routine, Gaius did not accompany him. Instead, he sought out his father's counterpart, the aging Paquius Proculus, and offered to act as his assistant. Proculus was delighted, and Lucius, despite feeling somewhat slighted, could not find it in his heart to object. Indeed, after some consideration, he realized this was the best way for Gaius to learn about the day-to-day requirements of city governance. As a result, Gaius spent a great deal of time in the streets of Pompeii, inspecting public works like the fountains at major intersections, and reporting on their condition to Proculus.

Within the house, all was silent. Ariana was almost mute, speaking only when necessary. Though sympathetic, Clodia was constrained by concern for Lucius's reputation. The mood of the servants echoed that of the masters; even the friendly joking of the kitchen slaves was subdued, and other household tasks were carried out in silence. There were no more long, mellow meals in the warm twilight, no more recitations of Horace or Ovid. Meaningful conversations occurred only between Lucius and Clodia, and these, too, were brief, as Lucius often returned late from the Forum or the baths.

For two or three weeks, Ariana had remained indoors, even though Clodia, kind-hearted as ever, had not forbidden her from taking her afternoon walks. She had spent the time in her *cubiculum*, lying on her bed and staring at the ceiling, or turning her face to the wall and weeping bitter tears. Eventually, however, her innate high spirits had returned, albeit in subdued form. She began smiling and chatting again, but only with Clodia, and though she resumed her walks, she kept them short, going a little way along the Via Nola toward the Nola Gate, then turning around and returning to the House of the Faun. Her natural curiosity seemed to have deserted her.

A similar shadow enveloped the House of the Vettii. Claudius devoted every spare moment to his studies of philosophy and literature, even taking most of his meals in his *tablinum.* Julia virtually ignored him. She visited Rufus as often as she could, even though he was far less available than he had been before Clemens's arrival. To the surprise of many who knew her, she began devoting a great deal of attention to Aurelia and Julilla, who were approaching womanhood. She bought ankle-length *stolae* for them and taught them how to arrange their hair; she took them to the shops and the women's baths and the theater. They even attended poetry readings in the roofed Odeon next to the theater—an attempt, no doubt, to make them appear less frivolous. Her efforts were reflected in the girls' faces, which glowed with new-found self-confidence. Julia basked in the compliments of friends who began noticing them. They were growing tall and shapely, and like Marcus, they had inherited their father's good looks. They had not, however, developed their brother's mercurial personality.

As for Marcus, he had a new passion: He wanted to know everything there was to know about gladiators. Whenever he could, he hung around at the gladiators' school, watching the training of new recruits using wooden swords. He haunted the training areas and the barracks, trying to absorb every detail of what he imagined to be a glamorous life. He even asked the school's manager if he could help out in any way; the man merely laughed and told him to keep out of the way. Undeterred, he roamed around the edges of the field, listening to the men as they joked and swore between bouts. In this way, he learned a great deal that would have made even Julia blush. He longed to be able to fight like them, to win fame in the arena and perhaps have an affair with a lusty Pompeiian matron. Perhaps, when he was older, the trainer would give him a lesson. Some of the older youths took lessons (without their parents' knowledge), and Marcus envied them. *Someday I'll be like them. Then Gaius had better watch out!*

◆ ◆ ◆

Gaius was standing in the Via Stabiana, watching a couple of workers as they dug through the thin layer of soil covering a lead pipe. The pipe, which carried water to the Stabian Baths, had apparently broken, and the men were trying to find the break and repair it. When they had done so, Gaius would inform Proculus and receive his next assignment.

He looked north and saw a brief flash of white, and somehow he knew it was Ariana crossing the Via Stabiana as she returned from her afternoon walk. Impelled by some unknown force, he left the men to finish their work and walked quickly to the House of the Faun. He knew where he would find her. He strode through the atrium and the small garden, across the mosaic of Alexander and into the large *viridarium* at the back of the house, with its fountains and statues, and a marble bench at one end shaded by a cluster of small olive trees and oleanders. On the bench sat Ariana.

She was sitting perfectly still, staring down at her hands, which were clasped in her lap. Her hair was bound back in an indifferent fashion, her *stola* not fresh, her feet dusty. Her expression was a blend of sadness and resignation. She resembled a carving on a grave stele: the silent matron mourning a lost child, the young wife weeping for a husband killed in battle. She did not react when he approached and knelt before her.

"Ariana, my love, my goddess …"

He looked up, seeking her eyes, yearning for a response; there was none.

"I'm so sorry. I'm so terribly sorry!"

She said nothing. She wanted to forgive him, but her hurt was deep.

"Ariana, I didn't mean to hurt you. Please forgive me. I love you, only you. I'll never love another!"

Still she was silent, but finally she sighed and put a hand on his head.

"I love you too, Gaius."

He laid his head on her lap and she stroked his hair. After a moment he looked up at her again. She was smiling through her tears. Filled with happiness, he rose and sat beside her, taking her in his arms.

"Someday we'll be together, we'll find a way, I promise," he assured her.

◆ ◆ ◆

It was midsummer, and Pompeii was consumed by election fever. The city was choosing its two magistrates—the *duoviri.* One of the incumbents, Caecilius Jucundus, was running for reelection. The other, Octavius Quartio, had recently died, and Lucius Tullius was seeking that office. Running against him was Statius Rufus.

As it was not considered appropriate for a candidate to seek votes himself, others sought them on his behalf. Throughout the city, walls were whitewashed to erase the previous year's inscriptions. During the night, professional writers, accompanied by lantern-bearers, covered them with new testimonials in red or black paint; by this means, individual citizens or professional groups (the dyers, the goldsmiths) expressed their support for one candidate or the other. These inscriptions carried a single message: They stated that the candidate was of good moral character, and followed the statement with a request—*oro vos faciatis* ("I ask you to elect him"). All other statements about a candidate—his past actions, his suitability for the office he sought, his promises to reduce taxes or improve the roads—were made in private: at dinner parties, in conversations at the baths, during chance encounters in the streets.

For Lucius, the move from *aedilis* to *duovir* would be a natural and logical progression, and he had long planned to seek the higher office. When Quartio died, Lucius thought the time was right. Contrary to his expectations, Suedius Clemens governed with a light hand and had succeeded in restoring order and decorum to the *Comitia.* Indeed, it might be a particularly opportune time to become a *duovir,* with Clemens's presence serving to deflect or diffuse any criticism that might come his way. He had expected to run unopposed, or to be opposed by one of the more experienced councilmen, such as Vascula or Aper. *But no,* he realized, *they won't run until both positions are open so they can serve together. What a pair!* He had been stunned when Rufus announced his candidacy.

"What on earth is he doing?" he asked Clodia and Gaius as they shared an evening meal. "He's much too young, and he hasn't even served as *aedilis* yet. It would make much more sense for him to run for *aedilis,* especially since the position is open. And though I hate to say it, his work as Clemens's *procurator* has given him the experience he needs. But *duovir?* He doesn't have enough experience for that. And he lacks judgment ..."

"Lucius, you know you can't use that against him. Even if people know what's going on—and they probably do—it would be in bad taste," Clodia warned.

"You mean the affair with Julia?" Gaius asked, to the astonishment of both parents. "Don't look so surprised. You're quite right, Mother, everyone knows what's going on!"

"Yet they write testimonials on their walls as if he were a model of fidelity and sobriety!" Lucius grumbled.

Gaius smiled in sympathy; then turned serious. "Father, I've heard something that might interest you."

"And what is that?"

"I've been spending a fair amount of time with the men working on the pipes and fountains ..."

"Yes, I know. Go on!"

"Well, the men talk among themselves, and sometimes I hear what they're saying. There are complaints about the taxes ..."

"There are always complaints about taxes!" Lucius interrupted.

"Yes, but this is different. If I understand what they're saying, the figures don't add up."

"What do you mean?"

"That Rufus is collecting more than he should, and keeping some of it."

Lucius sat for a moment in stunned silence. Then he said,

"Son, that's a very serious accusation! You can't make such a claim without evidence."

"You're right, Father, and I'm not making it in public. I don't have evidence, only rumors. I just thought you should know."

"Well, now I know, and there's nothing I can do about it, at least not now. But it still doesn't answer my question: Why in the world is he running for *duovir?*"

"There's only one possible explanation," said Clodia.

"And what might that be?"

"He's running because *you* are. He's running against *you*!"

"My dear, that doesn't make any sense. We've always been friendly, even though we've been on opposite sides ... Oh, wait a minute. *That's* it! Samnites versus anti-Samnites, *again*. Why can't he leave it alone?"

"Apparently because he feels so strongly about it. He genuinely believes the Samnites are trying to take over the government, and he's dedicated himself to preventing them from doing so."

"You may be right. But he must know his chances of defeating me aren't very good."

"Maybe he's not expecting to win. Maybe he's just running for the sake of opposing you and attracting attention to himself. Or maybe his chances are better than you think they are."

"In what way?"

"He could be spreading rumors about you. It wouldn't surprise me."

"What kinds of rumors?"

"I don't know, Lucius. I just think he's the kind of man who would stop at nothing to get what he wants."

The three of them sat in silence for a while, lost in thought. Finally Lucius said,

"I'll need someone to speak on my behalf. We could ask certain people to dinner and let them know their support would be appreciated ..."

"We'll do that," Clodia agreed. "But that's not enough. You need someone with a good reputation to back you, someone who can't be accused of any personal interest in the outcome. Perhaps Claudius ... Oh, no, what am I thinking!"

"No. Unfortunately, he *does* have a personal interest ...

"How about Proculus?" Gaius suggested.

"Proculus?"

"Why not? He's reputable—after all, he's an *aedilis*. He's known to everyone; he doesn't have a personal interest in the outcome (though he's hinted once or twice that he hopes you'll win). Also, I think he likes me!"

"He's not in the habit of giving dinner parties, though he certainly has the means."

"He'd do it for *you*, I'm sure of it. Would you like me to ask him and let you know what he says?"

"That would be very kind of you, Son," Lucius assented, his generous smile illuminating his face. Gaius smiled back. Amity had been restored between father and son, and Ariana, standing nearby in case Clodia needed her, felt a wave of relief.

◆ ◆ ◆

As it turned out, it was not necessary for Proculus to give a dinner party on Lucius's behalf. In the midst of the campaign, Claudius divorced Julia. While everyone had assumed he was absorbed in his philosophical studies and oblivious to Julia's adultery, he had been aware of it and had decided to take action. Conscientiously following the required procedure, he began by sending a freedman of the house—Petronius—to convey his message to her: *Tuas res tibi agito* ("Take your belongings away!"). Then, in the presence of seven witnesses, he publicly expressed his wish to divorce her *propter mores*—that is, for misconduct.

Shocked and disoriented, Julia protested vigorously, but soon realized she had no recourse. She was forced to gather up her personal belongings and leave the house; as she left, she repeated the parting formula, *Tuas res tibi habeto* ("Keep your belongings to yourself!"). Though she would later be able to reclaim her dowry, at first she had nothing but her clothing and jewelry. Accompanied by her maid, she walked through the streets of Pompeii, an edge of her *palla* drawn across her face, until she reached the vestibule of Rufus's house. There the door slave, following his master's orders, denied her entry; Rufus had grown weary of her.

Julia Vettia had nowhere to go.

◆ ◆ ◆

The whole city was abuzz. Already excited by the election, the citizens of Pompeii were now served up a delicious feast of gossip. No one blamed Claudius, but Rufus had both defenders and detractors. Many people understood that he was under no obligation to receive Julia, but the sight of her and her maid wandering through the streets had aroused their sympathy. Julia eventually found shelter with a friend, and it was said that she would soon move into one of the apartments rented out by the enterprising landlady Julia Felix. As sympathy for Julia Vettia rose, Statius Rufus's reputation sank. And when it came time to vote, Lucius Tullius was elected *duovir* by a three-to-one majority.

◆ ◆ ◆

Julia Felix owned a large estate that covered two adjacent *insulae*. She had combined these, eliminating the road between them, and then subdivided the buildings into a number of shops (with *pergulae*) and apartments, along with a public bath house. An inscription at one of the entrances read, "In the estate of Julia, daughter of Spurius Felix, to let: elegant baths for respectable people, shops with living quarters above, and apartments on the upper floor. From August 1 next to August 1 of the sixth year, for five years. The lease will expire at the end of the five years."

Claudius divorced Julia in mid-July. On the first of August, she moved into one of Julia Felix's apartments. As it was customary for the children of a divorced couple to live with their father, Aurelia and Julilla remained in their childhood home. Marcus, however, was furious with his father and would have nothing more to do with him; he went to live with his mother. Julia hoped to find another husband before her lease expired.

For the first few days, both Julia and Marcus had no inclination to leave their rooms. There was no sign of Julia's erstwhile haughty demeanor; her self-confidence had vanished, and she could not bear the thought of encountering anyone she knew. *What could they say? "My dear Julia, I'm so sorry to hear that your husband divorced you and your lover refused to take you in!"* Despite the pleas of her maid, Julia would not allow her to help her dress or arrange her hair. She sat for hours staring out at the large cultivated gardens at the rear of the complex of apartments and shops, paralyzed by shock and anger. She realized she had seriously misjudged—not to mention betrayed and insulted—her husband. Over-confident and insensitive, she had given up a lifetime of wealth and status for a few afternoons of illicit pleasure. When she thought about Rufus, she burned with shame. She now saw what she should have seen all along: He had never made her any promises, never wished for anything beyond those few afternoons. For that matter—now that she was being honest with herself—neither had she.

While she sat brooding, Marcus wandered aimlessly from room to room, consumed with anger. He hated his father. *Why did he do it? How could he!* Of course he had overheard the gossip, but he had refused to believe it even as his ears burned. Nor could he forgive Claudius for failing to acknowledge Ariana as his daughter, even though he knew it was Julia who had insisted on it. Adrift in a sea of conflicting emotions, he began constructing fantasies of a future in which he was tall and strong, a gladiator perhaps, or at least a soldier in one of Rome's legions—that was it! He'd run away and join the army! With such thoughts, he whiled away the time until eventually his restlessness drew him out of the apartment to explore his new surroundings.

Julia Felix had thought of everything. Her tenants could satisfy many of their needs right there: Food and wine was available in the shops; there were baths and a swimming pool; the large garden with fruit trees planted in the middle could be reached from all directions and was a pleasant place in which to stroll—and enjoy an apple or a juicy pear when they ripened. The paintings in the public rooms portrayed a wide variety of scenes, from everyday life in the Forum to mythological themes and Egyptian fantasies. At one end of the inner courtyard was a shrine dedicated to the Egyptian goddess Isis. Her cult, much more emotional than the stiff and solemn official religion of the Empire, was immensely popular among slaves and freedmen, who were attracted by its promise of a better life to come, and it had gradually taken hold among the upper classes as well. The temple of Isis, recently repainted, occupied a small precinct near the theater; there, priests performed daily ceremonies in her name. But each afternoon, Julia Felix presided over a simpler ceremony in her courtyard.

Marcus spent a day examining all this, even entering the private house at one end, where he glimpsed Julia Felix herself seated in her *tablinum*, conferring with her steward. The tall woman with steel-gray hair impressed him with her clear speech and authoritative bearing. Suddenly she looked up and saw him.

"Come here, young man. Don't hide in the shadows like a mouse!"

Marcus approached reluctantly.

"Who are you?"

He told her, and she asked him if their rooms were satisfactory. He merely shrugged. He had not paid any attention to the rooms. She looked at him curiously for a moment. An intelligent woman who had dealt with all kinds of people for many years, she could sense the turmoil within him. She was also well aware of his mother's situation.

"If you're not too busy, I could use a little help," she told him. "Would you mind checking on the flow of water in the bath house? I've heard complaints that the water's too hot; there may be an obstruction in the cold-water pipe."

He stared at her in surprise, then nodded and left the room. She turned back to the steward and laughed. "All that boy needs is something useful to do," she said.

◆ ◆ ◆

When Marcus returned to the apartment, the words tumbled out as he told Julia about the gardens and the shops and Julia Felix and the water pipes in the baths. She immediately recognized the insight and kindness behind Julia Felix's action and sought her out to thank her.

"Think nothing of it," said Julia Felix. "The boy is full of natural curiosity. I just gave him something to be curious about."

"I appreciate it," said Julia. "He's been very moody lately."

"Tell him he can stop by here whenever he likes; I can find plenty of things for him to do."

"That's very kind of you."

As the weeks went by, Marcus and Julia became increasingly integrated into the life of the sprawling community that was Julia Felix's establishment. They became acquainted with the shopkeepers and the gardeners, chatted with neighbors in the baths, and took some of their meals in the little *caupona* attached to the *thermopilium* that sold hot prepared foods both to residents of the apartments and to passers-by on the Via dell' Abbondanza. Marcus became the steward's unofficial assistant, running errands and checking on anything that needed maintenance. Never before had he been given responsibility for anything, and the experience transformed him. His moodiness and despondency evaporated like fog on a sunny day. Soon he was well known to everyone in the establishment, and wherever he went, he encountered a smile or a friendly greeting, which was returned in kind. He no longer thought about gladiators or the army; he was absorbed in his daily activities and for several weeks did not even venture outside the Villa of Julia Felix.

Somewhere in the back of his mind, however, his feelings about Gaius and Ariana simmered, and from time to time his dark moods returned. He would stop whatever he was doing and go off by himself, staring at the ground and brooding over the fact that there seemed to be little he could do to prevent Gaius from making love to Ariana. His own desire for her had subsided, but his hatred and jealousy of Gaius were as strong as ever. He would get even with him somehow, perhaps not yet, but before too much longer. In the meantime, there was much to keep him occupied from day to day.

Julia's recovery took longer than her son's. Though she gradually developed a daily routine that included shopping, walks, and other activities that brought her into contact with other people, she kept her thoughts to herself. She sold much of her jewelry and began dressing more simply so as not to draw attention to herself. Unconsciously, she was following the example set by Julia Felix, who wore no jewelry and eschewed the fine fabrics favored by the wealthy women of Pompeii—though she could certainly have afforded them. Indeed, Julia Vettia was increasingly falling under the spell of Julia Felix. The older woman was so self-possessed, so competent and yet so kind and understanding. Julia was grateful to her for taking an interest in her son, but more than that, she sensed that in Julia Felix she might find the wisdom she knew she lacked. Perhaps Julia Felix could help her find a way out of the dark forest in which she found herself, lost and alone. She began seeking excuses to visit the older woman, who would receive her in her *tablinum* but often invited her to sit with her in the peristyle that flanked the courtyard, which was attractively planted with laurel and flowering oleander; in the center was a long, rectangular fish pool with miniature bridges and marble niches for small bronze statues of nymphs and cupids. Resting in the shade, they drank chilled wine and spoke lightly of events in their little community—of the birth of a daughter to one of the tenants, or the impending arrival of cooler weather, signaling the need to harvest the ripe fruit from the trees in the garden. And, with a little gentle questioning, Julia Felix learned the story of Julia's life.

"And did you ever consider asking him to take you back?"

"No! That wouldn't be possible!"

"Why not?"

"Because … because …"

The older woman sat quietly as Julia searched for the words to express her guilt and remorse. The words did not present themselves, but tears crept from the corners of her eyes and slid down her cheeks. Julia Felix reached across and took her hand.

"We all make mistakes, Julia, and the world doesn't come to an end. You'll make a new life for yourself, you'll see."

Unable to speak, Julia merely nodded. A cloud that had cast a shadow over the courtyard moved on, allowing the sunlight back in.

XII
FEBRUARY, 75

Life in the House of the Faun took on a new coloration after Lucius took office as *duovir.* As one of Pompeii's highest officials, he had many more responsibilities, and they kept him occupied in the Forum for most of the day. In the evenings, he hosted numerous dinners in an effort to maintain amicable relations with all the members of the *Comitia,* regardless of their adherence to one faction or the other. He did not, however, invite Statius Rufus to dine with him.

Clodia, with Ariana's help, planned and supervised the meals and entertainment. The best silver and bronze dishes were used, and on more than one occasion, Petronius was borrowed from Claudius's household to prepare his specialties—especially his roast suckling pig. Eumelos was called upon for recitations; musicians played the harp and flute as the guests relaxed over dessert. Lucius purchased his entire supply of fine wines from Claudius's establishment, and Claudius himself could often be seen among his dinner guests.

It was a restful time, a time of peace in the household and amity among its members. Occasionally, when there were no guests for dinner, Lucius, Clodia, Gaius, and Ariana would enjoy a quiet meal together. They would chat about the events of the day, and Gaius would recite his favorite poems. On one midwinter evening, he treated them to one of Horace's most famous odes:

Vides ut alta stet nive candidum
Soracte, nec iam sustineant onus
silvae laborantes, geluque
flumina constiterunt acuto?

Dissolve frigus ligna super foco
large reponens atque benignius
deprome quadrimum Sabina,

o Thaliarche, merum diota.

> Do you see how tall Soracte stands, shining with snow, and the forests bend under their heavy load, and now the rivers are frozen by the sharp cold? Chase away the cold, Thaliarchus, by putting logs on the fire, and be generous in pouring the four-year-old wine from Sabine jars.

"Just substitute Vesuvius for Soracte," he said with a smile.

For several months, Gaius and Ariana had gone about their day-to-day lives without attempting to be alone together. And for several months they had been content to let their love speak through their eyes rather than their lips. But as Ariana approached her sixteenth birthday, her feelings became more intense and she found it more difficult to hide them. Gaius, too, found that he must make a great effort to restrain himself whenever he saw her. Each, in fact, was burning with desire for the other.

At about this time, Clodia, wearied by her added responsibilities, caught a chill. Throughout the days and nights she shivered, no matter how many *stolae* and *pallae* she wore, no matter how much charcoal was heaped on her brazier. Ariana was kept busy bringing her warm barley broth and replenishing the coals in the brazier, or sitting beside her as she lay shivering beneath a pile of blankets. Lucius came into the room from time to time to see if there was any change in her condition; he would take Ariana's place and sit beside his wife, holding her hand between both of his in a fruitless attempt to send some warmth her way. Then, with a sigh, he would relinquish his seat to Ariana and return to his duties in the Forum.

After three days, Clodia finally stopped shivering and drifted into a sound sleep. Ariana adjusted the blankets around her so she would stay warm. Exhausted herself, she stumbled dazedly from the room in search of her own bed; without knowing how, she found herself in Gaius's arms.

He held her for a long time as she leaned against him, resting her head on his shoulder. Then he raised her face to his and kissed her slowly, lingeringly. Eyes closed, she felt as if she were in a dream: Mythical landscapes passed before her, peopled with gods and goddesses, cupids, nymphs, and fauns. Through them, in hero's garb, strode Gaius, and as he approached, she opened her eyes and looked into his. "Ariana, my love," he whispered.

There were several small rooms at the rear of the house that were used for storing old furniture and other household goods—extra pots and dishes, braziers (during the summer), and the like. They found a room whose contents included a pile of old quilts and blankets. A shaft of sunlight slanted through an opening high in the outside wall, and in the hazy light they knelt on the blankets and embraced again.

They were on fire. She made no protest as he slipped her *stola* over her head and pulled off his tunic. He paused for a moment to admire her slim body, then reached out and touched her breasts. She moved close to him and they kissed, rejoicing in the sensation of warmth and closeness as they pressed against each other. All thoughts of life outside their little room vanished, all fears of being discovered evaporated. Their entire world was in each other's arms.

Though neither had made love before, they were not unaware. No one in Pompeii who was not blind could have missed the many paintings and mosaics portraying lovers engaged in their favorite pastime. Indeed, Pompeiians believed they had a special relationship with Venus, and that she brought them good luck and prosperity. But for Gaius and Ariana there was no need to call up images from the works of artists; impelled by love and desire, they followed their natural instincts to their inevitable conclusion.

It was not what they had expected.

There was some awkward fumbling, then a moment of sharp pain for Ariana. She stiffened and lay still. He withdrew and lay beside her, quietly waiting. Then she turned toward him, and he took her in his arms.

"Are you all right, my love?" he whispered.

"I don't know … Could we stay like this for a while?"

They lay on the blankets, watching the ray of sunlight slowly trace a path along the wall above them as the dust motes glinted in the light. After a while he began kissing her and stroking her breasts and belly. Soon they were both aroused again, and this time their joining was more successful. Yet still they sensed that something was lacking. They had not taken flight, not reached the glorious heights they had imagined. Still, just being together was bliss. They could have lain there forever.

Eventually, however, they noticed that the sun was no longer shining through the opening in the wall. Hastily they dressed and, with a last quick kiss, left the room separately, Gaius going to his study in the *oecus*, Ariana to Clodia's room. Clodia was only half awake, and did not notice Ariana's flushed face.

Clodia spent the next two days in bed, and Ariana spent much of that time caring for her. But on each of those days she and Gaius were able to meet for an hour or two in their love nest at the back of the house. With each encounter, they became more adept, better able to satisfy each other. But still it was not enough. They needed more time together, time to explore and learn about each other, yet they knew the present arrangement could not last. They were certain to be discovered, and neither wished to face the consequences.

"Gaius …" she said hesitantly as they parted on the third day.

"I know, my love," he replied. "We must stop meeting here."

"What are we going to do?"

"I don't know."

They kissed and went their separate ways, their future as uncertain as ever.

◆ ◆ ◆

"Father …"

Gaius was standing in the entrance to Lucius's *tablinum.*

"Yes, Son, come in. What is it?

"Father, I want to marry Ariana."

"You know that's not possible."

"Couldn't you free her?"

"Not until her thirtieth birthday. Even if it could be done sooner, it would not be possible. I can't allow you to marry a freedwoman. We've spoken of this before."

They looked at each other for a moment. Neither was angry, but both were determined.

"I will marry no one else," Gaius finally said, and left the room.

◆ ◆ ◆

A few weeks later, Ariana realized she had missed her monthly courses. At first, she thought she might be mistaken, might have misremembered how long it had been since the last time. But as days and then weeks went by with no sign, and she began to feel ill in the mornings, she knew she was with child.

She did not tell Gaius; indeed, she told no one. She became silent and withdrawn, doing only what she was required to do and ceasing her daily walks. She knew she would be sent away; it was only a matter of time.

Then one day she was so ill she could not leave her bed, and soon she was bleeding heavily and racked by cramps. Now it was Clodia's turn to care for Ariana. A slave brought fresh rags and took the blood-soaked ones away. Weeping at the pain, Ariana placed a fist in her mouth to avoid crying out. Clodia sat beside her, occasionally wiping her sweating forehead and offering her dates and chilled wine. She thought she knew the cause of the girl's distress.

After a few hours, the pain eased, but Clodia remained at Ariana's side. To pass the time, and perhaps deflect Ariana's thoughts from her condition, she began talking about her own early life.

"When I was your age," she said, "I was living in Herculaneum, in the villa of Claudius Pulcher. Actually, it's just outside Herculaneum. It's a huge place, stretched out over a series of terraces facing the sea. Gods, what a view! I loved to sit in the little semicircular portico at the end of the garden, which was open in the back so you could look out over the water. I would sit there for hours, watching the boats and the seabirds and the waves breaking against the rocks.

"Claudius Pulcher was my uncle. I was living in his house because my parents had died of a fever a few years before, and my uncle had been kind enough to take me in. I was grateful, but I never felt as if I belonged in that grand house with its many rooms, its statues and peristyle courts—it even had a swimming pool! I felt lonely and out of place, which is why I spent so much time looking out at the sea. Also, my uncle had an excellent library—he was steeped in Greek culture, and he collected the works of the Greek philosophers as well as many Latin texts. There were busts of Epicurus, Zeno, and Demosthenes in the corners of the room. I spent a lot of time there, as I could read well enough. My father had had me tutored along with my brothers—'Why not?' he had said. 'She's as bright as they are, and it won't cost me any more!'

"Of course, I took part in the life of the family—the dinners, the trips to the theater or the games, the outings in the countryside. And I met all the eligible young men of Herculaneum, Pompeii, and Oplontis—that is, the ones from the best families. That's how I met Lucius.

"Lucius could have married anyone he chose. He was the most sought-after young man in the whole region, not just for his wealth but for his noble Samnite heritage. But his father was a particular friend of Claudius Pulcher; they shared that love of all things Greek that you find so often in the best families. So Lucius and his father were frequent guests at my uncle's dinner parties. I had a few conversations with him; sometimes we talked about what we'd been reading, and I guess that impressed him, since most of the women he knew had no interest in literature, if they could read at all. I was hopelessly in love, and I mean hopelessly: I didn't dare to even dream of marrying Lucius Tullius! I was, after all, an orphan, a poor relation. Well, not that poor, actually, and my brothers would have provided a dowry of sorts, but certainly nothing to entice a family like the Tullii.

"As time went by, though, Lucius began to feel as I did. I could see it in his eyes and the special smile he gave me whenever we met. You know that wonderful smile of his! One day, he asked me to walk with him in the *viridarium*—we both loved the fountains and the statues, especially a delicate little pig in bronze, and a pair of elegant deer. We strolled through the garden, and when we got to the portico at the back, we stopped to admire the view. And then, without saying anything, we embraced. Then he asked if I would consent to marry him. If *I* would consent! By then the tears were streaming down my face, and all I could do was nod.

"So he went to his father and my uncle, and they approved, and my uncle very kindly provided a decent dowry, and we were married. I was eighteen at the time.

"I was so happy to be living in the House of the Faun. It's a big house, but it's not as grand as Pulcher's villa, and I think it has more dignity. Its decor hasn't been changed with each new fad that comes along. I love the little faun, and of course the mosaics, especially that one of a cat and two ducks in the atrium. I love the *viridarium,* with its fountains and the shady peristyle around it. I've always felt at peace here.

"I was surprised when I didn't have a baby in the first year or two after we were married. It was actually three years later that Gaius was born. It was a difficult birth, but thankfully he was a strong, healthy baby. And so like his father! People smiled when they saw them together. They still do.

"After that, another three years went by before I was with child again. It didn't go well. I was sick all the time, and weak and tired. When the baby came early, I was glad—until I saw how tiny she was, and how frail. She lived only a few weeks. I wept and wept. I didn't want to go on living, but Lucius was so good to me, he spent as much time as he could with me, and held me and comforted me. Finally I recovered, but I wasn't as strong as before; sometimes I was too weak to get out of bed in the morning. And it was clear that I couldn't have any more children.

"So I devoted myself to raising Gaius to become as fine a man as his father, and doing whatever I could to help Lucius in his career. Nothing else interested me, though I did enjoy going to the theater, and sometimes we would hire litters and go on outings in the countryside. Like that time after you came to live with us, when the four of us went out for a day in the country. Do you remember?"

Clodia had been leaning back in her chair with her eyes closed as she reminisced. Now she opened her eyes and looked at Ariana. Looked at her and saw that she was sleeping, her dark lashes curling over her cheeks and a peaceful smile on her lips. With a smile on her own, Clodia pulled the blankets up over the girl's shoulders and left the room.

◆ ◆ ◆

A few days after her recovery, Ariana resumed her afternoon walks, and one day, as she set out along the Via Nola, she found Gaius waiting for her at the Via Stabiana. He took her hand, and they continued toward the Nola Gate. When they had traversed most of the way to the gate, they came to a part of the city that had suffered considerable damage during the most recent earthquakes. Some of the houses had been demolished and converted to agricultural land, others left as they were, in ruins. The residents did not have the means to rebuild and had moved away. The walls of the modest houses were still standing, but the roofs had collapsed, the tiles scavenged for use elsewhere. The gardens, untended, had grown wild. In one of them, Gaius and Ariana found a marble bench, and after brushing aside the leaves and twigs that had accumulated on it, they sat, his arm around her waist, her head on his shoulder.

Gaius knew Ariana had been ill, but he did not know the nature of her illness. When she told him, he turned pale and held her closer.

"Oh Ariana, my love, I'm so sorry!" he whispered.

"I'm better now," she said.

He told her about his brief conversation with Lucius, and she shrugged and said his father's attitude was not surprising. Then they were silent. There was nothing more to be said. They kissed a few times—brief, sweet kisses with little passion—and after a while he rose to return to the Forum while she went back to the House of the Faun to resume her duties as a household slave.

XIII
SEPTEMBER, 75

It was his manservant, Nabucco, who finally informed the authorities of Rufus's illicit activity. The son of a Syrian slave, Nabucco had managed to buy his freedom, but, like many other newly freed slaves, he had chosen to remain in his master's household. Rufus's establishment was a comfortable one, and Nabucco's duties were not onerous, but the man despised the master for his rabble-rousing and his casual treatment of women, and resented his stinginess. The sums of money traditionally given to slaves and servants during the Saturnalia were paltry in Rufus's house, even though the master could easily afford much more. But Statius Rufus was nothing if not charming, and when Nabucco came to him with complaints, he easily dispelled them with a grin and a pat on the shoulder.

For the past year or two, Nabucco had become increasingly restless, and he was considering leaving Rufus for another master, or perhaps learning a trade. The latter would entail some hardship, however; he would have to apprentice himself, and he could hope for little comfort in his living arrangements. At best, he might expect to be given a cramped portion of a tradesman's *pergula,* sparsely furnished and, if he was lucky, curtained off to provide a modicum of privacy. So he stayed on, increasingly discontented—and increasingly disgusted as he observed Rufus's affair with Julia.

When he overheard Rufus and his three accomplices arguing over how to divide up the proceeds of their tax-skimming operation, he knew the time had come to act. He memorized some of Rufus's more incriminating statements. Then he quietly packed his personal belongings and left them with a friend on his way to the magistrates' offices at the south end of the Forum.

As it happened, Caecilius Jucundus was ill, leaving Lucius Tullius to receive Nabucco and hear his accusation. Remembering his son's remarks during the campaign the year before, he was not especially surprised. But he was in a difficult position. Having defeated Rufus in that election, he could be seen as holding a grudge; it could even be rumored that he had persuaded Claudius to divorce Julia at that particular moment in order to improve his chances. The guilty parties must be arrested, but Lucius felt unable to give the order himself. So he advised Nabucco to stay with his friend until he could find a new place to live, and admonished him not to leave Pompeii because he might be called upon to testify. Then he sought out Suedius Clemens.

Clemens was incensed. He had prided himself on restoring order to the disorganized Pompeiian government, and anticipated returning to Rome and receiving the Emperor's praise as well as other, more tangible rewards. Now he was told that the very men he had trusted to carry out his directives had betrayed him. He ordered their immediate arrest and imprisonment pending a trial.

"You'll have to preside," he said to Lucius, and no amount of protest would change his mind.

◆ ◆ ◆

"I feel very uncomfortable about this," Lucius said to Clodia that evening. "How is it going to look, me sitting in judgment on Rufus?"

"You're a magistrate, it's your duty. Surely people will understand that."

"I wish Jucundus could do it."

"So do I, but I hear he's quite ill. You'll just have to make the best of it."

"Yes, I know. But it means I'll have to be very, very careful."

◆ ◆ ◆

The first decision Lucius had to make was the selection of a prosecutor. In the increasingly litigious society of the early Roman Empire, there were plenty of advocates to choose among. Every day the Forum echoed with their harangues, some of them lasting as long as two hours and, of course, answered by equally long orations in behalf of the accused. At best, advocates were thought of as windbags; at worst, as sleazy bribe-takers. *No, I can't use one of them,* thought Lucius. *This is a serious case, not a spectacle in the arena.*

As the accusation had been made against a member of the *Comitia,* the case would be heard by the *Comitia* acting as a court, with Lucius presiding. He could not choose anyone from that body to serve as prosecutor, but he needed someone with sufficient legal knowledge. A former member of the *Comitia* would be appropriate—someone who had served with honor but had not gone on to become an *aedilis* or *duovir*, someone who was not weakened by advancing years, whose mind was still sharp. *Someone like Munatius Faustus. Yes, Faustus would be the perfect choice.*

Munatius Faustus came from an old Samnite family, but his paternal grandmother was descended from one of Sulla's veterans, and he had never been closely linked with the Samnite faction—which in any case had developed only in his last year or two of public service. During his many years in the *Comitia,* he had been a voice of reason, always trying to focus his colleagues' attention on the ultimate goals and possible consequences of any proposal under discussion. He was a slim, fairly tall man, and in his later years his hair had turned white but had not fallen out, giving him a dignified look that was lacking in some of his shorter, balder contemporaries. Being more of a thinker than an actor, he had not been interested in seeking higher office and had retired from the *Comitia* to live a quiet life while still following the actions of the municipal government with keen interest.

Lucius sent a slave to Faustus to ask if he might visit him, and when the response was positive, he set out across town to Faustus's modest home, ironically located not far from Rufus's grander establishment; the latter was already surrounded with gaping citizens abuzz with gossip about the arrest. Faustus welcomed Lucius politely, led him into his *tablinum*, and offered him a seat and a glass of chilled wine.

"I think I know why you're here," he said.

"I'm here to ask you to serve as prosecutor in the case against Statius Rufus," Lucius replied. "I know you've retired from public life, but you're well suited to the task: Your reputation for impartiality, your clear thinking and reasonable ideas ..."

"Please, Lucius, there's no need to flatter me. I accept, but on one condition."

"And what is that?"

"That the men arrested with him be treated leniently. The crime, if it truly occurred, is Rufus's doing, not theirs. They were looking only for a few more *sesterces* to feed their families. You know how it is."

"Yes, I know, and I agree. But we *will* frighten them into telling us what they know. You can't object to that."

"No, of course not."

◆ ◆ ◆

As the day of the trial approached, Lucius spent little time at home. Gaius also was kept busy with his work for Paquius Proculus. There was always something to attend to, as rebuilding after the earthquakes, both the big one almost fifteen years earlier and the less severe ones three years ago, seemed never to end. A matter of special concern was the condition of the public water supply. The pipes running under the main streets had been damaged in the quakes and never properly repaired, so there were constant ruptures that required immediate attention. Other public works ordered by Clemens were also under way, and one of Gaius's assignments was to report on them to Proculus, who in turn informed Clemens of their progress.

One afternoon, however, Lucius and Gaius almost ran into each other in the atrium as both were heading out for a quick visit to the baths. Laughing, they stopped to look at each other in mock surprise—"What are *you* doing here? I haven't seen you in ages!"—and then proceeded together to the Forum Baths, even though both would have preferred to go to the more luxurious Stabian Baths. On the way there they chatted, each getting a quick update on the other's affairs. Not much was new about Gaius's daily life other than its heightened pace, but he had found time to read a new scroll Claudius had lent him that contained translations of Aristotle's *Politics* and *Ethics*.

"That doesn't sound like your usual fare," Lucius teased. "Aristotle was many things, but he definitely wasn't a poet!"

"I know, and believe me, I'm quite ready to go on to something lighter. But there's something about Aristotle's ideas that's gotten me thinking. I don't know how applicable they might be to our government here, but they certainly seem to have played an important role in Athenian democracy."

"What ideas are those?"

They had reached the baths and were about to enter the changing room. Gaius paused and said,

"Could we sit in the peristyle for a while? I'd love to talk to you about these questions, but it might be difficult while bathing!"

Lucius agreed, and they found a bench in the shade. A slave brought them some chilled wine.

"It's like this," Gaius began. "In the *Ethics*, Aristotle shows how the individual citizen can lead a good life. In the *Politics*, he demonstrates that such a life can be attained only in a well-ordered society. So the state is the chief means by which the citizen can attain happiness, which is achieved through virtuous action. This means, according to Aristotle, that every state has been formed for a specific purpose: to enable its citizens to pursue virtue, rather than power or wealth."

"Not very realistic, I'd say," Lucius commented.

"Maybe not. But wait, there's more. Aristotle believes the function of the state is to teach citizens to follow the ways of virtue. That is, the purpose of government is to promote the virtue of citizens so they can lead the best life and so the state, as an aggregate of citizens, can also lead the best life. So you see, he's saying the citizens and the state are really the same thing and have the same goal. And that goal is all-important. He even believes that in the ideal state there will be no war, because aggression is not a virtuous action. Everything is directed toward the goal of virtue, and therefore happiness.

"Now here's where I have a problem. We've always associated Aristotle with the 'Golden Mean,' the idea that we should seek moderation in all things. But if individuals and the state are directing all their actions toward achieving happiness through virtuous action, I don't see where moderation comes in. It seems like a contradiction."

"I see what you mean," said Lucius. "I haven't read any of Aristotle's works, but I've heard discussions of them at some of the dinners I've had to attend in the last couple of years. (Too many, I'm afraid. Little by little I feel myself growing heavier, and there's no time for exercise.) Anyway, some of my hosts have invited philosophers to contribute to the discourse—mostly those Stoics who are so popular these days, but also one or two with more Platonic leanings. Well, you can imagine the discussions, especially when it comes to virtue. It's been defined a hundred different ways. But I remember one of them saying something to the effect that virtue is 'a mean state'—'mean' in the sense of 'moderate'—one 'that lies between two vices, the vice of excess on one side and the vice of deficiency on the other.' So maybe what Aristotle's saying is that the *right* action, the one that will get you closer to your ultimate goal, is a decision derived from the balancing of opposed forces."

"Yes, I see!" said Gaius. "I remember now: Aristotle wrote something about a ship: 'A ship which is only a span long will not be a ship at all, nor a ship a quarter of a mile long; yet there may be a ship of a certain size, either too large or too small, which will still be a ship, but bad for sailing.' If you apply that to the state …"

"… you'll find that the state must be contained within certain limits if it's to be effective. Thus, moderation helps achieve the purpose or goal of the state."

"That's excellent, Father!" Lucius exclaimed happily.

"But Son, why do you think it could apply to Athenian government and not Pompeii's?"

"Because Athens was a democracy. There was no king or emperor. Here, for example, Clemens, acting on the Emperor's authority, could simply order that

Rufus be executed. Oh, there might be a show trial, but the outcome would be predetermined."

"Clemens *does* have that power," Lucius agreed, "but he's a man of moderation, and I've come to respect him a great deal. We'll have a trial, and it *won't* be a show trial. As for whether Rufus will end up being executed, that I can't say, though I doubt it. And that reminds me, there's something I need to ask of you."

"What's that?"

"Remember last year, during the election campaign, you told me you had heard rumors about Rufus, and about the tax numbers not adding up?"

"Yes, I remember, but surely you're not suggesting that I ..."

"No, of course not. I just wondered if you could give me the names of the laborers who were talking about him so we can interview them. I promise you they'll come to no harm."

Gaius pondered the question for a moment and then agreed, but he also made a suggestion: "Why don't you offer to include them among your clients so they can receive the daily *sportula.* That way they'll be less afraid to tell you what they know."

Lucius consented, and father and son made a quick pass through the baths before heading back to the House of the Faun.

◆ ◆ ◆

Because of the seriousness of the charges and the intense interest the case had aroused at all levels of Pompeiian society, the trial would be held in the Basilica, the largest space available other than the theaters and the arena (though there were some who suggested, privately, that the arena would be a more appropriate setting). Situated at the southwest corner of the Forum, the huge building had a large, unroofed vestibule at one end. Here, four magnificent columns divided a flight of stairs to create five entrances into the main hall. Inside, a peristyle of brick ran along all four sides, its columns echoed by half-columns set into the walls opposite them; between the half-columns, the walls were painted to imitate large blocks of stone, interrupted by two entrances along the side walls. At the far end stood the tribunal, a tall platform surrounded by a set of slender columns. Access to it was provided by a mobile wooden structure that could be quickly removed if necessary to guarantee the magistrate's safety. The wooden ceiling was carved in a pattern of rectangles, and the space was flooded with light entering through openings in the upper portions of the side and end walls. On the long exterior wall were posted the *Acta Diurna,* or "Daily Doings," copied from a similar list that was posted in Rome's Forum each morning.

The Basilica lacked the stately dignity of the Capitolium, but it made up for it in its monumental size and importance. On most days, it was the center of life and activity in Pompeii. It was the meeting place of merchants and bankers, who mingled in its vast space and conducted business there. Vendors set up stalls and displayed their wares: crockery, tools, shoes, fabrics, garlands, perfume. Auctions took place there. More important trials were held there; less serious matters were resolved in the magistrates' offices nearby, so as not to interrupt the city's commercial activities—its lifeblood.

On the day set for the trial of Statius Rufus for grand larceny, crowds completely filled the hall, spilling through the entrances onto the piazza of the Forum. On the tribunal was the magistrate's chair; on benches below him sat the prosecutor, the defendants, and other parties to the proceedings. The *centumviri*—the members of the *Comitia*—would serve as the trial court, and a section in front of the tribunal was roped off for them. Behind these swarmed the public, so closely packed together, and so vocal, that the atmosphere was stifling and it was difficult to hear the proceedings above the noise of the crowd, which sounded like an undifferentiated roar (though one could occasionally hear an especially loud comment—"He should be thrown to the lions"; "I always knew he was up to no good!"). There were no food or wine vendors in the Basilica that day, but there were many outside, and they did a thriving business. It may not have been a show trial, as Gaius had feared, but it certainly constituted a performance for the people of Pompeii.

The day of the trial, which took place in early October, was overcast, with a damp, chilly wind that did nothing to improve the temper of those who were forced to stand outside the Basilica, straining to hear what was going on inside. As Lucius, Faustus, and the *centumviri* entered the building, they were met with a loud and indistinguishable mixture of applause, complaints, and suggestions. Rufus's three accomplices were brought in through a back entrance, but Rufus himself, having been arrested and released on his own recognizance, arrived alone and entered through the vestibule, traversing the passage hastily created for him with his head held high and no change in his expression despite the taunts and invective of the crowd, none of whom even considered the possibility that he might be innocent. He took his seat on the bench assigned to him and stared out at his former colleagues, still with no change of expression.

The Basilica was so crowded that all the people in the space behind the roped-off area were jammed together. It seemed as if all of Pompeii was there, though of course that would not have been possible. Clodia and Ariana were not present, nor was Claudius. Gaius had managed to gain a position near the front, leaning against one of the pillars of the peristyle. From this vantage point, he was able to survey the crowd as well as the tribunal. Among the former he noticed Marcus, who had taken a place similar to his on the other side of the hall. Their eyes met; Gaius ventured a smile, but Marcus turned away as if he had not seen him. He had grown taller and more muscular than when Gaius had last seen him, and was more handsome than ever. *He looks more and more like Claudius,* Gaius thought. *Actually, he looks a lot like Ariana! If he were a woman …* He tried to imagine Marcus in an ankle-length *stola* and *palla,* with long black hair arranged in a simple but becoming style. He did not succeed, but he kept glancing at the younger boy, seeing similarities he had never noticed before. *Could it be …?*

Now the crowd was quieting down, if the continued murmuring and occasional bursts of laughter and taunts could be considered quiet. Having ascertained that all the key participants were present, including Rufus's advocate, Lucius opened the proceedings.

Munatius Faustus began with a summary of the charges: that Rufus, with the help of his three co-defendants, had abused the office of *procurator* by manipulating the tax rolls so the amounts recorded were lower than those actually collected. He emphasized that over a period of almost two years the discrepancies had added up to a substantial total—estimated at several thousand *aurei*—and that this constituted a major theft from the people of Pompeii, especially the laborers and other freedmen, for whom even the legitimate tax amounts created significant hardships. He then called upon Nabucco to present his evidence to the court. Nabucco repeated what he could remember of the conversation he had overheard between Rufus and his co-defendants. Faustus thanked him and indicated that he could be seated, but at that point Rufus's advocate—Larcius Licinius, a notorious member of his profession who was widely known as Lupus Licinius,"The Wolf," for his shaggy gray hair and aggressive style—rose and requested permission to ask Nabucco a few questions. Nonplussed, Nabucco remained standing as Licinius asked him to repeat the exact words he had overheard. Naturally, there were some minor differences between the statements he made to Licinius and those he had made to Faustus, and the advocate pounced on these as evidence that Nabucco's account could not be viewed as accurate. After all, he was a mere servant; how could he be trusted to give accurate testimony? In fact, what could be motivating him to testify against his own master, who had housed and fed him for many years? Could he perhaps have been bribed?

At this there was a roar from the crowd, accompanied by a burst of applause that seemed to go on forever. Faustus and Lucius exchanged glances. Evidently Licinius—or rather, Rufus—had hired a large number of professional applauders. These were hangers-on who spent their days lounging around the Forum, drinking and playing dice. They were available for hire by anyone with a spare *sestercius.* The more respectable spectators began to realize they were in for a day of discomfort and annoyance: No matter how carefully the proceedings were conducted or how convincing the arguments—or unconvincing, in the case of the defense—the trial would take place in the midst of a mob, accompanied by continual uproar and periodic bursts of hired applause.

Lucius did his best to maintain order. He stepped to the front of the tribunal and waited calmly until the mechanical applause finally ceased. Then he declared that if the crowd failed to behave with appropriate respect for the speakers on both sides of the case, the trial would be moved to the Curia and the public would be excluded from the proceedings. There were grumbles and a few catcalls, but the noise gradually subsided.

Faustus then called on Rufus's co-defendants. These three men, whom Rufus had selected to assist him when he was made *procurator,* were lesser-known members of the magistrates' and *aediles*' staffs—functionaries who performed various tasks, including collecting taxes. Rufus had assumed, correctly, that they were unlikely to arouse suspicion as long as they carried out their duties in the accustomed manner. Small increases in tax rates were rarely questioned, though they might be met with halfhearted protests and complaints. There were taxes on imported wine and olive oil; a tax levied for supplying the Emperor's legions; a tax for the maintenance of the public baths and aqueducts. All these taxes were collected in the Forum, and Rufus's accomplices had continued the practice, simply informing each citizen of the amount owed, receiving it, and recording the payment.

When one of these men described the system Rufus had devised for skimming a couple of *sesterces* from each payment, storing the money in a safe in his house and periodically paying a percentage to his accomplices, pandemonium broke loose in the crowd. Many turned to each other with expressions of agreement: They *had* noticed that the tax rates were a little higher, but they had assumed this was normal. Again, however, "Lupus" Licinius had an effective response. He rose to speak, and his paid applauders clapped loudly for several minutes. Just as Lucius was preparing to carry out his threat and move the trial to the Curia, the clapping ceased and Licinius began his argument.

"Citizens," he began, "my colleague has made a very serious charge, one that cannot be sustained unless it is proven with irrefutable evidence. And what you have just heard is *not* evidence!"

Another burst of applause, this one cut short by Licinius himself, who raised a hand to indicate that he had more to say.

"Why is it not evidence? My friends, it's quite obvious that these men have been threatened with dire punishment. To avoid being sold as slaves or sent into the arena to face gladiators or wild beasts, they have agreed to provide the testimony you just heard. But how can you believe the words of a man who speaks under duress, out of fear of slavery or death? Such words are no better than fabrications, little stories made up to cast doubt on the character of a fine man like Statius Rufus, a man with a long record of service to the government and people of Pompeii!"

Loud cheers and applause, again cut short by Licinius; he now directed his remarks to the *centumviri*, who were seated just below him.

"Members of the court, it's your responsibility to consider the evidence, such as it is, that is placed before you. Don't be misled by assertions of wrongdoing made by individuals who have most likely been bribed or threatened. Such assertions cannot be taken seriously, and my client denies them emphatically. How could anyone imagine that one of the noblest and best-known citizens of Pompeii is capable of such a petty crime? Why would he even be tempted? He has wealth enough to live comfortably and doesn't need a few extra *sesterces.* I propose that this case be closed and the defendants allowed to go free with no stain on their reputations. There's no credible evidence on which to base any judgment, let alone a judgment of guilt."

This speech was met with a prolonged uproar—not just the applause of Licinius's paid supporters but also the jeers of those who were familiar with The Wolf's tactics, along with the hubbub of conversation among others in the crowd, many of whom had been convinced by his arguments.

Lucius stood and raised a hand. When the noise finally subsided, he announced that there was further evidence to be considered and the trial would be continued after an interval of two hours—that is, after all the participants had had their midday meal and rested for a while. Such a pause was customary, but Lucius hoped many in the crowd had heard enough and would be reluctant to return to the tightly packed hall, with its stifling air and incessant noise. He had a headache, and he was sure he was not alone. Besides, he wanted a respite from Rufus's arrogant gaze and Licinius's wolfish grin.

Gaius joined his father as he left the tribunal, and together they returned to the House of the Faun for a quick meal. As they crossed the atrium, Lucius patted the dancing faun's head as usual, but Gaius could see the fatigue in the set of his shoulders and the way his hand fell to his side after reaching out toward the little statue.

"Father, why don't you go sit in the *viridarium,* and I'll bring you some bread and olives, and a little wine," he suggested.

"Thank you, Son, I'll do that," Lucius assented.

They sat together quietly, by tacit agreement not commenting on the morning's proceedings. Clodia joined them for a moment, just to ask how they were feeling and if there was anything they needed.

"All I need is for it to be over," Lucius said with a sigh.

They finished their light meal and changed into fresh tunics, then set out for the Forum. The cool air seemed to revive Lucius, and he walked more quickly, with greater purpose in his stride. Gaius ventured a comment.

"Father, what are you going to do about Licinius?"

"There's little I can do as long as he keeps his supporters under control. But if he tries to turn the trial into a farce, I'll move it to the Curia. You can see he doesn't want that; he gets the crowd to quiet down just as I'm about to reach the end of my patience."

"And that is permissible?"

"That is permissible. But don't be too concerned, Son. Faustus is a quiet man, not much to look at compared to The Wolf. But he knows what he's doing. You'll see, The Wolf may discover that Faustus is no sheep."

As they returned to the Basilica, Lucius was disappointed to find that, if anything, the crowd was even larger and more raucous than before, fortified by the cheap wine and sausage pastries sold by the vendors in the Forum. When all the parties had reassembled and he sought to resume the proceedings, it was more difficult than ever to quiet the crowd. Finally the noise subsided and Faustus was able to call his next witness, one of the laborers Gaius had identified. The man, dressed in a shabby tunic and worn sandals, was very shy; he barely spoke above a whisper. In response to gentle questioning by Faustus, he told the *centumviri* about the conversations he had had with some of his fellow laborers when the taxes were being collected. At the time, they had doubted that the amounts were correct: They remembered paying ten *sesterces*, but now they were required to pay twelve. A difference of even two *sesterces* was important to them, as they earned very little and had many mouths to feed. It was only in the last two years that the amounts had risen. They had complained among themselves, and even mentioned the matter to the tax collectors, but they had been told in no uncertain terms that the amounts were correct and must be paid.

During this testimony, the crowd had become surprisingly quiet. Many of the onlookers were laborers themselves, or unemployed freedmen who lived on the *sportula* distributed by their patrons, which was equivalent to the wages of a workman. They, too, had many mouths to feed and were careful with their *sesterces.* The laborer's words had clearly aroused their sympathy.

At this point, Licinius stood and began speaking in his usual aggressive tones. He disdained to even glance at the laborer, and instead addressed the *centumviri.*

"Citizens of Pompeii," he said, "surely you're not going to be taken in by this flimsy testimony, the words of a mere laborer. All these men know is how to swing a pick; they have no learning; they can't do sums, let alone speak correctly. Moreover, what you've just heard is mere rumor; there's no substance in it—it's merely the casual chatter of men with little to occupy their minds. Again, I insist that this cannot be considered evidence!"

The advocate's paid applauders went into action, but their shouts and clapping were the only sounds in the huge hall. Many of the other onlookers were silent, while some were saying to each other, "The Wolf has gone too far this time!" A persistent muttering could be heard, which continued after the applause had finally ceased. Sensing the mood of the crowd, Licinius declined to speak further and took his seat.

Faustus now called another witness: one of the clerks who kept the tax records. The man stood, holding in his arms a large scroll. When asked what the scroll contained, he replied that these were the records of the taxes collected in the past five years for the maintenance of the Emperor's legions. Every citizen of the Empire was required to pay a specified amount each year to support the legions. That amount was decreed in Rome and was a matter of public record. The amounts required of different classes of citizens varied, but those were also a matter of public record.

"And what is the amount required of a common laborer?" Faustus asked him.

"Ten *sesterces.*"

"And has that amount been changed at any time in the past three years?"

"It has not."

"And do your records show that the correct amount has been collected from these laborers in the past two years?"

There was complete silence now. All eyes were on Faustus and the clerk. Even Rufus looked uneasy as the man opened the scroll. He found the section where laborers' payments for the current year were recorded. There was a list of names, and opposite the first dozen or so names was recorded a payment of twelve *sesterces*. This had been crossed out and replaced with ten *sesterces*. The amount recorded opposite all the remaining names was ten *sesterces*.

"Could you explain why the amounts were changed?" Faustus asked him.

"Umbricius Scaurus (he pointed to one of Rufus's accomplices) and I were seated at a table on the day the laborers were to pay the legionary tax. As each man came up, Scaurus told him to pay twelve *sesterces*. I recorded the amount, but then Scaurus told me to correct the records: He said each man had paid ten *sesterces*, not twelve. I protested, but he said I was old and obviously hard of hearing, and if I didn't do as he said, he would have me dismissed for incompetence and make sure I couldn't find another position anywhere in Pompeii."

Pandemonium broke loose in the Basilica. Licinius leapt to his feet, but even his well-trained voice could not be heard over the jeers, taunts, and expressions of outrage that rose like a chorus from the crowd. There was nothing Lucius could do to quell the uproar.

◆ ◆ ◆

The next morning, the court reconvened in the Curia, with Suedius Clemens presiding. Lucius had reported to him in detail on the events of the previous day (as had others), and he had decided to take matters into his own hands.

"It's no reflection on you," he assured Lucius. "Rufus has not only wronged and cheated the people of Pompeii; he has betrayed *me: I'm* the one who appointed him *procurator*. So I want to see this through to the end."

The Curia was, of course, much smaller than the Basilica; there was room only for the *centumviri* and the litigants themselves, who sat on benches at one end of the room. Outside, the throngs of would-be observers, prevented from entering, strained to hear the proceedings over the grumbles and quarrels of their fellow citizens.

Clemens began by asking that the record of the proceedings be read; then he asked Licinius if he had any questions for the clerk who had testified about the tax records on the previous day. Again The Wolf disdained to question such an insignificant witness. Instead, he launched into a long laudatory speech about Statius Rufus, in which he again referred to Rufus's many years of service to Pompeii. He reiterated his claim that the testimony of the previous day's witnesses could not be considered evidence because all of them could have been bribed or intimidated. It wouldn't surprise him, he ventured to say, if there were actually a conspiracy among members of the Samnite faction in the *Comitia* to eliminate a popular leader of the anti-Samnites ...

At this point, many of the *centumviri* looked at each other in disbelief, but Clemens's presence kept them from protesting audibly.

Besides, Licinius went on, Rufus was well off. Why would he stoop to such an unworthy activity when he was already wealthy?

It's true, thought Lucius, along with many others. *What would motivate him to do such a thing? Certainly he was disappointed by the outcome of last year's election, but there are always other years. The Wolf* does *have a point:* Why *did he do it?*

But now Licinius was bringing his somewhat rambling remarks to a close, asking Clemens to dismiss the charges and release an obviously blameless man with his reputation intact. The crime, if it had actually occurred, must have been committed by the three tax collectors, who had conspired among themselves to shift the blame to Rufus. As for Nabucco, he deserved to be crucified for lying about his patron, while Rufus deserved the court's sympathy for having unknowingly harbored such a viper in his home.

From outside the walls arose the applause of the paid applauders, one of whom must have been listening at the door during Licinius's harangue. Clemens ignored it, however, and turned to Faustus.

"Do you have anything to add?" he asked.

"Yes," said Faustus. "I call Julia Poppaea, formerly Julia Vettia, to testify!"

There was a moment of shocked silence during which a guard led Julia from the small side room where she had been waiting. She was dressed in a plain *stola* and *palla* and wore no jewelry; her hair was arranged in a simple, yet attractive, style. Rufus turned pale when he saw her.

"Is there anything you wish to say to this court?" Faustus asked her gently.

"Yes, there is," she replied. She took a few steps forward until she was standing directly in front of the assembled councilmen. Then she addressed them in quiet, even tones.

"My fellow citizens, I come before you humble and repentant. You all know that two years ago I engaged in an affair with Statius Rufus, for which my husband—my former husband—Claudius Vettius justly divorced me. I had wronged and betrayed him, and I deserved my fate. I wish to state that I sincerely regret my actions and have vowed to live the rest of my life—as much as the gods may grant me—in an honest and virtuous manner."

This speech drew gentle murmurs of approval from the *centumviri,* which ceased abruptly when Clemens raised a hand and gestured to Faustus to continue.

Rufus's face was flushed, and he was looking at the ceiling, the floor—anywhere but at Julia or his fellow councilmen. For once, The Wolf had nothing to say.

"Do you wish to add anything that is relevant to the current proceedings?" Faustus asked Julia, again treating her with the utmost deference.

"Yes, I do," she said.

"And what might that be?"

"Well, when Rufus and I … Sometimes after we …" She had lost some of her composure and was floundering; Licinius sensed an opportunity and prepared to pounce, but Clemens stopped him.

"Give the witness a moment to collect her thoughts," he ordered.

Julia stood still for a moment, her head bowed. Then she continued.

"Rufus and I often had conversations about what was going on in our lives. On one occasion, he told me he had to go to Rome on a matter of business. He didn't tell me what it was, but later, after he had been appointed *procurator,* I asked him how he had managed to obtain the position when there were so many candidates to choose from. He told me that when he went to Rome he met with a client of Clemens, who promised to speak to Clemens on his behalf. Apparently he did so, with the result that Clemens appointed Rufus *procurator.* Rufus had to pay the client a large sum for his assistance, and that's why he needed additional funds."

Licinius leapt to his feet and attempted to discredit Julia's remarks, but though he was speaking as loudly as he could, he could not be heard over the outraged shouts and jeers of the normally decorous *centumviri.* Despite the uproar, he tried to convince the court that the manservant could have been bribed, the tax collectors intimidated; that Faustus could not prove that any "extra" taxes had been channeled to Rufus; that the laborers' memories could not be trusted and the clerk was elderly and probably hard of hearing; and finally that Julia was obviously seeking revenge against Rufus for locking her out of his house on the day Claudius divorced her. The *centumviri*—those few who actually listened to him—were unconvinced, and Clemens, remembering the conversation with his client that Julia had referred to, knew without a doubt that Rufus was guilty.

When the uproar finally ceased, he asked the *centumviri* to confer among themselves and reach a verdict. The witnesses were released, the three tax collectors returned to their cells. Faustus asked one of the guards to escort Julia to her apartment. Rufus and Licinius sat silently in the side room; Clemens, Lucius, and Faustus chatted quietly in another room until one of the councilmen came to summon them. They resumed their seats.

"Have you reached a verdict?" Clemens asked the *centumviri.*

"We have," replied their spokesman.

"And what is it?"

"Statius Rufus and his three co-defendants are guilty of the charges against them."

There was a roar from the crowd outside the Curia, whose doors had been left open, but guarded, so the verdict could be heard. Then there was silence as Clemens pronounced his sentence.

"Statius Rufus, you are guilty of a serious crime against the people of Pompeii, one that merits the most severe punishment. I could order your execution, or perhaps some entertainment in the arena during the next games. Your wolfish friend could keep you company. Rufus and Lupus, the fox and the wolf—now *that's* food for thought …"

Rufus's proud bearing had vanished, and he was visibly shaken. He could not believe Clemens would actually consider execution, and he shuddered at the thought of facing death in the arena, an object of scorn and derision to those he had robbed. And what kind of "entertainment" was Clemens thinking of? Something involving a wolf and a fox …

With these thoughts swirling through his mind and his limbs weak with fear, Rufus was actually relieved when Clemens merely sentenced him to permanent exile from the city of Pompeii. His house and wealth, including his slaves, would be confiscated; he would be permitted to take with him only his clothing and personal possessions. He would be given enough money to hire transport to whatever destination he chose, so long as it was within the borders of Italia. (His former colleagues understood from this that Rufus was actually being allowed to travel to Rome, where he likely had acquaintances who could help him build a new life and career.)

The tax collectors would each be given ten lashes and relieved of their duties.

The records clerk would be allowed to retire with a pension.

The laborers identified by Gaius would become Lucius's clients, and would collect the standard *sportula* when they attended him in his atrium each morning.

And so, after a trial that would provide grist for Pompeii's gossip mills for weeks to come, the crowd dispersed and the city's public life slowly returned to normal—with one exception: Suedius Clemens assumed a much more active role in its day-to-day governance.

XIV
MAY, 76

In the ensuing months, life in Pompeii resumed its normal course. Clemens presided over the *Comitia* and ensured that the city's governance proceeded smoothly. The Saturnalia was celebrated with more than usual gaiety as citizens of all ranks rejoiced in their orderly and prosperous lives. In early spring, games were held in honor of Apollo, and shortly thereafter, on a warm, sunny morning in mid-May, Julia Poppaea and Munatius Faustus were married.

Faustus had admired Julia from the moment he met her, and Julia appreciated his calm intelligence and gentle manner. After Rufus's trial, he visited her on several occasions; they walked in Julia Felix's gardens and found that they had much to say to each other. During the Saturnalia, he asked her to marry him and she accepted. Julia Felix, who had been in favor of the match from the beginning and done everything she could to encourage it, graciously released Julia from the remaining obligation on her five-year lease. Marcus could have gone on living in the apartment, but Faustus persuaded him to come and live with them, and Julia Felix suggested to Faustus that he arrange for the youth to be tutored in mathematics and geometry, where his true interests clearly lay. At seventeen, Marcus was too old to continue working for Julia Felix's steward—and indeed, he had again begun roaming the streets of Pompeii in search of something, anything, that might interest him. With appropriate training, he could become an engineer, a profession that was not well represented in Pompeii, where so many educated men were politicians, financiers, or advocates.

Another interesting development that occurred at about the same time was Clemens's move to Rufus's house, which was now city property. Since his arrival in Pompeii, Clemens had lived inconspicuously in a small house not far from the Forum. Assuming he would be returning to Rome within a year or two, he had not tried to integrate himself into the city's social life. But now his outlook had changed. After Rufus's trial, he had decided to make his presence felt more directly and visibly. He took over Rufus's house and hired painters and mosaicists to redecorate it, leaving only the best works from the previous decor. (Though Julia never mentioned it, when she and Faustus dined there she was pleased to note that Clemens had retained the exquisite scene from *Iphigenia in Tauris* in the refurbished *triclinium.*) And in an ironic twist, Clemens brought in Rufus's former manservant, Nabucco, to serve as his house steward.

◆ ◆ ◆

Meanwhile Gaius had sought out his former tutor, Kineas, and persuaded him to teach him Greek. Kineas was delighted to resume work with his favorite student, and Gaius learned quickly. After cutting his teeth on Xenophon's *Anabasis* and enjoying the works of his favorite lyric poets—especially Sappho—in their original form, he progressed to Herodotus and then to Homer. Herodotus's *Persian Wars* he relished for its vivid and often fanciful descriptions, giggling like a girl at the historian's straight-faced account of winged snakes flying from Arabia to Egypt each spring, only to be devoured by ibises. But it was Homer who held him spellbound.

All educated Romans were familiar with the works of Homer, though for the most part only in translation. Few actually learned Greek, but those who did so were, without exception, impressed by the elegance, flexibility, and sheer nobility of that ancient tongue. After reading the *Iliad,* Gaius understood why Virgil had been reluctant to embark on his own epic, the *Aeneid,* even requesting that all copies of it be destroyed after his death. The *Iliad* was a grand and complex work, and it was doubtful whether even the *Aeneid* could hope to equal it. But the *Odyssey*—oh gods, the *Odyssey*—what a splendid tale, what endless entertainment, what depths of human emotion! Gaius could not contain himself: For several weeks, he spoke of nothing else to family, friends, even casual acquaintances.

It was a source of frustration to him that on the rare occasions when he and his parents could share a quiet meal, he could not recite portions of Homer's epics in the original Greek. He wished he could demonstrate to them the vigor, the clarity of the language, the intense beauty of it. But his enthusiasm was unbounded, and even when he read to them from Latin translations, they were able to get a feeling for the original through his gestures and tone.

"Listen to this," he would say. "Listen! Here Poseidon flies into a rage at Odysseus and stirs up a terrible storm. Here's what Homer writes:

> With that he gathered the clouds together, grasping his trident in his hands,
> and roused the waves from the deep, and whipped all the winds into storms,

> shrouding land and sea alike in thick clouds. And night sped down from the sky. The East and South Winds clashed, and the raging West and North, born in the bright air, drove onward a huge, rolling wave. And Odysseus's knees trembled, and his spirit quailed, and groaning he spoke to his own great heart: "Oh, wretched man that I am! What's to become of me now?"

"Isn't that wonderful?" he asked, and before they could answer, he plunged on. "Can't you imagine yourself in the middle of the sea, with the wind howling and the waves breaking over you?"

"I certainly can!" Lucius said, and Clodia and Ariana nodded in agreement. But Gaius hardly noticed.

"And that's in Latin. You can't imagine how amazing it is in Greek. And another thing: We think of Homer as using little epithets like 'sandy Pylos' and 'rosy-fingered Dawn' just to fill up space, to make the lines come out even. But there's more to it than that. For example, in Greek, *rhododactylos* can mean 'rosy-toed' as well as 'rosy-fingered.' Can't you just see 'rosy-toed Dawn' tiptoeing toward us each morning on her little pink toes?"

Lucius threw back his head and laughed. "Son, you're amazing. I had no idea you had such a vivid imagination!"

Gaius smiled back. Though he was almost nineteen, he still valued his father's praise. But his mind was teeming with further observations, and he paused only briefly before continuing.

"And then there's all that talk about how clever Odysseus is—'Odysseus of many devices,' or 'crafty Odysseus.' But in Greek, *polumechanos* can be interpreted a bit less positively, as meaning 'shrewd' or 'cunning.' And I have to say, I don't think Odysseus is much of a hero. First he loses all his ships and men. Then he doesn't make much of an effort to get home to his wife; in fact, he stays with Calypso on Ogygia *for seven years!* If he was so crafty, he could have found a way to get off that island in a couple of weeks. And he's very selfish. He barely gives a thought to Penelope and Telemachus throughout all those years of wandering. But oh, what a sly dog he is! The way he insinuates himself into his own household without being recognized, and kills all those greedy suitors—it's incredible!"

"Well, he *does* get some help," Lucius put in.

"Sure, but it's only a couple of farm hands. And Telemachus, of course. Actually, Telemachus is the character I respect the most. He …"

But it was growing dark, and though she had greatly enjoyed the conversation, Clodia wished to retire.

"I'll look forward to hearing more about the *Odyssey* next time we're together," she said to Gaius with a gentle smile. "And maybe you could recite the scene where Odysseus and Penelope finally recognize each other. I've always loved that part of the story. No matter what you say, they *did* love each other!"

◆ ◆ ◆

Every morning, Ariana would wake at dawn, slip into her *stola*, and go out into the *viridarium,* where she would stand for a few moments looking up at the sky, assessing the day's weather while enjoying the peaceful splashing of the fountain nearby. Every morning, Gaius would join her there, standing behind her with his arms around her waist, bending forward to kiss her cheek as she leaned back against him. And every morning his greeting to her was the same: "Ariana, my love, my goddess!" And she would reply, "I love you, Gaius."

Then they would go their separate ways, Gaius to the Forum, Ariana to Clodia's *cubiculum,* where she would help her mistress dress and confer with her about the management of the household, in which she played an increasingly active role. Clodia's illness the previous year had made it clear that she could not shoulder the entire responsibility alone, and she now depended on Ariana to oversee much of the meal planning and preparation. The cook did not mind: At sixteen, Ariana was more beautiful than ever—tall and slim, with shining black hair and glowing skin. She dressed simply, but Clodia insisted that her *stolae* and *pallae* be made from good fabrics and in colors that suited her, especially the soft rose that complemented her complexion so well. Unconsciously, also, Ariana imitated Clodia's speech and manner, so that to the casual observer the maid might appear to be a younger version of the mistress. One who looked more closely, however, might notice that Ariana, though always gentle and polite, did not often laugh. And that she sometimes stopped in the midst of her work and closed her eyes for a moment, seeming to lose herself in a dream. Then she would open her eyes, shake her head sadly, and go on with the task at hand.

By tacit agreement, she and Gaius spent little time together other than those brief morning encounters in which they reaffirmed their love. They knew there was nothing they could do to change their situation, yet they continued to believe in a future together. For now, they must live in the House of the Faun almost as brother and sister—and indeed, in most of their interactions with Ariana, Lucius and Clodia treated her more like a daughter than a servant.

And certainly life was pleasant in the House of the Faun. The members of the household liked and respected one another, and at the daily gatherings in the *lararium* they mingled and conversed as equals. It was a rather large household by Pompeiian standards, befitting Lucius's status as *duovir,* yet Lucius and Clodia knew the name of every slave or freedman under their roof and provided liberally for their welfare. It was a happy household, and Ariana and Gaius were as happy as they could be under the circumstances. But it was not enough, and they knew it.

Summer arrived, and the pace of life slowed. There were fewer meetings of the *Comitia,* and formal dinner parties were replaced by informal gatherings of close friends. Ariana had fewer responsibilities, and more time to spend as she chose. As was her custom, Clodia would rest for an hour or two after the midday meal, but she no longer required Ariana to attend her during the afternoon. Ariana therefore braved the heat and made her way to the public gardens on the southern side of town. She had heard about them and always wanted to visit them, but had never had enough time. It was a long walk in each direction, and she wanted to spend some time in the gardens as well.

She prevailed on Manlius to find her a straw hat like those she remembered from her years on the farm; then, dressed in a lightweight *stola* and sandals, she walked along the blazing streets to the gardens, where a few umbrella pines provided some shade. She strolled along the walkways for a while, admiring the well-tended plantings, especially the profusely flowering oleanders, and then sat on a bench at the southernmost side of the gardens, where the land fell away toward the harbor and the sea.

From her vantage point, she could watch the activity in the small harbor—mostly fishing boats, but also ferries carrying people between the seaside towns of Stabiae, Pompeii, and Oplontis. Nets were spread on the shore to dry. Nearby were the little village where the fishermen lived and the warehouses where the local wine, the region's chief export, was stored before being carried to the larger port at Puteoli to be loaded onto the huge merchant ships that sailed to every corner of Our Sea and beyond. Farther north, she could see the salt pans and the buildings where *garum,* the fish sauce made from brine that Pompeiians consumed in huge quantities, was produced. To the south, connected to the harbor by a short canal, was the sandy delta at the mouth of the Sarnus River. The horizon was obscured by a lavender haze, but closer to shore, the azure sea sparkled in the bright sunlight.

She rested her elbows on the marble balustrade running along the edge of the gardens and watched as fishermen guided a heavily laden boat to a dock where their colleagues waited. With much shouting and gesticulating, the boat was made fast and the catch unloaded. Ariana could not make out the contents of the heavy baskets that were being taken ashore, but she could imagine the silvery fish, the octopi and squid that would be rushed to the *macellum*—the market on the west side of the Forum, with its walls lined with small shops and a fish pond in the center—to be sold to those who planned to include them in their evening feasts.

And then suddenly someone was standing beside her. Startled, she looked up and saw Gaius smiling down at her.

"How did you know I was here?" she asked in wonderment.

"I asked Manlius if he'd seen you, and he told me about the hat. He also said you'd mentioned the gardens, so I decided to see if I could find you. It wasn't too difficult: You're the only one here wearing a hat!"

She laughed and took his hand. "Look at the sea!" she exclaimed. "Isn't it beautiful?"

He followed her gaze and realized that this scene, so familiar to him, was new to her.

"I'd say more interesting than beautiful," he said thoughtfully. "There are other places that are more beautiful. Just across the harbor—you can't see it because of the haze—there's an island called Capreae. The views there are the loveliest in the world, I'm convinced of it. I'll take you there someday, and you'll see for yourself. They say it was the home of the Sirens, whose seductive song no one could resist but Odysseus—and then only because he put wax in his ears. And that's where the Emperor Tiberius built all those villas—twelve of them! Can you imagine?"

She leaned against him happily and he put an arm around her shoulders. They stood together for a few moments, quietly enjoying the view, then sat on the bench and chatted like old friends who have not seen each other in a long time. For while they saw each other every day at the House of the Faun, they had little opportunity to engage in conversation without others present. They relished the chance to do so now, and the afternoon slid by quickly as they discussed everything from Rufus's trial to Gaius's recent infatuation with the *Odyssey.*

"Did you see your parents' faces when you told them about 'rosy-toed Dawn'?" she asked, smiling at the memory.

"I certainly did!" he said with a laugh. "I really enjoyed that evening. But it ended too soon. There was much more I wanted to tell them. Especially about Telemachus."

"Why Telemachus?"

"Well, usually when people think about the *Odyssey*, they think of Odysseus and his wanderings, all the different places he went and the strange creatures he saw, and all the things that happened to him. They think of the *Odyssey* as an adventure story, a rather messy afterthought to the *Iliad.* Or they think of faithful Penelope, waiting twenty years for her husband to come home."

"Yes, I often imagine what it must have been like for Penelope," Ariana commented. "It would have been so easy for her to believe Odysseus was dead and marry someone else. But what brings me to tears is poor old Argus ..."

"That sweet, loyal hound," Gaius agreed. "It's so sad that he died right after Odysseus came back. But as I was saying,..."

"About Telemachus ..."

"About the *Odyssey.* Everyone sees it as a story about Odysseus, or about Odysseus and Penelope. No one pays much attention to Telemachus, but in reality he's a central figure—perhaps *the* central figure—in the story!"

"I doubt if many people would agree with you."

"No, they wouldn't. But look at the story. It's *Telemachus* who has to keep the household intact while Odysseus is gone. *He* has to defend his mother against the suitors. *He* goes to Pylos to see if Nestor has any news about his father. *He* faces the aristocrats of Ithaca in council and demands that they respect the rights of his family. And while he's doing all this, Odysseus is living with Calypso on Ogygia. *For seven years*!

"Then Odysseus finally gets home, and he manages to kill the suitors. But who's standing beside him, throwing the javelin and wielding the sword? Who makes the arrangements in the household so Penelope and the 'good' maids will be out of the way during the fighting? And who orders the armor locked up? Wise Telemachus. *Wise Telemachus.* That's one of Homer's epithets that I think fits really well."

"So Telemachus plays an important part in the story. I see that. But I think you're going a bit far when you call him the central figure."

"Maybe I am," Gaius admitted. "But it galls me that he's constantly overshadowed by his father so no one pays attention as he develops from a youth into a man, and a strong and wise man at that."

"Maybe you see a little of yourself in him," Ariana suggested. "Do you feel overshadowed by your father? After all, he's the most respected man in Pompeii, and without realizing it, he may be standing in your way. You've reached the age of manhood yourself, haven't you? And while I'm sure you're performing a worthwhile service for Paquius Proculus, you can't do that for the rest of your life. You need to strike out on your own, gain a place in the *Comitia,* establish your own household ..."

Gaius shook his head. "He's not standing in my way," he insisted. "Except in the matter of marrying *you*, and you know I'm going to marry you as soon as I'm able to, no matter what he says. But in some ways, you may be right. It's time for me to get started on my career in city government, and perhaps I've been held back a little by my father's prominence. That is, without realizing it, I may be intimidated by his success. Like Telemachus: For a long time, he doesn't feel mature enough to take charge of Odysseus's household, and in fact he can't—the suitors move right in and start devouring his flocks, and there's nothing he can do about it. But eventually he becomes aware of his own ability and joins his father in getting rid of the suitors. Actually, they work together. And I've worked with my father on some matters—behind the scenes, as it were. No, he's not standing in my way. I just have to decide what I want to do and set about doing it."

Ariana noticed the ambivalence in Gaius's remarks but did not comment on it. Instead, she remarked that he was fortunate to have a father, and such a fine one at that. After that, they said little. She was content to sit beside him, with her head on his shoulder, as the late-afternoon sunlight slanted through the branches above them and bathed the gardens in a golden glow. After a while, a gentle breeze blew in from the sea, and they knew it was time to go home.

"Let's meet here again," Gaius suggested. "Why don't you leave your hat with Manlius, and whenever he tells me you've borrowed it, I'll know where to find you."

She agreed, and they headed back to the House of the Faun. Neither was aware that Marcus Vettius had been standing in the shadow of a tree not far from them, watching them and listening intently to their every word.

XV

SEPTEMBER, 76

Alomila was ill. She vomited frequently and could keep nothing down, not even water. Afraid she might die—or perhaps so miserable she wished she could die—she sent for Ariana. Asking Manlius to tell Clodia where she had gone, Ariana set out for the Vettii's farm, jolting along the rough road in the produce cart.

She came softly into the darkened room where Alomila lay, and took the place of the old woman who was tending her. She sat beside the bed, dipping a rag into a bowl of cool water and gently laying it on her mother's forehead. Stroking her sweat-dampened hair, she asked, "What is it, Mama? Why did you send for me?"

Her mother said nothing as a spasm crossed her face. Then, in a weak voice, she said,

"Ariana, I've never been so sick. I'm afraid I'm going to die, and before I do, I want you to know who you are."

"Mama, I can see you're very ill, but I don't think you're going to die. You probably ate some tainted food. And I know who I am. I'm your daughter. That's all I need to know."

"Don't you ever wonder about your father?"

"My father was a slave in Claudius Vettius's house. I know that."

"That's what you've been told, what everyone's been told. But it's not true." Alomila turned away and retched, but the spasm soon passed.

Ariana sat and stared at her mother, unable to answer. She was beginning to glimpse the truth. After a while she whispered,

"My father wasn't a slave?"

"No."

"Then who was he?"

"Haven't you guessed?"

Ariana went rigid at the realization that her long-suppressed suspicions had been correct. Feeling as if she would faint, she reached for her mother's hand and asked,

"Is Claudius Vettius my father?"

"He is," said Alomila, and vomited.

Dazed and angry, Ariana stumbled from the room, motioning for the old woman to return to her post. She walked quickly to the back door and out into the midday glare. The world seemed to be swirling around her. She must find a place to sit still and think. There was a patch of shade behind the goat shed; she lurched across the yard and slumped down. For a few moments, everything went dark.

When she came to herself, she began looking at her situation in a new light. If she was Claudius's daughter, did she not have some rights beyond those of an ordinary slave? Could he not free her if he wished? Could he grant Alomila her freedom and thus improve Ariana's status? These hopeful thoughts were interspersed with periods of despair marked by abundant tears. *How could Claudius do such a thing? And Lucius, he must have known. Does Gaius know? If he does … And what about Marcus?* Despair turned into anger as she looked back over her life and imagined what might have been. Finally, filled with new resolve, she returned to her mother's bedside.

◆ ◆ ◆

Ariana stayed at the farm until her mother recovered from her illness—which apparently, as Ariana had guessed, had been caused by something she had eaten. Once Alomila, much weakened, could leave her bed, Ariana bade her farewell and went back to the city. She immediately sought out Clodia and apologized for her absence, explaining that her mother had been extremely ill, but had recovered. Clodia, kind as always, suggested she get some rest before resuming her household tasks, but Ariana insisted on going right back to work, checking on the supplies in the kitchen and helping Clodia plan the evening meal. At dusk, however, she asked to be excused and went to her room, where she fell into bed without pausing to take off her *stola*. She slept soundly at first, as the long hours spent caring for her mother had exhausted her, but toward morning her sleep was troubled, and finally she rose just before dawn and slipped into the *viridarium* in search of a few moments of peace. Gaius found her there.

He came up behind her to greet her as usual, but she turned on him furiously and pushed him away, her eyes blazing. "You knew, didn't you," she whispered fiercely. "*You knew!*"

Stupefied, he stumbled backward, then found his footing and stood staring at her.

"Ariana?"

She went on glaring at him, and when he reached for her hands she snatched them away.

"Ariana, my love, what's this all about? Please tell me!"

"Do you mean to say you don't know who I am?"

Suddenly he understood. "Ariana, did your mother tell you who fathered you?"

"*Fathered* me? *Fathered* me?"

"I'm sorry, my love. Did she tell you Claudius Vettius is your father?"

"Yes, and you *knew* it, didn't you!"

"Ariana, I swear to you by all the gods, I didn't know. But the last couple of times I saw Marcus, for a moment I thought I was looking at you. And I started wondering. But that was all. I've never heard anything about your parentage other than what you yourself were told as a child."

She continued to stare at him in disbelief, but now, when he approached and took her in his arms, she did not protest but rested her head on his shoulder, her tears dampening his tunic until he said, with a little laugh,

"Let's give the other shoulder a chance, shall we?"

Silently she obeyed, the tears continuing to flow until he took her face between his hands and kissed her, kissed each eyelid, then the tip of her nose, and finally her lips, murmuring "Don't cry, my goddess, don't cry. I love you!"

Distantly they became aware of the stirring of life in the household. The kitchen staff was at work, heating water and preparing bowls of porridge for those who preferred a warm breakfast; running to the bakery for loaves of fresh-baked bread for those who sought simpler fare. Soon there would be activity in all parts of the house, including the *viridarium.* The gardener would arrive, and slaves would carry in buckets of water from the *impluvium* and begin watering the plants. It was time to leave.

"Get your *palla* and meet me in the atrium," Gaius instructed her. "We're going to pay a visit to Claudius Vettius."

◆ ◆ ◆

Openly holding hands, they traversed the short distance between the House of the Faun and the House of the Vettii. There they shouldered their way through the throng of clients in the atrium and reached the entrance to Claudius's *tablinum.* The door was open, and Claudius, seated at his table, was engrossed in a newly acquired scroll, enjoying a few quiet moments before dealing with his clients' most urgent petitions. The sudden appearance of Gaius and Ariana startled him, and at first he could only stare at them. Then, seeing them together, he realized why they were there. He rose and greeted them, signaling to a slave to close the door. Then he motioned to them to be seated and offered them some wine.

Normally polite, on this occasion Gaius was in no mood for pleasantries. "Is it true?" he demanded.

Claudius looked at them, studying their faces, Gaius's angry, Ariana's tear-streaked. Gaius looked back, noticing the similarities between Claudius and Ariana: the high cheekbones, the rich black hair, the slim build. Even their eyebrows had the same smooth curve. Only Ariana's eyes were a dark blue, Claudius's a soft brown. "Tell us. Is it true?"

"I assume you're asking me if it's true that I'm Ariana's father. Yes, it's true," Claudius replied, looking sadly at Ariana. "And before you go on with your accusations, listen to what I have to say."

Gaius made as if to speak, but Ariana forestalled him. "Please, Gaius, I want to hear what my father is saying." Gently but firmly, she emphasized the words "my father."

Claudius and Gaius looked at her in surprise, but the moment passed, and Claudius continued.

"When your mother"—he nodded at Ariana—"first entered this house, I was a much younger man. I had recently married, and my wife was with child. I was proud of my household and my beautiful wife, and eagerly anticipated the birth of my son—somehow I knew it would be a son. Yet at the same time, there was friction between Julia and me. I didn't realize it then, but we weren't well suited to each other. There were constant arguments—little battles over unimportant things like which wines we should serve our guests, or whether my toga was draped properly. And as her belly grew larger, her temper grew worse, until I was actually avoiding her much of the time.

"Of course, there were times when we quarreled and made up, and then we were the sweetest of lovers for the next two or three days. But then it would start all over again, until I was almost out of my mind. I didn't understand what was happening. All I wanted was a little peace and quiet in my own house. One evening, we were having a quiet meal together—I remember watching some birds bathing in the fountain in the *viridarium* and thinking how pleasant it was—when out of nowhere she started shouting at me, and crying, and accusing me of all sorts of things. She said I wasn't paying enough attention to her or providing for her needs—by all the gods, I couldn't imagine what she needed that I wasn't providing! She had her fine *stolae* and *pallae,* and a maid and a hairdresser, and all the ointments and perfumes she could ask for. But there wasn't anything I could say to appease her. Finally she threw her wine cup on the floor and went to her chamber. It was pretty clear that she didn't want me to follow her.

"Well, by then I was angry too. I sat for a while and finished my wine. Then, as was my right as master of the household, I sought comfort with one of my slaves. That slave was Alomila. She was pretty and sweet, and above all, *quiet*. She gave me what *I* needed: a little peace! I started spending my nights with her, and Julia didn't seem to mind; at least, she didn't say anything at the time. She was getting pretty big, and I think she didn't want me to see her like that.

"Well, things went on like that until Marcus was born. I was so excited at having a son that I forgot everything that had happened in the last few months. I was the very image of a loving husband. I spent all my time with Julia. I showered her and the child with presents. I wanted to hold the baby all the time—Julia would laugh and ask me why didn't I nurse him while I was at it. Then I would give him back to her and watch as she nursed him: the perfect picture of mother and child. Of course, after a few weeks she found a wetnurse and let her own milk dry up. She didn't want to look like a mother, she said; she wanted her body to return to its former shape.

"I was a bit disappointed that she was less enthusiastic about being a mother than I was about being a father, but I didn't let it bother me. After a few weeks, I went back to her bed and stopped sleeping with Alomila. And Julia responded to all the attention she was getting by becoming much nicer and more reasonable than she'd been for months. For a while, things seemed to be going very smoothly: I was thrilled to be a father, I had a beautiful baby boy, and my wife seemed happy.

"Then it became evident that Alomila was with child. Julia noticed it before I did, which is why I didn't have a chance to get the poor girl out of the house and prevent all the uproar and unhappiness that followed. Julia came in here and started screaming at me and calling me every low thing she could think of. I was a worm, a lizard, I was the muck in the alleyways. How could I have done this to her, she who had been a faithful wife and had just borne me a fine son? She wouldn't admit that she had driven me away, nor would she grant that I had the right to lie with a slave in my own household if I wanted to. She insisted that Alomila be sent away, and I agreed because it was obviously the best thing for her. I arranged for her to go live on the farm, and made it clear to the manager that she must be treated kindly. When her time drew near, and without consulting Julia, I arranged for a midwife to be at hand. When I received the news of your birth"—again he nodded at Ariana—"I told Julia I was going to make a tour of my country properties—that is, the farm and vineyards—and consult with the manager. If she guessed I was also going to see you, she didn't indicate it. So I rode out to the farm and saw you: a pretty baby, with features much like Marcus's even then. I gave Alomila some money and saw that she was comfortable. And in fact, she seemed to be happy living on the farm—she liked caring for the goats and chickens, she told me, and enjoyed an occasional ramble in the fields. I saw that it would be a good place for you to spend your childhood, and so I took a good long look at you and went home.

"Seeing how much you looked like Marcus, and like me as well, it troubled me that I couldn't let others know I had a daughter as well as a son. Somehow Julia sensed how I felt, because one day she came to me and said, 'I won't allow you to acknowledge that child as yours.' Naturally, I was irritated by her arrogance, and I asked her what made her think she could give orders to me. She insisted on what we all know: Any child of a slave is also a slave. I responded that I could easily free Alomila and acknowledge you as my daughter if I chose to do so. Then she started crying and threatening to divorce me if I acknowledged you. And she *did* have that right. The prospect of losing her and having to raise a child by myself was not one I was prepared to face, so I gave in: I promised her I wouldn't tell anyone I was your father, and that I'd let it be known that you had been fathered by one of the household slaves, whom we immediately sold. But I had some demands of my own: Julia would never speak to anyone about the matter, and she wouldn't interfere with my efforts to make sure you were safe and well cared for. That's where we left it, and I must admit she kept her side of the bargain, even after you were brought back here to help in the kitchen."

Gaius was shifting restlessly in his seat, waiting for a chance to speak. When Claudius paused, he plunged in right away.

"Claudius, this all happened—what, sixteen years ago? Why can't you forget all that and acknowledge that Ariana is your daughter? After all, she looks more like you and Marcus each day, and pretty soon everyone's going to notice. Besides, Julia isn't here anymore, so there shouldn't be a problem."

"There *is* a problem, Gaius," Claudius countered. "Actually, there are a couple of problems. One is that I made a promise and I won't break it …"

"A promise to *Julia*! Look how she repaid you!"

"That's not the issue here. I also have my daughters to think of. Before long they'll be of marriageable age, and it'll be difficult to find good husbands for them if they have a sister whose mother is a slave."

At this, Ariana began weeping; Gaius put an arm around her shoulders and attempted to comfort her. "Don't cry, my love. I promised you we'd find a way, and we will."

"Claudius," he continued, "as you can see, Ariana and I are in love and intend to marry. When your daughters marry, their husbands will have as brother-in-law the son of Lucius Tullius, one of the most respected men in Pompeii. And you're widely known as a successful merchant and an able scholar—surely people will consider that more important than who Ariana's mother happens to be. Besides, they'll remember Julia's affair; if anything, they'll think you were entitled to find a little comfort with another woman ..."

"Gaius, you're going too far," Claudius broke in. "It's not for you to judge Julia or myself for our actions, past or present. Wise as you are for your years, you're still young and inexperienced in these matters. As things stand now, I cannot and will not acknowledge Ariana as my daughter ..."

"As things stand now," Gaius interrupted. "Does that mean you might reconsider sometime?"

Claudius looked at him thoughtfully. He saw before him an intelligent and serious young man, one whom he would welcome as a son-in-law, one whom, despite his earlier remarks, he considered mature and responsible. When the time came, he would make a good husband and father.

"Gaius," he said, "I value our friendship and would be pleased to call you my son. Yes, I might reconsider my decision at some time in the future. In the meantime, I'm asking you to be patient. I have much to think about before I can do anything more."

He looked at Ariana, whose lovely face was turned toward his, her eyes full of hope. "Ariana," he said, "between us, you are indeed my daughter. For now, this has to remain a private matter, but be assured that I *do* care about your well-being—I always have—and will continue to care. I personally am not opposed to your marriage to Gaius; I'm afraid the obstacles you face reside in the House of the Faun, not in this house."

"We'll overcome those obstacles," Gaius vowed. "In the meantime, would you consider freeing Alomila?"

Again Claudius looked at the young man for a moment before responding. *He's a fine young man, better than any father-in-law could hope for. I should do everything to encourage him. But there are others to think of ...*

"I could free her, certainly. There's no reason not to. But I don't think that would help your cause very much. Your father's opposition is based on other considerations. But yes, if you wish it, I'll free her."

At this Ariana sprang from her seat to embrace Claudius. Tentatively he stood and returned the embrace; then, embarrassed, he gently pushed her away.

"Thank you, oh thank you so much," she whispered as she wiped away her tears with a corner of her *palla.* "I can't thank you enough. And I'm sure she'll want to go on living and working on the farm; it's her home, and she's happy there."

"Consider it done, then," he said. He escorted the two young people to the vestibule and watched as they headed home, hand in hand.

◆ ◆ ◆

The atrium of the House of the Faun, like that of the House of the Vettii, was filled with clients, some hoping for a brief word with Lucius Tullius, others content merely to receive their daily *sportula* and be on their way. This time, Gaius and Ariana did not push their way through to the *tablinum;* they simply asked Manlius to tell Lucius they wished to speak to him. Lucius was not entirely surprised; he had heard about their abrupt departure that morning, and believed he knew the reason for it. He dismissed his clients and invited the young couple into the *tablinum.* He seated himself, and asked them to be seated as well. But Gaius remained standing, not even bidding his father good morning.

"You *knew*, didn't you! You've known it all along!" he accused him, barely suppressing his anger.

"If you mean I knew Claudius is Ariana's father, you're right, I've known it for a while," Lucius responded calmly. "But I haven't 'known it all along,' as you put it. I began to suspect it after Ariana came to live here and I saw how much she looked like Marcus. And like Claudius. After you had your little fight with Marcus"—he looked sharply at his son—"I spoke to Claudius about the matter, and without actually admitting you're his daughter"—he glanced at Ariana—"he agreed to speak to Marcus about it. You may have noticed that Marcus's behavior changed after that."

"So Marcus knows."

"Of course he knows!"

"It sounds as if everyone knows except us. And all this time you've tried to prevent me from loving Ariana, even though she's not really a slave, she's the daughter of your good friend Claudius Vettius ..."

"Gaius, stop right there. You know the facts. Alomila is a slave, and any child of a slave is also a slave. And though you may have forced Claudius to admit he's her father, he hasn't acknowledged it publicly. Which means Ariana is, and remains, a slave—though in this house we don't treat her as a slave, and Clodia loves her almost as a daughter ..."

"Claudius has freed Alomila," Gaius interrupted.

"That changes nothing."

"Father, you could free Ariana if you wanted to. You know you could. I realize Augustus's manumission laws were necessary, but there are always exceptions. You've practically admitted you don't view Ariana as a slave, regardless of her legal status. If we could persuade Claudius to acknowledge her ..."

"Even then, Son, it wouldn't be possible for you to marry her. Whatever changes might occur in her legal status, it would still be common knowledge that her mother was a slave. For the sake of our family's reputation, I can't permit such a marriage."

At this, Ariana hid her face in her hands, and Gaius, with an angry look at his father, leaned over and put his arms around her. "Don't cry, my love," he pleaded, "Don't cry. I'll marry no one but you, I swear it by all the gods."

Lucius could not help but be moved by this scene, and he found his resolve wavering. He loved Gaius beyond measure, and he was fond of Ariana. He sat for several moments with his head bowed, looking down at his clasped hands. *Would it be such a bad thing if they married? It wouldn't hurt me personally: I'm already a magistrate, and I have no further ambitions. What if people* do *talk behind my back? They're always gossiping about* something. *They'd talk about this, then they'd move on to something else. No, it wouldn't hurt me. But it might hurt Gaius's chances. Even if Claudius acknowledges her as his daughter ... But if Gaius was already a member of the Comitia, maybe then ...*

He raised his head and spoke to them in a gentler and more conciliatory tone.

"Gaius and Ariana, please listen to me. I know you love each other, and Gaius, I believe you when you say you won't marry anyone else. But even if Claudius acknowledged Ariana—and there's no guarantee that he would—there'd be gossip, some of it malicious. There are bound to be people who are envious of a family like ours. Look at Rufus ..."

He paused for a moment as the memory of the trial flooded over him. *That poor man! I never really understood what drove him ...*

"But there's more to it than mere gossip," he continued. "There's your career. If you and Ariana marry, there'll be those who consider you unsuitable for a seat in the *Comitia*. When you seek office, they'll find ways to slander you. But if you were already a councilman and known for sensible public service, as I'm sure you will be, such a marriage would attract less comment. It won't be long before you're eligible to run for office, and once elected, you could establish a household of your own. At that point, though I would still be opposed to the match, I wouldn't try to prevent it, provided Claudius does his part."

Gaius had been listening intently, but was not convinced. "Father, I don't care about gossip, and I don't think anyone could stop *your* son from gaining a seat in the *Comitia*. This is all about Ariana's legal status, and that can be changed. There are plenty of marriages between citizens and freedmen or freedwomen; it's nothing unusual. I can't believe the reputation of the Tullii would be damaged by a marriage between Gaius Tullius and Ariana Vettia. We could even give her a Roman name—Arria—when she's freed, so it would be Gaius Tullius and Arria Vettia; who's going to complain about that? Not very many people even *know* Ariana; she's here in the house with Clodia most of the time. The people who see her most often are your dinner guests, and they're all decent, respectable people—and many of them are indebted to you for one thing or another. They wouldn't cause any trouble. Father, you could allow this, you *know* you could!"

Lucius looked at him sympathetically. Had their positions been reversed, he would have made the same arguments. He sighed, put his hands on the edge of the table, and stood.

"Son, you make sound arguments, and I believe that in time I might be persuaded. For now, though, I remain opposed to this marriage. No Tullius has ever married a freedwoman. And another thing: It may not be a good idea for the two of you to continue living in the same household. Perhaps if Ariana went to live with her mother on the farm—I'd have to get Claudius's permission ..."

"No, Lucius, please, no!" A tearful Clodia burst into the room. Manlius, knowing how important Ariana was to her, had alerted her to the discussion taking place in the *tablinum*.

"*Please* don't send her away," she begged. "I need her with me, I *depend* on her! *Please* don't do this!" She rushed over to Ariana, who was still sitting in the chair Lucius had assigned to her, mute and tearful. Now Gaius and Clodia, with Ariana seated between them, were facing Lucius, all three opposed to his will and expressing their desires in different ways, but with considerable effect. He no longer knew what to say. He sat and stared back at them. There was love in his eyes, but also confusion. He was used to being obeyed without question by all the members of his household, including his wife and son. Now, for the first time in many years, he was unsure of himself. Finally he reached a decision, knowing it was unsatisfactory but unable to come to any other conclusion.

"All right, my dear," he said to Clodia. "She may stay here and continue with her usual duties. And Gaius," he turned to his son, "seeing how matters lie, I won't try to prevent you from spending time with Ariana, provided you're discreet about it. In the meantime, I'll confer with Claudius about recognizing her parentage; perhaps after his daughters are married, he'll be more willing to do so. And we should start planning your political career. It's been good for you to work for Proculus, but you've been doing that long enough, and it's time to move on to something else."

Gaius was somewhat mollified by Lucius's tone and began to hope his opposition to the marriage would eventually fade. But he would have preferred a more definite promise. He briefly considered making such a demand, but thought better of it. Then Lucius rose, signaling to Manlius to being him his *pallium*.

"I have to go to the Forum; I've already spent too much time here. I'll go directly from there to the baths. I hope we can enjoy a quiet meal together this evening. And Gaius ..."

"Yes, Father?"

"I know this is difficult for you. Please bear with me. Let's not let this matter come between us—I want the best for you, you know that. We'll talk again, and maybe in time we'll come to a decision that'll satisfy both of us."

He turned to leave, then turned back. "And Son,..."

"Yes?"

"Would you read to us again tonight? You know how we all love to listen to you! I believe you've been reading the works of that new young author, Plutarch, the one who's been writing about the lives of famous men. Has he written a life of Alexander the Great?"

Gaius nodded.

"Well, maybe you could read us some of that."

Gaius nodded again, and Lucius left for the Forum, absently patting the dancing faun on the head as he passed through the atrium. Clodia and Ariana went to Clodia's room to sort through the chests of *stolae* and *pallae* in preparation for the cooler weather to come. And Gaius, exhausted by the morning's events, went to his *cubiculum*, where he lay on his bed for over an hour, staring at the ceiling and wondering how long it would take to overcome all the obstacles standing in the way of his marriage to Ariana.

XVI
OCTOBER, 76

As it turned out, they did not dine together that evening, as Lucius was detained in the Forum. And in the ensuing weeks there were numerous dinners, both at the House of the Faun and elsewhere, that occupied the attention of all of them. Finally, on a warm evening in early October, they were able to have a quiet meal together in the *viridarium*. After they had eaten, Gaius kept his promise to read to them from Plutarch's *Life of Alexander*.

"You need to understand," he began, "that Plutarch's intent was to write about lives, not histories. What he meant was … Oh, let *him* explain. Listen: 'The most glorious exploits do not always furnish us with the clearest discoveries of virtue or vice in men; sometimes a matter of less moment, an expression or a jest, informs us better of their characters and inclinations, than the most famous sieges, the greatest armaments, or the bloodiest battles whatsoever.' So if you expect to hear about Alexander's victory at the Battle of Issus, so dramatically portrayed in our mosaic, you're going to be disappointed."

He paused, and they all glanced toward the mosaic floor of the hallway leading into the garden where they were sitting. The scene seemed alive, the slanting late-afternoon light tinting the helmets and spears of the combatants with an orange glow as a triumphant Alexander overwhelmed the army of Darius, the Great King of the Persians.

"Plutarch tells us almost nothing about the battle itself," Gaius went on. "He spends more time describing Darius's tent, which Alexander's men refrained from pillaging and reserved for their commander. 'Here,' he writes,

> when Alexander beheld the bathing vessels, the water-pots, the pans, and the ointment boxes, all of gold curiously wrought, and smelt the fragrant odors with which the whole place was exquisitely perfumed, and from thence passed into a pavilion of great size and height, where the couches and tables and preparations for an entertainment were perfectly magnificent, he turned to those about him and said, 'This, it seems, is royalty.'

"Darius, you understand, had fled the scene," Gaius reminded them. "And Plutarch was very impressed by Alexander's actions after the battle. Listen to this:

> But as he was going to supper, word was brought him that Darius's mother and wife and two unmarried daughters, being taken among the rest of the prisoners, upon the sight of his chariot and bow, were all in mourning and sorrow, imagining him to be dead. After a little pause, more affected with their affliction than with his own success, he sent Leonnatus to them, to let them know Darius was not dead, and that they need not fear any harm from Alexander, who made war upon him only for dominion; they should themselves be provided with everything they had been used to receive from Darius.

"Only for dominion," Clodia broke in. "Only for dominion! How much comfort do you think that gave to those poor women? Even as royal prisoners, they could expect little but royal slavery. They were given to Alexander's commanders as concubines, weren't they?"

"That was the custom, it's true," Gaius admitted. "But Darius's family was spared. Alexander kept his promise, and provided luxurious quarters for them where they could live in privacy. In fact, later on he got the idea of blending Persian and Greek culture. He took to wearing Persian dress, and he ordered his officers and men to marry Persian women. He himself married Stateira, a daughter of Darius. Naturally, there was a lot of grumbling among the Greeks, especially when large numbers of Persian men were enrolled in the army. It bothered them that a conquered people were being given a status equal to theirs. There was a mutiny, but Alexander executed the ringleaders, and the rest fell into line."

"What about Roxana?" Ariana asked, somewhat breathlessly. Lucius and Clodia looked at her in surprise.

"Who was Roxana?" Lucius asked.

"Roxana was the daughter of a Sogdian baron," Gaius explained. "Alexander fell in love with her and married her. Plutarch doesn't tell us much about her …"

"Did he marry her before he married Stateira?" Ariana persisted.

"Yes. It was during his Asian campaign. Here's what Plutarch writes:

> As for his marriage with Roxana, whose youthfulness and beauty had charmed him at a drinking entertainment, where he first happened to see her taking part in a dance, it was, indeed, a love affair, yet it seemed at the same time to be conducive to the object he had in hand. For it gratified the conquered people to see him choose a wife from among themselves, and it made

> them feel the most lively affection for him, to find that in the only passion which he, the most temperate of men, was overcome by, he yet forbore till he could obtain her in a lawful and honorable way.

"So she *was* his wife, not a concubine," Ariana said, with an emphasis that again drew curious glances from Lucius and Clodia.

"Apparently," Gaius agreed.

"Why are you so interested in Roxana?" Clodia asked.

"Because she was my ancestor!" Ariana declared proudly.

Lucius and Clodia looked at each other with raised eyebrows, but Ariana continued:

"When I was a child, living on the farm, my mother told me all about it." She leaned back in her chair and closed her eyes, remembering. Then, in the silence, she began to speak.

"This is what my mother said, what her own mother had told her: 'Ariana is the name of a vast land far from here, a proud land where many tribes—Arachosians, Bactrians, Sogdians—roam with their herds, and warriors fight on horseback. My mother's people lived there, had lived there for hundreds of years ..."

She continued with her mother's story—her ancestors' life on the plains, the arrival of Alexander, the young girls dancing and Roxana's flashing eyes, her marriage to Alexander.

"And she named me Ariana so I would always remember where I came from," she concluded.

When she had finished, the only sound in the garden was the splashing of the fountains. Even Gaius, who had heard the story before, was entranced. Finally Lucius rose and put an arm around the girl's shoulders.

"You understand, don't you," he said kindly, "that there's no way to determine the truth of what you've just told us."

"I realize that," she said. "But I know it's true."

◆ ◆ ◆

During those golden autumn days, there were many afternoons when Ariana and Gaius met in the public gardens and sat together on the marble bench overlooking the harbor. Sometimes one of them would point out something of interest—a sea hawk flying overhead, or an unusually shaped cloud on the horizon—and they would exchange a few words. For the most part, though, they were quiet: holding hands, occasionally stealing a kiss when no one else was near. On cooler days, Gaius would put an arm around her shoulders so his *pallium* enfolded them both, and in their warm cocoon they leaned against each other and whispered, "I love you."

At times, they spoke about their future, their words a mixture of sadness and hope. It was evident that Lucius would not allow them to marry unless several aspects of their situation were changed. Claudius would have to acknowledge Ariana as his daughter, and for that to happen, he would have to be satisfied that his other daughters' chances of making good marriages would not be affected. Ariana would have to be freed and her Roman citizenship restored. Gaius would have to launch his political career and attain a position and reputation that would make him immune to malicious gossip. And during the years it would take for all this to occur, Ariana could not be seen to be with child.

They had waited so long to begin their life together, they felt they could wait another year or two—except for one difficulty: They were consumed with desire. At meals in the House of the Faun, it was all they could do to avoid gazing longingly at each other. Each day at dawn, when he embraced her in the *viridarium,* he held her longer and kissed her more passionately. Sometimes, when they sat on the bench in the public gardens and he enfolded them in his *pallium*, with his other hand he reached beneath her *stola* and sought her breasts, fondling them until the nipples were hard and she was flooded with desire.

◆ ◆ ◆

Ariana went to see her mother, and as they walked in the fields between the rows of dry stubble, their *pallae* wrapped tightly around them to ward off the early-November chill, she told her everything. Alomila listened in silence, but without surprise; slaves carried gossip along with everything else they carried on the donkey and mule carts that made their slow, lumbering way between the farm and the city. Finally she took her daughter by the shoulders, turning her so they faced each other.

"Ariana," she said, "I know nothing I say will turn you from the path you've chosen, but you must be prepared for great sadness. You're young, you're full of hope, but there's little chance you and Gaius will ever be able to marry. You must face facts."

"But Claudius has freed you, hasn't he?" Ariana objected, her eyes brimming.

"Yes, he has, and I'm very grateful," Alomila replied. "But that was a matter of little importance to him. He knew I wouldn't go anywhere else, and he doesn't have to pay me much for the work I do here. Admitting you're his daughter ... well, that's quite another matter. And even if he did, there's still Lucius ..."

"Mama," Ariana broke in, "Gaius and I ... we ... we can't spend the rest of our lives waiting for Claudius and Lucius to change their minds. We *love* each other. We *need* each other. But if I ..."

"If they see you're with child, they'll send you away. I know. How well I know!" Alomila interrupted her. She stood still for a moment, silently gazing at the tall mountain in the distance, its shoulders wreathed in clouds under a cold gray sky.

"Mama, isn't there something I can do," Ariana persisted. "Some herb or berry? I've heard there are old women who know these things. What about the woman who tended you when you were ill? Is she one of them?"

"No, she isn't," Alomila replied. "But there *is* something you can do. It's not foolproof, but it'll reduce the risk." And as Ariana listened closely, she told her what she knew about a woman's monthly cycle—the "dangerous" times and the times when it was less likely that she would conceive. "There are things Gaius can do, too," she pointed out.

Ariana nodded, blushing. Then she hugged Alomila and whispered,

"Mama, I love you. You're so good to me!"

"I love you too," Alomila replied, and mother and daughter turned and walked back to the farmhouse, arm in arm.

◆ ◆ ◆

Manlius had been steward of the House of the Faun since well before Gaius's birth. He loved the boy as if he were his own son, and on occasion he had served as his confidant on matters Gaius felt were too delicate to discuss with his father. It was thus that Gaius had learned most of what he knew about sexual relations, as well as how to alleviate his physical needs when they became too intense. Manlius had offered to accompany him to the *lupanar,* but Gaius had declined. "I can take care of myself," he said. Much of this had occurred when the boy was thirteen or fourteen, before Ariana's arrival in the household.

As love was born and grew between Gaius and Ariana, Manlius observed them with sympathy. As a former slave, he thoroughly understood Ariana's situation. Had she and Gaius not been in love, a few sexual encounters between them would have drawn no comment; masters—and their sons—often slept with female slaves. But he was aware of what had taken place between Claudius and Alomila, and he knew Ariana was their daughter—knowledge he never mentioned to anyone. He also knew Gaius had sworn not to marry anyone but Ariana, and he believed it.

So when Gaius came to him for advice, he did not try to dissuade the youth from pursuing his heart's desire. Manlius had come to care for Ariana almost as much as he did for Gaius, and he had quietly assisted them in the matter of the straw hat. He told Gaius he had known about their meetings in the storage room at the back of the house and made sure the servants were kept busy elsewhere. Gaius blushed and thanked him, realizing yet again that there could be few secrets in a large and busy household like theirs.

"We were happy in that little room," he said, "but we were afraid we'd be discovered and separated, so we stopped going there. After that, we decided to stay apart and keep hoping … But it's not enough, Manlius. It's not enough for either of us. I'm a man and she's a woman, and we love each other in every way …"

"I know," Manlius assured him. "It's quite evident. And you *do* have the right to sleep with her. Why don't you?"

"I don't want to sleep with her because it's my *right!*" Gaius exclaimed. "I don't want to take her to my bed, take my pleasure and send her away. That's not what this is about."

"You don't have much choice," Manlius reminded him. "But I understand. You wish to be together as equals. At least, equals in your hearts and in your thoughts. And to tell you the truth, I don't think Lucius and Clodia would object, as long as you're discreet. Suppose I arrange a room for you, a nice room with a bed and other furnishings. You'd just have to go through the little side atrium to the room in the far corner, which is empty at the moment. Early afternoon would be the best time, when Lucius is at the Forum and Clodia's resting. The servants will be busy elsewhere; I'll see to it."

"Manlius, you're a true friend," Gaius told him gratefully. "If there's ever anything I can do for you,…"

"Don't mention it," Manlius replied with a smile. "All I want is for you and Ariana to be happy."

◆ ◆ ◆

About a week later, on a chilly November afternoon, they arranged to meet in the room Manlius had provided for them. Gaius arrived first, Ariana a moment or two later. Gaius had the presence of mind to close the door before they threw themselves into each other's arms. They hardly glanced at the pleasant little room in which they found themselves, not noticing the brazier glowing with coals, the two wooden chairs placed nearby, or the newly washed, brightly-colored quilts piled on the bed.

Over and over, Gaius had imagined this moment: how he would kiss her, first on the lips, then in the sweet little hollow below her throat, then, after sliding her *stola* from her shoulders, on the soft, smooth tops of her lovely breasts. He had dreamed of stroking her legs and belly before finally placing his hand between her thighs and arousing her to new heights of ecstasy …

He had imagined, he had dreamed; but when the moment came, there was no room for dreams; there was only blazing desire. Aware that her need was as great as his, he quickly shed his tunic while she stepped out of hers. Slipping under the topmost quilt, they abandoned themselves to the passion that drove them, helpless to resist. They felt as if they were in the grip of some omnipotent god. Almost immediately, they were fully aroused, and a moment later, their bodies came together, straining to merge and become one.

Afterwards they lay in each other's arms, warm and contented beyond words. Soon both were lost in a dreamless sleep that completely relaxed and renewed them. After a while they awoke, almost at the same moment. They looked into each other's eyes and smiled. "Ariana, my love," he whispered; "I love you, Gaius," she replied.

The afternoon was almost over, and they must leave their warm bed to return to their respective tasks. "Tomorrow?" he asked. "Tomorrow," she agreed.

◆ ◆ ◆

The next afternoon began like the one before: They fell into each other's arms, kissed hungrily, then tore off their garments and quickly slid into the bed. Again they came together as one, reaching a pinnacle of pleasure beyond anything either had ever imagined. This time, though, they did not fall asleep afterwards. They spent the next hour exploring each other, an odyssey of touching and stroking, mingled with warm kisses. She rejoiced in his firm muscles and gentle touch. He was entranced by her body: its long, slim lines, the smooth curve of neck into shoulder, of waist into hip, the breasts like ripe fruit on which he nibbled gently.

"You are truly a goddess," he told her. "No mortal woman could be as beautiful as you! Even Aphrodite …" (he had been using the Greek names lately, since reading Homer's epics) "even Aphrodite can't compare with you!"

"Hush, Gaius, don't say such things!" she admonished him.

"But I must!" he insisted. "You're my goddess, my Goddess Ariana …"

She sat up and put one hand over his mouth, while with the other she stroked him lightly on the belly and thighs. Aroused, he pulled her down on top of him. Her dark hair enveloped his head and shoulders; with one hand, he held her face against his and kissed her, a long, slow kiss, while with the other he reached between her legs and coaxed her to a state of eager desire; then he entered her, moving slowly, rhythmically, his hands now on her hips, holding her against him. Lost in the fragrant darkness of her hair, they closed their eyes and gave themselves up to the love that possessed them.

◆ ◆ ◆

As Manlius had suggested, they were discreet, though their affair was common knowledge within the household, if not outside its walls. After the first few days, they met less frequently, but with no less anticipation and desire. As the weeks passed and they grew to know each other more intimately, their pleasure became more intense. At the same time, they became more relaxed with each other, more playful. Sometimes they simply lay side by side, like children, making up stories to tell each other, or devising little epigrams like Martial's:

Pomponius, when loud applause
Salutes you from your client-guests,
Don't fool yourself: good food's the cause
And not your after-dinner jests.

Lucius and Clodia were, of course, aware of their affair. Indeed, it would have been difficult to conceal it, as Ariana glowed like Venus newly risen from the sea, and Gaius could be heard laughing happily at any hour of the day. Even if they had missed these signs of the young couple's happiness, they could not have missed the significance of Gaius's choice of after-dinner recitations. He had gone back to his early favorites, Horace and Catullus. Especially Catullus. One evening, with mischievous intent, he plunged into one of Catullus's most amorous offerings:

Quaeris quot mihi basiationes
Tuae,…?

> You ask, Lesbia, how many of your kisses are enough for me, and more than enough. Count the grains of Libyan sand in silphium-producing Cyrene,

> between the oracle of sultry Ammon and the sacred tomb of ancient Battus. Or count all the stars that in the silent night look down on the furtive loves of men. Only then will you know how many of your kisses are enough, and more, to satisfy mad Catullus ...

The implications could not have been more obvious, especially as Ariana responded by blushing to the roots of her hair. Taking pity on the poor girl, Gaius switched to his favorite works by the Greek lyric poets, reciting his own translation of a fragment from Alcman:

> Asleep are the peaks and ravines, the headlands and beds of mountain streams, and the creeping crowds of animals that the black earth nourishes, and mountain beasts and the generation of bees, and the whales in the depth of the purple sea. Asleep are the tribes of birds with tapering wings.

And one from Anacreon:

> We call you happy, Cricket, because on the twigs of the trees, having drunk a bit of dew, you sing like a king. For all this belongs to you, what you see in the fields and whatever the woods nourish. You are the farmers' friend, bringing harm to no one. You are honored to mortals, sweet prophet of summer!

In this way, as the days grew shorter and the Saturnalia approached, life in the House of the Faun proceeded in peace and happiness. All knew that changes lay ahead, but none could foretell their nature, and no one wanted to disrupt the comfortable and predictable life of the household as it unfolded from one untroubled day to the next.

XVII
MARCH, 77

Suedius Clemens was both frustrated and relieved. Frustrated, because the Emperor had not recalled him and he was forced to remain in what he thought of as a rather backward provincial town, far from the exquisite pleasures and fascinating political life of Rome. Rome was, after all, the nerve center and heartbeat of the Empire, and he wanted to be there. But he was aware that Vespasian knew all about the unfortunate Rufus episode; Clemens himself had been required to submit a report, and there was always a large band of informers who were eager to provide embarrassing details in exchange for a *denarius* or two. Had he chosen to do so, Vespasian could not only have recalled him but put him on trial for incompetence. But he did not. Hence Clemens's feelings of relief mixed with disgust at his "exile."

Seeing that the fates had decreed that his stay in Pompeii would be considerably longer than he had anticipated, Clemens decided to make it more interesting. He would leave his mark on the city by sponsoring several architectural and engineering projects, some of which were destined to bear his name. There were plenty of buildings and monuments adorned with the names of famous Pompeiians, both men and women. Eumachia, a priestess of Venus and a member of an ancient Samnite family, had sponsored the construction of a building in the Forum to house the wool market, and had arranged for an inscription that included not only her name but that of her son Marcus Fronto. After the major earthquake fifteen years before, repairs had been made to the amphitheater with donations from Cuspius Pansa and his son, who were rewarded with statues of themselves placed in niches added to the outer wall on either side of the main gate. Holconius Rufus, a forebear of the infamous Statius Rufus, had paid for the renovation of the theater, including the facing of the steps and seats with marble; his name was prominently inscribed on a bench at the center of the area reserved for public officials.

There were also plenty of opportunities to repair or improve more mundane, yet essential, parts of the city's structure. The system for supplying water to houses, public fountains, and the growing numbers of baths and swimming pools was a patchwork of pipes and tanks. These were connected to the *castellum aquae*—a squat, square tower located just inside the Porta Vesuvio. The *castellum aquae* received and stored the water that flowed into the city over a branch of the aqueduct extending from Avellinum, in the mountains eighteen miles away, to Misenum, the navy's headquarters at the northern end of the Bay of Neapolis. The aqueduct had been reinforced some years before, but the pipes inside the city were subject to constant rupture and hasty repair, a situation made worse by the big earthquake and the series of quakes a few years later, which had been less severe but had caused a disproportionate amount of damage. A complete overhaul of the water system would be an important and worthwhile undertaking, Clemens thought, but it would disrupt people's lives and fill the city with the disorder of construction. It would do little to enhance his popularity.

No, he needed to come up with something more visible and less disruptive, something later generations could point to with pride. Something like the renovation of the theater sponsored by Holconius Rufus. *How could a snake like Statius Rufus come from the same family?* Clemens wondered. *Or was the first Rufus just like the second? Did he pay for the marble seats in order to distract attention from some less honorable activity?* He shook his head angrily, trying to free his thoughts from the persistent memories of the trial and its unfortunate effect on his career.

Marble does *make an impression,* he admitted. *The first Rufus knew what he was doing in that respect.* Apparently, Holconius Rufus had made his mark: There was a statue of him just outside the Stabian Baths; it showed him in the dress and pose of a military commander, a reference to his honorary title of military tribune. *I wonder what he did to deserve* that? Clemens asked himself, and again shook his head in disgust. *Why am I wasting my time on him?* he berated himself. *Because you're jealous!* whispered a little voice from deep within. *Wouldn't it be wonderful if the citizens of Pompeii honored you with a statue like that one? But not standing in front of the baths. It must stand at the center of the Forum!*

Obviously, Clemens could not commission a statue in his own honor. But the idea of marble remained in his thoughts, mingling with his fantasy of a statue in the Forum. He remembered that Augustus had used marble to transform Rome—"I found Rome a city of brick; I left it a city of marble," he had boasted. Could Clemens do the same for Pompeii? *"I found Pompeii a city of brick; I left it a city of marble!"* He laughed at the thought, but it stayed with him, and in the ensuing weeks a plan took shape, one that looked better each time he examined it. It satisfied all his requirements: It would be both beautiful and practical; it would not disrupt citizens' everyday lives; and it would earn him their lasting respect and gratitude. Clemens would sponsor the renovation and beautification of the Forum. Perhaps then he would be rewarded with a statue of his own.

Pompeii's Forum, like that of all Roman cities, was the center of public life. It was a large, rectangular plaza surrounded by temples, public buildings, and fish and produce markets. Along the west side stood a row of statues on pedestals: Romulus, Aeneas, Caesar, and some of Pompeii's more illustrious citizens. All administrative and legal business took place there; most public religious ceremonies were held there; it was the scene of elections, trials, and the announcement of municipal edicts; the Curia, where the *Comitia* held its meetings, was there; all kinds of goods and services were bought and sold in and around the Forum square—everything from fresh fish to legal advice. And in addition to all this, it was the favored locale of idlers, gossips, and shysters, who filled the Forum from dawn to dusk, adding to the clatter and clamor of those who were there on legitimate business.

At any hour of the day and into the night, the Forum was thronged with shopkeepers, ironworkers, farm carts, vegetable sellers, cattle merchants, tradesmen, politicians, beggars, philosophers declaiming, lawyers arguing, and slaves bearing messages for their masters. It is doubtful if any of them stopped to look at the condition of the crowded square where they conducted their business. If they had, they might have noticed that the buildings on the long sides of the rectangular area looked like the teeth of an old woman—some missing, some broken, many discolored or shifted to create a snaggle-toothed effect unbecoming to a prosperous, well-governed city like Pompeii. Or so Clemens concluded. He vowed he would transform the old religious and commercial center into the most elegant forum in Italia.

But how to accomplish this? The existing buildings could not be moved or destroyed, and the Capitolium at the north end must remain the most important edifice in the Forum, as required both by imperial decree and by Clemens's strong instinct for political self-preservation. Clemens could add a building in his own name—something like the Eumachia Building, which served a variety of functions but whose main purpose was to bear her name and her son's. But the spaces available were inadequate, and in truth, there was no need for another building of that sort.

A marble pavement for the entire square? Too expensive, even for Clemens, and besides, it would not take long for the marble to be covered by the dirt and detritus deposited by the crowds who filled the square each day. Besides, who ever looked down, unless it was to retrieve a dropped coin or adjust a sandal strap? Clemens wanted something that would be clearly visible, practical, and beautiful. Something involving marble. Day after day he pondered the question, examining every corner of the Forum as he passed through on his way to the magistrates' offices. And one early spring morning, as the pale sunlight glinted off the sides of the Basilica and the temples, he looked northward from the entrance of the magistrates' building and was inspired.

He would sponsor the construction of a peristyle that would extend around three sides of the Forum, leaving the north side open so the Capitolium would be unobstructed. The irregularities of the facades on the other three sides would be hidden, and the peristyle would provide shelter when it rained, and shade during the hot summer days. It would be like the peristyles around most private gardens, only much larger. And built of marble.

Clemens stood there for a long time, imagining the unifying effect the peristyle would have on the disorganized perimeter of the Forum, considering the types and quantities of marble required, and dreaming of the statue that would eventually be commissioned in his honor. *I need an architect, and a good one!* he thought.

◆ ◆ ◆

Not long after reaching his decision, Clemens went to see his friend Munatius Faustus, who invited him to take a seat in a comfortable *oecus* looking out onto a well-tended garden. There was nothing Faustus liked better than a good long chat with an intelligent man. And whatever else he might be, Clemens was certainly intelligent.

"And how's your lovely wife?" Clemens asked, after they had exchanged the usual pleasantries.

"Very well, thank you, but you won't get to see her today. She's out visiting Julia Felix."

"Ah, Julia Felix. What a woman! Pompeii wouldn't be the same without her."

And so it went, until Clemens came around to his plan for the Forum. After an initial expression of surprise, Faustus indicated his approval, though inwardly he wondered what could have motivated Clemens to undertake such an expensive project.

Clemens had been thinking of bringing in an architect from Rome, but his political instincts had warned him against attracting Vespasian's attention so soon after the Rufus episode. *Better include a statue of Vespasian in the plan,* he decided. *And put it on a large pedestal, where everyone can see it ... He'll have to be on horseback, or driving a chariot ...*

"So, how can I help you?" Faustus asked.

"I need an architect, a good one. Someone who knows the mathematical principles developed by the Greek architects when they built their great temples. Of course, we're not building the Parthenon here, but I'd like the effect to be dignified and pleasing."

"Why not hire a Greek architect?" Faustus suggested. "You could consult Kineas, Marcus's old tutor. He knows all the Greeks in Pompeii. He's the one who recommended Archytas when we were looking for someone to teach Marcus mathematics and geometry. And it's worked out very well. The boy learns fast—I'd swear by now he knows almost as much as his teacher. In fact,..." Faustus leaned his chin on his hand and thought for a moment.

"In fact?"

"In fact, when you hire your architect, you might consider asking him to take on Marcus as his assistant. I'm sure he'd be a great help, and it'd be good for him. After all, he's almost nineteen years old. He should be out in the world doing something useful." Faustus knew something was troubling Marcus, but as the youth was either unable or unwilling to confide in him, he contented himself by providing a comfortable home for him and letting him pursue his own interests. He was unaware of how often those interests took him to the *lupanar.* Julia too, though concerned for her son's welfare, did not spend much time with him or question him closely about his activities. Faustus might have sought out Claudius to learn more about his son's personality and interests, but he was prevented from doing so by a sense of decorum. It was Claudius, after all, who had divorced Julia and so alienated Marcus that he insisted on living with his mother instead of remaining in his father's household, as was customary.

"That sounds like a good idea," Clemens agreed.

◆ ◆ ◆

With Kineas's help, Clemens found his architect—one Phidias, who claimed to be descended from the famous Athenian sculptor Pheidias. As there was no way to determine the truth or falsehood of the claim, Clemens let it stand and, as promised, instructed the man to hire Marcus as his assistant. And as Faustus had predicted, it was good for him. Marcus soon became engrossed in the planning of the peristyle, energized by the challenge to his knowledge of mathematics and geometry, and grateful to both Faustus and Clemens for giving him the opportunity to begin his architectural career with so grand a project. For he no longer had any doubt about his future career: He would be an architect. His fascination with architectural design and construction was not new: He had grown up watching workers repair the buildings damaged in the great earthquake. Now he dreamed of rebuilding the city walls, redesigning the public gardens, constructing new, more beautiful public buildings—the possibilities were endless. He now spent all his time in the Forum, taking measurements and watching as Phidias sketched plans on large sheets of paper.

Clemens could also be found in the Forum at almost any hour of the day, either consulting with Phidias or wandering around the square, imagining how it would appear with the completed peristyle in place. He had considered using the white marble of Carrara, which had been popular since the days of Augustus, but Phidias had persuaded him not to use it because the intense Pompeiian sunlight would reflect blindingly from the white columns, creating an effect that was far from restful. So they decided on the beautifully varied, veined marbles imported from the Empire's eastern quarries, with a pavement of travertine and a ceiling of wooden beams. They also added a second story, with smaller columns of travertine and a roof covered with terra-cotta tiles. There would be staircases at intervals so people could climb to the upper story and look out onto the Forum square. On one side of the colonnade would be placed the statues of Pompeii's civic leaders, moved from their original positions along the west side of the Forum square.

Once construction began, Clemens watched eagerly as the columns were erected in their regularly spaced rows, following the rules of proportion laid down by the Greeks centuries earlier. He befriended the workmen, joking with them and ordering his slaves to offer them wine at the end of the day. The workmen were delighted at the prospect of several months of steady employment, with the promise of a bonus if they finished the job more quickly.

Pleased, if somewhat bemused, the people of Pompeii also spent much of their time in the Forum, watching the construction and wondering what lay behind it. Could the Emperor be planning a visit to their small city? Was Clemens building the peristyle as a penance for his role in the Rufus episode? Whatever the reason for the project, they appreciated its practical value as well as its grand effect—especially as the summer months approached and they could imagine the shady refuge the peristyle would offer during the heat of the day.

Thus, as the building progressed and the plan unfolded, everyone was happy—Clemens, Marcus, the workmen, the citizens of Pompeii. Everyone, that is, except Lucius Tullius.

◆ ◆ ◆

For a while after the trial of Statius Rufus, Clemens had taken a more active role in governing the city, presiding over the meetings of the *Comitia* and issuing edicts of his own, as he had in the early months of his administration. This had irritated some members of the city council, who had grown accustomed to his less obtrusive rule during the last year or two. But it had freed Lucius from some of his duties and allowed him to spend more time at home. Now, however, Clemens was absorbed in his Forum project, and Lucius was left to carry out all the duties of both magistrates, his colleague Caecilius Jucundus still suffering from a debilitating illness. So Lucius, too, was spending almost all his time in the Forum, but unlike Clemens, he was spending it indoors, in the magistrates' offices or the Curia.

At home, he was constantly occupied, either with the petitions of his clients or with the arrangements for the endless dinner parties he must host; with Clodia and Ariana's help, he had to decide whom to invite, whom not to invite to the same dinner, what forms of entertainment would be appropriate, and of course, what dishes to offer so the meal would be satisfying while not appearing ostentatious. For the first time in his adult life, he found himself wishing he was not one of the *duoviri* or even a leading citizen of Pompeii. For the first time, he could appreciate the idea of being an ordinary man, with little fame and few responsibilities. *Like Claudius,* he thought, with an unexpected twinge of envy. *Someone like Claudius, who can spend hours studying the works of Cicero or Aristotle ... Maybe it's time for me to retire.*

After abandoning himself to such thoughts for a few moments, however, he would mentally shake himself like a wet dog and go back to work at whatever task had been occupying him before he began daydreaming. No one knew of these thoughts, not even Clodia. All who dealt with him saw a pleasant, honorable, highly regarded civic leader, a man of medium height with sandy hair growing gray at the temples, and an engaging smile, a man who was always ready to offer assistance when it was requested. Only Clodia noticed that his hair was thinning and there were more lines around his eyes. She guessed his feelings but kept silent, knowing how devoted he was to Pompeii and its citizens, and knowing, too, that when the time was right for him to retire, he would do so.

Under these circumstances, Lucius was barely aware of Gaius and Ariana's affair and too preoccupied even to ask himself how he felt about it. In a distant corner of his mind, he knew he must somehow deal with their desire to marry despite his opposition and whatever social consequences might follow. *But not yet, not yet.* Gaius was still young, though a man and ready to begin his career. His career! That was something Lucius must deal with *now.*

◆ ◆ ◆

Responding to his father's summons, Gaius paused anxiously before entering the *tablinum.* Was this something to do with his sleeping with Ariana? Manlius had convinced him Lucius would not object, but had he been mistaken? He allowed himself a small sigh of relief when his father, after a brief greeting, launched into a speech about the importance of doing something worthwhile and making a name for oneself. Gaius barely stopped himself from grinning; it was so typical of Lucius.

They settled in to a friendly discussion of Pompeiian politics and Gaius's ambitions. For several years, it had been understood that Gaius would follow in his father's footsteps and choose a career in city governance. With his twenty-first birthday imminent, the time was ripe. But Lucius wanted to be sure his son was choosing a political career because he genuinely wanted to, not because he felt constrained to do so.

"There are alternatives," he reminded him. "For example, there's the estate in Sicily. The manager is getting on in years and will need to be replaced. But if you wanted to supervise the place yourself, and get a taste for that kind of life, we could arrange it. You could live the life of a country gentleman, like Horace on his beloved farm. It's a pretty place, with olive groves on the hillsides overlooking the sea, and the house is pleasant. The olive presses are in a separate enclosure …

"I know, Father, I went there with you once, don't you remember?"

"Oh, that's right! We had new presses made—the best ones are made here—and when we shipped them to Agrigentum, we went along to inspect the place. You were about ten years old, I believe. And you remember it?"

"Yes I do, Father. I was impressed with the orderliness of it all, and I agree, it was very pleasant. When the breeze came off the sea through the olive trees, all the leaves turned from green to a shimmering silver, like a school of fish …"

Lucius raised his eyebrows. "Perhaps you'd prefer a career as a poet?"

Gaius smiled. "No, Father, I get too much pleasure out of reading other people's poetry!"

"In any case," Lucius went on, "the olive oil business is an important source of our family's wealth, and we've always made sure it was managed well. We could, of course, hire a skilled freedman to take over, but I wanted to offer you the opportunity. Manlius could go with you, and perhaps one or two of the other slaves …"

Gaius looked at his father curiously. Was he proposing that he take Ariana away to Sicily, live with her there and give up his hopes of a political career? *No, that can't be it. Mother couldn't do without her. And it wouldn't really solve anything.*

Perhaps sensing his son's confusion, Lucius did not wait for an answer. "It's just that I don't want you to go into politics merely because I did," he explained. "I know we've talked about this before, but I need to tell you again that it can be very difficult, even frustrating … It's so much easier to deal with shipments of olive oil than with people … Oh, you know what I mean: In politics, the quarrels, the personalities, all the shouting—it can be a very tiring and tiresome profession. Don't go into it looking for praise or approval; you won't get it. You'll have people coming at you from all sides with conflicting demands, and if you try to help them reach a compromise, they'll all hate you. And if you *do* manage to accomplish something, the credit will probably go to someone else …"

"Father, why are you telling me this now? We've spent many hours talking about politics. I *know* what I'm getting myself into! Don't worry, it's *my* choice, and it's a genuine one. *Of course* it's because of your influence; *of course* I'm following in your footsteps. But that's what I want to do. I know there are alternatives. I've considered them. But this is my choice."

"Well, then," Lucius said with a smile. "We'll have to start planning your campaign for a seat in the *Comitia*. The elections aren't far away, and there are some vacancies."

"You mean you're not going to buy a seat for me by making a huge donation to Clemens's peristyle? The way Ampliatus did for his son, by rebuilding the Temple of Isis?"

Lucius looked startled. "Surely you're not serious!" Then he saw that Gaius was teasing him, and laughed.

"Did you know that boy was only six years old? Ampliatus got his son elected, but everyone was laughing at him behind his back. Besides, I've already made a donation to Clemens's project. He claims he's paying for it himself. Ha! He invites all the richest men in Pompeii to dinner and persuades them to contribute; *that's* how he's paying for it!"

After sharing a laugh at the many forms human folly can take, father and son got back to business. There was much to be done if Gaius was to win a seat on the *Comitia* in the upcoming elections, less than four months away.

XVIII
JUNE, 77

They were lying sprawled out naked on the bed, the quilts and brazier long gone. Summer had arrived early, and their little room was warm, almost hot, with the door closed and only one small shuttered window, high up on the outer wall. With Gaius's campaign for the *Comitia* in full swing, they met less often these days, but their need for each other was as strong as ever.

With her eyes, Ariana followed the lines of light shining through the spaces around the door and across the wooden ceiling. Lazily she watched the changing patterns of light and shadow, occasionally drifting into a pleasant daydream. She and Gaius were walking in the countryside, picking blackberries as they went along. Or they were sitting on a hillside, watching the fishing boats in the bay below them ... She slipped into a doze.

Gaius also was daydreaming, but his thoughts were on his campaign. *Father certainly knows how to manage a campaign,* he was thinking. *I hardly have a moment to myself. In fact ...*

He roused himself, remembering that Lucius had arranged to meet him at the baths later that afternoon. *He's probably rounded up another half-dozen important citizens to introduce me to. How am I ever going to remember all those names?*

He turned toward Ariana and, with a fingertip, traced the contours of her breasts, first one, then the other, then back to the first again. She opened her eyes and smiled. "My Aphrodite!" he whispered, and kissed her sleep-warmed lips. They wrapped themselves in each other's arms and remained still for a moment, savoring the touch and scent of their entwined bodies. Then desire overwhelmed them, leading them on toward the exquisite climax that left them satiated yet hungry for more.

"Gaius?" she said hesitantly, watching him dress and prepare to leave.

"What is it, my love?"

"Promise you'll never leave me!"

Amazed, he looked at her and saw the tears in her eyes. "Ariana, my goddess, you know I'll never leave you. I promised you long ago. Why are you asking this now?"

"I don't know," she said, the tears gaining strength. "I don't know! I'm just afraid something might happen ... things might change ..."

He sat on the bed and took her in his arms. "Don't cry, my love, or I'll be all wet before I even get to the baths!"

She laughed through her tears, and rested her head on his shoulder. "I'm sorry, I just can't help it!"

"Ariana, I've said it before and I'll say it again now, and if you want me to say it again tomorrow, I will: I promise I'll never leave you!"

Gently he rocked her back and forth, then kissed her.

"Shall we meet again tomorrow?"

She nodded, and he left her and went to join Lucius at the baths. She lay there a while longer, still quietly weeping. *I'm a slave. Just a slave. How can I dare to hope?*

◆ ◆ ◆

Almost every evening, there was a dinner party at the House of the Faun. It seemed as if everyone in Pompeii would have a chance to savor Lucius and Clodia's hospitality before midsummer. And indeed, Lucius intended to entertain, if possible, every member of the *Comitia*, the entire College of Augustales, all the top public officials, and anyone else of importance in the city. The unspoken *quid pro quo* was that the guests would paint testimonials to Gaius's character on the walls of their houses, and speak well of him if anyone should ask. Gaius was present at all the dinners, and Lucius always managed to involve him in the conversation in ways that would reveal his native intelligence as well as his familiarity with political and philosophical writings, Greek as well as Latin.

One evening, the party was more relaxed than usual, as the guests included Vascula and Aper, Claudius, and Proculus. As was often the case, Claudius's old cook, Petronius, had been borrowed for the occasion. The meal featured Petronius's specialty, roast suckling pig, along with fresh vegetables from the countryside. After everyone had been eating contentedly for a while, Lucius wiped his mouth and fingers and said, grinning,

"Do you know what happened the last time Petronius served up this delicacy?"

The other guests, their faces turned toward Lucius, missed Claudius's questioning look.

"It seems Petronius has a new assistant in his kitchen, a good, strong girl they've brought up from the farm. He's getting on in years and needs help with the lifting and carrying. Anyway, Claudius was having a little dinner that I was honored to attend ..."

Claudius was looking studiously at his hands, which he had dipped in the water dish and was carefully wiping with his napkin.

"... and Petronius cooked a suckling pig, as they're in season, you might say. But when he had the pig laid out on the serving tray and was surrounding it with—what was it, Claudius? braised figs, I think; I don't exactly remember. Anyway, when he was almost finished, he called the girl over and told her to carry the tray to the *triclinium.* 'And make sure there's an apple in the mouth,' he said. 'There must be an apple in the mouth!'

"The girl just stood there looking at him, but he was busy, so he shouted at her to get on with it, and set about preparing the dessert. The girl was still standing there, but finally she went to the pantry and found an apple, and then she picked up the tray and brought it in to us. We were waiting expectantly—Petronius's roast suckling pig is famous, as you know—so we were all looking toward the doorway when she came in, carrying the tray with the pig on it, her mouth wide open with the apple sticking out of it, and tears streaming down her cheeks!"

There was a moment of shocked silence; then they all burst into laughter. When they could finally speak again, Claudius tried to assure them that every word was true, but instead he began laughing again, and the others joined him. They were making so much noise that Clodia sent Ariana to find out was has happening, and her appearance in the doorway, her face flooded with doubt, sent them into further gales of laughter. She stood there a moment, mystified, then turned to go. Gaius hastened after her.

"Don't worry, my love, it has nothing to do with you. I'll tell you all about it tomorrow!" And with a quick kiss, he left her and went back into the room.

"Mother was afraid we'd gone mad," he said, chuckling.

When they finally managed to stop laughing and had caught their breath, Lucius announced that there would be no harpist or flute-player that evening. "Instead," he said, "I'm going to ask you to resolve a paradox."

Surprised and curious, the guests looked at one another, then at him.

"I'm sure you've all heard of Zeno of Elea," Lucius continued. "The Greek philosopher who believed the basic matter of the universe is single, indivisible, and unchanging."

Vascula and Aper nodded, but it was obvious they had never heard of Zeno. Claudius contented himself with a knowing smile and a glance at Gaius.

"Well," Lucius went on, "From this, Zeno concluded that motion is impossible, and he wrote a book of arguments to prove his point."

His guests were both amused and intrigued. "How in the world could he have imagined that motion is impossible?" asked Proculus.

"His reasoning is rather complicated," Lucius answered, "and, frankly, absurd. But what I want to pose to you tonight is one of his arguments, known as the paradox of Achilles and the tortoise."

Claudius's smile broadened.

"It goes like this: If a tortoise is given a start in a race against Achilles, Achilles will never be able to overtake it, because when he arrives at the tortoise's starting point, the tortoise will have moved ahead to a new position, and when he reaches *that* position, the tortoise will again have moved ahead, and so on indefinitely. On this basis, the tortoise must always be ahead of Achilles, even it it's by the tiniest possible distance."

Aper was incredulous. "You mean Achilles couldn't outrun a tortoise?"

"Not me; Zeno," said Lucius. "Theoretically, at least."

"But that's ridiculous. Achilles ran much faster than that!"

"Yes, on the face of it. But how would you counter Zeno's argument?"

The guests sat for a few moments in puzzled silence. Then Vascula said,

"Achilles took bigger steps?"

"Of course he did," said Lucius. "But that's not what the philosophers say."

"What do they say?"

"Gaius, you've read about this recently, haven't you?" said Lucius, turning to his son. "Why don't you tell us?"

With a smile, Gaius said, "Well, I'm no philosopher. But I read Aristotle's explanation, and it goes something like this: What Zeno's trying to prove is that if the tortoise has always moved ahead of where it was when Achilles tried to catch up with it, it would take an infinite number of such episodes for Achilles to catch the tortoise. In other words, he would never catch it, because it would always be ahead of him. The counterargument is that in fact, the total distance required to catch the tortoise is finite, and Achilles easily covers that distance in just a few strides."

There were still some puzzled looks. Then Gaius continued.

"Zeno posed another paradox that's similar to the one about Achilles and the tortoise. He divided the distance to be covered by a runner in a stadium into a geometric series—one-half plus one-fourth plus one-eighth, and so on—and claimed that the distance, having an infinite number of divisions, could never be covered, and that therefore motion is impossible."

"Which is clearly false!" said Proculus.

"Yes," said Lucius. "But we're indebted to Zeno nonetheless."

"And why is that?" asked Claudius.

"Because, at least according to Aristotle, he invented the dialectic, one of the basic tools of philosophy, and one you're probably already familiar with, if you stop to think about it."

Vascula and Aper looked at each other quizzically; Proculus stared back at Lucius, his mind a blank.

"Socrates!" said Claudius. "Plato and Socrates!"

"That's right," said Lucius. "Socrates used the dialectical method with his students in his efforts to uncover the truth about various qualities, such as virtue or beauty, and Plato reported the resulting conversations in his Dialogues. You know: *Crito, Phaedo,* the *Republic,* the *Symposium, Timaeus …*"

"Of course, I remember now," said Proculus. "You just came at it from behind, if you know what I mean."

"Yes, I *do* know, and I apologize," said Lucius with a smile. "But tell me, what do you think of Plato's notion of a philosopher-king?"

Again the room fell silent. Then, to the surprise of some of those present, Vascula ventured an opinion.

"I'm not sure it's very practical. Kings don't have time to sit back and think about virtue or beauty. They've got to deal with all kinds of things every day: edicts, trials, taxes—the whole business of governing."

"That's right!" Aper chimed in. "Just look how busy *you* are, Lucius."

"*Me*!" Lucius exclaimed. "I'm no king, just a public servant. And we all know serving the public is an endless task. No, I was thinking of Vespasian, or perhaps Clemens …"

"Well, it looks as if Clemens has plenty of time to think about beauty, judging from that project of his in the Forum," Claudius commented. And with that, the discussion turned to what had come to be known surreptitiously as "Clemens's Folly." While there were varying opinions about how beautiful the new peristyle would be, all agreed that it was impressive, would provide much-needed shade in summer, and was a boon to Pompeii's always-hungry labor force. Soon dessert arrived, and with it the guests enjoyed another cup of wine. A short while later, all but Lucius and Gaius retrieved their cloaks and headed home.

◆ ◆ ◆

The next evening was a rare one, with no dinner guests, and Lucius, Gaius, Clodia, and Ariana were able to enjoy a quiet, simple meal. They were sitting in the shady portion of the *viridarium*, where slaves had placed some chairs and a couple of small tables. Gaius had recounted the story of the kitchen maid and the apple, and they had shared a laugh, but now they were silent, watching the play of the afternoon light on the spray escaping from the fountains. A sense of profound peace enveloped them; each wished the moment could last forever. Finally Lucius roused himself and asked Gaius if he felt like entertaining them with a selection from one of his favorite poets.

"But no more love poetry," he admonished. "Let's hear something more exciting."

"There's a new translation of the *Iliad*," Gaius said. "It was done by an up-and-coming writer in Rome, one Publius Fagelsius, who's getting a lot of attention these days. Claudius lent me the scroll yesterday; I haven't had a chance to look at it yet, but ..."

"No, Son, not the *Iliad*, not tonight, anyway. How about something from the *Metamorphoses*?"

"All right," said Gaius, and went to find the scroll.

"Let's see," he said upon returning. "There's Apollo and Daphne—I think I read you that one not long ago. Io, Phaethon, Diana and Actaeon ..."

"Oh no, not that one, please," said Clodia. "That poor boy, torn to pieces by his own hounds!"

"Well, what about Perseus and Andromeda? Not the whole thing, just the part where the monster comes to get her."

They agreed.

"All right, here's the exciting part," Gaius said. "Remember, Perseus is wearing Mercury's winged shoes." And he began reciting:

> Look out to sea! Swift as a diving, tossing,
> Sharp-prowed ship that cuts the waves, propelled
> By the sweat-soaked arms of galley slaves, the monster
> Approached, churning the water with its chest
> And sending up spray on either side; plunging,

It came as close to shore as a Balearic
Sling could send its shot. Perseus, leaping
From the earth beneath him, vaulted to midair;
The monster saw his shadow on the sea
And plunged to tear at it. Then, as Jupiter's eagle
When he has found a snake in a broad meadow,
Turning its mottled body in the sun,
Falls on the unseeing creature from the air,
And, wary of the snake's forked tongue,
Grips its scaled neck and sinks his claws within it,
So Perseus dove upon the raging monster,
Thrusting, hilt-deep, his sword into its shoulder.
Burning with its gaping wound, the monster reared
Its bulk in the air, then dived, veered like a boar
When it has been surrounded by quick hounds,
Loud with the kill. Perseus, dodging, swayed
Past snapping jaws on agile, dancing wings;
Then, as the beast rolled its soft belly upward,
Or bared its neck, his curved sword stabbed
At the back grown tough with sea-wet barnacles,
At the flanks, or at the thin, fishlike tail.
The beast vomited purple blood, and Perseus's wings,
Damp with salt spray, grew heavy;
He saw a rock that pierced the shifting waters
And leaped to safety on it.
With his left hand grasping a ledge
He plunged his sword three times, and then again,
Into the monster's bowels.
Then all the shores and the halls of heaven,
From which the gods looked down on Perseus,
Echoed with great cheers; Cepheus and his wife,
Cassiope, saluted their hero as a gallant
Bridegroom who had saved the glory of their house.
And now the girl, released from her chains, stepped forward,
The cause for which he fought, and his reward.

"You know," Clodia commented after he had finished, "it's striking how hard the heroes of those tales have to work to win a wife. They have to go to the ends of the earth, kill all kinds of monsters, retrieve rare treasures like the Golden Fleece or the Golden Apples of the Hesperides. Nothing's ever easy for them."

"Unless they're gods, of course," Lucius pointed out. "Look how easy it is for Zeus. He can change himself into a bull, a swan, even a shower of gold!"

"I suppose it's meant to make us grateful we're mere mortals," said Gaius, with a smile and a glance toward Ariana, who ventured a little smile in return. "On the other hand, sometimes I think it might be easier to slay a wild boar than to win an election in Pompeii."

"What do you mean, Son?" Lucius asked, concern in his voice. "Your campaign is going very well, as far as I can see."

"Yes, Father, it is," Gaius agreed. "I'm just a little worried by something I saw this morning. You know, there are five of us competing for three vacancies on the *Comitia* ..."

"Yes, I know," Lucius began, then stopped himself. "Sorry, Son, I didn't mean to interrupt. Please go on."

"Well, probably due to your good reputation, a lot of people have had testimonials to my character painted on their walls. My name is all over town!"

"It certainly is!"

"But this morning I was walking around in the eastern part of town, over toward the Nola Gate. You've encouraged me to try to meet as many people as I can, just to introduce myself, perhaps chat a little, and that's what I was doing. But there weren't many people around, so I just walked to the gate and back, and on the way I saw fresh paint on some of the walls. It looked as if my name had been painted over and another one painted on top of it."

"That happens sometimes," Lucius said. "People change their minds."

"Yes, I know, but this is different. It's not just at scattered houses here and there. It's in a large area, as if someone in the middle started it and it spread outward from there."

"That *is* curious," Lucius agreed. "Tell you what. Let's go there in the morning and take a look. Maybe we can find someone who'll tell us what's going on. There are all kinds of possible explanations—rumors, bribery ... Once we know the cause, maybe we can do something about it."

"All right, Father, thank you," said Gaius.

They sat together quietly, drinking a last cup of wine, as the evening shadows filled the *viridarium* and the stars began appearing in the sky above.

◆ ◆ ◆

Lucius and Gaius left the house just after dawn, walking quietly through the almost-deserted streets. The rising sun shone in their eyes and cast long shadows behind them. Birds called sleepily from hidden gardens, their twittering conversations mingling with the gentle splashing of hundreds of fountains. The people of Pompeii loved fountains; even the humblest garden had its little fountain and fish pond, and throughout the city the public fountains, each topped by a grotesque face with water gushing from its large mouth, offered refreshment to passers-by.

As they approached the Nola Gate, Lucius saw for himself what Gaius had described. During the summer, the outer walls of Pompeii's houses were used as giant electoral signboards advertising the good qualities of one candidate or another. It was a simple matter to paint over the previous year's slogans and replace them with new ones. But here the current year's testimonials to Gaius's good name had been painted over, and as soon as the paint was dry, an opponent's name had been painted in the blank space. There was no pattern in the names—each of Gaius's four opponents was given wall-space throughout the neighborhood.

"It's clearly directed at you," Lucius said, his brow furrowed in thought. "But why? Have you any idea where this animosity is coming from?"

"No, Father, I really don't," Gaius replied. "I'm not well acquainted with the other candidates, but I've met them, and they seem pleasant enough. I don't think this is their doing."

"No, I don't either," Lucius agreed. "Someone else has been at work here, someone who wants you to lose the election. Or simply someone who hates you for some reason. Tell me honestly, Son, is there someone you've antagonized? Has something happened that I don't know about?"

"No, Father, nothing has happened, or nothing I'm aware of. Frankly, most people seem to like me, and many respect me, mostly because of you. I can't think of anyone who might hate me."

They had turned around and were walking back along the Via Nola toward home. The city was beginning to come to life; slaves were running errands, and laborers were leaving their houses and setting out for work. On a hunch, Lucius stopped one of them and asked him if he knew anything about the candidates for the *Comitia*. Though obviously in a hurry, the man paused to consider.

"Well, there are those four whose names you see on the walls around here," he said. "There's not much to choose between them. There was another name—Gaius Tullius—but it's been erased. Everyone knows he's a fornicator, probably an adulterer as well. I wouldn't vote for him, nor would anyone I know!"

The man spat in the gutter and went on his way, leaving Lucius and Gaius to stare at each other open-mouthed. Finally Lucius said,

"Have no fear, Son, we're going to find out who's spreading these rumors. But right now I have to go home and meet my clients. In the meantime, why don't you go see if you can find out anything from Julia Felix. She knows everyone in Pompeii and could probably tell you what he or she had for breakfast!"

Gaius did not answer. He was leaning against one of the newly painted walls, head down, a hand over his eyes. Disbelief flooded his senses; tears were not far away. Finally Lucius put an arm around his shoulders and tried to comfort him.

"Gaius, I know this is a shock, but you mustn't let it cause you so much pain. You're young; you haven't been through an election before. There are always rumors about candidates, believe me, though I'll grant you I've never seen walls being repainted. We'll find out who's behind it, and by all the gods, we'll find a way to turn it to your advantage. After all"—he gave a little laugh—"by now everyone in Pompeii already knows your name!"

If he had hoped to get his son to smile at that observation, his hopes were disappointed. Gaius's face could have been carved from stone.

"Come, let's go home and get something to eat," Lucius finally said. "This afternoon I'll go with you to talk to Julia Felix."

XIX
JULY, 77

Julia Felix was sitting in her *tablinum*, chatting with two of her tenants, when Lucius and Gaius arrived. She gave them a knowing glance and turned to the two women.

"Here are two friends of mine, Lucius and Gaius Tullius. Lucius and Gaius, these are my tenants—and friends—Corelia and Terentia."

"A pleasure," they all said at once, and laughed. After a few remarks about the weather, the tenants took their leave.

"Come again soon," said Julia Felix with a smile. "I want to hear more about your wonderful grandchildren!"

After they had gone, and she had waited a moment to forestall eavesdropping, she turned to her new visitors. "You want to know about the walls," she said without preamble.

"Do you know …?" Gaius began eagerly, but Lucius put a hand on his shoulder. "Not so fast, Son. Let her tell us."

Julia Felix leaned back in her chair and looked at them thoughtfully, her glance finally resting on Gaius long enough to cause him to lower his eyes.

"Well. No, Gaius, I can't say I know for sure who's behind this, but I think I can guess."

No one spoke. Gaius looked up expectantly.

"As you know, I meet and talk with a lot of people in the course of my work," she continued. "And I hear rumors. Lots of them. And I know that until a few days ago, everyone was talking about the election and a lot of people were planning to vote for you, Gaius."

"And then something changed," Lucius prompted.

"And then something changed. It began as a whisper but soon turned into a typical Pompeiian gossipfest. Someone has convinced most of the workers of Pompeii that your character is deficient in some way and they should vote for one of the other candidates."

"But who started the rumor?" Gaius asked, his distress causing his voice to tremble.

"As I said, I can only guess," Julia Felix replied. "But I've been told that the rumor started among the laborers working on Clemens's Folly—"

She broke off and smiled. "You won't tell anyone I called it that, will you?"

Lucius laughed, and Gaius managed a little smile.

"Well, the person those men talk to most often, day to day, is Marcus Vettius."

She paused. The two men looked at each other in silence.

"Now, as I recall," Julia Felix continued, "you once got into a fight with that young man over a girl. Is that so?" She looked searchingly at Gaius.

"Yes, but that was a long time ago!" he said. Then he thought for a moment. "It's true we never liked each other, and after the fight, it was worse. Mostly we tried to avoid each other. Once I tried to be friendly, but he turned away. I guess he still doesn't like me, but is that enough of a reason … I mean, from what Father says, no one has ever gone this far before. He would have to *really* hate me, and I haven't done anything …"

"Haven't you?" Julia Felix asked. "What about the girl? Isn't she that beautiful young woman who used to be the Vettii's kitchen maid and now lives in the House of the Faun? Forgive me for saying so, but most people know who she really is."

Again there was silence. There was nothing more to say. Finally Lucius thanked her, and he and Gaius left the Villa Felix. They walked home slowly, both of them deep in thought. Finally Gaius turned to his father, his expression a mixture of frustration and embarrassment.

"How does he know? Our slaves don't gossip, and I believe we've been discreet."

Lucius looked at him in disbelief. "Do you think he couldn't guess? One has only to look at the two of you!"

"But he hasn't seen us together."

"What about your meetings in the public gardens? Could he have seen you there?"

Gaius stopped in his tracks, unable to respond. *Of course! He spied on us there. But I didn't know Father knew about those … What's the matter with me? Father knows everything that happens in our house! Manlius must have told him. I can't blame him; that's his job. So Father must have given his permission before we even …*

With an effort, he turned his attention back to the immediate problem.

"What am I going to do? What *can* I do?"

To his credit, Lucius refrained from commenting that Gaius had gotten himself into this situation and must find a way to get himself out. Instead, once again he put an arm around his son's shoulders and led him home.

"Son," he said, "I'm sorry this has happened, and I can see it's very distressing for you. But you're going to have to be strong. Don't let people know you're upset. Go about your daily activities as if nothing has happened. I'll go talk to Faustus and see if he and Julia can get Marcus to stop spreading his rumors. Then we'll see about reviving your campaign. Don't worry, we'll get through this, and before long you'll be sweating on a bench at the back of the Curia, listening to old men's speeches and wishing you hadn't won this god-cursed election!"

◆ ◆ ◆

That evening Lucius sent a slave to see if Julia and Faustus were home and would receive him. It was not customary to visit someone in the evening unless invited, but he wanted to make sure both of them were home. He did not want to deal with Julia alone.

They replied that he would be welcome, but he could sense the puzzlement behind the response. With a shrug, he threw a *pallium* over his shoulder and walked to the home of Munatius Faustus and the former Julia Vettia, now Julia Faustia. They greeted him cordially and invited him to share a cup of wine with them. It was evident that they had just finished their meal, since they were sitting in the *triclinium* and looking out toward the *viridarium*, enjoying the fading light and the evening breeze just as Lucius and Clodia often did. A shadow passed over his thoughts. *These lovely, quiet evenings! How many of them are left to me?*

Julia had changed radically. While still attractive, she no longer wore her hair in elaborate arrangements or flaunted expensive jewelry. She dressed simply, in plain *stolae* and *pallae* with narrow embroidered borders. And she had refrained from redecorating Faustus's house, though her touch could be seen in some of the furnishings in the atrium and the *triclinium*, and in the statuettes scattered throughout the *viridarium*. These were far more fashionable than anything Faustus would have acquired. *He probably doesn't even notice the difference!* thought Lucius. Faustus had always been more interested in substance than in appearance.

It was obvious that Julia's second marriage was a success. She and Faustus sat together companionably, their conversation ranging over many subjects, with no sign of discord. *What is it that makes a marriage succeed?* Lucius wondered. *Why was Julia unable to get along with Claudius—despite having three children by him, so the problem obviously wasn't in the marriage bed ... And Claudius is so honest and intelligent. But she betrayed him and he divorced her. Now here she is, completely changed, happily married to a man who isn't that different from Claudius. Well, he's different in one way: He doesn't aspire to be a scholar. Maybe* that *was the problem—Claudius was so engrossed in his scrolls that he didn't pay enough attention to her. So she did whatever she could to get his attention—even if it meant destroying the marriage …*

He realized that Julia and Faustus were looking at him expectantly. They had discussed the weather and Clemens's Folly, and were coming around to the election. Since Gaius was a candidate, it was obviously Lucius's turn to comment.

"Actually, that's why I came to see you," he said. "Perhaps you've heard about the walls being painted over?"

They nodded.

"Well, there's evidence—indirect evidence—that Marcus may be behind it. You know he's never liked Gaius—"

"Why should he?" Julia interrupted, a spark of her former self showing. "Gaius gave him a black eye in a silly fight over a slave girl. I always said that girl was nothing but trouble!"

"That girl, Julia, is a mature young woman who serves my wife faithfully and well. Whoever is at fault in this situation, it's not Ariana." Lucius did not raise his voice, but Julia knew she was being reprimanded.

"I can't believe Marcus is even paying attention to the election," Faustus interceded. "He's so involved in Clemens's … Clemens's peristyle. He's in the Forum from dawn to dusk every single day."

"That's just it," said Lucius. "The rumors started among the laborers working on the peristyle. Many of them live near the Nola Gate, where the walls first started being repainted. It's been spreading from there."

"That doesn't mean Marcus started the rumors. And by the way, what rumors are you talking about?" Julia countered.

But Faustus had heard enough. "I believe I understand, Lucius, and I don't think we need to discuss it any further. I'll have a little talk with Marcus in the morning."

Julia was about to protest, but a look from Faustus stopped her. Realizing that if they were to remain friends he must take his leave immediately, Lucius mumbled something about having to go home because Clodia was feeling unwell. Faustus saw him to the vestibule and handed him his cloak.

"Don't worry, my friend," he said. "Leave it to me. Gaius's name will be back on those walls within two days, and his reputation will be restored as well. You have my word."

"I am most grateful," said Lucius, and retraced his steps to the House of the Faun.

◆ ◆ ◆

Faustus was as good as his word. A self-effacing man with many friends and useful connections, he was able not only to convince Marcus that his actions were ill-advised but also to gain the cooperation of Clemens, the *aediles,* and several councilmen in countering the rumors. He even spoke to some of the laborers himself, explaining that whatever they might have heard, he could assure them the accusations were unfounded. Within two days, as he had promised, the walls of Pompeii were once again plastered with testimonials to Gaius's good character.

Marcus had agreed to stop spreading the rumors, partly out of respect for his stepfather but also because he knew he had already caused Gaius considerable distress; the actual outcome of the election did not concern him. Soon his attention was once again focused on his work in the Forum. Construction of the peristyle was progressing rapidly. Already part of it was in use, and the wine and pastry vendors had set up their stalls in the welcome shade.

Thus occupied, Marcus gave no further thought to Gaius and was startled, and rather frightened, when the latter suddenly appeared before him in the middle of the Forum. Involuntarily, Marcus raised his hands to protect his face, but Gaius made no move to harm him. Instead, he took him by the elbow and led him, unresisting, to one side of the square. He stood there, facing him, his expression unreadable.

"Why did you do it?" he asked quietly.

"You know why!"

"No, Marcus, I don't. I know you're aware that Ariana and I are lovers, but why does that concern you?"

"Because you're taking advantage of her. How can she refuse you when she's a slave in your house?"

"She could refuse me if she wanted to. I've never forced myself on her."

"I don't believe you."

"Why don't you ask her yourself? After all, she's your sister."

Marcus did not reply, but turned away, clenching his fists. "You're not supposed to know that," he muttered.

"Marcus, where have you been? It's common knowledge, though I'll admit Ariana and I didn't find out until recently. Listen to me, Marcus. I love her. She loves me. I've sworn to marry her, if it ever becomes possible. We have difficulties enough as it is. Please don't make it any harder for us."

"I still don't believe you. It would have been easy for you to persuade her. She doesn't have any choice, after all."

"All I can say is what I said before: Ask her. And another thing: If you pull another trick like the one you just did, I'll come after you, and I won't waste any time on words. Remember that!"

He turned and walked away without looking back. Marcus stared after him, stunned and confused. He stood still as a flurry of thoughts whirled through his head like a snowstorm. *Ariana's my sister. If she loves Gaius, and Gaius has sworn to marry her, and he makes her happy, I should be pleased. But I hate Gaius. I don't want him anywhere near her. But what if she's really happy with him? She* does *look happy when she's near him. Why should I interfere? I still love her and want to protect her. But what can I do as long as she's a slave in the House of the Faun? Where Gaius is free to do whatever he likes with her …*

Unable to come to an acceptable conclusion, he gritted his teeth and forced himself to put aside his feelings and concentrate on the day's work.

◆ ◆ ◆

Gaius won his seat on the *Comitia*, but he took little pleasure in the outcome. Of the five candidates, he placed second, but one of his rivals placed a close third. The winner of the most votes was Quintus Quartio, the son of Octavius Quartio, one of the wealthiest men in Pompeii. Lucius suspected that Octavius had bought a seat on the *Comitia* for his son by making a massive donation to Clemens's Folly, but he kept his suspicions to himself.

In this way, Gaius's political career was launched, though there would be little activity in the Curia for the next month or two. Pompeii baked under a blistering sun, and its citizens spent their days with only one goal in mind: finding someplace cool. Those who could afford to left the city for their—or their friends'—seaside villas, which lined the shores of the Bay of Neapolis from the tip of Cape Misenum to Surrentum, and abounded on nearby Capreae. Those who remained behind sweltered. The baths were so crowded that they offered no relief; even the *frigidarium* was warm. All the swimming pools in town were in constant use, and there was little exercising in the *palaestra*. Even the gladiators trained only briefly, very early in the morning.

Though he could easily have afforded a villa by the sea, Lucius had chosen not to build or purchase one. He did not like the idea of moving his family and slaves to a different residence two or more times a year, as was customary among wealthy families, considering such a lifestyle wasteful and ostentatious. Besides, he and Clodia loved the House of the Faun, and they had devoted much time and thought to making it a pleasant, welcoming home. So they spent their summers there, escaping the worst of the heat by spending much of their time in the shaded portion of the *viridarium*, soothed by the splashing of the fountains.

Gaius spent many hours in his *oecus*, studying the writings of any scholar, Greek or Roman, who had ever written anything about history, philosophy, or government. In the evenings, he and Lucius discussed and argued over the ideas of Plato and Aristotle, Cicero and Seneca. Clodia rarely joined them; she was suffering from severe headaches. Ariana spent her days sitting by her mistress's bed and placing moist cloths on her forehead, or in the kitchen with the cook, trying to conjure up meals that would appeal to her. Her appetite had vanished; she was subsisting on fruit and water and growing noticeably thinner.

Gaius and Ariana met a few times in their little room, but it was so hot and confining that they spent most of the time simply lying side by side, holding hands and dozing. After the excitement of the election, there was little to talk about, and the prospect of marrying and having their own household seemed as distant as ever. He had tried to interest her in the philosophical ideas he was studying, but without success. "It's much too hot for philosophy," she said, and that was that.

◆ ◆ ◆

Toward the end of August, the heavy blanket of heat began to lift, and a slight breeze occasionally wafted through the streets and alleys of Pompeii. It was still very hot. The city remained almost immobilized, but now there was some faint hope of relief. People began making plans for the coming weeks, inviting one another to dinner not on a specific date but "as soon as it gets cool again." In the countryside, the grape harvest began, a festive time during which the grapes were picked by nimble fingers and pressed by dancing feet, after which the crushed grapes were stored in huge clay containers called *dolia* to ferment. Later the wine would be brought to the city in animal skins and transferred to *amphorae* for sale.

Clodia's headaches became less severe.

Then one day the city woke to find itself engulfed in a storm the likes of which no one had experienced before—or at least could remember. The Sirocco—a hot, humid wind born in North Africa—swept across the sea, thrashing the waters and producing voluminous clouds. The wind began to roar like the lions that were occasionally hunted in the amphitheater—another import from North Africa. When a late, gloomy dawn broke over the city, people looked from their doorways to see the streets filled with swirling clouds of dust. Any object—a jar, a sandal—that had been casually left outside was picked up and smashed against the walls of the houses. Loose tiles flew from the rooftops. The men who drove the carts bringing produce from the countryside abandoned them and sought shelter for themselves and their donkeys and mules; the contents of the carts were scattered by the wind. Fearful citizens peering from their houses stood a good chance of being pelted by vegetables, or worse. Then it began to rain.

Southern Italia normally received a moderate amount of rainfall, enough to provide good growing conditions for olives, figs, and many kinds of vegetables and fruit, and to fill the lakes from which water was carried to towns throughout the region. It rained from time to time, not heavily, but steadily for a few hours; then there would be sunshine for a week or two. But on this day it did not merely rain. The water came down in sheets, then was blown sideways by the rampaging wind. The *impluvium* of the House of the Faun was a large one, but it lacked the capacity to absorb so much water, and before long the atrium was flooded; the little faun appeared to be wading through the water, which rose almost to its knees. The *viridarium* likewise was drenched, many of the statues knocked over. Soon it, too, was no longer able to absorb the quantities of water falling into it, and the marble floors of the peristyle were flooded. Clodia asked Manlius to set slaves to work mopping floors throughout the house, and to try to protect the mosaic of Alexander. He covered the mosaic with a pile of quilts, held down by the heaviest objects he could find, including Lucius's chair from the *tablinum* and a couple of small bronze statues from the *viridarium*. And still the rain came down and the wind crashed through the streets.

The family huddled in the *triclinium* and ate cold food. Throughout the city it was the same. No one dared go outside, for fear of being struck by falling tiles. Though the storm had its origins in a hot African wind, within a few hours the rains had chilled the air, and the citizens of Pompeii, unused to the cold after a long, sweltering summer, were shivering. Slaves were sent to fetch cloaks. No one dared light a brazier, so blankets and quilts were fetched as well. Clodia was wrapped in them from head to toe; Gaius looked at her and laughed.

"You look like an Egyptian mummy!" he said.

With that, the tension in the room dissolved. Gaius and Lucius began making jokes about what certain members of the *Comitia* might be doing at that very moment, some of which made Ariana blush. Clodia asked Gaius if he had read anything about weather in the course of his studies. He told them what little he knew about the Sirocco. Then Lucius asked him if he knew anything about fire-mountains.

"Not much has been written about them," Gaius replied. "Pliny mentions them in his *Naturalis Historia*—you know, that huge book he's been working on for years. Parts of it are circulating among people like Claudius ... Anyway, all he says is that some mountains have fires within them that produce smoke, which comes out through cracks in the rock. That's what causes that plume of smoke we see coming from Vesuvius."

"But some, like Aetna, send out flames and burning rocks and make thundering noises."

"Yes, but Vesuvius isn't one of them."

"I know. But this summer I noticed that the cloud of smoke coming from Vesuvius was taller and wider than before. I wonder if it means anything. Does Pliny say anything about what causes a fire-mountain to throw flames into the sky and send out rivers of burning rock?"

"No. Nor does he mention anything about the amount of smoke coming from the mountain. Maybe the larger amount you saw had something to do with the unusually hot weather."

"Well, let's see what happens when it gets cool again. I'll bet there won't be as much smoke. Vesuvius may be a fire-mountain, but it's never done anything like what Aetna does. People have been farming up there and growing grapes for hundreds of years without any sign of the kinds of things Aetna's famous for."

"True," Gaius agreed. But he could not help wondering whether the two mountains might be more similar than they seemed.

◆ ◆ ◆

The winds and rain continued at full force all day and into the evening, sometimes accompanied by thunder and flashes of lightning—"like snakes' tongues," Ariana said—but sometime during the night they departed as suddenly as they had arrived, and when it was over they had swept away the heat of summer and left a clear sky filled with stars. The morning dawned cool and sunny, and the streets of Pompeii were filled with people strolling, greeting friends and neighbors, and enjoying the first fresh air they had breathed in several weeks. The Forum was crowded with the curious, who wanted to see if the new peristyle was still standing. It was. Once that had been ascertained, they spent the morning exchanging accounts of their experiences during the storm and patronizing the vendors whose stalls began appearing, as if by magic, soon after dawn.

The long, hot summer had come to a sudden end, and during the ensuing weeks the city came back to life. The days were cool and sunny, the nights pleasant. People spent as much time as they could outdoors, commenting on the weather as if they had never experienced anything like it. Gaius happily took his seat as a backbencher at the sessions of the *Comitia*, wisely refraining from speaking, but listening intently. As Lucius had predicted, he found the speeches of his older colleagues largely devoid of meaningful content.

Clodia's health improved with the return of cooler weather, and Ariana had more time for herself. Though Gaius was fully absorbed in his new career, he joined her as often as possible in their little room. The joy returned to their lovemaking, and in the pauses between those passionate encounters, they amused themselves with little jokes about Gaius's fellow councilmen. Neither said anything about their hopes of marriage and a future life together.

XX
DECEMBER, 77

Autumn was beautiful that year. It seemed as if the city had been blessed by the gods, and everyone was happy—though one can never know what takes place in the private rooms of houses or in the secret chambers of people's minds and hearts. Though Gaius, Lucius, Clodia, and Ariana were all very busy, they snatched whatever time they could to dine together in the glorious evenings. One day they hired litters for an outing in the sparkling countryside, stopping by the Vettii's farm so Ariana could greet her mother, and then swinging northward toward Vesuvius to observe the stream of smoke emerging from the top of the huge mountain. Gaius had an odd feeling of dread. Was it possible that the fire within the mountain was growing? Could it heat the rock within until it burst forth and flowed down the mountain like the burning rivers for which Aetna was famous? To allay his fears, he vowed to search for more information about the inner workings of fire-mountains. *Maybe one of those early Greek scientists knew something we don't. Archimedes, perhaps? After all, he lived in Sicily. He figured out why and how things float. He might have figured out why and how Aetna exploded. I'll see if Claudius has anything of his. Or maybe Lucretius, in* De Rerum Natura. *I'll ask Claudius.*

But Gaius had little time to pursue his inquiries. In December, all thoughts and plans centered on the Saturnalia, which would be especially lively as Clemens had ordered games and a grand feast to celebrate the formal opening of the renovated Forum and the unveiling of the new statue of the Emperor Vespasian mounted on a tall horse. Privately, he was hoping the *Comitia* would vote to commission a similar statue of him in gratitude, and he even ventured a hint or two to some of the council's more influential members. Gaius got wind of it and told Lucius, who laughed long and heartily.

"I should have known! There exists no man whose motives are completely unselfish."

"Not even you, Father?"

"Not even me!"

◆ ◆ ◆

As the residents of the House of the Faun were making plans for their own celebration—Manlius would be "king" that year—startling news arrived: Claudius Vettius was taking a new wife.

Claudius had long realized he needed to remarry. His daughters were of marriageable age, and he had no idea how to go about finding appropriate husbands for them. Besides, he had to admit he was lonely. True, he valued the time he could devote to his studies, and by dint of much labor and perseverance he had achieved his dream of becoming a scholar, both in fact and by reputation. And his days were full, what with supervising his wine-importing business (though a manager did most of the day-to-day work), carrying out his duties as a member of the College of Augustales (though these were largely ceremonial), fulfilling his obligations to his clients (which required a great deal of time, if not thought), and, of course, reading his beloved scrolls. But at night he slept alone. He would not sleep with one of the women of the household—*that's caused me enough trouble to last for several lifetimes!*—or even consider visiting the *lupanar.*

Finally he decided to act. He sent a slave to Julia Felix (*She knows everyone!)* with a letter asking her to suggest a potential wife. And, in her typically direct fashion, she sent his messenger back with a definite recommendation: "You could do no better than to marry Cornelia Jucunda."

Through discreet inquiries, Claudius ascertained that Cornelia Jucunda was a widow several years younger than himself who lived in a fine house in Herculaneum and owned a farm and vineyard not far from his own. Never having borne children, she occupied herself with learning all she could about viticulture, often walking through the vineyards with her manager, and was not above tying up a few vines herself. She also—and this was the clincher for Claudius—had studied Greek, and was a devotee of the lyric poets. It was said that she could recite the entire works of Sappho from memory, with an eloquence that left her listeners speechless—at least those who understood Greek.

He sent another message to Julia Felix, asking her to arrange an introduction. Julia, who relished her success as a matchmaker, immediately set out for Herculaneum to persuade Cornelia to allow Claudius to pay her a visit.

It was intended to be a marriage of convenience, but they took to each other almost immediately. After several hours of uninterrupted conversation, spent strolling around her *viridarium* and then through the public gardens nearby, she invited him to share her evening meal. Later, she invited him to share her bed. By the next morning, the plans for their marriage were largely complete.

They would wed at his house in Pompeii, which would be more convenient for most of their guests, but then—to the surprise of his long-time friends—he would go to live with her in Herculaneum. Aurelia and Julilla would stay with them until they married—which would be soon, Claudius was sure, as Cornelia proposed to throw herself into the task of finding husbands for them with the same energy she devoted to all her endeavors. Cornelia's Samnite ancestry would help in attracting potential husbands, and between them they could provide ample dowries for both girls. Once married, the girls would live in their husbands' homes, and the House of the Vettii would be empty. Claudius would arrange for it to be kept clean and would see that any needed repairs were made as it awaited its future occupants—perhaps Marcus, or even Ariana. In a corner of his mind, Claudius harbored the possibility of acknowledging Ariana as his daughter and offering the house to her and Gaius if Lucius ever allowed them to marry. One could never tell what the gods might ordain for the young couple—or anyone else, for that matter.

◆ ◆ ◆

Faustus's advice, his father's remarriage, the pleasure of working at something he did well—whatever the reason, Marcus felt a change taking place within him. His thoughts, which had always chased each other around and around like a puppy chasing its tail, began to settle into a calmer pattern. Gradually he accepted the fact that Ariana was his sister, and he no longer thought of her as a woman whom he wanted but could not have. And he realized that she could do far worse than marry Gaius Tullius, if such a marriage were possible. Though there was no love lost between him and Gaius, it was clear that there was nothing to be gained from trying to interfere any further. Besides, he had more important things to think about—in particular, his first commission (on Phidias's recommendation): to design a new peristyle and *viridarium* for a Roman senator's villa at Stabiae.

◆ ◆ ◆

It was clear and rather cold on the first day of the Saturnalia, but nothing could keep the citizens of Pompeii from thronging to the Forum for the dedication of the peristyle and the unveiling of the statue of Vespasian. As usual, the ceremonies began in the Capitolium with sacrifice and prayer. Then Clemens, wearing a thick woolen toga with a purple border, stood on the steps of the temple and welcomed the populace. In a brief speech, he dedicated the renovated Forum to the city's three protectors: Jupiter, Juno, and Minerva. Then the *pontifex maximus* led a procession consisting of the members of the College of Augustales and the *Comitia*, along with the *duoviri* and other public officials. Lucius and Gaius walked together, and Clodia, watching from a covered litter with Ariana beside her, smiled proudly.

The procession descended the steps of the Capitolium and crossed the square to the statue of Vespasian. There was another sacrifice and further prayer, and the coverings were removed from the statue. The crowd cheered loudly, as much in anticipation of the feast to come as in appreciation of the huge bronze statue on its marble pedestal.

Knowing that not everyone could fit into the Forum, Clemens had arranged for tables of food to be set up at several other locations throughout the city, including the public gardens and the *palaestra*. Many people spent the day wandering from one table to another, feasting happily on sausage pastries and honey cakes. Wine flowed freely, and by evening the streets of Pompeii were crowded with raucous throngs of people in various states of inebriation, some singing, some brawling, some making love in darkened doorways. Long before then, the residents of the House of the Faun had gone home and barred the doors. They would welcome guests later in the week.

◆ ◆ ◆

On the second day, they crowned their "king." Lucius draped Manlius in his best toga and led him to a chair in the atrium, where the entire household had gathered shortly after dawn. Everyone was smiling; Manlius was well liked.

"Hail, King of the House of the Faun!" proclaimed Lucius. He knelt, along with all the others except Clodia, who sat in a chair nearby. After a moment, he looked up and asked,

"And what are your commands for this day, O King?"

Manlius looked around at the expectant faces. Everyone in the household loved this celebration. They loved the change of pace, the reprieve from their usual tasks, the opportunity to visit friends or kin, and most of all the feeling of equality and friendship that permeated the occasion. Had they stopped to think about it, they might have recognized that it was merely a more overt manifestation of the climate that prevailed in the House of the Faun throughout the year. They felt fortunate indeed.

Manlius began by speaking to the five youngest slaves, three men and two women, all between the ages of fifteen and twenty.

"Timon, Quintus, Junius, Tertia, and Claudia," he said, "this is my command to you: You will each tell Ariana your favorite dish and ask her if she knows how to prepare it. If she says yes, you will check to see what ingredients are required, and if we don't have them in the kitchen or the storerooms, you will go to the market and purchase them; Lucius will give you whatever coins you'll need. I can tell you right now that someone will have to go fetch more *garum*, since it's used in almost every dish we serve!"

The young slaves looked at each other and grinned, then turned toward Ariana as Manlius continued.

"Ariana, you'll prepare those dishes, and any others you wish. Gaius, you will assist her. You are commanded to do whatever she asks."

There were winks and smiles all around. Ariana blushed.

"We'll dine early this evening—just before sunset," Manlius went on. "Timon and Quintus, when you come back from the market, you will arrange the benches and tables in the *triclinium* for our meal. Then you'll be free to do whatever you like for the rest of the day—until the evening meal. That goes for the rest of you as well"—he gestured toward the remaining members of the household. "Yesterday I brought home some of the pastries and cakes from Clemens's feast. You'll find them set out on a table in the kitchen. Please stop there and have a bite to eat before you go out."

"Lucius, my command to you is to attend Clodia and do whatever she asks," Manlius said with a smile. "The litter is available—I hired it for the whole week. I suggest you accompany her on a short outing in the morning—just down to the public gardens to take in the view of the harbor and the sea. Then she'll probably want to rest. While she's resting, you'll go to the theater and reserve seats for all of us."

"Oh, I almost forgot," Manlius continued. "Gaius, if you can spare a few moments from your work in the kitchen"—he smiled as Gaius blushed in his turn—"you'll prepare a recitation for this evening. Or—wait, I have another idea. Do you have any of Plautus or Terence's plays?"

"Of course I do!" said Gaius.

"Then I have a further command. You, Lucius, and I will meet in your *oecus* just before the evening meal, and you will assign each of us a role from a scene of your choice. Then, in the interval between the First and Second Tables, we'll act out the scene. If there's a woman in the scene, you'll take that part. So choose carefully!"

Gaius laughed. "I'll obey your command," he said.

◆ ◆ ◆

Ariana was in the kitchen, checking the food supplies and setting out the utensils she would need. She had sent Gaius out for coals. She looked up to see Claudia, the youngest of the slaves, approaching her timidly. It was Claudia who did most of the cleaning in the rooms bordering on the *viridarium*, including the mistress's *cubiculum*. She admired Ariana, who had a higher status among the slaves but was always kind to her. When Claudia had bled for the first time, Ariana had found clean rags for her and sat with her, explaining the nature of womanhood as her mother had done for her.

"Hello, Claudia," she said with a smile. "Have you made your choice?"

"Yes," the girl replied, "but I don't know if you … That is, I haven't eaten it since I came here, but I know you can cook many things …"

Claudia's shyness was getting the better of her. Ariana helped her along.

"Just tell me what you'd like, and I'll let you know if I think I can make it."

"Well," Claudia began, "it's a sweet. I thought we could have it after the meal. It's very good, and it would go well with the wine … we'll be having a sweet wine with dessert, won't we?"

Ariana hid her impatience with a smile.

"Of course we will. Now tell me, what's this wonderful dessert?"

"It's cheese-and-sesame sweetmeats!" Claudia said, returning her smile. "I watched the cook in my former home making them. You boil milk and put flour in it …"

"Oh, I know how to make those!" Ariana interrupted her. "Petronius used to make them when I lived in the House of the Vettii …" She paused, remembering those long-ago days when grumpy Petronius would yell, "Where have you been, girl?" whenever she returned from the bakery with the warm loaves clasped to her chest. Even now, Petronius was busy planning the wedding feast he would prepare for Claudius and Cornelia when they married on the first day of the new year. Then he would go with them to Cornelia's house in Herculaneum. She was surprised to feel tears pricking at her eyelids. She would miss old Petronius.

"All right, I'll make cheese-and-sesame sweetmeats for dessert," she finally said. "We have the flour and oil, and I think we have sesame seeds and honey, but you'll have to get the milk and cheese. Get two *sesterces* from the master and go to the market. Here, take this pitcher. We'll need a pitcher of milk—any kind will do. And you'd better take a large bowl for the cheese—we'll need a soft, sheep's-milk cheese for this. You know, the kind they make on the farms around here, with fluffy curds in a little liquid."

"Yes, I know the kind," said Claudia happily. "Thank you, Ariana!"

One by one they came to her with their requests. Timon wanted bream baked in cheese and oil; Ariana told him he would have to get the fish—a porgy would do if bream was not available—and some hard cheese; she would have Gaius break up the cheese and pound it in a mortar. He would also have to shovel coals into the small domed oven that sat next to the brick-and-tile cooking hearth, which stood at waist height, topped with a gridiron on which were placed the earthenware pots and metal pans used for boiling and frying.

Quintus requested roast kid or lamb, but when she reminded him that neither would be available in midwinter, he changed his request to roast hare.

"Do you think you can catch a hare?" she asked jokingly.

He laughed and said no, but he was sure he could find a good one in the market. "You can find anything there—I could get you a wild boar if you like, or some pigeons, or sausages, garlic, figs ..."

"Just a hare," she said, smiling. "And get some more *garum* while you're at it," she said. "We've got enough onions and herbs, and wine. We'll have to boil the hare and then roast it right away, to make room for Timon's fish."

Quintus grabbed a jar for the fish sauce, went to Lucius to get a few *sesterces*, and dashed off on his errands.

As luck would have it, Junius and Tertia requested celery puree and squash with dates, respectively, and Ariana found that all the ingredients for these dishes were at hand. But she decided to add one or two dishes of her own, and sent the two of them out to buy a couple of small chickens—which Gaius would have to pluck—as well as leeks and some almonds and hazelnuts; she would make a honey nut cake to accompany Claudia's sweetmeats.

Now all I need to do is think of a stuffing for the chicken. Sausage and chestnuts? No, something a little more interesting. Oh, I nearly forgot: We'll need bread!

As soon as Gaius returned with the coals, she rushed to find Lucius before he left with Clodia in the litter.

"Master," she said hurriedly, "I need a few coins for bread."

"Don't worry about the bread," Lucius said. "I'll stop by the bakery on the way back and pick up a couple of loaves."

"That would be very helpful. Thank you," she said. "Would you mind seeing if they have any barley rolls while you're there?"

"Certainly," he replied, favoring her with his sunny smile. "And Ariana,..."

"Yes?"

"Don't try to do too much. We'll be happy with whatever you do!"

"I understand, and thank you. But I'm enjoying this. When I have my own home, I think I'll do a lot of the cooking."

He smiled again and turned away to see to Clodia's needs. It might be many years before Ariana had a home of her own.

◆ ◆ ◆

She planned the meal carefully, determining when she would have to start cooking each dish so they would all be ready at the right time. To her surprise, when Claudia and Quintus returned from their errands they volunteered to stay and help, and she found their assistance invaluable. She set them to chopping vegetables and pounding spices, and sent them to the market for ingredients she had overlooked, or when supplies of honey, oil, or flour ran low. Soon the kitchen was pleasantly warm, and filled with savory aromas and lively chatter. Sometimes Gaius and Ariana paused for a brief kiss, but both were so interested in the planning and preparation of the meal that they took more pleasure in working side by side than in the love play they might have enjoyed had they been alone.

There was no time to make sausage pastries or other appetizers, so Gaius offered to go to the Forum and see what the vendors were selling. He returned with a variety of little delicacies—small pieces of seasoned meat on sticks, dried apricots, honey-glazed shrimps, and, of course, sausage pastries and olives. Then he had an idea.

"Ariana," he said, "suppose I take a blank scroll and write out everything we're having tonight. Then, when we meet in the *triclinium,* I can read it so everyone will know what's coming. I'll also include the entertainment—which reminds me, I'd better go look through my collection of plays to see if I can find a scene to act out, as our 'king' has commanded."

"All right," Ariana agreed. "But don't be long. I need you!"

He came over to her and whispered in her ear.

"I won't be long, my goddess. I need you too, more than I can say."

They gazed at each other with love and hope, and with a quick kiss he went to his *oecus* to look for an unused scroll.

◆ ◆ ◆

The sun was sending its slanting beams into the *viridarium,* illuminating the fountains and reflecting off the columns into the winter *triclinium,* where the benches and tables had been grouped informally so everyone would have food within reach and could chat with one or two others seated nearby. Manlius ordered Lucius to mix the wine and water and fill the drinking cups, and Lucius, after fetching a jug of good Samnite wine from the storeroom, happily complied. He poured some of the wine into a large *krater* and, from a silver pitcher, added enough water to weaken the wine without causing it to lose its flavor. Then he poured a libation to the Lares, seeking their protection for every member of his household.

Gaius produced his scroll and announced the evening's fare:

"The *Gustatio*: sausage pastries, honey-glazed shrimp, grilled mushrooms, olives, dried apricots.

"The First Table: bream baked in cheese and oil, roast hare, chicken with leek and pine nut stuffing, celery puree, squash with dates and ginger.

"For entertainment: a scene from *Miles Gloriosus*. Lucius will play the part of Palaestrio; Manlius will play Sceledrus; and I'll be Philocomasium."

There was a brief silence, followed by giggles.

"The Second Table: honey nut cake and cheese-and-sesame sweetmeats!"

There were smiles all around, and a few shouts of approval from the younger slaves. The level of anticipation was high and rising.

Gaius rolled up his scroll, and he, Ariana, and Lucius passed among the slaves and freedmen, giving each a napkin and a small bowl of water for washing their fingers, and setting baskets of bread and barley rolls on the tables. Clodia and Manlius were seated in the place of honor, at the back of the room near a glowing brazier; Ariana had sent Tertia to fetch an extra shawl for her mistress. Quintus and Claudia went to the kitchen and returned with trays of appetizers. Soon the room was abuzz with chatter as members of the household shared accounts of their day's activities. Some had visited friends or family members in other parts of the city; some had gone for brisk walks outside the gates, reveling in the fresh air and the sight of the harbor below and Vesuvius in the distance.

"Did you notice the plume of smoke coming from the top of the mountain?" Lucius asked.

"Yes, actually, I did," said Timon. "Do you know what causes it?"

Gaius explained that some mountains had fires burning within them that caused smoke to escape through cracks in the rock. He did not mention Aetna, though lately he had been wondering why Aetna was so fearsome while Vesuvius seemed so tame.

It was time for the main course, and Gaius, Ariana, Quintus, and Claudia each went to the kitchen and brought back a platter laden with succulent meat and vegetables. Ariana, hot and tired after her long day in the kitchen, had managed a quick bath and a change of *stola.* Having had plenty of time to prepare the meal, and all the help she needed, she had outdone herself. Smiles and compliments came her way from all sides as everyone in the room reveled in the tasty fare. *This is what it means to be happy,* she thought. *If only it could last forever! If only …* She shrugged off the sadness that, yet again, threatened to creep into her thoughts. This was an evening for celebration.

Now it was time for the entertainment. Gaius had copied each actor's lines on a separate scroll, and now Manlius stood in the space between the tables and the doorway, with the *viridarium* behind them glowing in the pink-and-orange sunset. On each side were oil lamps, which provided enough light for them to read their lines. They did so with gusto, making faces and exaggerating their gestures. Somehow Gaius had obtained an elaborately styled wig—the last resort of some Pompeiian matron whose hair was thinning—and he donned it now, along with one of Ariana's *pallae.* Accompanied by Lucius, he strutted through the doorway, swinging his hips in an exaggerated parody of a woman's walk.

"Remember what I told you, now," said Lucius, in the role of Palaestrio.

"How many times do you think I want telling?" replied Gaius—that is, Philocomasium—speaking in a high-pitched voice.

"The question is whether you're clever enough to do it."

"I've enough cleverness to spare to teach ten innocent girls a few tricks. Go on with your scheme; I'll stay over here."

The room echoed with laughter, and the actors themselves were hard pressed to perform the scene without dissolving into giggles. Passers-by in the street looked at each other questioningly; the House of the Faun was not known for loud revelry. Finally the noise subsided, and Ariana and her two assistants brought in the dessert. Now the room was quiet as everyone enjoyed the sweets, accompanied by some of Lucius's good wine.

Finally someone remembered that they had been planning to go to the theater that evening, but by then no one wanted to leave.

"Let's not go," suggested Lucius. "Why don't we stay here and choose another scene to act out. Gaius, can you suggest something? Perhaps a scene from *Pseudalus*?"

He could and did, and they spent the rest of the evening acting out scenes from their favorite comedies. Finally they were too sleepy to continue, so they contentedly bade one another goodnight.

They did not suspect it then, but it was the last time they would all celebrate the Saturnalia together.

XXI
MARCH, 78

"Father," said Gaius, slipping into Lucius's *tablinum* as the last of his clients departed, "I've finally found something more substantial about fire-mountains. It's in Lucretius's *De Rerum Natura.* I don't know why I didn't think to look there before."

"And what does Lucretius say?" asked Lucius, glad to be distracted from the pile of petitions on his table. They were always the same: requests for exemption from taxes due to age or illness; pleas for manumission of relatives; requests for assistance in finding work as a laborer or as a servant in a reputable household …

"Listen," said Gaius. "Here's his explanation:

> I will now turn to the specific question, by what means that suddenly quickened flame spouts from the stupendous furnaces of Aetna. First, then, the whole interior of the mountain is hollow, honeycombed with basaltic caverns. Next, in all the caves there is air and wind, the wind being produced by disturbance of the air. When this has been thoroughly heated and in its raging has heated the surrounding rocks and earth where it comes in contact and extracted their content of fire ablaze with leaping flames, it wells up and flings itself skyward by the direct route of the gaping throat. So it scatters fire and ashes far and wide, rolling dense clouds of murky smoke and discharging boulders of staggering weight. There can be no doubting that this is the work of wind at its most tempestuous.
>
> Furthermore, along one extensive stretch the sea dashes its waves against the roots of this mountain and sucks back the undertow. From this sea subterranean caverns penetrate all the way to the depths of its throat. It cannot be doubted that by this channel a blend of wind and water from the open sea is forced into the heart of the mountain. From here it spouts out, shooting up flame, volleying stones and disgorging clouds of sand. For at the very summit

> there are *craters* or "mixing bowls," as the Sicilians call them, which we term "throats" or "mouths."

That must be why the Greeks use to say the king of the winds, Aeolus, had imprisoned all the winds in caves beneath Aetna!"

"That's very interesting!" said Lucius. "So winds blow from the sea into the interior of the mountain through subterranean caverns ... or, as the Greeks would have it, are trapped there. Then the fire inside the mountain is stirred up and heats the rock around it ... But if water enters the mountain through the same caverns, why doesn't it put out the fire, or at least prevent it from 'shooting up,' as Lucretius puts it?"

"I don't know. I think there's a flaw in his reasoning, but I'm not sure what it is. Besides, Vesuvius isn't right beside the sea the way Aetna is, so I doubt if there are subterranean caverns bringing wind and water into it."

"Don't be too sure, Son. It's fairly near the sea, and there may be some connection. There are a lot of caverns in this region. Remember the ones on Capreae?"

"Yes, I do. And that beautiful blue light in the ones that open onto the sea. But somehow I think the fire inside Vesuvius, and Aetna as well, has some other cause. Something beneath the mountain—and I don't think it's the wind—makes the fire burn more strongly and heat the rocks around it, and makes that plume of smoke escape from the top of the mountain. Something deep within the earth. I can't imagine what, but whatever it is, it's extremely powerful. There's nothing we can do to stop it if it flares up and shoots fire and ashes from the top of the mountain. It's truly in the hands of the gods."

"Do you really think Vesuvius could start sending out flames the way Aetna does?"

"I think it's possible. Even though the mountain has always remained quiet, just sending a little smoke into the sky, that doesn't mean something couldn't change. Vesuvius looks a lot like Aetna. And did you notice that Lucretius speaks of 'basaltic caverns'? There's basaltic rock all around us; the whole city is built on a huge slab of basalt. Where do you suppose that rock came from?"

"You don't mean to say ...?"

"It's only a guess. But there's something else ..."

"What?"

"Just something I read in a treatise by Vitruvius. You know, the architect. It's mostly about architecture, of course, but he makes some interesting remarks in passing. Among other things ..."

"Among other things, what? Come on, out with it!"

"Among other things, he says he believes fire has always smoldered beneath Vesuvius and in ancient times was spewed out onto nearby fields. He also compares Vesuvius to Aetna, implying that the same thing could happen here."

"Well, Son," said Lucius after a short pause, "as you say, there's nothing we can do about it. It's in the hands of the gods. But while you're here, there's something else I'd like to discuss with you."

"What's that, Father?"

Lucius rose and paced around the room for a moment, his expression troubled. "Gaius," he finally said, "you must have noticed that your mother hasn't been well since last summer. She tries to hide it, but each day she seems weaker, and the cold weather afflicts her almost as much as the heat did. I think she may be in pain, though she doesn't complain. She's spending a lot of time in bed, rolled up in quilts, either sleeping or resting. Or she sits near a brazier, wrapped in her *palla*. She doesn't eat much, though I keep trying to tempt her with little treats, and several times Ariana has made those cheese-and-sesame sweetmeats we enjoyed so much during the Saturnalia."

They both fell silent, remembering that glorious evening.

"If she agrees—and perhaps even if she doesn't—I'm going to call in a physician," Lucius continued. "And Son, I'm going to resign from my position as magistrate. I want to spend more time with Clodia, and besides, it'll give my successor plenty of time to prepare for the election."

Gaius was stunned. The thought of his father not playing a key role in the governance of Pompeii had never entered his mind. *But of course he was bound to retire sometime. I should have foreseen it …*

He was startled to notice, for the first time, that his father's hair was now entirely gray. *When did* that *happen?*

"Father, are you sure you want to do this?" he finally said. "You're the most respected man in the city; everyone comes to you for advice, looks to you for guidance. You're the voice of reason, you …"

"Son, there comes a time for every man to step down, before he becomes too old or unsound of mind. I can't concentrate on my duties while I'm worrying about Clodia. And there are plenty of younger men who are qualified for the position of *duovir*—Vascula, Aper …"

Gaius gave a little laugh. "Not unless they can serve together. Those two seem to think they're twins!"

"Well, I've no doubt the campaign will be an interesting one. And you and I will decide who's the best man for the job and paint his name on our walls!"

◆ ◆ ◆

As winter made its slow traverse toward spring, one day after another dawned cold and wet. The dampness crept into every corner of the house, and no matter how many coals were heaped on the braziers, the rooms were chilly and people shivered. Clodia took to her bed. Ariana spent most of her time sitting beside her, occasionally coaxing her to eat a little barley broth or drink some honeyed wine. Sometimes Lucius came to sit beside his wife and hold her hand. She seemed to diminish before his eyes, and she no longer smiled at him or chatted happily about anything and everything. Little tendrils of fear began curling through his thoughts. *Surely she'll recover when the sun comes out and the days are warmer …*

But she did not recover. Though Lucius called in the best physicians in town, they could not fathom her ailment and there was nothing they could do for her. As the damp, wet days gave way to sunny, windy ones, she grew weaker and weaker. She ate almost nothing, and drank only a little water. By now it was obvious she was dying. Ariana sat mutely beside her, helpless, tears streaming down her cheeks. Lucius, equally helpless, padded around the house, staring vacantly at the paintings and mosaics, eating very little himself. From time to time, he stood in the doorway of Clodia's *cubiculum* and gazed at his wife, who no longer responded; then he would wander away, perhaps to sit in his *tablinum* and rifle through the growing pile of petitions, then push them aside and bury his head in his arms.

For a while, Gaius left the house each morning and hastened to the Curia, but his thoughts wandered and he could not concentrate on the debates. One day he left the council chamber in the middle of a long speech and did not return. He went home and sat in his *oecus*, staring at his scrolls in their buckets along the wall. Then he, like Lucius, went to his mother's room and stood in the doorway. He looked at Ariana, and she shook her head mutely.

On the first day of spring, the wind subsided and the sun shone brightly from a clear sky. The fountains in the *viridarium* sparkled in the sunlight. Lucius wrapped Clodia in her *palla* and carried her into the garden, where he sat on a bench and held her in his arms. She managed a little smile, and laid her head on his shoulder. He bent down and kissed her. "I love you, Clodia, don't leave me," he pleaded.

"I love you, Lucius," she whispered. And then: "Lucius, will you do something for me?"

"Anything!"

"Let them marry!"

He held her close, rocking her in his arms. "I'll speak to Claudius," he finally said.

He carried her back to her bed and covered her with quilts. She smiled again and closed her eyes. He sat beside her and held her hand. Gaius and Ariana joined him. They sat with her all day, saying almost nothing. Manlius brought them bread and olives and a little wine. Clodia remained motionless, with her eyes closed. Toward evening, she gave a little sigh, opened her eyes, smiled gently at them, and was no more.

◆ ◆ ◆

Lucius fell to his knees beside the bed and rested his head beside Clodia's. Gaius and Ariana left him with her and stumbled blindly to their own little room, where they lay in each other's arms and wept. All night they lay there, and in the morning—another beautiful morning full of hope—they rose disconsolately and went to find Lucius.

Lucius sat in his *tablinum*; he had ordered the door slave to turn away all clients. He looked up at them, saying nothing. They went over to him and knelt beside him, one on each side, leaning their heads against his shoulders. He reached around them with his arms and gathered them into an embrace, in which they stayed for several moments, weeping. Finally Ariana went to the kitchen to see if she could find something for them to eat.

Then they began making the arrangements for Clodia's funeral.

◆ ◆ ◆

They washed her, dressed her in her best *stola* and *palla*, and placed her on a couch in the atrium so visitors could pay their respects. Word had traveled fast. They were amazed at the number of people who filed silently through the atrium, walked slowly past Clodia's couch, and then took a moment to express their condolences to Lucius. It seemed as if all of Pompeii had known and loved her. Only then was it apparent that Clodia had been the mainstay of the House of the Faun. In her quiet way, she had befriended everyone she met, be he magistrate, merchant, or laborer. Lucius's clients told him how she had always had a smile or a kind word for them as they waited in the atrium with their petitions. The baker came to the house with several loaves fresh from the oven, saying, with tears in his eyes, that it was the least he could do. People whom Lucius barely knew came up to him and told him—as if he had not known—what a sweet and gentle person Clodia had been, always ready with a greeting, always concerned for their welfare, the most unselfish person in the world. All day the visitors came, and all day Lucius and Gaius stood in the atrium and listened as they spoke in praise of Clodia. Around noon, Ariana brought them some bread and a jug of water. Late in the afternoon, Claudius and Cornelia came over from Herculaneum—how had they heard the news so soon? It turned out that Manlius had sent messages to many of Lucius's friends and colleagues.

Before Claudius left, Lucius took him aside.

"There's something I need to speak to you about," he said.

"I think I know what it is," said Claudius. "Why don't you and Gaius come to our house sometime in the next week or two—after the funeral—when you feel ready …"

"We will," said Lucius. "Thank you."

All that evening and far into the night, Lucius and Gaius accepted condolences. Ariana and Timon offered wine to them and their guests, and Manlius set out baskets of bread and olives. Most of the members of the *Comitia* had come and gone, and still new faces appeared at the door. Finally the last of the visitors departed, and the house was silent. Lucius would not leave Clodia to rest alone in the atrium, so Manlius had another couch set up for him. Ariana and Gaius went to their room and immediately fell into a deep sleep. Sometime in the early morning hours, they woke and made love, then went back to sleep. The sun was high in the morning sky when they rose to find the rest of the household already awake. No one said a word when they emerged sleepily from the room where they had never before spent an entire night together.

The funeral procession left the house a little before noon. The bier on which Clodia lay was preceded by a small group of musicians playing flutes and lyres; Lucius disliked the more usual, and much louder, combination of trumpets and hired mourners. The bier was draped in white cloth with a gold border, and beside it walked Timon and Quintus, bearing torches burning perfumed oil. Lucius and Gaius followed, carrying the *imagines,* wooden busts of the family's ancestors, and behind them walked Ariana and the rest of the household. As the procession wound its way toward the Porta Nuceria, it grew longer as friends and acquaintances, and even some strangers, joined it. When Lucius paused at the gate and looked back, he was amazed to find that almost two hundred people were trailing along behind him.

Outside the gate, in a cleared area between the city wall and the necropolis, was the open space where cremations were carried out. There, after Lucius called her name aloud for the last time, Clodia's body was placed on a pyre and burned. Lucius could not bear to watch this, so Gaius and Ariana led him away, back through the Porta Nuceria to a bench on one side of the nearby *palaestra*. There they sat, looking out over the open area where a group of young men were engaging in a series of desultory wrestling matches. A few tattered sparrows pecked in the dirt near their feet. Again Lucius, seated between Gaius and Ariana, put his arms around them as they sat in silence and waited.

At last Manlius arrived to tell them the ashes had been collected and placed in an urn with the customary coin, ready to be taken to the tomb. Knowing Lucius's wishes, he had also asked the crowd, including the musicians, to disperse. Only members of the household and close friends would be present for the burial.

They made their way to the tomb of the Tullii, which, along with many others, was located in the necropolis that extended for some distance along the road leading from Pompeii to Nuceria. It was a popular location, and tombs belonging to families from all social backgrounds, from freedmen to *duoviri*, were crowded together, interspersed with shops, inns, country houses, and orchards. The styles of the tombs were equally diverse—some resembled small houses or temples, others were simple monuments. That of the Tullii contained a chamber with a set of niches in which the cinerary urns of family members and slaves were placed. They placed Clodia's urn in an empty niche next to the one containing the ashes of the infant daughter who had died so long ago. It was covered with a stone slab pierced by a tube through which liquid offerings could be poured. Lucius would later commission a marble *columella*, a bust of Clodia with an inscription, to be placed in the niche with her ashes. Each year, on her birthday and on the anniversary of her death, he and other family members would visit her tomb and make a small sacrifice there, a libation of wine or olive oil, afterwards holding a feast in her honor.

Lucius knelt on the floor of the tomb while the others went outside to give him some privacy. "Oh, Clodia," he said amid his tears, "why did you leave me? I love you so much! Oh, Clodia, my only love, my wife ... You were the heart and soul of our house—you were always there, you always knew what should be done, and I—I didn't tell you how much I appreciated it, how much you meant to me. Why did you leave me? I can't bear it!" He leaned against the wall below the niche, his head in his arms, sobbing. Ariana and Gaius came back and knelt beside him, resting their heads on his shoulders.

He seemed to take some comfort from this, and after a while he rose, took their hands in his, and walked from the tomb into the sunlight.

◆ ◆ ◆

During the next few weeks, as spring blossomed outside, in the House of the Faun there were people living but there was no life. Daily routines unfolded as usual, but without the friendly chatter and laughter of happier times. Lucius saw his clients in the morning and spent the afternoons reading the historical and philosophical works Gaius recommended; it was something he had always planned to do when he retired, but he derived little pleasure from it now. Sometimes he simply sat in the *viridarium,* listening absently to the splashing of the fountains and remembering how Clodia had enjoyed sitting there, with Ariana beside her. He thought back to the early years of their marriage, when they had planned the garden together and watched as the gardener arranged the plantings, benches, and statues according to their wishes. Gaius worried about him—he seemed to age visibly from one day to the next.

Gaius, though grieving deeply, dealt with his grief by spending many hours outside the house. He threw himself into his fledgling career, taking an increasingly active part in the doings of the *Comitia.* Though he had yet to make his first major speech, he spent a great deal of time with his colleagues, either at the baths or at the many dinner parties to which he was invited; he was rapidly becoming as popular as his father had been. Though Lucius was invited to the dinners as well, he always declined with thanks.

It had been taken for granted that Gaius and Ariana would go on sleeping together in their little room, and for a while they did. But after a few weeks, with Gaius spending most of his evenings elsewhere, Ariana returned to her own *cubiculum.* There she found sleep slow to arrive, and often she would rise during the night and sit for a while in the *viridarium*, gazing at the moon and stars and praying to Hera for guidance. For Ariana had discovered that she was with child.

XXII
AUGUST, 78

Gaius fidgeted uncomfortably as he sat with his fellow backbenchers at the rear of the Curia. In his haste to be among the first to arrive at today's session, he had forgotten the little cushion he usually brought with him. The stone bench felt harder than ever. Nor was that the only reason for his discomfort. The speech he was listening to was more than usually dull—he had no idea what the aging councilman who held the floor was trying to say. And he regretted having left the house in a hurry, without greeting Ariana or finding out how his father was feeling. He had spent little time with either of them lately, unwilling to dwell on the mourning that seemed to cloak the House of the Faun in an unending darkness.

This morning's speech aside, life as a city councilman had become more interesting in recent months. The *Comitia* had indeed voted to commission a statue of Suedius Clemens in appreciation of his efforts on behalf of Pompeii, but Clemens was disappointed by it. It was a good likeness, but it was a typical standing pose, like those of all the other civic leaders lined up on pedestals in the Forum. No equestrian statue for him; one did not compete with emperors, past or present. Of course, there was the pillar that had been set up in the middle of the crossroads outside the Porta Nuceria, which bore an elaborate inscription stating that Clemens, the Emperor Vespasian's envoy in Pompeii, after investigating these events and taking appropriate measures, had restored the public land unlawfully occupied by private individuals to the town of Pompeii. Similar inscriptions had been placed at the Herculaneum, Vesuvius, and Marine gates. But this was not enough for Clemens, and though he tried to hide his disappointment, he gradually loosened his hold on the reins of government and left the *Comitia* to its own devices.

The territory was ripe for the reemergence of factions. In these times of prosperity, many saw an opportunity to further beautify the city, make more extensive repairs to the water system, reinforce the walls, or build a new temple. There were debates about how necessary these projects were, about how to raise the money, and, when it was evident that only higher taxes could produce the needed revenue, about whom and how much to tax. The anti-Samnite faction of past years was reborn, and to Gaius's amazement, it gained considerable momentum as many of the younger councilmen joined its ranks. If there were to be any new taxes, they insisted, the burden should be borne exclusively by the wealthier citizens, not by the laboring class—it should be borne by the *patrones*, not by the *clientes*. And since many of the *patrones* were of Samnite descent, the battle lines were clearly drawn.

Gaius had not yet made his maiden speech, but that day was not far off. He was determined that his first address to the *Comitia* would not be some aimless ramble like the one now droning in his ears. No, it would be meaningful, persuasive. He would marshal his arguments in an orderly fashion, with a beginning, middle, and end, as Aristotle dictated, and with all the eloquence of a Demosthenes or a Cicero, though without the excesses of the latter. But how could he establish a credible presence when his Samnite background was known to all? He would have to appear to support the anti-Samnites' position and then slowly, inexorably, break it down—a task made more difficult by the fact that he actually agreed with some of their ideas …

He looked longingly toward the doorway, beyond which he could see a small section of the new peristyle and part of the Forum square beyond. He could see people passing to and fro—vendors, beggars, citizens greeting one another as they went about their business. *Life goes on.* It was a platitude, but to Gaius at that moment it had the ring of absolute truth. *Life goes on.* But in the House of the Faun life seemed to have ended. Especially for Lucius.

Though he did not speak of it, Gaius was deeply concerned about his father's condition. Lucius was completely lost without Clodia. He had no ambitions, no plans, nothing meaningful to occupy his time. He almost never left the house; occasionally, on an especially fine day, Gaius could persuade him to go for a walk, but even then Lucius insisted on heading north toward the Porta Vesuvio and avoided the Forum, where he might encounter friends and acquaintances, with their sympathetic glances and awkward attempts at condolence, which he could not bear. He continued to visit the baths, but he did so very early in the afternoon, when almost no one else was there.

What can I do for him? Gaius wondered, not for the first time. And again the answer came: *There's nothing I can do. Only time can heal such grief, and even then …*

Finally, thanks to all the gods, the long, dull speech was over, and with it, the day's work. As the councilmen rose from their seats and stretched their stiff legs,

Gaius smiled at his benchmates and made his way to the entrance. Ordinarily he would stay and chat with one or two colleagues, strolling in the shade of the peristyle, perhaps buying a couple of sausage pastries to munch on. But during August the *Comitia* met only occasionally, and only in the mornings; there were no pressing matters to discuss, and no one wanted to be outdoors in the hot afternoons. Gaius headed home, hoping to share a meal with his father. He had a new scroll: Livy's *The Early History of Rome*. It was tough going—Livy loved long, complex sentences—but it was worth the effort. He wanted to tell Lucius about it, perhaps get him to read it as well. Then maybe they could discuss it, compare their impressions, as they had in the old days. *The old days. Days gone by.* Suddenly he found himself close to tears as he realized yet again that the mellow evenings they had spent together, he and his father, his mother and Ariana, were gone forever. It was Clodia, gentle Clodia, who had maintained the balance and harmony of the household. *Without her … Without her …*

He leaned against a wall, buried his face in his arms, and wept.

◆ ◆ ◆

Ariana sat on the edge of her bed, staring at the cup on the table beside her. Alomila had been mistaken: The old woman at the farm was indeed a wise woman, but she kept her secrets to herself and shared them only after a great deal of persuasion. Guiltily, Ariana remembered the gold bracelet—one of Clodia's—she had bartered for the substance she was about to drink. The wise woman had given her just enough pennyroyal for a single dose, and had shown her how to prepare the infusion, but now she was on her own. There was no one to confide in, no one to help her through the coming ordeal.

Her mind wandered back over the years she had spent in the House of the Faun. She remembered the day she arrived, a none-too-clean kitchen slave, and Clodia had introduced her to the wonders of the bath, the comb, and the mirror. She remembered how kind her mistress had always been, how she had given her clean, well-made *stolae* and *pallae* and taught her how to manage her unruly mane of curly black hair. It had been a joy to serve her, and now she was gone.

There had been little for her to do after Clodia's death. She had lovingly cleaned and folded her mistress's clothes and stored them in chests, taken the covers off her bed and aired them, arranged her cosmetics and jewelry boxes on the table nearby, and placed her sandals in a row against the far wall. It was as if she was preparing the room for her mistress's return after a long journey, but this was a journey from which there was no return. Gradually the reality had crept over her, and she had wept yet again as she closed the door to Clodia's *cubiculum*. But she did not lock it. She knew Lucius went in there at night to kneel beside the bed and rest his head on the pillow.

After she had tended to her mistress's things, Ariana had nothing to do. She drifted aimlessly around the house, unable to think clearly, unwilling to approach Lucius and ask about her future. As for Gaius, he was almost never home. She knew this was his way of dealing with his grief, and she understood, but she missed him. More than that, she needed him. Once or twice, they had met in the *viridarium* at dawn, but only long enough for an embrace and a whispered "I love you." Sweet as his words were to her ears, they were not enough. At the core of her being, she knew he truly loved her, but there could be no denying that just now, when she needed him more than ever, he was not there. Little tendrils of anger began curling through her thoughts. *How could I have imagined he would love me forever? I'm just a slave. I can't even read! He's probably given up. Claudius isn't going to help us, nor is Lucius, and he doesn't want to talk about it any more. He's not just avoiding the house because it reminds him of Clodia. He's avoiding* me.

Eventually she wandered to the kitchen, the most familiar part of the house and the only place she could find sympathetic company. She began helping with the everyday work of chopping vegetables and stirring pots. Remembering their Saturnalian feast, the younger slaves occasionally asked her to prepare something special, provided the cook would not mind. He did not mind at all. The more work Ariana did, the less there was for him to do. And so, gradually, with no opposition, Ariana took over the cooking and began preparing the meals, often assisted by Claudia and Timon. They were a compatible threesome, and soon they had reorganized the kitchen and established a routine that resulted in tasty dishes for everyone in the household. Ariana took special care with Lucius's meals, trying to entice him to eat more by serving him carefully seasoned meats and fish and the freshest vegetables she could find. But he ate very little.

In the afternoons, she usually had a couple of hours to herself, which she spent outdoors despite the heat. She was a familiar sight in the streets of Pompeii, striding along, always wearing the straw hat Manlius had found for her. She explored parts of the city she had not seen before, pausing to peer through open entryways into the gardens of houses large and small, with their varied arrangements of fountains and statuary. It dawned on her that every homeowner in Pompeii was trying to re-create, on whatever scale was possible, one of the luxurious villas that lined the shores of the Bay of Neapolis. Even the smallest house might have a fountain set into the back wall of a tiny *viridarium*, a little jet of water framed by mosaics of birds and flowers.

Sometimes she went to the public gardens and sat on the bench she had shared with Gaius. She would gaze out over the busy scene below, where fishing boats were unloading the day's catch, past the waves splashing against the rocks, and across the wide bay to the distant horizon, where sky met sea in a purple haze. She would lose herself in that mist, her mind empty for a time, until finally—perhaps as a result of some shift in the nearby shadows, or some sound calling her back—she would come to herself. Then, with a sigh, she would rise and make her way home, stopping by the market on the way for some delicacy to include in the evening meal: figs one day, dates another, perhaps an octopus or a hare, depending on the season.

It was about six weeks after Clodia's death that she began feeling sick in the mornings. She noticed that her breasts were sore and somewhat enlarged. She knew what this meant, yet she continued to expect that her monthly courses would begin in just another day or two. She had lost track of time, and could not remember the last time she had bled. Finally she knew there could be no doubt she was pregnant. She kept a pot in her room so no one would see her vomiting.

She could not obtain the pennyroyal without visiting the farm, and her next visit was some weeks away. She thought of asking Lucius if she could go sooner, but decided against it. He would ask her if something was wrong, and she did not want to disturb him. Nor did she tell Gaius. She could not imagine how he might react. He might blame her for not taking suitable precautions—though now that she thought about it, she must have become pregnant the night after Clodia died, when she and Gaius made love, half asleep, just for the comfort of it.

So she had waited until she could visit the farm.

Now she sat on the bed and looked at the cup of pennyroyal. She did not want to bear this child—or did she? Could she conceal her condition long enough to allow Lucius to recover from his grief, so she and Gaius could speak to him about their long-delayed marriage? She thought not. It was going to be difficult enough without a child in the mix. And another thing: Even if Lucius finally allowed them to marry—and provided Claudius acknowledged her as his daughter—there were bound to be delays, and her child would be born a slave. She could not bear the thought.

She reached for the cup and drank the infusion.

An hour later, Tertia found her in the latrine, doubled over, her body racked by cramps. Young as she was, Tertia knew something about the world. She guessed what was happening and, without a word, helped Ariana to her feet, gave her a damp rag to wipe herself with, and accompanied her to her room, where she helped her into her bed and sat with her until the pain began to subside.

◆ ◆ ◆

The dog days of August had arrived, and the *Comitia* was no longer in session, even in the mornings. Gaius found himself at loose ends. In the morning, he wandered around the Forum square, stopping now and then to greet an acquaintance or chat with a friend. But there was little to chat about. The city was wrapped in its summer torpor.

He spent an hour or two at the baths, ending with a swim in the pool. Somewhat refreshed, he sat on a bench in the shade to rest; a slave brought him some water. It was early in the afternoon, and no one he knew was there. Sitting half-asleep on his bench, he opened his mind to thoughts he had long pushed to one side: his dear mother, gone; his father, sick with grief; Ariana ... *Ariana, Ariana. What must she be thinking? But I couldn't help it, I just had to get out of there. I hope she'll understand. Oh, I'm sure she will; she knows how much I love her. I know, I haven't been there for her lately. I meant to pay more attention to her, but ... But what? Am I just making excuses? Could it be that I don't really love her? No, that's ridiculous! I just haven't been myself since Mother died. I'm sure she'll understand ...*

These thoughts, and the underlying guilt, spurred him to act. He headed straight home and sought out Ariana in the kitchen, but she was not there. Timon and Claudia were preparing the evening meal, and something in their faces when they looked up at him made him uneasy.

"Do you know where Ariana is?" he asked them.

"She's in her room," said Claudia. "She's not well."

He turned on his heel and ran to Ariana's *cubiculum*. There he found Tertia, who had fetched some water and a cloth and was wiping Ariana's forehead. Ariana lay limply on the bed, the covers thrown off, her face flushed, yet pale. He nodded to Tertia, who handed him the damp cloth and left the room.

He sat beside the bed and stroked Ariana's forehead.

"I'm here, my love," he whispered. "I'm here."

◆ ◆ ◆

She had waited too long. The wise woman had warned her, but she had not heeded the warning. There was a little bleeding and a great deal of pain, but at the end of three days Ariana knew she was still with child. She did not tell Gaius, allowing him to believe she was suffering the ill effects of eating tainted food, coupled with exhaustion caused by too much activity in the hot weather. Why?

She did not know herself. He stayed with her throughout her illness, soothing and comforting her and apologizing for having spent so little time with her during the previous weeks. But a kernel of anger remained deep within her. She could not explain it; perhaps she blamed him for her condition, perhaps she felt that his apology was not enough to make up for her loneliness and distress. All she knew was that, while she still loved him, she could not remain under the same roof with him unless they were married. And that prospect seemed no closer than ever.

Neither Gaius nor Ariana knew of Lucius's final promise to Clodia, a promise he had yet to honor. He had intended to visit Claudius not long after her funeral, to see what could be done. After all, Claudius's two daughters were betrothed, and Gaius's career was flourishing. And Claudius had sent a slave to tell him he would be welcome any time. He understood that Lucius did not feel ready to spend time in company, but perhaps he would like to spend an afternoon with his old friend, looking over his latest literary acquisitions and borrowing whatever he liked. But Lucius kept postponing the trip. He was weighed down by lethargy; his mind was clouded. His health was beginning to suffer, despite Ariana's efforts to entice him to eat more and Gaius's attempts to persuade him to accompany him to the Forum or the baths.

Time passed, however, and the heat diminished. Early one morning, Lucius heard the patter of rain on the roof tiles, and looking out from his *cubiculum* he saw the leaves in the garden glistening; a cool, moist breeze played around the peristyle, and he felt refreshed. For the first time in many months, he thought about the day ahead and not about the years past. He realized he had been neglecting his family and friends, that they cared for him and he for them. It was time to get on with his life, and in particular to honor the promise he had made to Clodia on the day of her death.

You're right, my love, he thought. *They belong together, and it's high time I did something about it.*

He dressed and went to his *tablinum* to receive his clients as usual; Ariana brought him some bread and olives. He thanked her with a smile. She smiled back, pleased to see he was himself again, and went about her work.

When the clients had departed and Lucius was rolling up the last of the petitions and placing it in a pile for later consideration, Ariana came in again, bringing some wine and a jug of water. Again he thanked her, but this time she did not return his smile. Instead, she remained standing opposite him, looking at him with an unusually serious expression on her face. He sensed that she had something important to tell him, though he could not guess what it might be.

"What is it, Ariana?" he asked.

"Master …" she began.

"Please, you know you can call me Lucius!"

"Lucius … I have a favor to ask of you."

"I'll be happy to do whatever I can."

"I'd like to leave the House of the Faun and go live with my mother."

He was stunned. It was the last thing he could have expected.

"But why, my girl? Haven't you been happy here?"

"I've been very happy here, and I wish I could stay. But I'm with child, and I want to be with my mother, who can care for me and help me when the baby is born."

Lucius was even more stunned than before.

"With child?"

"Yes. About four months."

"Have you told Gaius? No, you can't have, he would've come straight to me. Why haven't you told him?"

"I didn't want to trouble him. He has more important things to worry about. And besides, it wouldn't make any difference. Unless we can marry, I can't go on living here."

Lucius was silent for a while, considering her words. He had to admit she was right.

"Gaius will be very upset."

"He'll recover."

He was taken aback by her apparent lack of fear or sentimentality, but he admired her strength of will. And he knew she was right about Gaius. He would be frantic at first, but in time he would understand that Ariana had made the right choice.

"I'm going to go visit Claudius soon," he finally said. "I'll ask him to accept you back into his household. With Clodia gone … Though I must say you've been doing a wonderful job in the kitchen. I'll certainly miss your cooking!"

She merely nodded. She had nothing more to say.

"Well," Lucius continued, "you may as well go whenever you're ready. I'm sure Claudius won't object. And Ariana …"

"Yes?"

"Thank you for … Thank you."

She shook her head sadly, and he could see tears starting from her eyes. Without meaning to, he stood up and opened his arms. She came to him and rested her head against his shoulder. He held her a moment; then she pulled away from him and left the room. He sat down again, staring blindly at the pile of petitions. He really would miss her.

◆ ◆ ◆

She left the house in the early afternoon, taking only the *stola* and sandals she was wearing and the mirror and comb Clodia had given her. Despite the distance she had to cover before nightfall, she went on foot. She wanted to breathe the fresh air and enjoy her first views of the countryside in several months. Once she reached the farm, she knew she would be set to work. She hoped she would be allowed to help out in the kitchen. She was also looking forward to being with her mother for more than a few hours. She gave little thought to how Gaius would react when he discovered she had gone.

As she walked, she found herself humming in time with her steps. A flock of swallows wheeled in the sky above her, and the trees and bushes, still damp from the morning's rain, shone in the sunlight, which was becoming stronger as the clouds dissipated. Ariana walked more quickly, a spring in her step. She felt as if she were returning home, not leaving the home in which she had lived for over ten years. She felt strangely happy. Whatever might lie ahead, she was shedding a heavy burden of care and distress. She would be with her mother; she would have her child; the rest was for the gods to decide.

XXIII
OCTOBER, 78

Ariana settled easily into life on the farm where she had lived as a child. After a week or two, she felt as if she had never left. She and her mother were glad to be together again, and Alomila did everything she could to ease Ariana's transition to a considerably harder life than the one she had enjoyed in the House of the Faun. There was no question of her working in the fields, but she remained a house slave and was expected to behave as such and to perform whatever tasks were required of her. Before long, however, she had convinced Publius, the manager—and the cook, an aging freedman named Sextus—that the best place for her was in the kitchen, and it was there that she spent her days, rising before dawn to prepare porridge and bread for the field workers, then helping the cook with the meals for the house slaves. The work of maintaining the kitchen and pantries fell to her, and she spent much time rearranging the system for storing foods and utensils so the items used most often would be closest to hand. As she did this, her thoughts strayed to Claudia and Timon, who had so happily assisted her in what she was beginning to think of as her "other life," and she realized she missed them very much. She had no such help here, but she did have her mother's love and care, and the respect of the other household slaves—especially after they had tasted some of the simple, but well-seasoned, dishes she prepared with fresh-picked vegetables from the kitchen garden and new-laid eggs from the henhouse. As time passed, she found she enjoyed the challenge of inventing new dishes using the resources available to her—not only vegetables and eggs but also olives, cheese, figs, grapes, and occasionally a newly killed and plucked chicken. Rarely were other forms of meat consumed on the farm; the livestock was reserved for the household in Herculaneum. True, the field workers sometimes trapped hares or pheasants, and in recompense they were allowed to share the resulting meals. For many days after sampling Ariana's roast stuffed pheasant, they greeted her with broad smiles each morning.

Claudius visited the farm occasionally, and on one of those visits, Ariana shyly approached him and asked if she could make a suggestion having to do with the kitchen. He paused before answering, taking in the sight of a mature, graceful woman, her belly swelling gently with the child she carried. *My grandchild* ...

"Certainly," he finally said. "What's your suggestion?"

"As you may know," she said (though he had probably never noticed), "there's no way for heat and smoke to escape except through the doorway, so when we're roasting something or cooking for many people, the room gets very hot and the smoke stings our eyes. Would it be possible to make an opening in the ceiling so the smoke could go out that way? Perhaps something could be done to keep the rain out, a little tile roof over the hole ..." Her voice trailed off, and she blushed. Sometimes she forgot she no longer held the privileged position she had enjoyed in the House of the Faun. Here, she was a kitchen slave. It was not her place to make suggestions to the master.

But he dispelled those feelings with an enthusiastic response. "Ariana, that's an excellent idea! Why didn't we think of it before? I'll have it done right away. And thank you for suggesting it."

They smiled at each other and went their separate ways.

◆ ◆ ◆

On the pretext of searching for mushrooms in the woods beyond the fields, she was able to resume her daily walks, though in a completely different landscape. She soon became familiar with the area—the hills, streams, and woods, the best blackberry bushes, the damp spots where mushrooms thrived. Taking a basket with her, and always wearing a straw hat—one her mother had found for her when she missed the one Manlius had lent her—she greeted the workers as she walked along the paths separating the various fields, some planted with vines and olive trees, others with barley and spelt, still others with rows of beans, and the lowest, marshiest ones with sweet cabbage, a local delicacy. Some fields were left unsown so they could "rest." The wooded areas bordering the farm were owned by Claudius and Cornelia, but they left them standing except for an occasional harvest of firewood. There, Ariana could be alone with her thoughts and her memories.

She had not forgotten Gaius, nor did she doubt his love for her or hers for him. *Someday, somehow,* she thought from time to time, but then shook her head and went on with her daily routine. As she often told herself, it was in the hands of the gods.

It was on a sunny, blue-skied day in mid-October that she saw him standing at the far edge of the cultivated portion of the farm, where a cart track divided the fields from the woods. He was dressed only in tunic and sandals, it being too warm to carry a *pallium*, even thrown over a shoulder. She knew immediately that it was he; his sandy hair gave him away, as well as the white linen of his tunic, much brighter than the gray-brown homespun of the field workers. She stopped, shifting her basket from one arm to the other, needing a moment or two to slow the beating of her heart. Then she approached him, pretending at first that she did not see him, then glancing toward him with recognition, then finally dropping her basket and running until they met and fell into each other's arms.

◆ ◆ ◆

"Oh, Ariana, why? Why did you leave me? When I got home and found you gone, I couldn't believe it, and when Father told me about the baby I was so shocked! Oh, Ariana … I wanted to run after you right away, but he persuaded me not to. He said you needed to get away, you needed some time … I was so upset, I said things I shouldn't have, but he … he held me and kept on talking to me. He kept saying it was your decision, you knew what you wanted, I should leave you alone. And after a while, I saw he was right, you were right, things couldn't go on the way they were—except I didn't know about the baby. If only you'd told me!"

He was practically babbling, and tears were streaming down his cheeks. She drew away from him and held his face between her hands, looking into his eyes.

"Listen to me, Gaius," she said, her voice calm and strong. "Listen to me! I love you, I'll always love you, don't ever doubt it. I wasn't running away from you. I simply couldn't go on living there. How could I have stayed there? Even with loose clothing, I couldn't have kept my condition secret very long … and then people would be talking about me … about us. Your father would be embarrassed. And don't forget, I'm still a slave. A slave who's with child by the master's son. People would wonder why I wasn't sent away. Think of all the gossip. I couldn't stay inside the house all the time, and even if I did, someone would tell someone else, and it would spread, and soon it would be all over town. Besides, a lot of people know I'm really Claudius's daughter. How would *he* feel? He'd probably be embarrassed too, and then would he be willing to free me? This way I can have the baby here, with Mama to help me, and the child will grow up here, among people who love him, and he'll be healthy and happy, and no one will point a finger at him and whisper about him behind his back."

"But why didn't you tell me?"

"I don't know, Gaius; I don't know. I suppose I was afraid you'd go straight to Lucius and Claudius and demand that we be allowed to marry immediately. But we both know that's not going to happen, at least not now. So my baby will be a slave. I couldn't bear the thought, not while I was living in your house almost like a freedwoman. Because I have to say I'm grateful to your mother … to your parents … for their kindness, for not treating me like a slave. But I'm still a slave, and here it doesn't trouble me so much. Here, I can just do the work of each day and wait for my baby to arrive, and spend time with my mother, and sometimes enjoy walking in the fields or the woods. It's not a bad life, really …"

"I have to admit it seems to have done you good," he said, reaching out to feel her rounded belly. "You're more beautiful than ever. I mean it! Oh, Ariana … But let's not stand here any longer. People can see us. Let's go find a place to sit, maybe in the woods over there."

"That's where I was headed anyway," she assented. "I was going to get some mushrooms. Come with me. I can't stay long, though."

They found a clearing where the grass was dry enough, and sat with their backs against a large tree. He put an arm around her and kissed her. For a while they said nothing, leaning against each other and looking at the vista they could glimpse between the trees. A downward-sloping hillside, more fields and woods, and finally the sea.

"This is a beautiful place," he finally said. "I can see why you like it here. But oh, my love, I miss you so much! I would have come to find you a long time ago, but Father insisted you didn't want me to come after you …

"He was right. I needed some time to adjust to … to everything. But I'm glad you came, Gaius. I've missed you too. I wish … Oh, never mind."

"I know. You wish things were different. So do I. But listen, Ariana. Father's gone to Herculaneum to see Claudius a couple of times. They're talking things over. After all, this"—he patted her belly—"this'll be their first grandchild! It may still take some time, but Ariana, my love, now they're both on our side! Father will agree to our marriage if Claudius acknowledges you as his daughter, and he seems willing to do so after Aurelia and Julilla are married. Then of course he'll find a way to arrange for your manumission, even though you aren't yet thirty. So you'll be free, and so will our child. There's still the question of restoring your free birth so you can be a citizen rather than a freedwoman, but Claudius promised me he'd look into it."

She looked at him mutely, hope glowing in her eyes. Then he held her as the tears flowed.

◆ ◆ ◆

In the ensuing months he came to see her once or twice a week, and they finally had a chance to walk together through the countryside and enjoy the juicy sun-ripened blackberries. *It's what I always dreamed of doing,* she reminded herself, even though in her dream she had not been a slave. Their love became a deeply rooted thing; in the few brief hours they spent together, they shared their innermost thoughts and feelings. Though at first they had made love hungrily, as if to make up for lost time, as time went by they felt less need for physical contact. It was enough just to be together.

As the days slid gradually from summer to autumn, they would walk for a while in the golden afternoon light. Then they would find a shady spot and sit, leaning against a tree or a boulder. Then, with an arm around her shoulders, he would tell her about everything he had seen and done in the preceding few days. With the arrival of cooler weather, the *Comitia* was back in session and the usual round of dinner parties had begun. He amused her with snippets of gossip overheard at the dinners, but when she asked him about his activities in the *Comitia,* he grew serious.

"You know," he said, "this is what I've always wanted, ever since I was a child. I wanted to be just like my father. I admired him—still admire him—so much, and I hoped I could someday be as influential and respected as he is. To be able to do some good, to prevent shallow men from making harmful laws …"

"And now?" she asked, hearing the uncertainty in his tone.

"And now I'm not so sure. I'm not Father, I don't have his skills, his persuasiveness—"

"But Gaius, you're young. He has many years of experience; you're just starting out."

"It's more than that, Ariana," he said, leaning his head back and looking up through the lattice of leaves above them, still mostly green, but with touches of yellow and orange. *It's too beautiful, too beautiful,* he found himself thinking. *It can't last*—though what exactly could not last was unclear. After a moment, he turned to face her.

"I think I may have made the wrong choice," he said. "Understand: Father didn't insist I go into city government. I was making my own choices. And I was comfortable with those choices. Until now."

"Something must have happened to make you feel this way. What is it?" she asked. He was gazing up through the leaves again, entranced by the patterns they formed and re-formed as the passing breezes disturbed them.

"It's my speech," he finally said. "I worked on it all summer. I used up so many scrolls, you can't imagine. I threw them all away. It's just no good. And I have to come up with something very soon. It's expected of me. Not just because I've been a councilman for a year now, but also because I'm the son of Lucius Tullius."

She turned and kissed him on the cheek. "It sounds as if you're trying too hard," she said. "You need to forget about that speech for a while. Listen—" she gently put a hand over his lips as he began to protest. "Here's what I think you should do. Don't try to write anything for—oh, about ten days. Don't even go into your *oecus*. Don't talk to Lucius about it, or your colleagues. If they ask, tell them you're thinking about it and it'll be ready soon. And spend the next ten days doing something else: Go to the *palaestra* and the baths, go for walks (without me, I'm too slow). Oh, I know what you could do: Go out the Porta Vesuvio and walk north; see how far you can go up the side of the mountain. I'll bet you can see all of Pompeii from there, and Herculaneum and Nuceria and Stabiae as well. Then come back here and tell me all about it."

"Ariana—"

Again she stifled his protests, this time with a kiss that held within it a world of promise. He responded in kind, and before long his worries and doubts evaporated in the warmth of their embrace.

◆ ◆ ◆

Ariana's suggestion was a good one, but Gaius did not follow it. Instead, he continued to struggle with his speech, spending his mornings in the *Comitia* and his afternoons in his *oecus*, followed by a quick trip to the baths. Finally, by mid-October, he had something he could live with, though he still was not entirely satisfied with it. It was clear and concise, well reasoned, with a logical flow of ideas supported by convincing arguments. But it lacked passion. And he had to admit he lacked passion as well. *In truth, I don't really care who pays which taxes. No matter how hard I try, I can't make myself care. But I've* got *to get this over with.*

Gaius's maiden speech was not a success. He argued—convincingly, he thought—that it was in the best interests of *all* the people of Pompeii to be able to enjoy beautiful temples, theaters, and monuments, to bathe in well-tended baths with athletic facilities and swimming pools, to walk and play in spacious public gardens, and to avail themselves of all the other amenities of a prosperous city. The costs of building and maintaining those facilities and amenities should be shared by all, even servants and laborers, because all would have access to them. A system of taxation should be devised that would require all citizens to contribute something, but would place the lightest burden on those who were least able to pay. Even if they paid only a few *sesterces*, they would still have a stake in their city. The wealthy should pay more—there should be a tax on the luxury items only the wealthy could afford: the jewelry, the cosmetics, the imported wines, spices, and other delicacies. It should not be too difficult to devise such a system—there were highly trained accountants and clerks in the magistrates' offices who could be assigned to work on it; he was confident they could come up with a good plan before the end of the year, one that would be acceptable to all and could be put into effect on the first day of the new year. Before very long, the public treasury would contain enough funds for all the projects his colleagues had proposed.

He had hoped to unite the opposing factions, and in that at least he succeeded: They were united in their opposition to his proposals. It was all very polite, of course—one did not intentionally antagonize the son of Lucius Tullius. But one after another, Gaius's senior colleagues stood and spoke against his plan. The anti-Samnites could not condone any addition to the burdens already borne by the poorer citizens; the Samnites were categorically opposed to any kind of luxury tax. Neither side addressed his notion of all citizens having a stake in the well-being of their city—it seemed to have had no impact at all. Finally Vascula gained the podium and made a gracious speech thanking Gaius for his valuable contribution to the council's debates and suggesting the meeting be adjourned.

◆ ◆ ◆

Gaius was distraught. "Father, where did I go wrong?" he asked that evening over a light dinner.

Lucius was sympathetic. He knew exactly how his son felt; it had happened to him, too, early in his career.

"Son, it was an excellent speech," he said. "There was nothing wrong with it. You simply made the same mistake all beginning speakers make: You concentrated entirely on yourself and your ideas; you didn't consider your audience."

"My audience? The *Comitia*? No, Father, it can't be. I was thinking about them all along. I wanted to put an end to the disagreements that have taken up so much time and get on with the business of governing. There are lots of things that need to be done, and the *Comitia* does nothing but argue about who's going to pay for them. I offered them a fair solution, but it seems they weren't even listening."

"They probably weren't. Because you weren't really speaking to them, you were speaking to yourself."

"Father!"

"No, listen to me. You have to put yourself in their place. What did any individual member hear when you were laying out your arguments? Each one heard something he was strongly opposed to. And as soon as he heard it, he stopped listening. He may have looked as if he was listening, but behind that polite face he was thinking about other things. He had already decided to oppose you."

"I can't believe it. It's a reasonable plan, it really is."

"Of course it is. But you'll have to find some other way to present it. They need to feel as if they're *getting* something, not *giving up* something. I know it's difficult, but if you want to persuade people, you have to understand them. That means putting yourself in their place, trying to think the way they think, to have the same feelings, desires, and fears. These things can't be learned by reading philosophical works. You need to put aside your scrolls for a while, Son, and spend more time listening to people. Go out into the city and talk to anyone you meet. Ask him about his family, his work. Listen to what he says. You'd be surprised how much wisdom lies hidden in the words of a sausage vendor in the Forum or an attendant at the baths. You should also talk to women—after all, they're the real rulers of their households. Talk to Julia Felix; she's one of the wisest people I know. And, Son ..."

He paused, remembering the early years of his career. How miserable he had felt after each setback, how exasperated he had been—still was—when selfish interests interfered with his efforts to advance the public good. It was all so long ago.

"Yes, Father?"

"Don't worry, you'll learn fast, and before long you'll be the best speaker in the *Comitia*. Just remember: You can catch more flies with honey than with vinegar."

Gaius thanked him with a smile, but inwardly he grinned. *He hasn't changed,* he thought happily. *He hasn't changed at all!*

◆ ◆ ◆

He went to see Ariana, taking with him a couple of Clodia's *stolae* and a good warm *palla*. Ariana protested, but he insisted she accept them. "Father wants you to have them, and I know Mother would have sent them herself if she'd been alive. But then, of course, you wouldn't have left."

"Perhaps, perhaps not," she said. "Let's not talk about that. Have you made your speech to the *Comitia*?"

He told her the whole story, and she took him in her arms and held him a long time. Cooler weather had arrived, and they spent less time outdoors. They lay together on her narrow bed in a little room beside Alomila's, warmed by a brazier full of coals. A curtain was drawn across the doorway, but the kitchen and pantry were nearby and they could hear everything that went on there—the chatter of the slaves, the chopping of vegetables, the banging of pots on the stove, the splashing of water in the basin. Soon she would have to get back to work, supervising the preparation of the evening meal. And sunset was earlier these days; he would have to make part of his homeward trip in darkness.

He sat up and looked down at her. She was lying on her back, her belly pleasantly round, her hair spread around her head like a shining cloud. Her dark blue eyes gazed up at him with love and concern. She raised her arms to him and he bent over and kissed her.

"I'll come again soon, my love," he said. "Be sure to keep yourself warm and eat well. I want you to be strong and our baby to be healthy."

She smiled. "Don't worry about me, Gaius. I'm eating very well. And when I go out, I'll wear the warm *palla* you brought me. My thanks to Lucius. And to your mother, whom I loved as if she were my own."

They looked at each other with tears in their eyes, and exchanged a lingering kiss. Then he set off for the House of the Faun as the sun drifted downward toward the sea and the shadows lengthened.

◆ ◆ ◆

Winter came early that year; by mid-November there was a chill in the air, and for much of November and early December a cold rain fell. Ariana gave up her afternoon walks and spent almost all her time indoors. There was much to do: Meat had to be smoked or salted; vegetables preserved in honey and vinegar; lentils, nuts, figs, and olives prepared for storage. There would be little fresh food for several months.

Though she was growing larger and heavier each day, Ariana helped with this work as much as she could. She could not stay on her feet very long, but there were many things she could do while seated. So she sat on a stool beside the kitchen table and shared jokes and stories with the cook and the kitchen slaves. She was no longer self-conscious about her relationship with Gaius, but she did not say much about him. *I know they're curious*, she thought. *Too bad!*

As the Saturnalia drew near, she spent much of her time preparing some of the dishes for the celebration—a more muted affair on the farm than in town, to be sure, but still a festive event, a respite from work and a time for feasting. With Alomila's help, she made sweet buns, roast hare with herb sauce, thrushes stuffed with crushed olives, ham in pastry, fried squash, beets with mustard, and cakes filled with honey and soft cheese. These, accompanied by a good local wine, went far to make the occasion a happy one. The field slaves joined the household staff for the day, and small gifts were exchanged. Work on the farm could be halted only briefly, however, and on the following day everyone was back at his or her assigned tasks.

The Saturnalia was observed in a more perfunctory way at the House of the Faun. Lucius gave the usual gifts to the members of the household and allowed them to spend the week as they wished. He also bought seats at the theater for them, and gave them coins with which to buy food and wine from the vendors. He and Gaius did not celebrate, but they spent much time together in conversation or reading; Gaius now shared the *tablinum* with his father, a glowing brazier set between them. Manlius brought them their meals, which had been prepared beforehand, and made sure they had water and wine at hand. They had been invited to several dinner parties, but both had declined, saying they would be happy to accept invitations in the new year.

Toward the end of the week of festivities, Gaius came to see Ariana. In a fold of his *pallium* were two small scrolls and a little leather pouch. After greeting Alomila and the others, he led Ariana into her room, where they sat together on the bed and kissed. Then he took the pouch from its hiding place and handed it to her.

"What's this?" she asked, suspecting nothing.

"Look inside and find out!"

She untied the drawstring and opened the pouch. Glinting up at her was a gold ring set with a small emerald, elegant in its simplicity.

"Oh, Gaius!"

"For you, my love. So you'll think of me when I'm not here."

"You know I think of you all the time!"

"It's also a token of my promise: I'll wed no one but you!"

He took the ring from her, reached for her left hand, and gently put the ring on the third finger. Her eyes bright, she put her arms around him and rested her head on his shoulder.

"I love you so!" she whispered.

They sat in silence for a little while as she admired the ring; then he produced the two scrolls.

"There's something I'd like to read to you," he said. "It's from the holy book of the Hebrews, which has been translated into Greek, but the language is a little unusual, so I wrote it down instead of memorizing it. Listen:

> Behold, thou art fair, my love; behold, thou art fair; thou hast doves' eyes within thy locks: thy hair is as a flock of goats, that appear from mount Gilead.
>
> Thy teeth are like a flock of sheep that are even shorn, which came up from the washing; whereof every one bear twins, and none is barren among them.
>
> Thy lips are like a thread of scarlet, and thy speech is comely: thy temples are like a piece of a pomegranate within they locks.
>
> Thy neck is like the tower of David builded for an armory, whereon there hang a thousand bucklers, all shields of mighty men.
>
> Thy two breasts are like two young roes that are twins, which feed among the lilies....
>
> Thou art all fair, my love; there is no spot in thee....
>
> Thou hast ravished my heart, my sister, my spouse; thou hast ravished my heart with one of thine eyes, with one chain of thy neck.
>
> How fair is thy love, my sister, my spouse! how much better is thy love than wine! and the smell of thine ointments than all spices!
>
> Thy lips, O my spouse, drop as the honeycomb: honey and milk are under they tongue, and the smell of thy garments is like the smell of Lebanon ...

Well before the end of his recitation, Ariana was blushing. He smiled at her and kissed her glowing cheeks.

"It's beautiful, though I find it a bit strange," she said.

"That's because the language is unfamiliar, my love. If you were to read more of the Hebrews' writings, you'd understand it better. Their language is rich in imagery, and very poetic. Here, listen to a little more:

> How beautiful are thy feet with shoes, O prince's daughter! the joints of thy thighs are like jewels, the work of the hands of a cunning workman.
>
> Thy navel is like a round goblet, which wanteth not liquor: thy belly is like an heap of wheat set about with lilies....
>
> Thy two breasts are like two young roes that are twins.
>
> Thy neck is as a tower of ivory; thine eyes like the fishpools in Heshbon, by the gate of Bathrabbim; thy nose is as the tower of Lebanon which looketh toward Damascus.
>
> Thine head upon thee is like Carmel, and the hair of thine head like purple; the king is held in the galleries.
>
> How fair and how pleasant art thou, O love, for delights!
>
> This thy stature is like to a palm tree, and thy breasts to clusters of grapes ...

Though Ariana was flattered by his words, she could not help giggling.

"Really, Gaius! I don't think my nose is a tower or my breasts are clusters of grapes! Though I have to admit it, my navel *is* starting to look like a goblet!"

He laughed. "Here, let me see!"

"No, I won't let you!" she said, folding her arms across her round belly.

"Please," he insisted. "Let me listen and see if I can hear anything inside."

"You might get kicked," she laughed, but she raised her *stola*, first checking to make sure the curtain was stretched all the way across the doorway. He gently stroked her belly, loving the warm skin and the thought of his child within. Then he knelt beside the bed and leaned over to rest his head against the smooth white mound.

"I don't hear anything," he said after a while.

"I don't know what you thought you'd hear," she said. "A heartbeat? But don't worry, I know the baby's alive. It moves around and kicks me quite often."

"My poor girl! How much longer?"

"Just another two or three weeks."

He stayed where he was for another moment or two, then began kissing her, moving upward until he found her breasts, larger now and rounder. He kissed one nipple, then the other, and grinned as they responded. He looked up and saw that her cheeks were flushed and her eyes bright with desire.

"Let's just lie here for a while," he said, and they stretched out on the bed. He stroked and kissed her in all the right places as she sighed with pleasure. Though he refrained from entering her, he brought her to an ecstatic climax, made all the more delicious as he placed his mouth over hers to prevent her from crying out.

After a while, he sat up and found the other scroll he had brought with him.

"I have something else to read to you, if you're interested."

She smiled up at him dreamily, her eyes half closed.

"Go ahead," she murmured.

"This one was written by Claudius Vettius, and it says, 'This is to certify that the slave woman named Ariana, daughter of the freedwoman Alomila, is hereby manumitted and is entitled to all the rights and privileges accruing to a freedwoman of the Empire of Rome.' It's signed by Claudius, and witnessed by Father and Suedius Clemens.

Ariana, our child will be born free!"

She did not hear him. At the word *manumitted*, she had fainted.

◆ ◆ ◆

"But, Gaius, how can this be?" Ariana asked, after she had recovered.

When he saw her in a faint, Gaius had rushed from the room in search of Alomila, who had grabbed a cloth, dipped it in cool water, and followed him back into Ariana's room. Almost immediately after the cloth was applied to her forehead, Ariana had opened her eyes and looked up at the two concerned faces peering down at her. She smiled and sat up with Gaius's help, grasped Alomila's hands, and told her the news. Now it was Alomila's turn: She did not faint, but she fell to her knees and put her arms around her daughter, weeping. Neither mother nor daughter could believe their good fortune; hence Ariana's question.

"In the end, it wasn't very difficult," Gaius told her. "Father and Claudius went to see Clemens. You may have heard that Vespasian is very ill, and his son Titus is effectively the Emperor now. Well, under the circumstances, Clemens feels safe in returning to Rome, so on the Kalends of January he'll be leaving Pompeii for good. He's been celebrating the Saturnalia like a madman: He's had tables of food set up all over the city; he's made offerings in the temples; he's gone to the theater almost every night; he's sent gifts to all the magistrates and councilmen—anyway, he's in a *very* good mood. So it seemed like a good time to petition him. Besides, he has a lot of respect for Father. Well, they told him the whole story—everything—and asked him to allow Claudius to free you even though you aren't yet thirty. A special dispensation. All it took was for Claudius to write this and the others to witness it, and here we are! Of course, it doesn't make you a citizen, but that can be fixed. Clemens promised to talk to Titus about restoring your free birth; only the Emperor can do that, you know ..."

Alomila stood and embraced him, the tears still flowing; then she wiped her eyes and went to tell the good news to the rest of the household. Gaius sat beside Ariana and kissed her.

"Are you happy, my love?"

"Oh, Gaius," was all she could say.

They could hear shouts and laughter in the kitchen, and the clatter of pots and bowls. Then Alomila spoke from the other side of the curtain.

"How would you two like to join us for a little celebration?"

Shyly they lifted aside the curtain and entered the kitchen. The long wooden table was covered with plates and cups, a jug of wine in their midst and the left-overs from the Saturnalia feast arranged on platters, along with olives, bread, and cheese. It was plain fare, but Gaius relished it, especially as he could recognize Ariana's touch in the stuffings and seasonings. The afternoon passed quickly as everyone congratulated Ariana and glanced admiringly at her gleaming new ring, whose meaning was unspoken but obvious.

Finally Gaius and Ariana excused themselves and went back into her little room. They sat on the bed, his arm around her. After a while she turned to him.

"When?" she asked.

"Not yet, but soon," he assured her. "Aurelia and Julilla will be married next summer, and as soon as they've gone to their new homes, Claudius will let it be known that you're his daughter. By then you'll be a Roman citizen, not just a freedwoman—father insists on that. And then we'll marry. We'll do it right, my love: You'll wear a saffron-yellow *palla* and a flame-red veil; you'll wear a garland of flowers on your head. We'll do it at the House of the Faun and there'll be lots of guests, and a priest will come to perform the sacrifice and Father will read the marriage contract and we'll sign it ..."

"You'll have to show me how!"

"I'll teach you," he said. He held her right hand with his and pretended to trace out a signature. "There: Arria Vettia."

"Arria?"

"That'll be your Roman name, the one Claudius supposedly gave you at birth. But you'll always be my Ariana. My Goddess Ariana."

She sighed contentedly and rested her head on his shoulder.

"And then," he continued, "there'll be a big feast, and afterwards we'll lead a procession of flute-players and torch-bearers to the House of the Vettii, which Claudius has offered to us, and when we get there, I'll pick you up and carry you over the threshold, and we'll begin a new life together."

Ariana said nothing, still resting against him. After a moment he realized she was half-asleep. It was already dark outside; time for him to leave.

I really don't want to go out in the cold and the dark, he thought. *Why not stay here? There's nothing to stop me, and I'm sure Father'll understand.*

Gently he helped Ariana lie down, and then he lay beside her, pulling up the quilts and adding his *pallium* to provide extra warmth. In the cool night they slept on her narrow bed, his body curled around hers.

XXIV
APRIL, 79

Gaius and Ariana were sitting on the bench beside the goat shed, leaning against the sun-warmed wall. Ariana was holding the baby, who was wrapped in a scrap of blanket with only his face exposed to the sun. It was the first warm day of spring, and they sat quietly, enjoying being together and admiring their son. Little Gaius had Ariana's dark blue eyes and Gaius's sandy hair, and showed signs of inheriting the fine features that made Claudius and Marcus so handsome. He was a delight in every way: healthy, strong, responsive. He ate and slept well, and was gaining weight rapidly.

Gaius was beside himself with joy. "My fine, strong son!" he kept saying. "He's beautiful! And those eyes—just like yours, my love."

Ariana smiled happily. Her joy matched his. Little Gaius had been born in mid-January, after many hours of labor that seemed to be going nowhere. Alomila had begun to worry, when suddenly Ariana cried, "He's coming!" Within a few moments the baby had made his appearance. Although the birth was by no means without pain, Ariana had been able to endure it and had suffered no ill effects. Almost immediately she was producing milk, and she found that nursing the baby gave her a deep sense of pleasure and satisfaction. After a few days, she returned to the kitchen and took over some of the cooking, even though as a freedwoman she was no longer required to do the work of a slave. But both she and Alomila were grateful for the home the farm provided for them, and they repaid the many kindnesses of the household staff by helping in a variety of ways. Indeed, though both were free, little had changed except for the arrival of Little Gaius.

"Let me hold him, Ariana," Gaius begged.

Gingerly she handed him the baby. "Be sure to support his head!"

"He's strong enough to hold up his own head."

"Please, Gaius."

He placed a hand behind the baby's head and gently rested him against his chest. Little Gaius obligingly belched and spat up on his father's tunic. Gaius smiled.

"Part of being a father, I suppose."

They sat contentedly for a while, the baby's head nestled against his father's cheek. Then Ariana, unwilling to have him out of her arms for very long, said she needed to feed him. Gaius handed him back to her, and she pulled down a shoulder of her *stola* and began nursing him. Little Gaius sucked intently, his blue eyes gazing up at Ariana's face. "Isn't he beautiful?" she whispered.

"He is, and so are you," said Gaius. "Maybe when he's done, I can have some of that, too," he added with a chuckle.

"Hush, Gaius!" she said, blushing.

"Ariana," he said after a while, "now that you're free, you can live wherever you choose. Couldn't you move back into town? It'd be easier to visit you, and Father would like to see the baby … his first grandchild …"

"Mama and I have thought about that," Ariana said slowly. "We thought about renting an apartment from Julia Felix—Mama's saved enough money—but the lease is so long … And besides, there'd be gossip. Julia Felix seems to be at the center of all the gossip in Pompeii. I'm sure she means well, but you know how it is. Someone says something, and the next person tells someone else, and before you know it, the story has been changed so much it has nothing to do with the truth. I *hate* gossip!"

He was startled by her vehemence, but said nothing.

"We also thought about getting a place in Herculaneum," she continued. "Not on the side with the villas, but on the other side, where the smaller houses are … but then we decided we're happy here, we'd like to stay a little longer. I know we can't stay here forever, but we don't feel ready to move yet."

"All right, my love, I understand. I'll tell Father all about Little Gaius, and maybe someday you could come for a visit—perhaps in the summer, when most people are indoors or at the baths."

"We'll see," she said.

The shadows were lengthening and the air was growing cooler. It was time for her to take the baby indoors and for Gaius to head home. He kissed both mother and child several times and finally left, walking briskly along the cart track, his *pallium* slung over one shoulder.

◆ ◆ ◆

"Father," said Gaius, over dinner on a balmy late spring evening, "do you know anything about the Fields of Fire?"

"Yes, a little," Lucius replied. "Why do you ask?"

"I went to a dinner party in Stabiae last night—Vasculus and Aper invited me to go with them. It was at one of those grand villas overlooking the sea … Fantastic view!"

"Yes, I know. I met your mother at one of those villas," Lucius said. A shadow crossed his face and he fell silent.

They sat quietly for a moment as each remembered Clodia in his own way. Then Gaius continued his account.

"Besides the host, Pomponianus—a relative of Aper's, I believe—there were a couple of other guests. One of them was Pliny—that is, Gaius Plinius …"

"Oh, that's Pliny the Elder. I've met him; he's the admiral in charge of the fleet at Misenum," Lucius interrupted. "Was his nephew with him—Gaius Plinius Secundus, better known as Pliny the Younger?"

"No, Father, just the admiral. He's a most interesting man. He's had quite a career: military service with the armies of the Rhine; *procurator* in Gaul, Africa, and Spain; counselor to Emperor Vespasian; and now commander of the fleet. Apparently he spends almost all his time reading and writing; I wonder if he ever gets any sleep. He seems to have an insatiable thirst for knowledge—he's been writing that *Naturalis Historia* of his for years and years, and he's still at it. When it's finished, he told us, it'll consist of 'twenty thousand important facts.' Remember that time when we were talking about Vesuvius, and I told you what he'd written about fire-mountains, especially Aetna? Well, he's very interested in Vesuvius—and the area around it. He wanted to know if the little tail of smoke above Vesuvius has gotten bigger or smaller at any time in our memory; he asked if the springs around here have ever run dry; he was very curious about the earth tremors we felt a few years ago …"

"I'm not surprised," Lucius put in. "Some people say he's trying to be the Roman Aristotle, Rome's expert in all the natural sciences—geography, geology, zoology, human physiology, medicine … you name it. And yet he strongly dislikes the Greeks—he thinks they're … how can I say it … soft? unmanly? A man of contradictions, I would think."

"That may be," said Gaius, "but he certainly was the center of attention last night. Everyone wanted to know what he'd seen on his travels—he told us about all kinds of things, you can't imagine. Things like the tricks elephants are taught, and how men dive for sponges, and the use of hedgehogs' quills to card wool. You'd have thought there wasn't anything he couldn't talk about. Not just mention, but describe in detail. But then he started talking about the Fields of Fire; he says they're more active now than before, and I was wondering if you'd ever seen them."

"Actually, I have," said Lucius. "I went to Puteoli once on a matter of business—it concerned our estate in Sicily. The man I went to see was the biggest importer of olive oil in the city. His son runs the business now—which reminds me, I should arrange for you to meet him. Anyway, we conducted our business, and then he asked me if I'd like to see some of the sights before I went home. He didn't say it, but I could see he thought Pompeii was a boring little country town and I must be excited to be visiting an important city like Puteoli. Well, to humor him I agreed, and he took me on a little tour.

"He showed me the Forum and the famous Temple of Serapis, and I admired them, and then he took me outside the city, along the coast to the northwest. Toward Misenum, actually. He wanted me to see the Phlegraean Fields—that's the Greek name for the Fields of Fire. It was really rather amazing. Spread out along the coast from Neapolis to Cumae are thirteen bubbling craters that emit sulfurous vapors and mineral waters. Many people think the water can cure a variety of illnesses. They come to Puteoli and Baiai to bathe in pools of hot mineral water. In Puteoli, the priests at the Temple of Serapis make a good living from the offerings people dedicate to the goddess when they think they've been cured. And of course Cumae isn't far from there—that's where the Sibyl is supposed to have lived and made her prophecies. The Greeks were very impressed by the Fields of Fire—they called the area Avernus and believed it was the entrance to the Underworld."

"That's very interesting, Father. Did you say the area is to the north of Puteoli?"

"North and northeast."

"So basically it's on the other side of Vesuvius from here."

"That's right."

"If the Fields of Fire are more active now, and there's more smoke coming out of the mountain, it would suggest that the fires inside the mountain are burning more fiercely than usual. I wonder what's causing that."

"I have no idea, Son. It seems to me it's like the weather. Sometimes we have rain for weeks on end, sometimes it's unusually cold, some years the Sirocco blows across Our Sea and turns the city into an oven …"

"Perhaps," said Gaius, unconvinced. "But I can't help feeling that there's something more to it, something we don't understand."

Their conversation turned to other matters, until finally darkness fell and they bade each other goodnight.

◆ ◆ ◆

One early summer day, Ariana and Alomila brought Little Gaius to the House of the Faun. They rode in the donkey cart, Alomila holding the reins while Ariana held the baby close in an effort to cushion him against the jolting ride. Arriving in mid-morning, they left the cart in the alley outside the house and entered through the small doorway used by the slaves so as not to disturb Lucius while he was seeing clients. They headed straight for the kitchen, where Timon and Claudia were busy preparing the midday meal. At the sight of the baby, Claudia let out a squeal that brought the rest of the household running. They crowded around the smiling mother and child, admiring the baby and asking all kinds of questions until Manlius good-naturedly told them to get back to work or there would be nothing for anyone to eat that day. Ariana and Alomila took the child into the small atrium in the servants' quarters, and sat there waiting for Gaius. The baby, not yet able to crawl but well aware of his surroundings, smiled at each new face and vastly enjoyed dabbling his fingers in the *impluvium*. One of the rooms opening off the atrium was the one where Ariana and Gaius had slept together, and she could not resist glancing into it. Nothing had changed; the bed, quilts, and brazier were as they had been when last used, except that there were no coals in the brazier.

Gaius left the Curia at the earliest possible moment and dashed home. As he entered the house, he passed the last of the departing clients. He ran to find Ariana and kissed her and the baby, greeted Alomila, and led the three of them into the main atrium to meet Lucius.

At the sight of Little Gaius, Lucius's heart melted. Wordlessly he held out his arms, and Ariana handed him the child. Lucius held the baby gently, examining every detail of his head and face, even lifting the bottom of the blanket in which he was wrapped to admire his tiny feet.

"Well, it looks like he's got all his fingers and toes," was all he managed to say. He passed the baby to Gaius and put his hands on Ariana's shoulders, looking into her eyes.

"It's good to see you again, Ariana. Welcome back to the House of the Faun!"

Tears sprang from her eyes and she reached out and embraced him.

"Thank you, Lucius," she whispered. "Thank you so much!"

They stayed for a light meal and part of the afternoon, sitting in the *viridarium*, their laughter blending with the splashing of the fountains. The younger members of the household kept finding excuses to see the baby: They brought olives and wine to the master, or found work to do in the rooms near the *viridarium*; the mosaic of Alexander was cleaned at least twice. Finally Manlius gave up and allowed them to come and go at will, as long as a little work got done and the evening meal would consist of something besides bread and water.

Little Gaius enjoyed himself immensely, smiling at everyone, nursing contentedly, and finally falling sound asleep, wrapped in his blanket and set in a large basket that Claudia brought from the kitchen. The others chatted amiably. Lucius wanted to know everything there was to know about his grandson, and as he listened, he looked lovingly down at the sleeping baby, whose face was a picture of peace.

◆ ◆ ◆

During his visits to the farm, Gaius had told Ariana about the doings of most of the people she knew, but there was one piece of news that gave rise to a great deal of discussion: Marcus and Claudius Vettius were reconciled.

Lately Marcus had made a name for himself as a designer of villas for wealthy patrons, especially the Roman senators and others who were building lavish villas along the coast overlooking the Bay of Neapolis. He planned both the layout of the rooms and their decoration. He was well versed in the latest fashions in painting and sculpture, and could satisfy his patrons' desire for the new and different, whether it be obtaining glass goblets from Puteoli or the three-legged tables that had recently become popular, installing windows in the *triclinium* so guests could enjoy the view as they reclined on their couches, or modifying the traditional house plan so a visitor entering the atrium would be met with a grand vista stretching through the *tablinum* into the *viridarium* and all the way to a large, mosaic-encrusted fountain at the far end. Though no one had yet found a way to produce clear glass, he could obtain thick, cloudy glass windows for the outer walls. He knew painters who could cover the inside walls with Egyptian fantasies or parks filled with birds and animals, separated into panels by graceful columns. His services were in great demand.

From time to time, he traveled to Capreae to direct the decoration of a new villa being built for a Roman financier. The owner's wife and daughter were already living there, enjoying their new summer home, with its splendid view of the bay, while also keeping an eye on Marcus and his laborers to make sure the owner's wishes were carried out. The daughter's name was Caecilia, and when Marcus met her his heart took flight. She was tall and slim, rather like Ariana, but her coloring was different: fair skin, red-brown hair, eyes like honey. *Caecilia, Caecilia*—her name mingled with every thought he had; he was distracted, he was falling in love. And sometimes she looked at him with a special light in her eyes, as if she might feel something for him. He hardly dared to hope.

His outward manner became very serious. He gave careful, measured instructions to his men; he spoke with infinite deference to Caecilia's mother; and he barely spoke a word to Caecilia. Inside, he was in turmoil, a seething mix of emotions he did not even attempt to name. But he spent as much time as he reasonably could at Capreae, and one day she allowed him a soft, sweet kiss.

From then on, he was a changed man. His heart sang. He smiled and laughed. Nothing perturbed him—even when a worker dropped a bucket of precious red paint and it spilled all over a newly tiled floor, he did not punish him but ran over to help clean up the mess. "Accidents happen," was all he said. The moodiness that had clouded his thoughts for years dissipated, and he felt incapable of holding a grudge or hating anyone—with the possible exception of Gaius Tullius, and even in Gaius's case he felt his animosity diminishing, banished from his thoughts by his yearning for Caecilia.

It so happened that some of Marcus's patrons were building or renovating villas in Herculaneum, and as a result he spent much time there as well. One spring morning he was walking past the entrance to Cornelia and Claudius's house and, to his surprise, was tempted to stop in and see his father. *Why should I still be angry with him?* he asked himself. *After all, Mother's happy with Faustus, and Father was justified in divorcing her for having that affair with Rufus. I've never understood what possessed her ... Anyway, I think I understand Father a little better now, and I haven't seen him for a long time. Why not give it a try? I've got nothing to lose, and besides, I could tell him about Caecilia.* At the thought of Caecilia he smiled and, still smiling, entered the house and asked the door slave to see if his father would receive him. Startled but pleased, Claudius agreed. He and Marcus sat in the *tablinum*, which was overflowing with more scrolls than ever, and conversed pleasantly as if nothing had ever gone wrong between them. Marcus described the work he was doing, and Claudius listened with interest. Claudius commented on one or two new scrolls he had recently bought, and Marcus listened with equal interest. Claudius invited him to share a meal and introduced him to Cornelia.

Since then, Marcus had made a number of visits to his father's house, and father and son were gradually becoming good friends. Marcus had not repudiated his mother, but neither Julia nor Faustus was particularly interested in his affairs. Once, somewhat hesitantly, Claudius asked Marcus how his mother was faring. Marcus shrugged.

"She's all right, I guess" he said. "She's changed a lot, you know. She's become a worshipper of Isis, and goes to her temple every day. Faustus doesn't mind; all he cares about is what's going on in the *Comitia* and what the magistrates are up to. He sees his clients, and then he goes to the Forum and the baths and has dinner with his old friends. He and Mother aren't together very much … during the day, that is."

As spring turned into summer, Marcus was busier than ever, and he took to staying overnight at his father's house. It was easier than making the trip from Pompeii to Herculaneum and back each day. And eventually he simply moved in with Claudius and Cornelia. There was plenty of room, and Marcus's presence made little difference, especially as he brought along his manservant to see to his personal needs. Also, the main business of the household that summer was preparing for Aurelia and Julilla's weddings. Marcus had never been close to his sisters, and now he kept out of their way, which was not difficult, as he usually left the house at dawn and returned late in the day. Sometimes he was away for several days, working on the villa at Capreae and hoping for a word with Caecilia. *Caecilia, Caecilia …*

"So it appears that Marcus will be Claudius's heir after all," Lucius was saying, as Gaius and Ariana listened intently. "I haven't had a chance to talk to Claudius much lately—they're getting ready for the girls' weddings, you know. But I don't think anything has changed. That is, he promised me …"

He paused, his brow furrowed.

"But Marcus might interfere? Is that what you're saying, Father?" Gaius asked, his anxiety evident. Ariana sat in silence, as still as a stone.

"We'll have to wait and see. By now, Marcus must know what Claudius intends to do, and I'm sure he knows you've been freed, Ariana, but … but I don't know if …"

"… if Claudius has told him about the child?"

"I don't know if Claudius has told him about the child, and if so, how Marcus feels about it, and about Claudius's plans. By the way, has Claudius seen Little Gaius?"

"No, not yet," Ariana said.

"Then I'll make sure he does," said Lucius. "Leave it to me. But there's another thing we need to consider."

"What's that, Father?"

"If Marcus is Claudius's heir, he'll not want you to live in the House of the Vettii. So after you're married, you'll need to find another place to live. Of course, you can stay here as long as you like."

Gaius and Ariana thanked him simultaneously, and they all laughed.

"We might arrange it the other way around," Lucius said thoughtfully. "You might be married in the House of the Vettii, and then the procession would come here. We'd actually plan a longer route for the procession; after all, it'd be a waste to have a grand procession and only cover a distance of two *insulae*!"

"If all goes well," Alomila asked, "when do you think the wedding could take place?"

"Well, Aurelia and Julilla will be married in early July, and then Claudius needs a little time to talk to certain people ... we should allow two or three weeks for that ... and by then the document of citizenship should have arrived from Rome ... how about the Kalends of September? An auspicious beginning for a new month and a new season, as well as a new family."

There he goes again, Gaius thought, but he smiled at his father and turned to Ariana.

"Would the Kalends of September suit you, my love?"

"Yes, Gaius," she whispered, her face aglow.

◆ ◆ ◆

Lucius was as good as his word. He went to see Claudius and persuaded him to plan a visit to the farm. It was not difficult—Claudius had been meaning to go there anyway to consult with his manager.

"Be sure to ask to see the baby," Lucius told him. "I promise you, you'll be delighted with him!"

Claudius agreed, and shortly thereafter he and Cornelia hired litters and made a tour of their country properties—his farm and her vineyards. It was a hot day, and when they arrived at the farm, they decided against inspecting the fields, accepting the manager's assurance that the crops were thriving and the daily deliveries of fresh produce would continue without interruption. They went indoors to rest and take some refreshment. Then Claudius sent for Ariana and the baby.

Ariana was nursing Little Gaius in her room off the kitchen. At Claudius's summons, she interrupted the baby's meal—despite his vocal protests—and held him up against her shoulder, where he belched, spat up a little, and finally was content. Hurriedly she changed her *stola* and his blanket, and carried him into the main room to show him to his grandfather.

It was love at first sight. Like Lucius, Claudius was speechless and simply held out his arms for the child. It was Cornelia who spoke.

"What a beautiful baby! And so strong and healthy! Obviously you're taking good care of him."

"Thank you," said Ariana, blushing. "Mama's a great help, and everyone here has been very good to me."

"I hear you more than make up for it with your wonderful cooking," Cornelia said.

Ariana looked surprised.

"Don't be surprised, my dear," Cornelia smiled. "You know how slaves gossip. My maid knows everything that goes on here because she's good friends with the man who delivers the produce to our house. But I wasn't trying to embarrass you. I mentioned it because I'd like to taste your dishes myself. Would you be willing to come and cook for us?"

Ariana did not know what to say. Apparently Claudius was unaware of Cornelia's plan, because he hastily handed the baby back to Ariana and turned to Cornelia.

"I, too, am eager to sample Ariana's cooking, but I expect she wants to go on living here for a while. Am I right, Ariana?"

"Yes, Master—I mean, Claudius"—Ariana stammered in her confusion. "I'd be pleased to prepare a meal for you someday, but for now I'd like to stay here and take care of the baby. He'll be crawling before long, and then walking, and I think this'll be a good place for him to explore without getting into too much trouble. He's so happy here, and moving to a new home just now might frighten him …" She hardly knew what to say, as she was unsure how much Cornelia knew. *Does she even know I'm Claudius's daughter? That he and Mama …*

Little Gaius saved her from further embarrassment by beginning to fuss and squirm in her arms. "Would you please excuse me?" she asked. "I think it's time for his nap, and I'll have to feed him first."

They nodded, smiling again at the baby, and she hurried back to her room, where she continued the feeding that had been interrupted, her thoughts swirling. *First Marcus and now Cornelia. Either of them could cause trouble if they wanted to. What are we going to do?*

She put the baby down and lay beside him. He nuzzled up against her and fell asleep. She was tired as well, but sleep was slow to arrive. She kept raising her left hand to look at the ring Gaius had given her, along with his solemn promise. Had Cornelia noticed it? If she had, would it have meant anything to her? Finally, exhausted by worry, she drifted off to sleep.

◆ ◆ ◆

When Gaius came to see her a day or two later, he found her moody and unsettled. The baby was fussy and demanding, and she had to feed him intermittently for almost an hour before he settled down for his nap and she and Gaius could talk.

He sat beside her on the bed, with one arm around her shoulders. With his other hand, he turned her face toward his and kissed her, first above each eye, then on the tip of her nose, and finally on her lips. She responded halfheartedly and he drew back, a question in his eyes. He could see tears gathering in hers.

"What is it, my love? Didn't Claudius like the baby?"

"Oh, he loved the baby," she said, "and so did Cornelia. Then Cornelia asked if I'd come and cook for them ..."

"She *what*? What on earth made her think you'd agree to something like that?"

"Gaius, she doesn't know. I'm sure she doesn't know."

He looked at her searchingly, finally realizing how deeply troubled she was.

"So she doesn't know," he said. "But she soon will. As soon as the girls are married. I believe their weddings are only a few days apart. I wonder why they didn't just have both of them at the same time."

"I knew those girls when they were little," Ariana said. "They were always very jealous of each other. Their mother didn't pay any attention to them until much later, and soon after that, Claudius divorced her. And *he's* never been interested in anything except his scrolls, you know that. And then, of course, Marcus went to live with Julia. You'd think Aurelia and Julilla would have grown closer after that, but they didn't. It was always a contest to see which one could have the best clothes and jewelry and hairstyles. Like their mother, before she married Faustus."

"Well, it'll all be over soon," Gaius assured her. "And then Claudius'll tell Cornelia, as well as the *duoviri* and certain other important people, that you're his daughter—which most people know anyway. And then we'll be married ..."

"I don't know, Gaius," she broke in. "I'm afraid something'll happen. Something will go wrong. We don't have the document of citizenship yet, and if it doesn't arrive in time, we'll have to wait even longer …"

"We won't wait any longer," he insisted. "Listen, Ariana: We're going to be wed on the Kalends of September, no matter what. If Claudius doesn't do what he says he will, if Marcus or Cornelia or anyone else tries to interfere, to Hades with them! I'm of age and so are you; we're both free to marry. Even if it doesn't happen quite the way we hoped it would, even if Father's upset because you're still a freedwoman, even if I have to leave the *Comitia*, whatever happens, we'll be wed. I *won't* wait any longer!"

He took her in his arms and held her a long time. Then they kissed, and after a while they made love, achingly, yearningly, until finally they slept. When they awoke, it was dark outside. Little Gaius also woke up and needed to be nursed. Gaius watched lovingly as the baby sucked eagerly, gazing intently into his mother's eyes. *There's no lovelier sight in the world,* he thought.

That evening they shared a meal with the household staff, and later, when the baby was asleep, he and Ariana made love again and then slept peacefully through the night in each other's arms.

XXV

AUGUST, 79

The dog days had arrived. No one went outdoors, unless it was absolutely necessary, until late in the afternoon, when those who could stand the blazing heat made their way to the baths to find a little relief. Never in the memory even of Pompeii's oldest citizens had there been such an unbearably hot summer. Conditions were not much better at the farm, where an occasional vagrant breeze did little to alleviate the discomfort felt by all—including Little Gaius, who suffered miserably from heat rash and protested noisily at being kept indoors all day. Little work was done in either the city or the countryside as all waited for the dog days to pass, yet each day dawned hotter than the one before.

Gaius came to see Ariana, dressed only in tunic and sandals and wearing Manlius's straw hat. He was carrying what looked like two small rolls of cloth. He found her in the kitchen chopping vegetables, pausing occasionally to wipe her forehead with a damp cloth. Little Gaius, completely naked, was lying in his basket, napping briefly between bouts of fussing that turned into loud wails whenever he grew hungry, which was far too often to suit Ariana. The heat, coupled with the baby's demands, was making her irritable, and when Gaius entered she merely glanced up at him and went on with her work. He leaned over and kissed her, at the same time depositing his two bundles on the table.

"Watch out," she said. "Whatever's in there is going to get dirty. This kitchen's a mess. No one feels like cleaning it up, least of all me. I swear, Gaius, I think I'm going to melt into a puddle!"

"I know what you mean," he replied. "Look at *me*!" He was drenched with sweat.

"So you'd better put those somewhere else. What're they for, anyway?"

He opened the smaller bundle, which contained a rolled-up scroll. He cleared a space on the table and spread out the cloth in which it had been wrapped, then unrolled the scroll so two or three columns of writing were visible.

"Do you know what this?" he asked.

"Gaius, you *know* I can't read!" she snapped at him. "Why are you teasing me?"

"I'm sorry, my love," he apologized, startled by her anger. "You read my thoughts so well, I forget you weren't taught to read mere words. Please don't be angry with me. I'll tell you what this is: It's Apicius's book on cookery! It's got everything in it. See, this part's about vegetables. Listen: 'Boiling Green Vegetables. A Vegetable Dinner, Easily Digested. Beets Cooked in Varro's Way.'—hmm, since when was Varro a cook?—Anyway, here's more: 'Young Cabbage Sprouts.'—He gives you six different ways to cook cabbage sprouts!—'Leeks and Beans. Field Herbs. Endives and Lettuce. Carrots and Parsnips.'—For each one, he gives you a couple of different ways to cook them."

He unrolled the scroll a little more, carefully rolling up the other end. "How about cooking up a bird or two? He's got directions for cooking ducks, partridges, wood pigeons, thrushes, figpeckers, pheasants, geese, chickens—and if you ever got your hands on an ostrich or a peacock, he'd tell you how to cook them, too."

Ariana was dumbfounded. "I never knew anyone wrote about cooking!" she exclaimed. "Oh, Gaius, I could learn so much from this. I could try all kinds of new things. How about figpeckers and beets? Or goose stuffed with young cabbage sprouts? Well, maybe not. But if I could read that, I would know what other cooks have done, and I could try to prepare the same dishes and maybe find ways to make them better. There's so much you can do with fresh herbs, and a rich sauce makes almost anything taste good!"

He smiled at her excitement. "Ariana, my love, when we're married I'll teach you to read, and you'll be able to read everything Apicius has written about cooking. And you'll cook wonderful meals for us and all the babies we'll have—but you won't have to do it all yourself. You'll have the best kitchen you can imagine, and two or three slaves to help ..."

"Not slaves, Gaius. Please. Not in our house."

"All right, my love. You'll have freedmen and women to help you with the cooking and the marketing and the babies."

"They won't be babies very long! Look at Little Gaius, he's growing so fast, he won't be a baby much longer."

The baby chose this moment to let out a wail that could mean only one thing. Ariana picked him up and began nursing him. Then she noticed the other bundle, still lying on the table where Gaius had set it down.

"What's in the other package?" she asked him.

He rolled up the Apicius scroll, wrapped it in its cloth, and then, equally carefully, unwrapped the other bundle. The colors of the garments it contained lit up the room. Gaius had brought her the saffron-yellow *palla* and flame-red veil worn by every Roman bride.

She almost dropped the baby as she reached out to touch the fine cloth. "Oh, Gaius!" was all she could manage.

"It won't be long now," he said, smiling happily. "The Kalends of September's just a few weeks away."

"Has Claudius … has Claudius told anyone …?"

"I don't know, my love, and I don't care. Whatever happens, we'll be wed on the Kalends of September!"

◆ ◆ ◆

A day or two later, Ariana had an unexpected visitor.

"It seems you have another suitor," Publius told her with a grin.

"What? Who?" asked Ariana, hardly believing her ears.

"Marcus Vettius!" said the manager, as Marcus came into the room, his fine features bronzed by long exposure to the sun, his slim frame clothed in a tunic of exquisite design, the unnecessary *pallium* slung over one shoulder. He smiled at Ariana's flustered expression.

"I know this is a surprise," he said, "but my father told me you have a fine baby boy, and I came to see him for myself and offer my congratulations. After all, you *are* my sister."

Ariana was speechless. All she could do was point to the baby, asleep in his basket.

"A good, strong child, I see. Are you both managing to survive in this heat?"

"Not very well," she said, "but it can't last forever. Marcus, what *really* brings you here?"

"I've got quite a lot of work in Oplontis, which as you know isn't far from here. I pass this way often. I was curious about you and the child, and there's something else as well …"

"What else?" she asked faintly, stunned by his presence and his friendly manner. Was this the Marcus Vettius who had followed her in the streets of Pompeii, forced himself on her, spied on her and Gaius, and received a black eye as a result? What had happened to change him? If she had been less preoccupied with her own concerns, she might have guessed that he, too, was in love. But she could not have known about Caecilia—*Caecilia, Caecilia!*—and the secret whispers, the stolen kisses. Nor did she know how much his work meant to him—how immensely satisfying it was. What had happened to change Marcus was very simple: For the first time in his life, he was happy. Truly happy.

"Ariana, I owe you an apology," he said. "I know I caused you and Gaius a lot of distress when the three of us were younger. Of course, I didn't know then what I know now. But that's no excuse. I behaved very badly to both of you, and I'm truly sorry. I've also apologized to Gaius, and I hear the two of you are going to be married, and I'd like to offer you my most sincere congratulations."

"You've seen Gaius?" she asked in amazement. Marcus had hated Gaius for years and avoided being anywhere near him at public events like the sacrifice and feast at the beginning of the Saturnalia, when they and their fathers usually stood or were seated close to each other. Since their conversation after the wall-painting incident, the two young men had not spoken a word to each other.

"Yes, I've seen him," Marcus went on. "As you may know, my sisters—my *other* sisters—were just married. By all the gods, what a commotion that was. Or rather, I should say 'those were,' because the weddings were separate affairs. It's just like those two to refuse to share a wedding, which would have saved my parents thousands of *denarii.* Anyway, Lucius and Gaius were among the guests on both occasions, and since I've made my peace with Claudius, I thought I might as well do so with Gaius as well. It wasn't too difficult: I apologized, and we shook hands."

She stared at him in disbelief. "So all of a sudden you're friends?"

"Well, that may take a little longer," he admitted. "But we're going to be brothers-in-law, and we might as well be decent ones, for your sake. Besides, I've grown up, Ariana. I'm not the sniveling youth I used to be. My work with Phidias was so interesting, and I enjoyed it and learned so much, that I stopped worrying about some of the things that used to bother me and make me disagreeable. And now I'm an architect myself—actually, more like an architectural designer. I've gotten commissions to design villas in Herculaneum and Oplontis, and one at Capreae—everything: the arrangement of the rooms, the style of painting in each, the layout of the *viridarium.* Of course, most of my patrons are wealthy Romans, so they have lots of money to spend on decoration, and I'm free to do almost anything I like, as long as it's in fashion. And I've met … but I came to see *you,* not to talk about myself. What I want to say is, I've spoken with Gaius, I'm glad he's going to marry you, and I congratulate you both on your beautiful baby. I hope you'll allow me to come to your wedding, which I hear will take place on the Kalends of September."

"And how did you hear that?" asked Ariana in wonderment.

"Oh, Ariana, don't you know by now that everyone in Pompeii knows everything about everyone else? Gossip travels faster than the wind. As soon as Aurelia and Julilla were married, Claudius started hinting that you're actually his daughter. Which everyone already knew, of course, but had never mentioned so as not to embarrass him. And then Lucius hinted to a couple of his friends that he no longer objects to Gaius's marrying you, since you're Claudius's daughter and Claudius is a good friend of his—and by the way, he already has a lusty little grandson—and word spread from there."

"But what about Cornelia?" Ariana put in. "After putting so much effort into finding good husbands for Aurelia and Julilla, and then arranging expensive weddings for both of them, what could she have thought when she was told there's going to be yet another wedding?"

"Well, for one thing," Marcus said, grinning, "Cornelia knew all along that you're Claudius's daughter. I was there when my father made up his mind to tell her, just after Julilla was married. He was beating around the bush, trying to tell her without getting her upset, but she just laughed and laughed. 'My dear Claudius,' she said. 'How could you imagine I didn't know? Everyone in Pompeii has known for years! And don't you think I noticed that ring she was wearing? You told me Gaius was the baby's father, so Gaius must have given it to her, which means they intend to marry. Actually, I knew something was afoot when you and Lucius went to Clemens to get permission to free her. So now there's going to be another wedding, on the Kalends of September.'

"Well, Claudius was relieved that she didn't start throwing things at him or something, but he was taken aback when she asked him who was going to pay for the wedding. 'Well, she's my daughter,' he said; 'she should be married from this house, like Aurelia and Julilla.'

"Cornelia put her foot down at that. 'Not from this house,' she said. 'The girl was a slave and the daughter of a slave. They've both been freed, and that's very nice, but I won't allow the marriage to be held here. You'll have to make other arrangements.' And there was nothing Claudius could do to persuade her otherwise.

"So he went to see Lucius, and the two of them made the arrangements, and provided the citizenship document arrives in time, you'll be married in our house in town and then go to the House of the Faun and live there until you can afford one of your own. It's all settled."

"And your mother?"

"She and Faustus will be invited; it's up to them to decide if they'll come."

"What about *my* mother?"

"I'm not sure how they're going to work that out," Marcus said. "They haven't told me all the details. But I'm sure that if you and Gaius insist, they'll find a decent way to include her."

"We *do* insist," she said simply.

They sat in silence for a while, not sure what to say next. Little Gaius started fussing and Ariana apologized, saying she needed to take him into her room and nurse him. Marcus took the hint and rose to leave.

"Ariana," he said, "listen to me. I'm serious. I really *am* sorry about those things that happened when we were younger, and if there's any way I can make it up to you, just let me know. You're my sister, and I love you as a sister. Please think of me as your brother, and call on me if there's ever anything I can do for you."

"Thank you, Marcus," she said, standing up with the baby in her arms. "I'll remember that. And thank you for offering the olive branch to Gaius. That was very good of you."

He took a step or two toward her and kissed her on the forehead. "Be well, my sister," he said, and went on his way.

◆ ◆ ◆

Sirius, the Dog Star, followed its annual path across the night sky, but the dog days showed no sign of waning. If anything, it became even hotter. The sun blazed down mercilessly on both city and country. The vegetables in the kitchen garden wilted despite desperate efforts to keep them watered. Dust rose in clouds from the unpaved tracks that criss-crossed the countryside. Springs and wells produced less water, and some showed signs of drying up entirely.

There were repeated sightings of giants roaming the land. Gaius wondered about these: Was the heat making people dizzy, or were the "giants" swirls of dust raised by the hooves of mules and the wheels of carts? To the supersititious Romans, the sight of a giant was a bad portent indeed. According to legend, when the gods defeated the rebellious giants they buried them beneath mountains. Mount Aetna was said to be the prison of the mighty giant Typhon, its noises his groans, its flames his breath. Of course, this was pure myth, and the sightings nothing but mirages, but they made him uneasy nonetheless.

Gaius did not make another visit to the farm for several days, and when he did, he hired a litter, set out at dawn, and stayed only a little while so he could make the return trip before the heat became unbearable. He found Ariana more irritable than ever. She was threatening to cut her hair.

"It's so hot, Gaius! It feels like a blanket. I could cut it off and sell it to a wigmaker in the city. There's always plenty of demand for wigs!"

"Please, my love, don't!" Gaius begged. "This heat can't last forever. Why don't you come back with me and stay in the House of the Faun until we're wed? You'll be more comfortable there."

"I don't think so, Gaius. Besides, I don't want to upset the baby any more than he already is. Poor thing, he's just miserable."

They glanced at Little Gaius, who was sitting in his high chair and adamantly refusing to eat the porridge Ariana was trying to feed him. Gaius could not resist a chuckle at the sight of the red-faced baby sitting in what looked like an overturned pot with the bottom cut out and two holes in the sides for his chubby little legs.

"You'll move to the house a few days before the wedding, won't you?" he asked.

"Yes, we will, if it's not too hot to travel. We'll need a couple of days to get the baby used to his new surroundings."

"He can stay there during the wedding," Gaius suggested. "I'm sure Claudia and Timon would be glad to look after him."

"Gaius, you don't know what you're talking about!" she snapped, still trying to stuff some porridge into the baby's mouth. "Do you want me to stand at the altar with milk stains on my *stola?* I'll have to nurse him just before the ceremony. Then Mama will take care of him, and she'll carry him in the procession. Tell your father not to make the route too long, or Little Gaius will make more noise than the flutes and cymbals."

"All right, my love," said Gaius contritely. "We'll arrange things any way you wish."

"Good," she said shortly. Giving up on the porridge, she lifted the baby from his chair and nursed him. Both she and Little Gaius calmed down, and after a while she smiled at Gaius.

"I'm sorry I snapped at you," she said. "I'm just not myself. It's just so *hot*, and the baby fusses and cries all day long. I think I must have nursed him at least a dozen times yesterday, maybe more."

"It can't last much longer," Gaius assured her. "It's never been this hot for more than two weeks; it *has* to end soon. Just a few more days, my love, and we'll bring litters to fetch you and the baby and Alomila. And a few days after that …"

The farm dogs suddenly began barking and howling; a moment later, the house shook. Pots and dishes fell from their shelves. Ariana clutched the baby to her breast.

"What's happening?" she gasped.

It was over before he could reply. They looked at each other, speechless, each remembering the tremors of several years before. Both had been much younger then, and terrified.

"An earth tremor," he said. "I must get back and make sure Father's all right. Ariana, if you hear the dogs howling like that again, grab the baby and get out of the house!"

"I will, Gaius," she said, still ashen-faced.

Giving her a quick kiss, Gaius left in a hurry. Ariana sat holding the baby for most of the morning, expecting more tremors. There were none, and finally she put Little Gaius in his basket, where he fell asleep almost instantly. Grateful for the respite, she dipped a pot into the basin of water in the kitchen and carried it to her room, where she washed herself, changed her clothes, and bound up her hair so it would not lie heavily on the back of her neck. Then she opened the bundle that lay on a table in a corner of the room, shook out her wedding garments, and held them up to admire them. *Not much longer now. Not much longer!*

XXVI

AUGUST 22–23, 79

"I just can't persuade Ariana to move here," Gaius said with a sigh. He and Lucius were sitting in the *viridarium*, hoping in vain to catch a faint evening breeze. "She says it's still too hot, she doesn't want to upset the baby. But Father, the Kalends is only ten days away. We'll never be ready at this rate! And what's delaying that document? It should have been here by now. It doesn't take long for a courier to get here from Rome!"

Lucius did not answer. He was looking intently at the wine in his cup. The surface of the liquid was trembling, even though he had put down the cup several minutes earlier and had not touched it since then.

"What is it, Father?"

"Look at your wine. Did you ever see it tremble like that before, when you hadn't just set down your cup?"

Gaius looked into his cup without touching it. "It's swirling as if the cup was moving. Do you feel anything?"

They had both felt the brief tremor a few days earlier. When there were no more tremors, they had forgotten about it. Now they looked at each other worriedly.

"Something's happening," Lucius said. "Look, it's still trembling. And there's another thing: I went to the baths today, and the water levels were low. They told me water isn't flowing into the *hypocaustum* at the normal rate. I wonder if there's a break in the aqueduct. Maybe that little quake the other day did some damage."

"Maybe," said Gaius. "But what you're saying reminds me of the questions Pliny was asking. He wanted to know if the springs around here had ever run dry."

"Did he say what it would mean if they did?"

"No, but he was also very interested in the Fields of Fire. He'd heard reports that they're unusually active. Some of the craters are spewing out a lot of sulfurous gas. I wonder if there's any connection. And now this trembling—obviously the ground's trembling beneath us, even if we can't feel it. I don't like it, Father. I don't like it at all."

"Do you think it's a warning of another earthquake like that big one we had about twenty years ago?"

"I don't know what to think. Did the springs and wells run dry before that one?"

"No, I don't think so."

Before Gaius had a chance to respond, the ground shook beneath them. This time the tremor lasted a few seconds—long enough for the wine to splash over the rims of their cups, but not much longer. Gaius leapt to his feet, but Lucius put out a hand to restrain him. "We're safer out here," he said.

"Ariana …"

"… is safer where she is."

"I must go to her."

"Don't worry about her, Son. These tremors aren't strong enough to knock down any walls. And there are plenty of people at the farm who can help her if she needs help."

"What if it gets worse? What if there's an earthquake during the night?"

"Then some people will be injured and some will die. It's in the hands of the gods, Son—or Fate, if you prefer. There's nothing we can do about it."

"Well, I'm not going to let her stay there any longer. Tomorrow I'm going to fetch her and bring her here, no matter what she says!"

◆ ◆ ◆

Just at dawn, all the dogs in Pompeii started barking and howling. The uproar woke Gaius, but before he could get out of bed, the room began shaking violently. Cracks appeared in the walls. He heard tiles falling from the roof, and people shouting. Then everything was still. The dogs were quiet, but the sounds of panicked people running and calling out increased. Panicked himself, Gaius grabbed the first tunic he could find and rushed from the room, slipping it over his head as he ran to find Lucius.

His father was not in his *cubiculum*; he had been awake and dressed before the tremor. When he heard the dogs, he stood in the doorway, clutching the wall. His room looked out onto the atrium, and he watched as the little dancing faun beside the *impluvium* seemed to come alive; he saw tiles slide down the sloping sides of the opening above the pool and splash into the water. The water in the pool was already splashing as the whole house shook. He noticed that the water level was low. Normally, the pool was full, not just with rainwater but with water pumped in from the public water system.

The shaking seemed to go on forever, but it was over in less than half a minute. People were shouting in the streets and alleys outside. Someone cried out in the servants' quarters. Lucius took a cautious step and felt the floor solid beneath him. Still stunned, he began walking around the house in an attempt to assess the damage. The sounds of voices and crying drew him to the kitchen, where he found Claudia sitting on a bench, holding one arm against her chest. Tears were streaming down her cheeks. The other kitchen slaves were clustered around her in varying states of undress. Timon was trying to persuade her to drink some water.

"I think her arm's broken," he said upon seeing Lucius. "A heavy jar fell on her." He pointed to the floor, which was covered with shards of pottery and the contents of the jar—green olives. Jars of food were kept on a shelf above the water basin, and it was Claudia's bad luck to have been standing at the basin when the tremor struck.

Gaius joined them, having followed the sound of voices. One look at Claudia told him the whole story. "Where's Manlius?" he asked. Suddenly he realized how much the household depended on its steward. Manlius could be counted on to know what needed to be done and how to do it.

"I'll go find him," said Quintus, and hurried out.

"We'd better take a look at the damage," Lucius said to Gaius. "Manlius'll take care of things here. Tertia, perhaps you could find a cloth to bind Claudia's arm and keep it still until Manlius can send for a physician. And Claudia, try not to move. Drink a little water, it'll help. And some wine."

Claudia managed a tremulous smile, and father and son left the kitchen to survey the rest of the house and the garden. They found several cracks in the walls, but nothing that could not be repaired by a good plasterer. The tiles that had fallen into the *impluvium* would have to be fished out and replaced; there were more tiles on the ground in the *viridarium*, and two of the small marble statues had fallen over.

It was strangely quiet in the *viridarium*. It took Gaius several moments to realize why, and when he did, he felt a chill of fear. The fountains were still.

"Father, look at the fountains," he said.

Lucius looked at them, then at Gaius.

"The water isn't flowing. And it isn't coming into the *impluvium* either. I *thought* there was a break in the aqueduct. It's probably worse now. We'd better talk to Manlius about how we can conserve water. This could turn into a serious crisis. Unless it rains, of course, but it shows no signs of raining anytime soon."

They looked up at the sky, a hazy pale blue bowl that seemed to trap heat against the ground. Less than an hour had gone by since dawn, and it was already hot.

"Father," said Gaius, "there may be a break in the aqueduct, but I don't think that's what's causing the problem."

"Well, of course there's a drought as well," said Lucius.

"I know. But springs don't run dry in a drought."

"Who says the springs have run dry?"

"In the last few weeks they've been producing less and less water. They're going to run dry."

"And you believe …"

"And I believe the cause lies beneath our feet. The same thing that's causing the springs to run dry is causing the Fields of Fire to flare up. And there's more smoke coming from Vesuvius."

"Well, whatever the cause, we're going to have to do something about our water supply," said Lucius. "In the meantime, we'd better go to the Forum and see what the magistrates are doing to keep order. If I'm not mistaken, they're going to need all the help they can get."

"All right, Father. But first let me get a clean tunic."

While Gaius went to his *cubiculum* to change, Lucius returned to the atrium, where he encountered Manlius. The steward had sent for a physician to tend to Claudia and was just coming to find Lucius. They held a brief conference about the water problem. Gaius returned, and Manlius told him a slave had come from the farm to let them know everyone there was safe. Gaius let out a sigh of relief. *Well, at least that's one thing I don't have to worry about. It looks as if she was right to insist on staying there.*

As they left the house, Gaius noticed that there were cracks running through the mosaic floor of the vestibule. But the greeting "AVE" was untouched. *A good sign,* he thought. *This house will always be a welcoming one.*

The streets were in turmoil. People were running in all directions, anxious to check on relatives and friends. The stone blocks along the sides of the Via Nola were unbroken, but they were littered with broken roof tiles. Several of the people who were running tripped and fell, got up slowly, and limped away. *There'll be as many injuries from panic and carelessness as from the quake itself,* Gaius thought.

They made their way to the Forum, walking slowly. As they neared the public square, the congestion increased. People were milling around, sharing "where were you when it happened?" stories and seeking news—who had been hurt, where was so-and-so, why was there no sign of the magistrates? Following some unnamed instinct, they gathered outside the Basilica as if they expected someone to come out and tell them what to do. Beggars, pickpockets, and food vendors, quick to recover from the shock of the quake, were hard at work.

"This is madness," said Lucius. "These people need a leader, and the *duoviri* aren't here. Do you see anyone from the *Comitia*?"

"It's not in session, Father. And anyone who can afford to has left town. That includes most of the *Comitia*, and I haven't seen any of the magistrates in weeks. Of course, there haven't been any dinner parties. The most popular meeting place in town these days is the latrine at the baths: twenty men at a time can sit there and gossip! But I haven't been there either …"

His voice was drowned out by the howling of dogs and the shouts of those who knew what it meant. The ground began to shake. *Oh no, not again!* Gaius grabbed his father's arm, and they held on to each other as the shaking grew stronger. By unspoken agreement, they sat on the pavement. Gaius had a glimpse of dozens of people embracing the columns of the peristyle surrounding the Forum. He found it oddly funny. *Look at them, holding on to Clemens's Folly. Will it still be standing two minutes from now?*

Time slowed to a crawl; a minute became an hour. Buildings swayed; statues crashed from their pedestals; those unlucky enough to have sought refuge beneath them were killed, or suffered serious head injuries and broken bones. There were screams. Gaius was unhurt but dazed. He thought he might be dreaming: faces, statues, roof tiles, the sky, the ground wheeled through his mind like dream images. He held on to Lucius: His father was real, he was here, now. It was not a dream. The shaking finally ceased, and there was a brief period of silence and stillness that, in Gaius's clouded mind, seemed to go on forever yet was only an instant. Then chaos: running, shouting, screaming people falling over one another and knocking over the vendors' stands, trying to force their way through the crowd, thinking now only of going home to see if their children were safe.

The peristyle was intact. *Good for you, Phidias!* thought Gaius. But now he was being shaken again. *Not again, please, Jupiter, not again!* But it was only Lucius shaking him. "Gaius, are you all right?"

He turned and stared at his father as if he had never seen him before. Everything was strange. He could not think clearly. He could not think at all. *But I* am *thinking. I'm thinking about not thinking …*

"Are you all right?"

Slowly he came to himself. "Yes, Father, I think so. How about you?"

"I'm all right. But look at this place."

The Forum was littered with broken pots, fallen statues, roof tiles, overturned food stands, and bodies—some alive, some not. There were fewer people as the crowds thinned. They could hear shouting and crying in the streets nearby. Some of the injured, helped by friends or slaves, were trying to stand; one man collapsed on a broken leg and cried out in pain.

Even the public-spirited Lucius had to admit there was no hope of maintaining order under these conditions. But there were things that could be done. "We should try to help some of these people," he said. "Let's at least hire a couple of litters and send them here to take the injured people home—if their homes are still standing."

If their homes are still standing.

They looked at each other with the same thought and headed back the way they had come. There was much more damage now than there had been after the earlier tremor. Walls had collapsed; some of the alleys were blocked. They had to go the long way around, by way of the Via Stabiana, which had been transformed into a sea of panicked people searching for friends or physicians, or simply hoping that if they stayed outside they would be safer than in their homes. Their houses were dangerous traps, with walls and ceilings threatening to fall at any moment. Many remembered the terrible earthquake of twenty years before, when almost no structure in the city had remained intact. They remembered, too, that it had been preceded by several smaller quakes. There could be more quakes today and tomorrow; they could be even worse than that one. People were crying, not in pain but in anticipation of disaster.

As they made their way through the throngs, Lucius held Gaius's arm so they would not be separated. When they tried to speak to each other, their words were drowned out by the uproar surrounding them. Finally they reached the corner of the Via Nola and turned toward home.

The House of the Faun was indeed still standing, and largely intact. The atrium was littered with roof tiles, and the marble-topped table where clients left their petitions had cracked. There was almost no water in the *impluvium.* As they passed the statue of the faun, Lucius absently patted it on the head. Gaius found the sight of that habitual gesture oddly comforting.

They went through the inner courtyard and the hallway with its mosaic of Alexander, undamaged. The *viridarium* was much as it had been that morning, though more of the statues had fallen over, and many had broken. They doubled back and went to the servants' quarters, where again, little had changed except that now many of the walls were cracked and the floor of the pantry was littered with broken jugs and spilled food. No one had been hurt; so far, the only injury was Claudia's broken arm. Manlius was already at work restoring order in the household. Knowing Claudia would not want to be alone, he had arranged a comfortable seat in the kitchen for her. It was fortunate that a physician had been found early that morning; it would be far more difficult now. Claudia's arm had been hastily set and bound, and she was drinking wine, accompanied by plenty of bread, to dull the pain. Timon and Quintus were busy cleaning up the kitchen, and the rest of the servants were going through the house and setting it to rights. Manlius knew broken statues could be replaced and cracked walls patched any time in the next few weeks. Right now, what was needed was a sense of order and routine. And food. He was giving the cook instructions when Lucius and Gaius arrived.

"I see you've taken charge as usual, Manlius. Thank you," said Lucius.

"I'm glad to see you're all right," the steward replied. "We were worried about you."

"Yes, we're all right, but there are many who aren't," said Lucius. He asked Manlius to see to the litters, and he and Gaius went to sit in the *tablinum.* Timon brought them some bread, olives, and wine.

They sat in silence for a few moments, glad be able to sit still for a while.

"We'll have to see about repairs right away," Lucius was saying. "There'll be a lot of competition for the services of plasterers and stonemasons."

Gaius did not answer. He was watching the trembling surface of the wine in his cup.

"It's not over," he said. "There's more to come."

"I know, Son. But let's hope it doesn't get any worse."

"I'm afraid it will, Father. I'm afraid it will." *Good thing Ariana and the baby are still at the farm. She was right to want to stay there—that house is sturdily built. They're probably safe.* He felt a pang of guilt; during the second quake and its aftermath he had not given a thought to Ariana and Little Gaius. *I'll go fetch them as soon as this is over,* he vowed.

Throughout the afternoon there were tremors and small quakes. Some of Pompeii's citizens, like Lucius and Gaius, tried to go about their daily routines as usual. Others crowded into the temples, making offerings to whatever god or goddess they thought was most likely to protect them from harm. The Capitolium was filled with anxious supplicants; the small temple of Isis near the theater could not hold all the people who crowded into it. At the villa of Julia Felix, Julia and her tenants gathered around the shrine of Isis in the garden. In other houses, people made offerings to the Lares, hoping their homes would at least remain standing. A wealthy merchant named Julius Polybius, who was planning to seek office in the next election, insisted that the workmen he had hired to redecorate his atrium remain on the job. They acquiesced grudgingly, but when a sudden tremor undid most of their afternoon's work, they departed in a body, ignoring his protests.

In the evening the tremors were almost constant, and the streets were filled with the shrieks and wails of people driven almost mad with fear. At any moment, they were certain, the earth would shake more violently than before. They feared being indoors, where ceilings and walls might collapse on them, but they did not feel safe outdoors, where they were equally likely to be struck by falling tiles or collapsing walls. People streamed through the city's seven gates, hoping to find safety in nearby fields or seeking shelter in the tombs of their ancestors, heedless of the possibility that those monuments, too, might collapse.

Gaius and Lucius were exhausted, but they sat together in the *tablinum*, knowing they would be unable to sleep and not wanting to be alone. They said little, merely sat and listened to the sounds of fear and panic echoing in the streets outside.

◆ ◆ ◆

After a restless night, Ariana had risen before dawn and dressed. She was sitting on the edge of her bed, going over and over in her mind what she would do if there was another quake. Then the dogs began barking; she snatched up the baby and ran outside. The ground shook and she stumbled backwards, holding him above her. It was over very quickly, but she continued to lie on the ground, clutching Little Gaius against her breast. His wails brought Alomila running from the house. Seeing Ariana motionless, she screamed, "No!" Ariana opened her eyes.

"I'm all right, Mama," she said.

The house slaves, some dressed, some not, came outside and joined them. Still dazed, they seemed to be walking in their sleep. No one had been hurt, but there were cracks in the walls. No one wanted to go back inside.

Alomila picked up the baby, and Ariana struggled to her feet. Her back hurt, but she could walk easily. She felt fortunate to have escaped with nothing more than a few bruises.

"Why don't we bring some bread and wine out here?" she suggested.

Publius assented, and a couple of the slaves went inside to fetch bread, a jug of wine, some water, and several cups. They sat on the ground and ate. Alomila and the manager were sitting on the bench beside the goat shed, their shoulders touching. Seeing them so close to each other, it dawned on Ariana that there might be something between them. *So* that's *why she stays on here and doesn't want to leave,* she thought. *But she said she'd go with me to the House of the Faun. I suppose she'll want to come back here afterwards …*

"We should send someone to tell Claudius we're all right," Alomila said.

"And Gaius," said Ariana.

The messages were sent.

The morning grew hot, and as nothing had happened for over an hour, the group was preparing to go back inside and get to work. Ariana was holding Little Gaius in her lap, nursing him, when the dogs began barking and howling.

"*Sit*, everybody. *Sit*!" Alomila yelled.

They sat, holding on to one another as the ground shook again. Tiles flew from the roof, some landing close by. Ariana put the baby on the ground and crouched above him. *They might fall on me,* she thought, *but they won't hit him!*

Finally the ground was still. She rose and picked up the baby, who was yelling lustily, offended by the interruption of his feeding. She carried him into the house and into her room, sat on the bed, and nursed him again. When at last he seemed satisfied, she laid him in his basket and went into the kitchen to survey the damage.

The floor was covered with broken dishes; a stack of them had fallen from their shelf. The table was sticky with spilled porridge. Water had splashed out of the basin onto the floor.

"Watch your step in here!" she called out to the house slaves, who were still outside. "Come on, it's over. We've got to clean this place up."

She supervised the work in the kitchen while Alomila checked the rest of the house. Gaius was right: The house was sturdily built, and the damage was minimal. Once the litter of broken crockery and spilled food was cleaned up, life at the farm could return to normal. But where was Gaius?

XXVII
AUGUST 24, 79

The tremors continued sporadically through the night, but the catastrophic quake that many had feared did not occur. By morning, the city was comparatively quiet. Believing the worst was over, the citizens of Pompeii tried to resume their everyday lives, as they had done in the past and expected to do in the future. This was especially true of the merchants and laborers. There was money to be made. People would need wine and bread. Business was booming in the taverns, and as Lucius had predicted, the plasterers and stonemasons were in great demand, as were the physicians. With weary eyes and much grumbling, Polybius's workmen resumed the task of redecorating his atrium.

For a few hours, calm prevailed. Throughout the city, people greeted one another with relief. Even the unnatural heat was forgotten as they shared stories about their experiences during the past two days. Those who had fled into the countryside began drifting back into the city. There were expressions of dismay when it was discovered that the public fountains were dry. The wine vendors did a brisk business, however, and the welcome news that a team of engineers and workmen had been sent to repair the acqueduct spread rapidly. Soon, thought the people of Pompeii, everything would be back to normal.

It was not to be. In midmorning, a new series of tremors and small quakes shook the city. Once again the streets echoed with the sounds of running feet, shouts, falling roof tiles, and barking dogs. Lucius and Gaius, who had ventured out to survey the situation in the Forum, made their way back to the House of the Faun, holding on to each other to keep their balance above the moving earth. When they finally reached the house, Gaius found himself gasping for breath and realized he was on the verge of panic.

"Father," he said, "I think we should leave the city. It's too dangerous here."

"I agree it's dangerous," Lucius replied. "But this can't go on forever, even though it seems that way. If we're careful, we'll be all right."

"I'm not so sure of that. I think we may be in for a lot more."

"But Son, it won't be any better anywhere else. The whole area's affected. Even the villas along the shore will be damaged. Where would we go?"

"I don't know. To the south, I think. Or eastward. As far away from Vesuvius as possible."

"Why Vesuvius? As I said before, the whole area's shaking. And it'll eventually stop. We've been through this before, though you wouldn't remember—you were just a baby."

"And this house? What happened to it?"

"There was some damage, but nothing that couldn't be repaired."

"I still think the mountain might ... Well, never mind. Anyway, I need to go fetch Ariana and the baby."

"Son, you don't want to do that. This isn't a good time to be traveling around the countryside. And the baby's probably upset enough already. Let them stay there, they're better off."

"I guess you're right. But I feel bad, not being with them."

"I understand. But be patient. I bet you this'll all be over by tomorrow, and you can go to them then."

They sat in the shade of the peristyle, looking out at the strangely silent *viridarium*, and shared a small midday meal of bread, olives, and wine. Lucius felt drowsy and decided to take a nap. Gaius remained where he was, uneasy, unable to concentrate on anything. He felt cold, and was trembling despite the heat of the day. He was about to go to his *oecus* in search of something to read when the ground shook violently, throwing him from his seat. *This is what fear feels like,* he thought. *I'm afraid. Deathly afraid.* He raced through the house and out into the street, where people had stopped in their tracks and were gazing open-mouthed and wide-eyed at the great mountain to the north.

An enormous cloud was billowing from its summit and rising far into the sky. After a while, the top of the cloud began spreading outward. "It looks like a mushroom," one of the spectators commented. "More like an umbrella pine," said another. "That's more smoke than I've ever seen coming out of Vesuvius," said a third. They spoke casually, as if they were watching something out of the ordinary, not something to be feared. Many, thinking it was just another quake, albeit more dramatic than most, turned away and went back to work, but some grew uneasy. "Do you think it might be a sign from the gods?" "A sign of what?" "I don't know ..."

Others began to feel a deeper sense of foreboding. There were some who had actually seen Mount Aetna and were afraid Vesuvius's activity was the first sign of something worse. They began thinking about leaving the city and heading south or east, away from the mountain. After all, if things did not get any worse, they could come back to their homes and resume their everyday lives.

In normal times, the prevailing breeze would have blown the smoke across the bay and out over the sea, but these were not normal times. There had been no wind at all for weeks. Now the wind arose and blew from the northeast, and the cloud of smoke above Vesuvius began crawling across the sky toward Pompeii. There was a series of thunderous explosions; huge gusts of smoke poured from the mountain, which soon became invisible, shrouded in clouds of smoke and ash. The sky grew dark, and ash began to fall from the sky onto the roofs and streets of Pompeii. There were claps of thunder and flashes of lightning. The ash-fall was so dense that day turned into night. *Lapilli*—small pebbles of pumice stone—began falling like hailstones. Children gathered up handfuls of them and threw them at each other, shouting and laughing.

Gaius dashed inside to find Lucius, who had been asleep for about an hour and was just waking up. "Is it an eclipse?" he asked. "I didn't sleep all afternoon, did I?"

"No, it's Vesuvius!" said Gaius. "Father, we've *got* to get out of here. It's bad and getting worse. It's dark because the sky's full of smoke and ashes. The wind's blowing everything this way. We've got to leave!"

Lucius raised a hand. "Not so fast, Son. Let's take a good look at the situation before we act."

"Father!"

In the pause that followed, they heard shrieks and wails. Amid the hail of *lapilli* were larger rocks that struck without warning. Injured people were lying in the streets or crawling to the nearest doorway to seek help. A blanket of ash covered everything and was getting deeper by the minute. Panic and chaos were spreading through the city. People streamed into the temples, convinced that the end of the world was at hand. Others rushed home and gathered up their families and a few belongings, the men grabbing their hoards of coins, the women whatever jewelry they could get their hands on. Those with more presence of mind snatched up pillows or tiles to protect their heads from the rain of ash and *lapilli.* They headed for the city's southern and eastern gates, trying to find shelter somewhere in the countryside or a nearby town. Meanwhile, those who had spent the previous night outside the city were trying to go home, collect some food and a handful of coins, and then set out to the east or south, or perhaps go down to the harbor and hire a fishing boat to take them out to sea. The Porta Marina, the Porta Stabiana, and the Porta Nuceria were jammed with people trying to pass through in both directions. Angry yells and fistfights added to the commotion.

Even the northern gates were filled with fleeing people, animals, and carts. Every loose dog in the city, driven by instinct, was running madly through the streets, between people's feet and the wheels of carts, growling and snapping as they dashed through the gates and escaped into the countryside.

"*Now*, Father!" Gaius insisted.

"All right, Son. Come, let's go talk to Manlius."

They called the household together in the atrium, where the *impluvium* was rapidly filling with cinders and *lapilli,* and the dancing faun had turned gray. Lucius could not refrain from wiping the little statue's face with the hem of his tunic.

"Gaius and I think it would be best if we all left the city," he said. "Each of you, put together a bundle of food and a water bag—especially the water, you're going to need it. I assume there's still a little water in the basin in the kitchen, and there may still be some in the cistern. Be ready to leave in ten minutes. We'll meet here and leave by way of the Porta Nuceria. I think we should try to go inland toward Nuceria ..."

"Forgive me, Master, but I must disagree," said Manlius. "Quintus and Timon went out a little while ago to see what's going on, and they say the road to Nuceria is almost impassable. Half of Pompeii is pushing through the Porta Nuceria and jamming the road. We need to choose a different route. I think we might be better off heading for Surrentum."

"The Porta Marina's jammed too," Timon put in.

"Then we'll have to try the Porta Stabiana and take the road to Stabiae. Then we can turn west toward Surrentum. I think most people will be heading east or south, so it shouldn't be as crowded."

"I won't be going with you," said Gaius unexpectedly. "I'm going to head out through the Porta Vesuvio and fetch Ariana and the baby. We'll take the coastal road and meet you at Surrentum."

"You'll be heading straight toward Vesuvius," said Lucius, looking pale.

"It's all right, Father, I'll be careful," Gaius replied.

"All right, everyone, go get your food and water, and whatever else you want to take with you. Manlius'll go with you. Gaius, do be careful. Those falling rocks are a menace, and it's so dark ..."

"I'll carry a torch, Father, and stay close to the walls as long as I can. But why aren't you going with Manlius and the others?"

"There are a couple of things I need to see to before I go. I'll catch up with all of you later," said Lucius. He gave his son a quick hug. Gaius felt tears pricking his eyes.

"Oh, and one more thing," Lucius said.

The assembled household stood in silence, waiting for him to speak.

"As of this moment, you are all free men and women. Gaius and Manlius are my witnesses. Go in freedom, and may you find peace and happiness wherever you go. Of course, if this house is still standing after today and you wish to return, you'll always be welcome here."

With tears in their eyes, the newly freed servants thanked him gratefully and ran to prepare for their journey. Soon thereafter they left the house. They tried to find a litter for Claudia, but there was none to be had at any price, so she was forced to walk with the rest of them, clutching her arm in pain. Timon carried her few belongings and her water bag.

◆ ◆ ◆

At Cape Misenum, Pliny the Elder was hard at work on his *Naturalis Historia* when his nephew burst into his *tablinum* and blurted out, "Uncle, you've *got* to see this!"

Pliny, who hated to be interrupted, looked up in irritation, but when he saw the excited expression on his nephew's face, he reluctantly rose and accompanied the youth to a vantage point where they could view the entire bay of Neapolis and the countryside beyond. When he saw the huge mushroom-shaped cloud, he was not sure at first what it was. But almost immediately he realized it must be coming from Vesuvius. An extremely curious man with a burning desire to observe natural phenomena up close, he ordered a light ship to be prepared to take him closer to the mountain.

"Are you sure that's wise?" asked Pliny the Younger. "It looks awfully dangerous. Look at that dark cloud moving toward Pompeii. That's no normal cloud; it must be full of ashes, don't you think?"

"You're right, it *does* look dangerous," his uncle replied. "We'd better send some ships over there in case they're needed for rescue operations. But I'm still going to go out myself and take a look."

Just then, a message arrived from their friend Rectina, the wife of Caesius Bassus, begging for assistance. They lived in a villa at the foot of the mountain, so the only escape route open to them was by sea. Pliny rescinded the order for his own light ship, and instead ordered several of the fleet's largest ships—quadriremes, with sails and four banks of oars—to be made ready. He embarked and headed straight toward the danger, heedless of the hot cinders falling on the ships. They tried to put in at Herculaneum, but boulders that had rolled down from the mountain blocked the shore. Pliny ordered his ships to continue toward Pompeii, but the sea was so full of ash and *lapilli*, and the air with smoke, that it was impossible to reach the shore. Because of the prevailing wind, the ships were unable to turn back to Misenum, so Pliny headed for the villa of his friend Pomponianus in Stabiae. There he would stay overnight, hoping to resume rescue efforts the next morning.

◆ ◆ ◆

At Oplontis, Marcus Vettius was directing work on the former villa of Poppaea Sabina, recently purchased by a Roman senator who had commissioned him to redecorate it. The quakes and tremors of the past few days had interfered with the work, but whenever any damage occurred, Marcus ordered his workers to repair it immediately. It was a challenging project, in which he was completely absorbed. The villa was immense, with a long, curved colonnade facing the sea, and the decorative scheme was the most elaborate he had ever attempted—every wall would be painted with architectural elements and mythological scenes; even the areas over the doors were to be painted with landscapes, and the door leaves would be decorated with winged Victories, peacocks, and incense burners, all portrayed in the finest detail. As for the mosaics … he could hardly bear to think of the hours of work they would require. A major concern was the low level of water, not only in the fountains but in the cistern. Wine was of limited value as a substitute, if his painters were to do the fine brushwork he demanded.

All the *aquarii* in the region were concerned about the aqueduct. After the earthquakes on the previous day, they had sent one another a series of messages in an effort to determine the extent of the damage and its location. If there was a break in the aqueduct far to the east, toward Nola, the repair crew would have to cart their supplies a great distance. Or maybe there was more than one break. Marcus's experience with water systems—he had studied them so he could install fountains and fishponds, as well as baths and large swimming pools, in his villas—warned him that the repairs would take much longer than most people imagined, and in the meantime there would be a serious water shortage. He had already had the villa's fountains shut off, even before receiving a message from the *aediles* stating that all possible measures must be taken to conserve water.

He was mulling over the problem when he heard Vesuvius's opening roar and, along with all the workers, turned to stare in awe as the huge cloud of smoke and ash billowed up from the top of the mountain. He had an unobstructed view of the rapidly rising and expanding cloud and the tendrils of smoke starting to creep toward Oplontis and Pompeii. Before long, ashes began falling on the villa, and soon thereafter a rain of *lapilli.* Seeing some fist-sized rocks among them, he began to think it might be wise to seek safety elsewhere—either out to sea or to the south. The villa was beside the sea and possessed a number of small boats; the owner was absent, but his slaves were present in the house. Marcus soon realized no one in the vicinity would be safe. He paused to think about Caecilia—*Caecilia, Caecilia!*—and decided Capreae was too far away to be affected. But he and his laborers, and the master's slaves, were at risk. And so were Ariana and the baby, on the farm not far from Oplontis.

It took him only a minute or two to make his plans. Calling together both the household slaves and his crew of workers, he gave them their instructions.

"If it were just ashes and a few *lapilli* falling," he told them, "I'd say we could simply stop work and go home for the day. But as I'm sure you've noticed, there are some bigger rocks among the pebbles, and they could do a lot of damage. I don't know much about fire-mountains, but I do know this: If Vesuvius is anything like Aetna, we're just beginning to see what it can do.

"So this is what I want you to do. Those of you who've been working on the paintings and mosaics, you can go home if you want to, but I'd advise against it. I think you should take one of the boats and head out of here. Go wherever you think you'll be safe; I suggest Surrentum. Sail if you can, row if you have to. You *do* know how to row, don't you?"

They nodded, not very convincingly. But Marcus knew that if they had to, they would find a way to get a boat moving through the water.

"The rest of you, I want you to get a couple of litters and come with me. We're not going far, just to a farm near here. We'll fetch my sister and her baby and bring them back here, and then we'll set out in one of the other boats. I'll pay you well for your help, and I promise that next time I get a chance to speak with your master I'll ask him to free you."

The slaves agreed willingly, and holding up his money pouch, Marcus promised to give each of them a *denarius* as soon as they got to Surrentum. They quickly readied three litters and, with Marcus riding in one of them and directing their steps, headed for the farm. The going was dangerous, as the ground was covered with a layer of hot ash and *lapilli*, but the distance was not great, and they arrived at the farm within an hour.

◆ ◆ ◆

Gaius struggled through the deepening layer of cinders toward the Porta Vesuvio. He finally reached the gate and passed through, but once outside, he could see nothing familiar. His flickering torch revealed an unbroken field of gray; he could not make out the roads or tracks, nor did he have any sense of direction in the darkness. He had not anticipated this setback, and stood still for a while, straining his eyes in all directions. The darkness was beyond that of night; it was like being in a sealed room without lights, except that occasionally he saw flashes of light in the distance. Eventually he realized that some of those flashes were not lightning but tongues of fire emerging from Vesuvius. They enabled him to make out the outer wall of the city as it sloped away to the left. With this minimal orientation, he set out westward, following the wall as long as he could. Then, using the flashes of fire from the mountain to guide him, he struck out across the trackless countryside. Under ordinary circumstances, he could have covered the distance in a little over an hour, but now, with so many impediments and little sense of direction, it would take much longer.

◆ ◆ ◆

In Pompeii, the layer of ash and *lapilli* on the streets and rooftops was growing ever deeper. Some roofs had collapsed under the unaccustomed weight. The temples were crowded with people who felt safer there than in their homes. Many people remained in their houses, however, believing them strong enough to withstand the onslaught.

As the afternoon wore on, the flashes of lightning became more frequent, briefly lighting up the gloom and offering glimpses of chaos and agony. The accumulation of ash and *lapilli* was over a meter deep. Blinded and choking, people sank into the drifts up to their thighs. In some places, bodies could be seen beneath the gritty surface—the bodies of those who had been felled by rocks as they tried to flee. As more ash fell and covered them, their forms became indistinct and created further obstacles to flight. The air was filled with the sounds of people screaming and calling out the names of loved ones from whom they had been separated in the darkness. Here and there were fires ignited by torches or oil lamps, dropped when their owners tripped or were struck down by falling rocks.

Julia and Faustus were among those who remained indoors. Faustus was getting on in years and reluctant to expose himself to the dangers that were only too evident whenever he went to his vestibule and looked out into the street. Nor did Julia relish wading through a hip-deep layer of hot ashes. They stayed inside and made an offering to their household gods, asking their protection during what promised to be a terrible night.

Julia Felix and some of her tenants took shelter in the temple of Isis with the priests; they brought along several jugs of wine and poured out a libation to the goddess, then drank the rest. The warmth thus produced gave them a feeling of confidence. All would be well by morning, and they would go back to the Villa Felix and resume their daily pursuits. Someone would have to clear the ashes from the streets, of course, but that was what slaves and laborers were for.

◆ ◆ ◆

At the farm, Ariana was beside herself with worry. Little Gaius had been crying incessantly all morning; she had nursed him several times, but each time he seemed to be asleep and she laid him in his basket, he started howling again. Then the tremors resumed, and she decided they would be better off outdoors. She took baby and basket outside and sat on the bench beside the goat shed. She nursed him again, and this time he did not wake up when she gently placed him in the basket. She was sitting there, leaning against the wall and dozing, when Vesuvius roared into action. Jumping to her feet, she stood and stared at the clouds of smoke billowing upward from the huge mountain. She remembered what Gaius had said. *It's a fire-mountain, and the fire's gotten much bigger. Look at all that smoke!*

Alomila, Publius, and the rest of the household rushed outside and gazed at the mountain, now transformed from a benevolent deity into a fiery monster. They watched in awe, and then in fear, as the huge cloud rose to an immense height, flattened out, and began moving toward them. Soon the first cinders and *lapilli* began falling on them, and they hurried indoors.

"We've got to get out of here," Ariana said to her mother. "Look: There are rocks falling as well."

They were peering out through the doorway as the sky darkened and lightning flashed. The mountain seemed to explode in fury, sending out huge clouds of smoke and ash. *Lapilli* rained down on the roof, sounding like a heavy rainstorm.

"Where do you propose to go?" asked Alomila. "It's the same everywhere."

"I don't know, I don't know!" said Ariana, close to tears. "I wish Gaius was here. Where is he? Why hasn't he come for us? Mama, what's going to happen to us?"

◆ ◆ ◆

In Herculaneum, Vesuvius's opening roar was cause for great alarm. The mountain towered above the town, and it was not long before boulders began rolling down its sides and crashing through walls and roofs. By midafternoon, many people were dead or seriously injured. The citizens of Herculaneum had had enough; they grabbed whatever they could lay their hands on and fled. Most took the coastal road south past Pompeii, but some, having sighted Pliny's fleet, made their way down the slopes to the beach and waited there to be rescued. Claudius and Cornelia were among them. They watched in dismay as the fleet turned away toward the darkness that now covered Pompeii and Oplontis like a shroud. The boat sheds that lined the beach were empty; anyone who could leave by boat had already done so.

"There are no more boats," said Cornelia. "We'd better go back up to the house and get some food. We'll have to take the road south like the rest."

They went back to the empty house. Their servants had chosen to flee on foot, and the slaves, newly freed, had gone with them. Cornelia was wrapping some bread and olives in a cloth while Claudius searched for a couple of water bags, when a boulder fell on the roof above them and demolished it. They both died instantly.

◆ ◆ ◆

When Marcus arrived at the farm, he found everyone preparing to flee to the south. The donkey cart was laden with bundles of food, a couple of pitchers of wine, and whatever water could be found. Ariana had wrapped the baby in one of her *pallae* and was trying to decide whether to bring his basket along; the cart was almost full already. She looked around her in confusion. What else should they take with them?

"We'll need torches," she said to Publius.

"And extra cloths for the baby," said Alomila.

"All right, but there isn't room for much more," the manager told them.

They went into the house and looked around to see if there was anything they were forgetting. Alomila had her bag of coins; she had been saving her small wages for many years. Sextus was fumbling in the kitchen, grabbing jugs and pots from the shelves; he was determined to take along as much food as possible. Ariana went to her room to fetch the baby's things. She glanced at the table in a corner and saw the rolled-up bundle lying on it. *My wedding veil and* palla*—I almost forgot them!* Snatching up the bundle, she rushed outside, just in time to witness Marcus's arrival.

"Marcus! What are you doing here?"

"I came to get you. I've got a boat waiting for us, but we'll have to hurry!"

"But, Marcus …"

"Don't argue, just get into that litter with the baby. Alomila, you can take the other one."

"What about Publius and the rest?" Alomila asked.

"They'll have to go along the road with the cart," he said. "Don't worry, we'll all meet up again at Surrentum."

"But … But what about Gaius?" Ariana cried. "Do you know where he is?"

"I have no idea. If he's got any brains, he's already left Pompeii and headed south. Or maybe east. No one's coming this way, you can be sure of that."

Ariana stood rooted to the spot, tears streaming down her cheeks. "I can't leave without him!" she wailed. "Why didn't he come for us? How could he just leave us here?"

"Ariana, be reasonable," Alomila admonished her. "He's not going to come here now. Maybe he should have come yesterday, but he didn't, and now he's going to have to look for you and the baby at Surrentum. You'll find each other, don't worry. Go with Marcus, it's the best way. The baby will be safer with you."

"But aren't you coming too?"

"No, Ariana, I'm going with Publius and the others," Alomila said firmly. "And Marcus, if you'll leave that extra litter with us, we can use it to carry some of our food and other things."

"All right," Marcus agreed. "You two"—he gestured to the slaves carrying the extra litter—"put that down and help carry my litter and my sister's. Is that the baby's bed?" He pointed to the basket.

Ariana nodded.

"Put it in here with me. And anything else the baby needs."

Alomila took her daughter's hand and led her to the second litter. "Come now, put your bundle in there and get in; I'll hand you the baby."

"Mama …"

"Go on, do as I say, it's for the best."

She leaned over and kissed the baby, then reached up to put her arms around her daughter. "I'll see you in Surrentum!" she said, and smiled.

◆ ◆ ◆

Toward evening, the roof of the peristyle in the Forum collapsed in several places. Many people still huddled under the lower ceiling, or took refuge in the buildings surrounding the Forum square. Fires were burning throughout the city as lightning struck exposed roof beams. More roofs caved in, causing many injuries and deaths. Some people who had hoped to be safe in their homes tried to leave, but by now the streets were almost impassable. Only those who were strong enough to wade through the chest-high layer of ash, *lapilli*, rocks, roof tiles, and other debris could get as far as the gates, and then they found the roads jammed with carts pulled by mules or donkeys, litters carried by slaves, women carrying wailing babies, and men trying to force their way through the crowds. More people were killed as rocks fell on the fleeing populace and those who fell were trampled underfoot.

◆ ◆ ◆

Gaius was lost. He held up his torch and looked around, but he could see nothing. Ashes and *lapilli* were raining down on him; it was like being buried alive. He felt panic swelling within him. Vesuvius was sending forth huge bursts of flame, but they illuminated nothing. He stumbled onward for a while, but when he looked again at the flaming mountain he realized he was heading northeast, away from the farm. It was obvious that he would not be able to make his way there in the enveloping darkness. Distraught, he sank to his knees in the ever-deepening ashfall. Reason deserted him: Without thinking, he dropped his torch into the ashes, where it was quickly extinguished. Now he was alone in the darkness. He wept bitterly as his hair filled with ash and each breath burned his throat. He pulled off his tunic and wrapped it around his face, but with each passing moment his will to survive diminished. Finally he curled up on the ground and lay still as the ashes and *lapilli* continued to fall above and around him.

◆ ◆ ◆

Manlius had guided his little band southward toward the Porta Stabiana. Before leaving the house, he had gathered up an armful of rags and handed one to each of his charges. Holding the rags over their noses and mouths, they made their way slowly along the crowded street, stumbling over stones, fallen roof tiles, and bodies living and dead, along with the throngs of panicked citizens trying to escape the awful fate overtaking them.

It was fortunate that they were heading for the Porta Stabiana. The Porta Marina was hopelessly jammed with people seeking to escape in the small fishing boats and larger merchant vessels moored in the little harbor just outside. From there, they could traverse the short canal that led to the River Sarno and thence to the bay, where the wind would blow them toward Surrentum or farther south. But the supply of boats was far too small to accommodate the crush of people trying to force their way onto them, and some capsized, dumping a load of screaming passengers into the canal before being righted and taking on another load. Some self-appointed captains used oars to beat off the throng and shove their boats out into the channel, and in this way a small number of Pompeii's citizens were able to flee their doomed city.

The majority, however, headed down the coastal road toward Stabiae, or out through the Porta Nuceria and along the western road. Manlius chose the southern route, believing it offered the best chance of getting as far away from Vesuvius as possible. Having sent his group on their way, he turned back to see if he could help Lucius. The older man was not as strong as he had been, and Manlius wanted to make sure he escaped safely. They had lived under the same roof for decades, and Lucius had always treated Manlius more as a friend than a manservant. As for Manlius, he was devoted to Lucius and would gladly have given his life for him.

Returning along the upward-sloping Via Stabiana was even more difficult than the outward journey, as he had to struggle not only against the deepening layers of ash and *lapilli* but also against the crush of people heading for the Porta Stabiana. Several times he was shoved aside and almost fell into the suffocating ash, but he managed to keep his footing and hold his torch above his head. Though the darkness was increasing as the ashfall turned from gray to black, there was enough light from torches, lanterns, and scattered fires to dimly light his way, and finally he reached the Via Nola and turned toward home.

◆ ◆ ◆

Something—perhaps a new outburst from the thundering mountain—brought Gaius back to awareness. He felt as if he was smothering, and in terror he flung his tunic away from his face and struggled to stand up. In the almost total darkness he was disoriented and hardly able to think. Finally he began taking stock of his situation. *I can't just die here without trying to go on, I can't! I've* got *to get out of here and find Ariana and the baby.* He realized that his only hope was to try to make his way back to the city and escape to the south, but without the light of his torch he dared not take a step in any direction. After standing still for a while, he found that he could hear in the distance the shrieks of despair, the screaming and wailing of the injured, bereaved, and terrified citizens of Pompeii. Using only those faint sounds to guide him, he struggled back the way he had come. It was not long before he encountered the crumbling outer walls. Partly in amusement and partly in despair, he realized that he had not gone very far.

He worked his way back to the Porta Vesuvio and along the Via Stabiana, recognizable only by its width. Lamps were flickering in some of the houses. He stumbled over a body and fell headfirst into the ever-deepening layer of ash. With a great effort, he struggled to his feet and leaned against the nearest wall, gasping and coughing. He was not sure where he was; in the heavy darkness, nothing was familiar. Finally, in the light cast by burning roof beams, he recognized the intersection of the Via Stabiana and the Via Nola. From there, he could make his way home.

The House of the Faun was shrouded in darkness. The door stood open, the welcoming "AVE" long since covered with ashes. He pushed his way through the vestibule and into the atrium, where the ash layer was shallower. He wept again at the sight of the little faun buried in cinders up to its waist, its laughing face covered with ash. *Lapilli* and stones were falling into the *impluvium* and piling up in the middle of the room. On the sides and in the back of the large room, the floor could still be seen. Gaius walked around the *impluvium* and into the *tablinum* in search of Lucius.

An oil lamp burned on the table, but there was no sign of his father. Only then did Gaius wonder why Lucius had stayed behind. He assumed his father wanted to place his most important documents and valuables in the strongbox that stood in a corner of the room. Perhaps he had done so, but the room was unchanged from the last time he had seen it—except for a scrap of paper on the table, apparently torn from the edge of a nearby scroll. Gaius picked up the paper and read: "Gone to be with Clodia. Don't try to follow me. *Omnia amor vincit.*"

◆ ◆ ◆

He sat in his father's chair and wept. "Why, Father, why?" he cried. "We didn't say goodbye. We never said goodbye! Oh, Father, why did you do it? You could have saved yourself. Don't you realize how much I need you? How much I've always needed you?" He sat, sobbing, oblivious to his surroundings. After a while, the lamp flickered and went out. He must go, but still he sat and wept. Then he heard footsteps. Could Lucius have returned? Full of hope, he stood and peered into the darkness. There was a glimmer of light, which grew stronger as Manlius entered the atrium, holding up his torch to survey the devastation around him.

◆ ◆ ◆

At first, Gaius did not recognize him. Manlius was wearing his old straw hat, which he had covered with a large rag, wrapping the rest of the rag around the lower part of his face. Gaius drew back in fear. He knew there must be looters prowling the streets. But at the sight of him, Manlius removed his strange headgear and strode forward in alarm.

"Gaius! What in the world are *you* doing here? And where's your father?"

"Oh, Manlius," was all the youth could say. The steward looked more closely at the dirty, tear-streaked face.

"What is it, Gaius?"

Mutely, the distraught youth gestured at the piece of paper bearing his father's message.

Manlius picked it up and read it, then let it fall from his hand.

"We've got to go find him," Gaius said.

"No, Gaius," said Manlius. "We must respect his wishes."

"But …"

"If you were Lucius, would you want us running around trying to save him when we can barely save ourselves? And what about Ariana and the baby?"

"Oh, Manlius," said Gaius again, the tears flowing once more. "It was so dark, and there were no roads. I got lost. I couldn't get to them. I had to turn back. I should have gone there before. Now I don't know if they got away. I don't know where they are, I may never see my son again …"

Gaius was giving way to despair. Manlius had returned in search of the father; now he took charge of the son.

"Gaius," he said, "listen to me. We're going to get out of here. I've sent the rest of them down the road to Stabiae. We'll go there too. Then we'll ask around and see if anyone has seen Ariana and the others. Once we've done that, I promise you I'll try to reach the tomb of the Tullii and persuade your father to come with me. You can stay in Stabiae or go on to Surrentum. If Ariana and the rest got away by boat, most likely they've headed there. Or you could take the inland road to Salernum. It might be a little safer there, and if it isn't, you can keep going south. We'll decide what to do when we get to Stabiae. See if you can find another tunic somewhere and come with me."

They left the house and struggled once more along the Via Stabiana. As night approached, the ashfall was increasing and contained more rocks and boulders. More and more people were being killed, either by the falling rocks or by the fires that were burning everywhere. Violent winds swirled through the streets, blowing the smoke and ashes into people's eyes and adding to the chaos. The air was filled with a malodorous gas, and those who did not cover their faces coughed and choked. The streets were crowded with desperate people who had finally decided to leave their homes, taking with them whatever valuables were close to hand; most carried small bags of jewelry or wooden boxes filled with coins, but some carried the tools of their trade—carpenter's tools, surgical instruments, religious paraphernalia. Others chose to remain in their homes, feeling safer there than in the swarming, ash-filled streets.

◆ ◆ ◆

At Stabiae, Pliny the Elder prepared to stay overnight at Pomponianus's villa, sending the quadriremes to Surrentum to await further orders. Pomponianus had already loaded his possessions onto his own boats, and planned to escape as soon as the wind dropped. But Pliny tried to reassure him. "There's nothing we can do now," he told his host. "But have no fear. By morning the wind will have carried all the ash out to sea, and then we can decide what to do." And, despite Pomponianus's protests, he went to bed and fell into a deep sleep. Before long, however, the courtyard leading to his room was piled so high with ash and stones that if he had stayed there any longer, he would have been trapped. So the servants woke him, and he joined Pompanianus and the villa's other residents in the *tablinum*. During the night, the house was shaken by a series of violent tremors and threatened to collapse, but outside, the shower of *lapilli* and stones was increasing. They debated the relative merits of remaining indoors or going outside; finally they decided to tie pillows on their heads and spend the night outdoors.

◆ ◆ ◆

Gaius and Manlius passed through the Porta Stabiana without incident and joined the vast numbers of Pompeiians fleeing to the south. Though thronged with carts, mules, litters, and hurrying crowds, the road was relatively clear, as hundreds of feet had pushed aside the piles of ashes and stones. Their pace picked up, and by the light of numerous torches, as well as the enormous tongues of fire flaring into the sky above Vesuvius, they could gauge their progress. When they reached the point where they must choose between the roads to Stabiae and Salernum, they turned toward Stabiae, hoping to rejoin the other members of their household and perhaps hear news of Ariana. Gaius was beginning to feel more hopeful. At least some of the citizens of Pompeii would survive this catastrophe, and he expected to be among them. And then he would devote all his energies to finding Ariana and Little Gaius.

What no one knew, either those fleeing to the south and east or those hiding in their homes in Herculaneum, Oplontis, and Pompeii, was that the worst was yet to come.

XXVIII
AUGUST 25, 79

All afternoon and into the night, Pliny the Younger and his mother had watched the drama unfolding across the bay. They watched as the fleet disappeared into the darkness; they went indoors to rest or study; and then, when there was no word from Pliny the Elder, went back outside to watch as Vesuvius belched forth great clouds of ash and cinders, huge tongues of flame, a rain of *lapilli* and rocks, and finally, mixed with everything else, evil-smelling gases that made their eyes water and their throats burn. Night fell, and still they watched, unable even to think of sleeping. Sometime after midnight, the top of the cloud towering above the mountain collapsed and a fiery surge headed down the mountainside, straight toward Herculaneum.

◆ ◆ ◆

Claudius and Cornelia had been fortunate. Among the first of Herculaneum's citizens to die, they had been spared the terror that now gripped the people of that ill-fated town. Screaming, running, trying to outdistance the surge as it fell upon them, none could escape. Everyone and everything in the path of the blast was incinerated. Those still waiting on the shore for rescue that never came were turned into charcoal. The entire town was buried under tons of molten rock.

◆ ◆ ◆

At about the same time, Gaius and Manlius arrived at Stabiae. The town was filled with people milling around, dazed and horrified, trying to decide whether to continue southward or wait for the ashfall to cease so they could go back to Pompeii, clear the debris from their homes, and try to resume their normal lives. Some were hopeful; others laughed at them. "Can't you see? It's over; the city's buried, or will be soon. You can't go back there!"

Claudia, Timon, and the other newly-freed slaves, who had spent most of their lives in the House of the Faun, were divided. The older ones were reluctant to leave; they hoped eventually to return to their familiar and beloved home. The younger ones argued for going on to Surrentum. There they might find new employment, or at least wait for news of conditions in Pompeii. Gaius and Manlius, after spending an hour searching the crowded market square, where most of the frightened fugitives had gathered, finally caught a glimpse of Claudia with her bound-up arm, and made their way toward her. They greeted one another with relief: At least most of the members of the household were alive, though Claudia was still in pain and the more elderly among them were half-dead with exhaustion. However, there was no news of Ariana and the baby. Gaius's heart sank.

"I'm going on to Surrentum," he declared. "Maybe they've gone there. In any case, I don't think it's safe here. It's still too close to that god-cursed mountain. Why don't the rest of you come with me?"

"I can't travel any farther," Claudia protested. Timon agreed; they were too tired to go on. Gaius begged them to reconsider. "It's dangerous here, I can feel it," he said. "*Please* come with me!"

He finally persuaded the youngest of the former slaves: Timon, who still carried Claudia's small bundle of belongings and her water bottle; Claudia, reluctant but unwilling to remain behind without Timon; and the three others: Tertia, Junius, and Quintus. The five of them had lived together in the House of the Faun for so long that they were almost a family. "You too, Manlius," Gaius insisted.

"Gaius, I promised I'd go back and try to persuade your father to join us," the steward reminded him.

"I know you did, Manlius, and I appreciate it. But you were right. Father doesn't want us to worry about him. He'll be inside the tomb, and perhaps he has a chance of surviving, but I know he'd want you to stay with us and help us escape. When it's over, you can go and see if he's still there. In fact, someone's going to have to go back and see if there's any hope of returning and starting over. I doubt if there is, though. We'll have to start a new life somewhere else, and I'd be honored if you'd all come with me, wherever we decide to go."

Manlius knew in his heart that Lucius would not survive; the tombs would be entirely covered with ash, and anyone within would suffocate. He tried not to think about it.

"I'll come with you," he said, his expression sad but resolved. He had served Lucius for many years and expected to do so for many more. But now their past life was dying before their eyes.

◆ ◆ ◆

In Pompeii, dawn arrived but darkness remained. Those who had stayed in the stricken city through the night were still debating whether to leave. There was no water, but neither was there much hope of escape. The layer of ash was so deep that anyone who left would have to crawl through holes in walls and roofs. A few succeeded in doing so, and began pushing their way along the barely discernible streets. They made little headway, and to make matters worse, early in the morning there was a massive earthquake that threw many of them headlong into the ashes, where they floundered and suffocated. Others, both indoors and outside, were killed by collapsing walls and ceilings. And now the mountain sent a surge of fiery gases and molten rock toward the city. The surge stopped just outside the northern walls, but it sent a lethal cloud of toxic gases through the streets. Some of the panicked citizens who were still trying to flee were felled by this new menace; others covered their faces with strips of cloth torn from their tunics and managed to survive, though the malodorous fumes made them ill and slowed their progress still further. Even in the face of these horrors, there were still a surprising number of looters rummaging through any empty house that remained standing, snatching up coins, silver goblets, jewelry, and anything else of value they could find.

A blood-red sun rose over the Bay of Neapolis, but its rays could not penetrate the darkness that covered the city, punctuated by the forlorn gleams of a few lanterns and torches. In the Temple of Isis, Julia Felix and her tenants finally decided to flee. As the temple was not far from the Porta Stabiana, they thought they might have a chance of escaping. They gathered up the few possessions they had brought with them and, accompanied by the priests, left the temple and struggled toward the gates.

A new series of tremors shook the ground. By now, all those who had remained in their homes were well aware that they had made a fatal mistake. A few made a last, desperate attempt to flee, but most were hopelessly trapped. They had no water; their lamps had burned down, and they were enveloped in total darkness. Faustus and Julia lay in each other's arms and waited for the inevitable end. Elsewhere, families and servants knelt at their household altars and prayed for deliverance. Some of Pompeii's few remaining citizens, wishing to avoid a more painful death, chose suicide. One of them was Lucius Tullius.

◆ ◆ ◆

With great difficulty, Lucius had made his way to the Porta Nucera and along the road to the tomb of the Tullii. His torch was burning low, but he could make out the entrance and feel his way inside. He found the niche that contained Clodia's ashes and, taking a flask of wine from a fold of his *pallium*, poured a final libation and drank the rest. He removed the cloak, folded it, and knelt on it. Then he spoke to his departed wife.

"Clodia, my love, my only love, I'll be joining you soon. If there *is* such a place as the Elysian Fields, I'll find you there and we'll walk together, arm in arm, as we did so often in our own *viridarium*. The House of the Faun is no more, but nothing can take away the life we had there. Nothing can take away my memories of you or my love for you. You were … you were a gift to me from the gods. And Clodia my dear, I've kept my promise. Gaius and Ariana will wed. They already have a son, Little Gaius, so your spirit will live on in our son and grandson. Oh, Clodia, my Clodia …"

He could no longer speak. Tears sprang from his eyes, and he wept for his wife, for himself, for his beloved home, and for the terrible fate that had overcome the city to whose welfare he had devoted so much of his life. Finally he was calm. He made himself comfortable, sitting on his *pallium* and leaning against the wall. His head rested between the niches containing the ashes of his wife and infant daughter. He felt for another, smaller flask that was suspended around his neck by a cord. Removing the stopper, he drank the poison it contained. His last thoughts were of Gaius, Ariana, and their baby. *They'll survive, I know they will, and they'll find each other, and life will go on. May they be blessed with healthy babies, and may the gods grant them a long and happy life, and …* His body slumped sideways and lay still.

◆ ◆ ◆

Alomila, Publius, and the other members of the group from the farm had passed Pompeii during the afternoon, following the coastal road to Stabiae. When they came to the place where the road to Salernum split off, some of the slaves chose that route in the belief that it would take them farther from Vesuvius in the same amount of time it would have taken to reach Surrentum. Publius and Alomila were determined to go on to Surrentum and rejoin Ariana and the baby, so the group was divided. Publius, Alomila, and two of the house slaves took the litter and some of the food and water from the donkey cart and set off along the road to Stabiae. Sextus, exhausted after several hours of walking, clambered onto the cart and wedged himself among the remaining jugs and water bags. With one of the field slaves leading the donkey, he and the rest of the slaves started out along the road to Salernum. But they made slow progress. The road was crowded with carts, mules, families trying desperately to stay together, barking dogs, all in a nightmare scene of dust, darkness, and falling rocks, occasionally lit by flares from the exploding mountain behind them. Before long the group split up, each of the younger men taking a water bag and a little food out of the cart and leaving Sextus to make his own way as best he could.

◆ ◆ ◆

At Stabiae, Pliny, Pomponianus, and the other residents of the Pomponinanus's villa had watched anxiously through the night as sheets of fire rent the darkness, briefly lighting up the desolate scene before them. In a vain effort to calm them, Pliny had insisted that what they were seeing were the burning houses of local farmers. No one believed him. Toward dawn, or what passed for dawn in the murky darkness, Pomponianus had had enough.

"I'm getting out of here," he announced. "Whoever wants to can come with me aboard the *Andromeda*—she's moored right over there."

The entire group, Pliny among them, headed for the shore, but when they approached the ship, they found that the sea was far too rough to for them to embark, so they sat forlornly on the rocky beach, waiting for conditions to improve. Pliny asked for a cup of water, drank it in one gulp, spread a piece of sailcloth on the ground, and lay down. He was lying there when the first wave of fire and poisonous fumes spewed from the mountain. The others started running along the shore. Two slaves tried to help Pliny to his feet, but in the suffocating air he could not catch his breath and collapsed. The panicked slaves fled.

◆ ◆ ◆

Not long afterward, Vesuvius emitted another fiery blast that raced toward Pompeii, spelling death for anyone left alive within its walls—and outside them as well. During the previous evening and through the night, fleeing feet had created narrow pathways through the ash-filled streets, and now the few people left in the city who were not huddling inside their houses—mostly looters and a handful who had waited until the last minute to leave the city—tried desperately to escape from the hot, sulfurous blast. They did not stand a chance. The surge stopped them in their tracks, felling them as they covered their faces with their arms. It was like breathing fire: a gasp for breath, a burning in the lungs, then suffocation. Julia Felix and her little band, just then reaching the Porta Stabiana, clutched one another in panic and a moment later were dead. Outside the city, any living creature that had not traveled far enough south or east suffered the same fate. Among them were old Sextus and the slow, patient donkey pulling his cart.

◆ ◆ ◆

At Misenum, Pliny the Younger and his mother watched, aghast, as the fiery surge enveloped Pompeii. Belatedly, they realized that they too must flee. Along with the rest of their household, they gathered up whatever possessions they could carry and, with slaves holding torches leading the way, set out to the north. As he was leaving the house, Pliny the Younger shouted "Wait! Wait just a moment!" He dropped the bag of coins he was carrying and rushed back into the house, blundering into walls in the darkness. Making his way through the rooms by feel and by memory, he found his uncle's *tablinum* and snatched up the scroll lying open on the table, along with two others stacked nearby. *Uncle will have plenty to write about when this is over!* he thought as he felt his way back to the vestibule, where his mother and the others were waiting impatiently.

Along with hundreds of other people fleeing from Misenum and nearby towns, they followed the coastal road that headed north past the Fields of Fire. The ferocious geysers of flame cast a ghastly orange light over them, and the fumes sickened them despite their efforts to cover their noses and mouths. Their eyes watered, and the ash-filled air made breathing difficult. But Vesuvius was sending most of its fury toward the south and west, and they were able to struggle onward without incident. After a couple of hours, weak and exhausted, they rested beside the road for a while, and it was then that they saw a strange sight: Carts standing on level ground began rolling backward, as if they had been going uphill, and the shore seemed to have expanded outward, leaving countless fish lying dead on the beach. Pliny the Younger was commenting on the remarkable scene when one of the slaves shouted, "Look! Look over there!"

Coming toward them was a thick cloud of ash and gases containing within it the glow of fire. They were doomed; helpless, they crouched and covered their heads with their arms. But the surge did not reach them. After a while, still fearing for their lives, they looked up cautiously and watched in disbelief as the haze thinned and a weak, livid light began filtering through. Hastily they gathered up their belongings and went on along the road toward Cumae.

◆ ◆ ◆

Alomila, Publius, and the two slaves who traveled with them had reached Stabiae late on the previous day. There they had rested and had a little bread and water, but Alomila, anxious to be reunited with her daughter and grandchild, had persuaded them to go on toward Surrentum during the night. The slaves carried the litter while Publius and Alomila walked ahead of them carrying torches. The road was clear of ash, and less crowded than it had been earlier, so they made good progress. They were well down the coast by dawn. Gradually the light grew stronger, though still hazy, with a red, angry-looking sun trying to shine through the smoky air. Even from that distance, they could hear the roar of Vesuvius as it spewed out the surge of fire and gas that doomed Pompeii. They turned and watched in horror as their beloved city was engulfed and the fiery cloud spread toward Stabiae. Anyone who had remained in Stabiae had no chance of survival. Among them were the older members of Lucius's household—the cook, the gardener, and the others who had been too tired to continue or unwilling to travel any farther from their lifelong home.

But it was not over yet. Now Vesuvius emitted its final blast—a huge surge of fire and gas and rock that sped westward across the bay, incinerating everything in its path. Any boat or ship in the bay—any craft that had not headed toward the north or south the day before or during the night—was destroyed. Charred timbers and bodies floated on the water's ashy surface. The mountain had spent itself, and now its rage subsided, leaving the survivors to watch in stunned silence as the smoky clouds lifted and hazy light began to illuminate the devastation of Herculaneum, Oplontis, Pompeii, Stabiae, and the entire surrounding countryside. In fact, there was little to be seen: Herculaneum was buried under tons of rock, Pompeii immersed in ash and *lapilli*, Oplontis and Stabiae completely destroyed.

XXIX

AUGUST 26, 79

Surrentum was a small town that hugged a hillside at the southern end of the curved shore of the Bay of Neapolis. It was a pretty, pleasant place, popular with summer visitors, who went there in August to enjoy the views and the cool sea breezes. But on the morning of August 26, 79, its population had swollen to more than four times its normal size. Every room in every inn, and in some private homes as well, was taken; every *caupona* was crowded with hungry customers; dozens of boats fought for a mooring place, and when these were all taken, people simply tied their boats to others and clambered from one to another until they reached the shore. In the central square—more of a marketplace than a true forum—crowds of hungry, anxious refugees were walking aimlessly, looking for missing loved ones and competing for the attention of the overworked food and wine vendors. Some of the survivors were so stunned that they could not walk or speak, but simply stood motionless, gazing at the scene around them without really seeing it, hardly believing they were still alive after the nightmare that had engulfed them.

Marcus and Ariana had arrived a few hours after leaving Oplontis, theirs being among the few small craft that had managed to cross the bay before it was too late. Speechless with fear, Ariana had clutched the baby to her breast and huddled in the bottom of the boat as the crew struggled to sail it through the increasingly choppy waves. Finally, when it was almost too dark to distinguish land from sea, they had seen the flickering lights of Surrentum and found a place in its small harbor to tie up the boat and scramble ashore. Marcus had installed Ariana and the baby in the best available room of a guest house at the edge of town, overlooking the sea. There she could rest and take care of Little Gaius while he sought news of Gaius and other members of either of their families who might have survived. Knowing the fate of Herculaneum, he had little hope for his father and Cornelia, but he thought it likely that Lucius, Gaius, and the others would head for Surrentum. There, assuming they had brought enough coins with them, they could hire boats, litters, carts—whatever they needed to go farther down the coast, or inland should they so choose.

So, after paying each of the slaves who had sailed their small boat through the choppy, ash-filled bay the promised *denarius*—and watched as they hastened into town to spend it on wine and sausage pastries—he lay down on a pile of sailcloth and rested. Then he, too, headed for the marketplace, where by some kind of unspoken agreement anyone seeking news of family and friends gathered to share whatever information they had and obtain whatever food or drink was available.

◆ ◆ ◆

Gaius, Manlius, and their companions arrived at Surrentum an hour or two before dawn. Desperate for sleep, they separated to search for accommodations, agreeing to meet at the center of the market square in the morning. Claudia and Timon, now an acknowledged couple, soon found a small room in a nearby house, which was fortunate, as Claudia was in considerable pain. Timon paid for the room, made her as comfortable as he could, and went out in search of a jug of wine and some food, as the small amounts they had brought with them had been consumed along the way.

Manlius and Gaius found a room in the home of Caecilius Jucundus. Jucundus and Lucius had served together as magistrates in Pompeii; Jucundus had been ill at the time of the trial of Statius Rufus, and soon thereafter he had resigned and moved to Surrentum. A banker as well as a politician, he was able to buy a luxurious house. After recovering from his illness, he had reentered local politics and was now one of the town's magistrates. He was greatly saddened by the news that Lucius was unlikely to have survived the destruction of Pompeii.

The other refugees from the House of the Faun scattered, each accepting any space they could find in a hotel or rooming house that was already overcrowded.

Manlius stretched out gratefully on the bed provided by their host, but Gaius was too anxious to sleep. Instead, he left the house and roamed the streets and the market square, gazing hopefully in the faint predawn light at every face he encountered. From time to time, he stopped and leaned against a wall, his eyes closed, practically asleep on his feet, but then he stumbled onward, dimly aware that dawn was at hand. Too tired to stand, he sat on the edge of the pedestal supporting the town's requisite statue of Augustus. From this vantage point, he watched as the wretched, worried refugees from Pompeii and Stabiae gathered in the marketplace to search for their relatives.

He could not help it: He fell asleep, only to wake with a jolt as he slid from his precarious seat. Hurriedly he stood and rubbed his eyes. *This isn't getting me anywhere. Maybe I'd better go back to the house and get some real sleep. But first I've got to drink a little water—if there is any. And a bit of bread soaked in wine would help.* He looked around for a public fountain or a food stand, and as he did so, he thought he saw a face he recognized. *Marcus? Could it be?*

All thoughts of food and rest left him as he rushed over to the handsome young man who was standing not far away, questioning the town's *aquarius* about the water supply. Apparently the engineer's response was satisfactory, because Marcus turned from him with a smile as Gaius approached.

"Marcus! Is it really you?"

"Of course it's me, who else would it be? By all the gods, Gaius, you look as if you could use some sleep."

"Never mind about that, Marcus. Have you by any chance seen …"

"… a beautiful black-haired young woman, with a baby she calls Little Gaius?"

"You've seen her? You know where she is?"

"Of course! I brought her here."

For a moment, Gaius could not say a word. He reached out and grasped Marcus by the shoulders, gazing into his face. There were tears in his eyes.

"You *brought* her here? How? Oh, Marcus, I tried to reach her but I couldn't. I'm so grateful—I'm forever in your debt! But where is she? Could you take me to her?"

"You ask so many questions, Gaius! I don't know which one to answer first," Marcus said teasingly. "No, don't get upset. I'll take you to her right away. But first let's buy some food and wine from this nice man who's just setting up his stand."

The vendor, eager to please his rich-looking customers, provided everything they needed, and Marcus paid him well. Then they hurried to the guest house where Ariana awaited them.

◆ ◆ ◆

At first she held back, still resentful at his failure to come for her in time. But almost immediately she relented and fell into his arms. They held each other for what seemed an eternity, tears streaming down their cheeks, kisses alternating with whispers of love—"Ariana, my goddess Ariana!" "Gaius, I thought I'd never see you again!" And then the stories: Gaius's fruitless attempt to reach the farm,

Marcus's unexpected arrival with the litters, Lucius's note saying he would stay with Clodia (at which Ariana wept again), the decision not to stay overnight at Stabiae, which saved their lives but doomed the rest of the household. And the questions: How was Little Gaius? Where were Manlius and the others? Where was Alomila? What about the rest of the slaves and freedmen from the farm? Was there any word of Claudius and Cornelia, Julia and Faustus, Aurelia, Julilla?

Along with the stories and questions, they shared the meal Marcus had thoughtfully provided. Gaius lay down on the bed and cuddled his son; a moment later, Marcus and Ariana laughed at the sight of the two of them fast asleep. But Ariana was worried about her mother. Alomila and Publius had started out at the same time as she and Marcus, but they were traveling slowly along the coastal road. Had they made the fatal mistake of spending the night at Stabiae, assuming they could find rooms? No, she felt sure they would have continued along the shore to Surrentum. As they parted, Alomila had said, "I'll see you in Surrentum."

Marcus, who seemed to have an inexhaustible store of energy, offered to go back to the marketplace and see if he could find out anything about Alomila, Publius, Sextus, and the others. Before he had gone very far, he spotted Manlius and the other survivors from the House of the Faun standing in a group near the center of the square, devouring hunks of wine-soaked bread and wondering what had become of Gaius. Marcus joined them and told them about the reunion of Gaius and Ariana, news that was greeted with joyful smiles and heartfelt thanks. Marcus was proud of his actions, but he insisted that it had been a simple matter to fetch Ariana and the baby and get them to Surrentum by boat. What he wanted to know, and they could not tell him, was what had become of Alomila and the others.

They were discussing their possible whereabouts, as well as what might have happened to the other members of both households, when Manlius caught a glimpse of a bedraggled woman carrying a torch, now extinguished, accompanied by three other exhausted travelers, two of whom were carrying a litter but set it down as soon as they entered the square. The four of them were looking dazedly around them, unsure of what to do next. He thought they looked familiar. Was that Ariana's mother, who had come with her to bring Little Gaius to meet his grandfather? It seemed so long ago …

"Look, Marcus," he cried. "Is that her?"

Marcus looked, and despite her ash-streaked face and the ragged *palla* covering her hair, he recognized Alomila, also noting that the man with her was the farm's manager, Publius.

"It's them!" he shouted, and he and Manlius pushed their way through the crowd toward them. Alomila was so exhausted she could hardly stand, but nothing could stop her from asking the question that overshadowed all others.

"Ariana?"

"Safe, and the baby too. Gaius is with them."

At which news Alomila collapsed, but Publius managed to catch her before she fell to the ground.

◆ ◆ ◆

Everyone crowded into Ariana's room. It was a scene of mixed emotions, with relieved embraces of those whose fate had been uncertain, mingled with many tears for those who had almost certainly perished. From time to time they all fell silent, struggling to come to terms with the enormous catastrophe that had overtaken them and the mixture of joy and guilt they felt as they faced the reality that they had survived while so many had not.

Gaius had woken from his nap and given the baby to Ariana for nursing. After a while, Alomila looked out toward the sea in astonishment.

"Look, everyone, the sun is shining!"

They all crowded through the doorway and into the central courtyard. It was true. The sky was blue, the sun yellow; there were a few clouds, but if one did not look northward, the vista seemed entirely normal. No one looked northward. There would be time enough for that.

"So the world hasn't come to an end, just our little part of it," said Gaius, with a sigh.

Again they paused to reflect on the events of the last three days. Not only had they all lost friends and relatives, but they were exhausted by their difficult, dangerous journeys. For now, though, they must not give way to grief. They needed to make some kind of plan for the future. As they spoke, an idea had been growing in Gaius's thoughts, and now he shared it with them.

"I don't think there's any chance we'll ever be able to go home," he said. He turned away for a moment, remembering the greeting "AVE" that had always welcomed guests to the House of the Faun. Then he went on. "It's gone, destroyed. But we still have the estate in Sicily, and we could live there, at least for a while. The manager of the oil-pressing business is about to retire, so Publius could take over that work. And Father had been talking about expanding the export business, which would be a good project for Manlius to oversee. I'm sure we can find work and a home for all of you, if you're willing to come with us. I believe Marcus has a couple of boats available. We can travel down the coast in them until we find a larger vessel for the crossing. Don't worry, Ariana, our estate's in Agrigentum, on the other side of the island from Mount Aetna!"

Marcus agreed to lend them his boats, but told them he'd be staying where he was. He thought of Caecilia and smiled, but decided to keep his secret a little longer. He would go back to Capreae soon. As soon as he could.

"There's going to be a lot of building and rebuilding around here," he said. Even if no one can build near Herculaneum or Pompeii, there are other places along the coast where people will buy land and hire architects to design villas for them. Just send the boats back here with their crews—I'll pay them and, I hope, have plenty of work for them. At the very least, we've got to find out what happened to Poppaea's villa, the one we were working on when Vesuvius went on its rampage. It may still be standing, in which case the senator will probably want us to finish the job and make whatever repairs are needed. I'm sure there'll be a lot of those. *If* it's still standing ..."

"Thank you for your offer, Marcus," said Gaius. "Let's see, how many of us are there? Me, Ariana, Little Gaius, Manlius, Alomila, Publius, Timon, Claudia, Tertia, Quintus, Junius ... Will that be too many for your boats?"

"Oh, don't worry about that. If necessary, we'll make two trips. But let's wait for fair weather and favorable winds. And if I were you, I'd go straight to the Temple of Jupiter Capitolinus—there must be one somewhere near here, every town has one—and make whatever offering of thanksgiving you can afford. You—all of us—are extremely lucky. I doubt if very many people got out safely after that first day."

"No, I don't think they did. I'm afraid that includes your parents and sisters, as well as my father."

"And poor old Sextus," put in Alomila. "I don't think he got far enough away, he was traveling so slowly. The others probably grabbed water bags and ran, but he had to ride in the cart."

"Someone's going to have to go back and look around," said Gaius thoughtfully. "It doesn't look as if anyone could be left alive in the whole countryside, but we should take a look anyway. My father ..."

"Gaius, I don't think there's any chance Lucius is still alive," put in Manlius. "But if Marcus'll go with me, I'll take one of his boats and see what I can find out. I doubt if we can even go ashore, but we'll go take a look."

"That's a good idea," Marcus agreed. "Then I can see what the situation is in Oplontis."

The two men, apparently having eaten and rested enough, went down to the docks. Fortunately, some members of Marcus's crew, having nowhere to sleep but in the boats, were resting there and were willing to row or sail toward Stabiae, depending on the wind, provided they stayed close to shore.

◆ ◆ ◆

The journey took several hours, and it was evening when they returned. "There's nothing left," Manlius reported. "We got as far as Stabiae, but there was so much rubble in the water, we couldn't go any farther. It's a curious thing, though: On the shore in front of Pomponianus's villa, I saw a tall man who seemed to be sleeping. We beached the boat and went to look, but he was dead. From your earlier description, I believe it might have been Pliny the Elder."

"That would be just like him," Gaius commented. "He was so curious about natural phenomena that he would risk his life to find out more. I hope his nephew got away. Maybe we'll meet sometime, and I can find out more about what Pliny was doing during those awful days. Writing careful descriptions of everything he observed, I'll bet."

"Well," Manlius continued, "while we were standing there, we looked up the coast toward Pompeii and Herculaneum. There's absolutely no sign of Herculaneum; it's completely buried. Pompeii is covered up to the rooftops in ash and other debris—you can just see the tops of some of the taller buildings. A couple of sections of Clemens's Folly are sticking up through the ashes, but that's about it. As for the necropolis … I'm sorry to say it looks as if it's completely covered. Unless your father changed his mind … But Gaius, I think he knew what he was doing. He probably took poison."

Gaius turned away. He knew Lucius would not have changed his mind. *Omnia amor vincit.*

"So much for the possibility of going home," he said, wiping the tears from his eyes. "We have to put the past behind us—though I'll never forget the House of the Faun …"

He was weeping openly now. Ariana handed the baby to her mother and went over and embraced him.

"I'll never forget it either, or your parents, who were so kind to me. It's something we'll tell our children and grandchildren about: the beautiful house where we met and fell in love …"

"And where we were going to be wed on the Kalends of September," Gaius interrupted. "Now I guess we'll have to wait a little longer. When we're settled in

Agrigentum, we'll send someone to Rome and find out what happened to that document the Emperor was supposed to sign and send to Claudius ..."

"Oh, no!" cried Ariana. "We're not going to wait. We'll be wed on the Kalends of September, right here!"

"But Ariana ..."

"Gaius, what's to prevent us? No one cares if I'm a freedwoman, and besides, you promised nothing would stop us! We'll find a priest, and Manlius will arrange for the ceremony and the procession—won't you, Manlius? You're so good at these things!—and we'll come here and you'll carry me through that doorway right there, and we'll start our new life!"

"But Ariana ..."

"What's this 'But Ariana'? What's to stop us?"

"Well, for one thing, you don't have your wedding garments ..."

"Yes I do!" she told him with a smile, pointing at the rolled-up bundle she had brought with her. "And I'm wearing the ring you gave me, which you can give me again. And I have my mother to give us her blessing, and Marcus will stand in for our father—you will, won't you, Marcus?"

Marcus nodded and smiled.

"So all we have to do is make a few arrangements, get some food and wine for the celebration, hire a couple of musicians, whatever kind you like, and ..."

"Just a minute, Ariana," put in Alomila. "We don't have a lot of money with us, and it would be more economical if Publius and I were wed at the same time. Not only that, but I wonder if Timon and Claudia ..."

At this, Claudia blushed to the roots of her hair, while Timon grinned from ear to ear. "Count us in!" he said.

◆ ◆ ◆

The Kalends of September was four days away. Those days passed quickly as everything possible was done to arrange for the celebration of three simultaneous weddings. Lodgings had to be obtained for Publius and Alomila, as well as a better place for Timon and Claudia than the little room they had found when they first arrived. Since many of the refugees who initially crowded into Surrentum had since traveled on down the coast, more rooms were available now, and even Marcus's crew no longer had to sleep curled up on sailcloth or sacking in the boats. Timon took the opportunity to find a skilled physician to reset Claudia's arm. Once free of pain, she reverted to her usual smiling self.

Jucundus offered to officiate, and suggested that his large atrium, with its beautifully painted walls and its floor covered with mosaics of birds and mythical creatures, would be an appropriate place to hold the triple wedding. His offer was gladly accepted.

And so, on the morning of the Kalends of September, Ariana and Gaius, Alomila and Publius, and Claudia and Timon were wed in the home of a magistrate of the town of Surrentum. Ariana wore the traditional white *stola,* saffron-yellow *palla,* and flame-red veil. Manlius had found appropriate garments for Gaius and the other two couples. On their heads, the three brides wore garlands of white oleanders. The magistrate, doubling as priest, sacrificed a dove and, after examining its insides, declared that the gods approved of all three marriages. Then, as Gaius had promised, he guided Ariana's hand as she signed the marriage contract: Arria Vettia. They joined hands and made their vows, and then the feast began.

Manlius and Marcus had scoured the town for whatever delicacies could be found. Not much was available, as the fleeing residents of Pompeii and Stabiae had consumed most of the town's food supplies. But they were able to obtain enough fruit, bread, and wine to make a decent meal, and one or two of the vendors offered to cook a few sausage pastries and honey cakes. By then, most of the town's residents had heard about the unusual triple wedding that was about to take place, and by the time the feast was over, a large crowd had gathered outside the magistrate's house to welcome the newlyweds and follow their procession. Smiling shyly, the three couples left the house, accompanied by Manlius, Marcus, and the others, along with a group of flute-players who had offered their services at no charge. The procession wound through the streets, leaving each couple at the entrance of their lodgings. Finally they arrived at Ariana's guest house. Amid much laughter and cries of "May the gods give you many children," and similar good wishes, Gaius lifted Ariana and carried her over the threshold. Tertia, who had cared for Little Gaius throughout the ceremony and the procession, gave him to his mother to be nursed, and then carried him to another room for his nap. Finally the newlyweds were alone.

"Ariana, my love, my goddess," was all Gaius could say as he put his arms around her and kissed her.

"I love you, Gaius," she replied.

She removed her garland, veil, and *palla*, and he his borrowed toga, and they sat together on the edge of the bed. Evening was coming on, and lamps had been lit throughout the house. There was a small one on a table at the foot of the bed.

"Shall we lie down together, my wife?" asked Gaius gently.

"Yes, my husband," said Ariana. "But first, would you please go get a piece of paper and a stylus?"

"Certainly," he said, raising his eyebrows. "But what do you want them for?"

"Just go get them, and I'll tell you."

He went to find the owner of the guest house, who (also with raised eyebrows) gave him a sheet of paper, a stylus, and a small jar of ink. Returning to their room, Gaius handed them to his bride.

"All right, what's this all about?" he asked.

"You promised to teach me to read," she replied. "I want my first lesson now. Just a short one. Show me how to read and write 'Gaius' and 'Ariana.'"

Smiling happily, he complied. She learned quickly, and soon the lesson was over. They set the paper aside and extinguished the lamp.

EPILOGUE

News of the eruption of Vesuvius and the fate of Pompeii and nearby towns reached Rome within a day or two. The Emperor Titus ordered that a rescue mission be sent to the stricken region as quickly as possible. However, when the rescuers passed Neapolis and attempted to continue toward Herculaneum, they found the coastal road buried under tons of rock. They turned back and tried to make their way around the mountain along the road to Nola. There they met some of the farmers who lived on the eastern side of the mountain. Because Vesuvius's fury had been directed mostly to the south and west, the farms on its eastern slopes had suffered little damage. The farmers told the rescuers there was no one left to rescue. They might travel a little way along the road from Nola to Pompeii, but they would see nothing but devastation. The city was buried, all its citizens departed or dead. There was no sign of life along the whole stretch of coast between Herculaneum and Stabiae. There was nothing for the rescuers to do but record their observations and return to Rome.

This they did, bringing with them not only a record of the devastation that had once been a thriving commercial and agricultural community, but also a startling description of the change in Mount Vesuvius. The once-beautiful cone-shaped mountain, with its gently sloping shoulders, had collapsed in on itself. It now lacked form. Its eastern and northeastern slopes had changed little, but on its southern and western sides it had been reduced to a misshapen pile of barren rock, its forests and vineyards replaced by bleak gray stone and hardened ash. The summit was no more; in its place, had anyone ventured to look, was a huge, smoking crater still emitting noxious fumes.

The report of the rescue mission has not come down to us, but one eyewitness account has. Pliny theYounger managed to escape, and at the request of the historian Tacitus, he wrote a description of the eruption of Vesuvius that is the only eyewitness account in existence. He also managed to preserve his uncle's writings, and Pliny the elder's *Naturalis Historia* was published posthumously in its entirety.

◆ ◆ ◆

In mid-September, Gaius, Ariana, Little Gaius, and their companions traveled safely to Agrigentum. There Gaius took over the management of his father's estate, and in time he expanded the business into wine production as well as the production and exporting of olive oil. He immediately freed all the house slaves and field hands, many of whom chose to stay there and continue working for good wages. There was plenty of work for Manlius, Publius, and the others, though they were free to seek opportunities elsewhere if they wished. After a year or two, Timon and Claudia moved to nearby Phintias—a small town, famous as the place where the tragedian Aeschylus died when an eagle dropped a tortoise on his gleaming bald head, mistaking it for a rock. Timon had a pleasant, outgoing personality, and he had always wanted to open a tavern where he could meet travelers from many places and listen to their tales. Claudia, who was rapidly becoming almost as good a cook as Ariana, happily assisted her husband in his new venture.

Gaius found that he enjoyed country life, and though he kept it to himself, he was relieved at not being expected to continue his career as a city councilman. He had already had doubts about his political skills, and now he was able to apply other abilities he had not realized he possessed: He was good at planning, managing, and most of all, keeping his workers busy and happy. He was rewarded with a thriving business that enriched himself and his family and would be passed down to his descendants for generations.

Gaius and Ariana had three more children, whom they named Lucius, Alomila, and Clodia. Ariana nursed them, played with them, and saw to their education along with her own. She also took over the management of the kitchen, the pantry, the meal planning, and a large part of the cooking. She experimented with every herb and spice she could lay her hands on—including exotic imports from Arabia and India, such as cloves and nutmeg—and enjoyed preparing meals that were not lavish but invariably were tasty and satisfying. As the Saturnalia drew near, she enlisted Timon and Claudia's assistance in the preparation of a feast that, had he known it, the Emperor Titus would have preferred over the elaborate dishes carried to him from his palace kitchens.

The Saturnalia was always a happy time for Gaius, Ariana, and their household, as well as Timon and Claudia's. But each year, on the twenty-fifth day of August, they would make a pilgrimage to the Valley of Temples, nestled in the hills above the city of Agrigentum. There, on the altar of the Temple of Concord, the priests would sacrifice a pair of white doves, and Gaius would pour a libation in memory of Lucius, Clodia, and all the other loved ones they had left behind in the ruins of Pompeii and Herculaneum.

GLOSSARY OF LATIN WORDS

aedilis: a city official, responsible for buildings and public works, supervision of markets, and organization of the games.

amphora: a large, two-handled, narrow-necked jar used to store wine or oil.

aquarius: the manager of a city or town's water system.

atrium: the large reception hall just inside the entrance of a Roman house.

aureus: a gold coin, equivalent to one hundred sesterces.

ballista: a catapult used in siege warfare.

basilica: a large public building used for commercial and legal activities.

bestiarius: a handler or caretaker of animals; also, a beast-fighter.

calidarium: the hot room in a Roman bath.

castellum aquae: a facility for storing and rationing water.

caupona: a dining area for customers of a snack bar.

centumvir: a member of the city council, consisting of one hundred men.

client: a person who is dependent on a patron for support and protection.

College of Augustales: an association of honorary priests.

colonia: a colonial town established as a result of trade or conquest, often settled by veteran Roman legionaries.

columella: a bust of a departed loved one, placed on a small column in his or her tomb.

Comitia: the town council.

compluvium: an opening in the roof over the atrium, allowing rainwater to fall into the pool *(impluvium)* below it.

cubiculum: a bedroom, usually small and used only for sleeping.

Curia: the building in which the town council meets.

damnatio ad bestias: an execution in which the criminal is placed in an arena with violent animals.

denarius: a silver coin, equivalent to half an aureus.

deus ex machina ("the god from the machine"): a device used in Roman theaters to create the illusion of a god descending from the heavens.

dolia: large clay containers in which crushed grapes are stored for fermentation; one dolium can hold one hundred gallons of wine.

duovir: one of the city's two magistrates *(duoviri)*, responsible for government finance, local justice, and elections.

faun: a young satyr; a forest-god.

fibula: a decorative pin used to secure a garment.

forum: a large open space at the center of a Roman town or city, surrounded by temples, markets, and public buildings.

frigidarium: the cold room in a Roman bath.

garum: fish sauce.

gustatio: the appetizer course of a Roman dinner.

hypocaustum: the heating system of a Roman bath house.

impluvium: a rectangular pool in the center of the atrium of a Roman house; a parallel opening above it, the *compluvium*, allows rainwater to fall into the pool.

insula: a city block.

Kalends: the first day of each month.

krater: a large bowl for mixing wine with water.

lapilli: small pebbles.

lararium: an altar to the household gods, the Lares and Penates.

lupanar: a brothel.

luxuria: luxury, extravagance, excess.

macellum: a market.

missio: reprieve from death when defeated in a gladiatorial contest.

oecus: a living room or study.

omnia amor vincit: love conquers all

palaestra: a wrestling school and exercise ground.

palla (pl. *pallae*): a woman's shawl or mantle.

pallium: a man's cloak.

paterfamilias: the (male) head of a Roman household.

patrician: a member of the aristocracy in a Roman town or city.

patronus: a prominent man who distributes money and favors to a number of clients, who come to his house each morning; also, the former master of a freed slave.

pergula: a room above a shop, where the shopkeeper lives.

peristyle: a court enclosed by columns; a Roman house often includes a garden surrounded by a peristyle.

pontifex maximus: the chief or high priest.

procurator: an official responsible for tax collection and enforcement of governmental edicts.

quadrireme: a large ship, with sails and four banks of oars.

retiarius: a gladiator who fights with a net and a trident.

Saturnalia: a week-long midwinter festival.

secutor: a gladiator who is lightly armed and depends on speed to catch his opponent.

sestercius: a bronze coin.

sportula: a small amount of money given by a patronus to his clients each day.

stele: an upright slab with a sculptured surface, used for commemorative purposes.

stola: a long tunic cinched at the waist, worn by adult women.

strigil: a metal tool used to scrape oil and dirt from the skin after exercising.

tablinum: a formal room near the front of a Roman house, where the head of the household receives clients and conducts business.

tepidarium: the warm room in a Roman bath.

thermopilium: a snack bar that serves a variety of hot foods.

toga: a loose outer garment worn by male Roman citizens, draped over the body in a prescribed fashion; worn on formal or official occasions.

triclinium: a dining room in a Roman house; some houses have several, both indoors and in the garden, to be used according to the seasons.

tunic: a sleeveless garment pulled over the head and reaching to the knees, worn by men and by children of both sexes.

viridarium: a garden in a Roman house, often enclosed by a peristyle or colonnade.

MODERN FORMS OF ANCIENT PLACE NAMES

Agrigentum	Agrigento
Baiae	Baia
Capreae	Capri
Neapolis	Napoli (Naples)
Puteoli	Pozzuoli
Salernum	Salerno
R. Sarnus	R. Sarno
Stabiae	Castellamare di Stabia
Surrentum	Sorrento

978-0-595-40519-0
0-595-40519-3

Printed in the United States
76583LV00004B/22-39